NICK PLACE
ROLL WITH IT

hardie grant books

MELBOURNE · LONDON

Published in 2013 by Hardie Grant Books

Hardie Grant Books (Australia)
Ground Floor, Building 1
658 Church Street
Richmond, Victoria 3121
www.hardiegrant.com.au

Hardie Grant Books (UK)
Dudley House, North Suite
34–35 Southampton Street
London WC2E 7HF
www.hardiegrant.co.uk

Cataloguing-in-Publication data is available from the National Library
of Australia.

Roll With It
ISBN 978 1 74270 433 3

Cover and text design by Lanz+Martin
Cover image courtesy of Matthias Lanz
Typeset in New Aster 9.5/14 by Cannon Typesetting
Printed and bound in Australia by Griffin Press

To my awesome boys, Will and Macklin.

To Chloé.

And to all of those who have been with me for the journey.
Chips, Shonko, Annie, Ronnie P and Patricia Rivers.
Amanda, Rich G, Rich H, Katey and everybody else.

Your support and love got me here. Thank you.

CONTENTS

1	A perfect shot	8
2	Reality bites	18
3	Ghosts and dreams	36
4	Life in the saddle	46
5	Friends of the planet	64
6	Riding with Rocket	72
7	Car shopping with the Wild Man	92
8	Lance Armstrong	100
9	Laver's day off	112
10	The Devil's Mockery	120
11	Showdown at the Soul Food Café	130
12	Spider senses	144
13	A nasty accident	154
14	Questions without answers	160
15	The Vegie Bar	166
16	The Mutant Children of Ossie Ostrich	176
17	Lost in Siberia	182
18	The Grevillea wing	194
19	Doing the Kew conga	200
20	Sewer life	208
21	The naked koala	214
22	The Vegie Bar, take two	218
23	Code 33	228
24	Stig cops a bullet	236
25	Nightmare Scenario	248
26	In the dark	256

27 It was probably nothing   264

28 A social call   278

29 The wallet   290

30 One minute to midnight   300

31 Taking care of business   310

32 77 Sunset Strip   318

33 Incident on Rathdowne   332

34 Punching your weight   338

35 The perfect shot (reprise)   344

Acknowledgements   348

CHAPTER 1
A PERFECT SHOT

Under different conditions, it might have been considered the perfect shot. People win gold medals in the Olympics for worse shooting.

The bullet had entered the body under the arm on the right-hand side and passed through both lungs, as well as the heart, before hitting a rib and deflecting almost exactly 90 degrees south, taking out several vital organs in the stomach region. But here's where the shot became close to magical. It ricocheted precisely off the top of the hip and pinballed straight up, actually leaving the body on its upward trajectory just long enough for the victim, in the process of looking down to see if he'd been shot, to receive the bullet right between the eyes. It then passed through his skull and nestled contentedly in the brain.

Needless to say, the victim, a known armed robber called Wesley Coleman, twenty-nine, of Thomastown (or the late 'Wasted Wes' as his motley crew of criminal friends would briefly mourn him) was dead long before his body made it to the tarmac of the airport car park.

His soul? Who can say? Maybe rising above his corpse to find his dead mother there, arms crossed and scowling at him, saying, 'So, that'd be right. Shot dead in a fucking car park.'

Back on earth, Detective Tony 'Rocket' Laver had a different set of problems, the first of which was that he was unlikely to be awarded any medals, gold or otherwise, for dusting a lowlife career criminal like Coleman.

In fact, Laver was trying to come to terms with the fact that less than three minutes ago he'd been asleep – and now he'd killed somebody for the first time in a fourteen-year police career.

It wasn't unreasonable that he'd been dozing on the job, despite the fact that he was kneeling in all-blue Special Operations Group overalls, feet spread to balance the load of equipment and Kevlar protective padding strapped to his body, his arms holding a high-calibre, fast-action semi-automatic rifle. Laver was Major Crime these days, right now part of a joint operation, but had spent enough time in the SOG to know what it was to wait, and how to switch on and off as required. Laver could sleep literally anywhere.

As it was, he'd been either squatting or kneeling in the unmarked delivery van for the best part of two days, with no sign of the armed robbery the surveillance dogs kept assuring them the gang was doing nothing but talk about. In the long-term car park of Tullamarine Airport, cars roamed aimlessly, looking for parks less than three suburbs from the terminals. There was the semi-regular rush of a plane in take-off. The distant hum of the freeway. Laver had closed his eyes to rest, confident that when the call came he'd be sharp.

So it was a shock to hear the barked 'Ready?' from his partner that day, SOG member Nathan Funnal; Laver's eyes flew open, his heart rate ramming from asleep to close to capacity in less than a second. Which, of course, it had done plenty of times before.

'They're here?' Laver blinking and trying to get a look at Funnal, jammed between him and the door in the cramped space of the van.

'Yeah, Rocket. Haven't you been listening to the dogs tracking them here for the last five minutes? What were you, asleep?'

'Don't be stupid.' Laver creaked off his knees to his feet, took a step back for a little more room, crouched, did some squats to get his legs moving and flexed his grip on the gun. 'Vision?'

'Nope. They're just pulling in off the freeway now.'

'And the van?'

'Just pulled in to the armoury, twenty metres to our right.' Funnal looked hard at Laver. 'You fucking were asleep. You're unbelievable.'

Laver grinned. 'It's all good, Spider. I'm wide awake now.'

Funnal, lanky and rail thin, all arms and legs under his Kevlar, shook his head in grudging admiration, peering out the tiny crack strategically placed in the apparently empty delivery van. 'Well, you better be awake enough to hit them hard and fast. If we can get them on the ground before they get their guns raised, we're a chance of getting out of this with no shots.'

Laver feeling his heart pumping now. Not sharing his partner's optimism. This gang had carried off five armed robberies on armoured vans and had killed three guards in the process. The police had finally made some inroads and started surveillance a month ago. The gang was a collection of hardened criminals with some dubious views on sexual equality, racial harmony and paying tax, if you went by their daily banter. It had also become clear that they were actually looking forward to the day a cop tried to foil one of their robberies; facing off against rent-a-security-guards was getting old.

Now a light-blue 80s-model Ford cruised through the lanes of parked cars, heading towards the cash armoury at the back of the car wash. Tullamarine Airport management had hoped this location would make it less obvious as a target for robbers, when in fact they'd made it pleasantly accessible and away from crowds.

A radio squawking on Laver's hip: 'Spider? Rocket? You good to go?'

'Affirmative, Doc. Say the word.'

Funnal motionless by the door. Laver, squatting beside him, moving his hand back off the radio to his gun. Locking eyes, not needing to see the crooks now. Doc doing that for them.

'Go! Go! Go!'

Funnal crashed open the van's door and they exited, low, crouched but running fast, aware of the similar blue-clad figures coming from the south and north, at tangents so no officers could be in the background of potential shots. The five bandits, barely out of their car, guns still dangling at knee height, taking the crucial half-second to register and react that they always did. By which time police guns were all over them.

One robber taking half a step to run but two SOG officers flanking him before he completed the thought, screaming at him to stay where he was, to drop the gun, to freeze.

Laver looking down the barrel of his gun as he slowed to a walk, still registering the four remaining, frozen bandits. Suddenly aware of one of them, the one with the bad afro hairstyle, raising his gun towards him. Laver yelling what he should yell, but the next few moments were strangely without sound. Not hearing his own voice, telling Coleman to drop it. Not hearing anything that Coleman yelled back, registering spittle flying from the man's mouth. Seeing the oddly silent flash of Coleman's gun and feeling the searing rush of something impossibly fast passing his right ear.

Wondering why he had let himself wait so dangerously long, surprised that he had such an aversion to killing now it came to it, after fourteen years of wondering what the moment would be like. Laver still in his cocoon of silence as he squeezed the trigger and watched Coleman jerk, spasm and fall right in front of him. Laver with no doubt he'd killed the man.

Fourteen years of carrying a gun, even doing his time in the Special Operations Group where wearing Kevlar and kicking in doors, guns drawn, was a standard work day. Being there as people died. Like the time Laver had entered a room only to find the serial rapist he was pursuing was hiding behind the door, shotgun ready. Laver swinging around to watch in mild surprise as his SOG partner, from outside a window and with a better view, unloaded eight rounds into the crim. The man had barely twitched – in fact, he'd been so still as the bullets hit that Laver had wondered if his partner had somehow missed. But he hadn't, not once. It wasn't like in the movies, where bodies get blown dramatically backwards. The rapist just froze, then toppled over.

Coleman got thrown around a little more by the magically perfect ricocheting bullet, but he was still very dead – and Laver didn't think for a moment that he would get any medals for it.

Instead, his ear still humming from Coleman's bullet, Laver saw his future in a flash, as though a TV news headline had been beamed into his head: 'Public and political outcry as sixth Victorian police officer in four months shoots to kill.'

Looking at Coleman's body, listening to the final barking orders of his SOG teammates telling the captured crooks to lie flat, to put their arms behind them, to not move a muscle while they were cuffed, Laver realised he was hearing again. Even so, he felt more than heard the approach of his best mate in the Force, Detective Senior Sergeant Mitchell Dolfin, usually Major Crime, currently with the Noble Taskforce into organised crime, gun dangling in his right hand by his hip.

Dolfin walked past Laver towards Coleman and gently nudged the lifeless form with a steel-capped boot.

'You let him get a shot off.'

'I know,' Laver said. 'I don't know why.'

'One thing's for sure, Rocket old boy.' Dolfin put a hand on Laver's shoulder. 'You picked a bad time to lose your virginity. Will I call the press conference or do you want to?'

* * *

The Wild Man had an aversion to flying, and so they drove. The Wild Man fundamentally refused to believe that something as big and heavy and metal as an airplane could fly. So it stood to reason that any plane with him on board, honestly believing it physically impossible for the plane to be airborne, would probably crash. Eighteen hours and four cars later, they were almost through New South Wales, approaching the Victorian border. Stig had taken the coast road to avoid cops on the Hume

Highway, sitting on 140 ks as they left Eden. He might grab another car around Cann River, or see if they could make it as far as Gippsland before they switched. Let the Wild Man terrify some holidaymaker in Lakes Entrance, just for the sport.

Flying would have been a lot easier, but it was safer this way. A leading drug baron like Karl Jenssen had ways of finding out if people had flown the state. Especially in Queensland, where there is a general understanding that most things are for sale. Even though the Wild Man and Stig were convincingly dead in the tangled wreck of a car down a deep ravine in the hills behind Byron Bay, not far from Nimbin, the drug capital of Australia, they couldn't be too safe. Hopefully the fact that two South African drug mules hadn't returned to J-burg would take months to filter back – and by then Stig and the Wild Man should be long gone, and rich.

Wildie seemed to know what he was doing, even saying he'd left a couple of bags of weed scattered near the wreck to help sell the accident. But not all of it. And not the bigger bag of white powder. The police would sigh at the loss of another couple of wastoids who shouldn't have driven after so heartily enjoying the local produce. The bodies were banged up and burned beyond recognition – what were the odds that both the victims' mouths would be smashed in the wreck, making dental identification impossible? – but they were the right size and weight, and there was Stig's wallet lying just to the left of a disconnected tyre. It was open and shut.

And the drugs they'd been carrying when they crashed? Gone, presumably burned. More than $2 million worth. Even Jenssen would feel that.

And wonder.

Hence the long drive south, swapping cars and putting a lot of miles in, fast.

Stig glanced at his co-pilot, currently asleep with his head tilted up against the window, bright-orange hair mashed against the glass, looking strangely childlike. His big, beard-enveloped mouth wide open, a hint of dribble collecting at the corner. Dreaming of God knew what. Stig still had no idea what made the Wild Man tick, but he was a good guy to have if you thought things could get nasty. Stig might even follow through on splitting the money with him, to avoid the unpleasantness of having to deal with all the other variations of that situation.

He thought again of how Wildie hadn't blinked at killing the South Africans and fixing the crash site. They were things Stig wasn't sure he'd be able to do, but the Wild Man shrugged that it was no different from finishing off a roo after you'd hit it and broken its legs. Stig didn't ask any more after that.

He stared into the night and drove, oblivious to the fact that, while he fretted about Jenssen and their immediate plans, the Wild Man was dreaming happily of penguins. The best thing about Wildie being asleep was that Stig didn't have to endure the hardcore rap making the car vibrate. Instead he could think about Melbourne and which people he should avoid when he got there. And who he wanted to see.

Like Louie.

Stig had lots of vivid memories of Louie, most of them naked and sweaty, but because of circumstances at the time he hadn't even said goodbye to her when he'd left. She may or may not know the details of his hurried evacuation from Melbourne by now, a couple of years on. But Louie would be interesting. Louie wouldn't like the Wild Man at all.

But Wildie would probably like Louie. A lot.

That could be a problem.

* * *

Jake's world was nothing but blue.

A light-blue world with a thin black line, spreading ever onward in front of his arms as he freestyled down the pool, goggles steadily filling with water but not so badly that he couldn't see. The dark shape of an approaching body loomed and Jake almost broke his neck, swimming awkwardly so he could look ahead instead of down.

The dark shape revealed itself to be a woman in a blue bathing suit splashing past, looking like she might be swimming off the effects of a pregnancy.

Not her.

The black line formed a T and Jake was at the end of lap thirty-eight. It gave him an opportunity to stop, adjust his goggles and take a moment to look around.

And there she was.

The same black one-piece bathing suit as always. The same endless legs rising to meet the suit and, above the taut flat stomach, the breasts that filled his dreams, slightly straining against the lycra. The same black swimming cap covering every single hair on her magnificent head. Those impossibly grey eyes. And no goggles – the only swimmer Jake had ever seen at the pool who didn't bother with goggles.

Jake prayed to, pleaded with, cajoled the gods of swimming to make her choose his lane, but she didn't. She squatted, showing the muscles in her sculpted legs before taking her weight on her arms and shoulders – man, those shoulders – and then was waist deep in the adjacent lane, waiting for a puffing, blotchy-skinned, overweight man to huff his way to the end and turn, then waiting a few more moments to begin her first lap. She duck-dived quickly to wet her head and shoulders and stretched her arms above her head, showing her armpits, bald and somehow stirring to Jake.

He clogged up the end of his lane as he tried to surreptitiously watch all of this, taking in her profile and trying not to ogle the side view of her breasts, now outlined beautifully by the wet bathers. He fiddled with his goggles, pretending there was a problem, until she took off, giving him one lightning glimpse of her perfect backside as water swallowed her and those arms began their distinctively smooth journey down the pool.

Jake was vaguely aware that this was probably beyond acceptable stranger lust, but that had become unimportant some time ago.

There was a gap in the traffic in his lane, so he swam and cased her one more time from afar as he slid away from the wall, her body disappearing ahead of him as those arms sliced through the water, barely leaving a splash as she moved, unlike every other swimmer in the Fitzroy Public Pool. At the deep end, Jake's neck again battled the forces of gravity and freestyle technique as he craned to watch her touch the wall and push on to lap two. He completed lap thirty-nine with the vision of her legs kicking in his head. He had only one lap to go, just as she began – beaten again by the clock.

If he wasn't out of the pool soon the traffic would be unmanageable, even as he headed to the Heidelberg Groc-o-Mart against the peak-hour rush. As assistant manager, it was up to him to be there by 8.30 am to set an example to the staff. Sighing, Jake pulled himself out of the pool, hovering for a moment with his weight on his arms, in case the girl was watching from her lane – giving her a moment to appreciate his physique. He had it all in his mind – the moment he would turn and find she was gazing, that she was quietly watching him. Their eyes would meet and it would be she who gulped, smiling in nervous anticipation.

Jake dragged himself out of the pool, fighting the dual urge to dig his Speedos out of his butt crack and take one more look at her. He lost one battle, looking over his shoulder into the end of her lane. She wasn't there. Almost at the other end of the pool already, she was in motion, leaving barely a splash in her wake.

Oblivious. As always.

Jake sighed and headed for the change rooms.

CHAPTER 2
REALITY BITES

It had been five or more years since the coffee chains had attempted their invasion of Melbourne – a European city happily stranded in the wrong hemisphere and boasting a strong population of Italian descendants, which meant a decent coffee was never far away.

The Starbucks invasion had been underwhelming, but it opened a door – and now there was a Gloria Jean's dominating the eastern side of Queen Street, near Little Bourke. A Hudson's Coffee offered yet more leather couches and mediocre lattes on Bourke Street's south side.

Watching the mid-morning coffee crowd thin, Tony Laver sat in Nick's, a coffee shop and restaurant that dated back to the early 1950s, as proven by décor that hadn't changed since its opening. It was home to a loyal clientele, spectacular and cheap pasta, and a series of black-and-white photos on the wall showing the owners with a lot more hair.

Laver pushed aside the local tabloid with the front-page headline 'COWBOY COP' and sighed.

He was refusing to admit the possibility of a hangover. He hadn't planned to drink last night. But then he'd arrived home to find a dead pigeon inexplicably in his apartment, like a demented gift in the middle of the lounge room – nothing obviously wrong with the apparently sleeping bird, although it was stiff as a board. Laver had been forced to remove it. He briefly considered a burial in the communal yard, but finally dumped it in the green waste bin, stopping only to check that the self-appointed ruler of the flats, Mrs Macleod, wasn't watching from behind her blinds.

It had unsettled him enough that he'd immediately felt the need for a drink. Plus Marcia was due at any time.

Things hadn't been great with his fiancée of two years before the shooting, but now he could feel his life unravelling. Or maybe he was just being paranoid.

Either way, last night he'd known he probably shouldn't be drinking in his state of mind, but then, post-bird, thought, 'Fuck it,' and poured himself a whisky while he waited for her to arrive. He was thinking about her first response when he'd phoned her and told her he'd shot a man: 'Oh for God's sake, Tony.' The same note of disdain she might have used if she'd caught him farting in a supermarket aisle. Not once in the call asking if he was okay.

Pondering that, he had another whisky as he got ready to watch the nightly news. And then he'd simply had to go a third, and a large one, when, second item, the police minister was shown giving the media a lecture about police ethics and trigger-happy cowboys who needed to be weeded out of the force. A man with red hair and a thin moustache stood by his right shoulder, looking stern and smug at the same time.

Another whisky got him through the sports segment – an under-performing Australian cricket team was the only target in the country facing more media heat than he was – before Marcia finally turned up, wanting to head straight out to catch the eight o'clock session at the cinema. Walking down the stairs to the car park, Laver, not completely ready to throw his career away on a drink-driving charge, suggested she drive, but regretted it immediately when she said, 'You've been drinking. You're pissed before we even go out.' She sniffed the air, as though he reeked of alcohol.

'A bird died. I had a whisky,' he said.

'Meaning six,' she wearily replied, brushing past him.

And he knew already how the night was going to go.

As she drove, Marcia didn't ask if he was okay or show any concern for her future husband's psyche after such a traumatic event, instead saying, in a wondering voice, 'Tony, are you for real? You sound surprised that this happened, that you killed somebody. Since when wasn't your entire life leading up to this?'

'What?'

'It's all about the job. It's all about you versus them.' Marcia taking on the persona of a movie preview announcer: 'Rocket and Flipper and the boys against the bad guys, armed to the teeth, in their own little dangerous world on the edges of society.' It would have been funny if there weren't such bitterness in her tone. Now back to her normal voice as she stared at him hard. 'How was somebody not going to die? You've had friends die.'

'You mean Richie? That was in Afghanistan, and he was in the army.'

Marcia looked sad as she pulled into the cinema car park. 'It's all big boys with big guns, Tony. I'm honestly surprised you're not smugger that you're finally in the killer club.'

Her mobile phone chirped. She hit her code to unlock it, smirked as she read and then started tapping out a text. Discussion over. Laver was speechless.

Did she honestly think he was proud to have killed somebody? Shit, be honest. Was he proud? He didn't feel guilt. He'd followed his training. He kept thinking about Coleman, lying there, oozing life. But Laver had been shooting *back*, not starting something. He'd waited longer than he was supposed to. Had almost been shot because of that pause. No way had he been trigger happy, or thrilled to shoot. Was that how Marcia really saw him?

Maybe it wasn't a hangover he was nursing. It was just a Life Headache. Who could blame him?

'Hey, Rocket,' said the barista from behind the counter. Laver looked up from his flat white. 'Some chick called Simone says they've phoned. It's time.'

Laver nodded. 'Thanks, Georgio. I was hoping if I kept my mobile turned off, they wouldn't know where to find me.'

'You're getting predictable in your old age, mate,' Georgio's partner, Nick, called from the kitchen.

'Gotta have some certainties in this crazy mixed-up world, mate,' Laver said as he stood up. 'Your coffee being drinkable is one of them.'

He threw ten dollars on the counter and headed for the door. 'You're too kind,' Georgio said. 'Everything all right, Rocket?'

Laver stopped at the door and looked back at Georgio and Nick, in their matching white Bonds T-shirts, at ease behind their counter, their lives uncomplicated by fatal shootings – at least, as far as he knew. 'I shot a bloke and now the assistant commissioner, no doubt accompanied by a few pollies, wants to have a chat. How do you think that's going to go?'

'Tony,' said Nick seriously. 'The coffees are on us.'

Laver smiled and took back the ten-dollar note, then shoved it in a charity tin for the Royal Children's Hospital. 'Thanks, guys. I'm sure they'll all recognise that they've never been in a crisis situation and will trust my professional instincts at the time.'

'That bad?' said Georgio.

Laver shrugged. 'What could go wrong?'

* * *

Deep in Melbourne's court and finance district, a long way from police headquarters where real cops lived, the lift climbed. Laver tried to judge how he felt. Empty? Resigned? Beaten? Not his usual suite of emotions. He took a deep breath and looked at his reflection in the mirror. Lined around the eyes, shaved patchily, a little haggard overall, he wasn't helped by the elevator's stark fluoro light. He looked like absolute shit for somebody thirty-five years old. Going on forty-seven.

Staring at his reflection. Cheer up, Rocket? No. 'Get it over with,' he said to himself, his voice suddenly loud in the confined space, and took a deep breath.

A chime announced that he was at level fifteen.

Laver automatically turned left out of the lift, walked down the corridor lined with fake mahogany and partitioned glass, creatively lit by row after row of covered fluoro lights. At the very end of the corridor was a heavy wooden door, opening into the office of Neil Broadbent, Assistant Commissioner for Police (Internal Administration and Personnel). Laver opened the door, winked bravely at Broadbent's secretary, Linda, who he noted had trouble meeting his eyes, and sauntered into Broadbent's inner office, wearing his broadest smile.

'G'day Neil,' he said.

Broadbent was sitting at his desk. Silver hair, frank, no-bullshit face, expensive tie struggling to rein in a career cop who should be in uniform or a cheaper suit, working the streets. Broadbent with his hands clasped on top of an A4 notepad. Looking stern.

'I think "Good morning, sir" might be a little more appropriate today, Detective Senior Sergeant.'

So, it was like that. Laver thought he might as well turn around and walk out now.

There were two other suits in the room. Reclining on Broadbent's leather couch, legs crossed and one designer shoe swinging, the smart money on an Italian brand, was Warwick Brunton, Assistant Commissioner (Crime). Laver had no idea why Brunton would be in attendance. The other man Laver hadn't met, but he immediately recognised him and knew exactly why he was there. Red hair and a thin moustache. Broadbent saw him looking and did the introductions. 'Detective Senior Sergeant Laver, this is Mr Jeffrey Strickland from the ombudsman's office. He has asked to be here as a government representative to see that this obviously delicate and unsavoury business is cleared up fairly and satisfactorily for all concerned.'

'Including me?'

Broadbent looked at him. 'Yes, Detective Senior Sergeant. Including you, as much as we can. Remember, you were the one who pulled the trigger.'

Laver knew he should just let that one pass.

But didn't.

'*After* being shot at. Okay, so what's the verdict?'

Broadbent pressed the 'record' button on a mini tape-recorder on his desk. Laver heard the click and stared at it.

'I'm sorry, Detective Senior Sergeant Laver, but at this stage we have no option but to demote you from your duties in the Major Crime Squad,' Broadbent said in a voice that suggested he was either reading or remembering well-rehearsed lines. 'Until such stage as an independent government investigation is completed into the shooting of Wesley Coleman by officer Detective Senior Sergeant Tony Laver, the said officer Laver will be re-assigned to the Mobile Public Interaction Squad, with the temporary rank of Senior Constable. His salary will remain at its current level for the duration of the aforementioned inquiry. When the inquiry is completed, Senior Constable Laver's rank, position within the Victoria Police Force and salary will be re-assessed, as will the possibility of criminal proceedings if required. Senior Constable Laver is with me now and has listened to these judgements. Do you understand your position, Senior Constable Laver?'

Laver put a lot of weight on, 'Only too clearly.'

'Yes or no, please, Senior Constable.'

Laver sighed. 'Yes. I understand my position.'

'Mr Strickland from the ombudsman's office is also present as a witness. Mr Strickland, are you satisfied that Senior Constable Laver's position has been clearly and fairly represented to him?'

'Yes,' said Strickland, leaning in towards the tape recorder.

Broadbent turned off the recorder and Laver turned to the politician. 'Mr Strickland, are you confident that, with these measures, the government's media smokescreeners can now distance the political cowards up at Spring Street from the whole police shootings crisis and land it instead on the heads of poor bastards like myself, trying to survive in sometimes extreme situations?'

Strickland took a long look at Laver, smirked and said, 'Yes, I'm very sure we can. Thank you for caring, Senior Constable.' He put an edge on the rank as he spoke.

You prick, thought Laver. But he shut up.

'Stay there,' growled Broadbent in Laver's direction, in what sounded a lot like an order. Broadbent showed Strickland out, murmuring, 'Thank you, Jeffrey, sorry business. I'll be in touch,' as the pair headed towards the lifts.

Through it all, Brunton hadn't said a word – just sat there, swinging his foot.

'Why exactly are you here?' Laver finally asked him.

'*Sir*,' corrected Brunton. 'Remember your rank, Constable.'

'*Senior* Constable, sir. Why are you here?'

'Just taking an interest.'

Brunton got to his feet, looked steadily at Laver and left the room.

Broadbent came back, closed the door and sat behind his desk. He opened the top drawer and placed the recorder in it.

'Merry Christmas, Rocket.'

'Shit, Neil. I can't even begin to tell you how fucked up this is.'

'What else could I do?' Broadbent replied wearily. 'It was a major win to keep you on full pay. The premier's office wanted you on bread and water. Maybe.'

'Fucking politicians.'

'One thing about Spring Street: when they decide to find a scapegoat, they don't muck around.'

'Who's that slimy Strickland guy?' Rocket asked, jerking his head towards the door.

'A cop, believe it or not.'

'Shut the fucking door. No way.' Rocket sat up straighter.

'Yeah, he was pushing for assistant commissioner status in Perth but then jumped sideways to play with the pollies over here. Never explained why he moved states all of a sudden. Must think he has a future in Canberra.'

'That explains a lot.' Laver stood and walked to the window. 'When's the inquiry?'

'Six weeks maybe ... depending on when people are available. The Christmas holidays will hold it back once the schools break up. Whatever the finding, the timing of the announcement will be vital too, given the other inquiries already running.'

'Whatever the finding?'

Broadbent didn't say anything. Laver turned back from the window.

'Neil, that sounded a lot like there was the possibility of more than one finding. The fucker fired at me first, remember?'

Broadbent rubbed his neck, exposing a sweat-patch fanning from under the armpit of his shirt.

'Yeah, yeah, I know.'

Laver gave him a long look. 'This is going to be okay, isn't it, boss?'

'Look Rocket, it should be, all right? What else can I say but that? Yes, all the evidence suggests you acted properly and in accordance with police regulations regarding handguns and self-defence. Every cop there swore you were probably too slow to fire, if anything. But the fact is you were the sixth Victorian cop to shoot someone stone motherless dead within a four-month period. One of whom was a fifteen-year-old kid with a kitchen knife, if you cast your mind back. You know and I know that the police force exists within a depressingly political world, especially here in Victoria where we have a reputation for being trigger happy – rightly or wrongly.'

Laver opened his mouth, but Broadbent's phone buzzed. He picked it up, said, 'When? Okay. Media Liaison in ten minutes. Thanks Linda,' and hung up. 'The seagulls are on their way already, looking for morsels. Strickland is fast on a mobile phone.'

'Or Brunton,' said Laver, sitting back down. 'What was he doing here?'

'Happened to stop by just beforehand and said he might as well stay for the show. Us assistant commissioners like to keep an eye on the Stricklands of the world as much as you do. Rocket, you spoken to the police union yet?'

'Tried to. Nobody's bothered to ring me back.'

'Nice to know you can rely on them when you need them, huh?' Broadbent stood and reached for his coat. 'I wouldn't watch the news tonight if I were you, Rocket.'

Laver stared past Broadbent, out the window to the wall of the next office building, and didn't say a word.

Broadbent was playing with his tie now. 'Rocket, I'm not going to lie to you. The pollies might win this. But I will do everything I can to protect you along the way.'

Laver still didn't speak. Broadbent walked around the desk and faced him.

'I know this sounds stupid, but just ride it out, mate. There's nothing you can do about the inquiry. You've made your statement, the coroner has made his, everybody from here to bloody Darwin has been or will be interviewed. It's out of your hands. It's not entirely out of my hands and you know I'll do whatever I can, so just relax.'

'Relax ...'

'Yeah.' Broadbent sounded almost surprised. 'Enjoy not having the responsibilities and stress of Major Crime for a while. Piss off at 5 pm and enjoy being home in time for dinner and a regular root for a change.'

Laver sighed and got to his feet. 'Yeah, you're right. Thanks for saving my pay packet, Neil. I do appreciate that and what you're doing. I'm just so fucking snaky about this whole process. It's got nothing to do with the fact the bastard was coming at me, firing, and I had to shoot. How are the other inquiries going? Will Shifter get off?'

Broadbent shrugged and grimaced. 'It's hard to say. It doesn't help him that the imitation gun was made of rubber. My kid's got one that looks more realistic.'

Broadbent looked at his watch and headed for the door but Laver stopped him. 'Hey Neil, I've got one more question. What exactly is the Mobile Public Interaction Squad?'

Broadbent couldn't help himself. He smiled. 'That's the best part. You're going to love this. You're joining the mountain bike police.'

'Huh?'

'Your job, as of now, is to ride around the city, tell tourists how to get from Bourke Street to Elizabeth Street, and occasionally give tickets to haphazard drivers.'

'You're joking. You're not serious.'

'Happy pedalling. And remember: try to relax.'

* * *

The Victorian Police Force being like any other government department, gossip travelled faster than a taxi between Lonsdale Street and St Kilda Road. By the time Laver stood at the squad room door, his squad was ready for him.

Steve Duncan was on the phone, saying 'What? WHAT?? Oh my God! Incredible!'

He spun around and put a hand over the receiver. 'Everybody, on your feet. There's a major pursuit taking place involving the Mobile Public Interaction Squad!'

'Seriously? Not those heavies from the mountain bike patrol?' gasped 'Spider' Funnal, who'd dropped by from the Soggies for the occasion.

'Apparently they're chasing some eleven-year-old kid on a dragster. The chase started at Flinders Street Station twenty minutes ago and they've made it all the way to the Arts Centre!'

'But that's gotta be two hundred metres!' gasped Mark Campbell.

Evelyn Calomoulous tore a sheet off the fax machine. 'It's coming in over the wire now! "Witnesses said the pursuit reached speeds of up to *thirteen* kilometres per hour!"'

Laver adopted a pose: arms folded, an eyebrow raised, scowling.

Duncan pretended to listen to the phone again, then slumped back in his chair in relief. 'It's over! It's all over! Apparently the cops had to call it off in case somebody collided with a lollipop lady at a school crossing or something.'

'Oh hi, Rocket. Didn't see you there,' said Funnel.

'Fucking hilarious,' Laver told the room, gathering his wallet, keys, and other stuff small enough to carry on a mountain bike.

Playtime over, a couple of squad members wandered over to commiserate. Duncan even slung a big arm over Laver's shoulder. 'You'll be right, mate. The inquiry will be a formality and you'll be back, hating the job as much as ever.'

'Maybe,' Laver replied.

He finished packing. Simone, the department PA, appeared at his desk. 'I'm really sorry, Rocket. But look at the bright side, you'll have plenty of time to do your Christmas shopping.'

Laver stared at her, then decided she was serious; she was sincerely trying to lighten his mood. 'Thanks, Simone. Pity a bike doesn't have anywhere to carry the parcels, eh?'

She played with one of his now-defunct Major Crime business cards, lying near a coffee mug full of pens. 'Well, I'll miss you, anyway, Rocket. I hope you're back here soon.'

Laver winked. 'She'll be right. Just don't let the bastards give away my desk.' He turned to the room. 'I'll see you bunch of low-life desk-bound no-hopers when I've got a better suntan.'

* * *

Jake slumped in his swivel chair. He was sure it could win some sort of prize for a lack of ergonomics if he ever got around to submitting it to the United Nations' Physics Institute or whoever it was that was in charge of RSI and that sort of thing. He pondered whether they would hand out anti–Nobel Prizes for design.

The office was gloomy, a crooked but effective white blind warding off the bright sunshine from outside. Jake's left leg was stretched and splayed to the front and side of his old oak desk. His right leg was bent underneath, twisting his hips so that his weight was balanced heavily on his right shoulder against the back of the ludicrously uncomfortable chair. An electric fan hummed and spun on top of the filing cabinet, listlessly shuffling the warm air around the tiny office.

Four small black-and-white TV monitors silently beamed out the findings of surveillance cameras placed unobtrusively around the supermarket's entrance and aisles, flicking occasionally from one camera to another. One screen showed a young woman pushing a trolley past the ice-cream fridge; next it switched to an old lady with a set jaw scrutinising the fine print on the back of a can of baked beans; now to a mother trying desperately to control two rampant toddlers. She finally got a hand on both of them just as an even younger child, riding in the trolley basket, reached out and swiped three packets of cornflakes to the floor. In aisle five, a shoplifter may as well have been loading up a wheelbarrow for all the notice Jake was paying to security. Jake didn't see a thing. He was staring at nothing in particular, his empty gaze landing somewhere about halfway across the blotter pad on his desk. The only movement came from his right hand, twisting and turning a ballpoint in clockwise and anti-clockwise circles.

She'd been there again this morning. Materialising at the end of his thirty-fourth lap, she'd still been swimming when he'd had to leave for work.

He couldn't believe he had never seen her enter or leave the pool in all those weeks of admiring from afar. He never seemed to see her until those legs materialised in front of his goggles. Part of the problem was that she never arrived until at least 8 am, and Jake couldn't hang around long enough to see what she looked like or where she went when she got out of the pool. Barry Paxton, his boss, was enough of a bastard that Jake couldn't afford to make himself late for work by hanging around the pool. The time clash only left him those few moments when they happened to be together at the end of the lane, but how do you land a pick-up line, even open a conversation, while dripping wet and gasping for air? Jake had never had much luck in green-light pick-up situations like late at a party or one-on-one in a nightclub, so the thought of making a move in the real world was beyond comprehension. The ballpoint twisted and turned some more.

The phone intercom buzzed loudly. Jake almost dented his head on the ceiling, black swimsuits evaporating in his head. 'Hello? What?' Jesus, he sounded like he'd just been woken up.

There was some static and then Georgi on checkout four was sounding strained as she said, 'A lady wants to know why one brand of baked beans is three cents dearer than a rival brand when they both appear to contain exactly the same ingredients.'

'Where's Barry?'

'Apparently in a meeting,' Georgi's voice crackled back.

'I'll come down,' Jake sighed.

At the tender age of twenty-three, Jake was already bored stupid with this job – but what else was there when you only had basic tertiary accounting? He looked at the monitors flicking around the aisles and saw an old lady, arms crossed tightly across her chest, looking defiantly at Georgi, who was slouched and carefully avoiding the woman's gaze as she waited for his reply. Jake sighed again, straightened to rearrange his legs and creaked clear of his bastard of a chair.

Walking past the frosted door to Barry's office – closed again, surprise – he could only make out the blurry outline of somebody leaning back in the guest's chair, legs crossed. Barry got to have meetings while Jake sorted out baked-bean conspiracies.

One day, if he worked really hard for five, ten, maybe a thousand years, all of this could be his.

* * *

Stig Anderson liked to let people think he was a movie star. Right now, in the Tramway Hotel in the backstreets of Fitzroy North, a watering hole for journalists and other heavy drinkers, he was loving being back in Melbourne. Feeling like he was home at last, he leaned on the bar, looking cool as could be, waiting for some babe to ask him what he did for a living so he could give her the stare and say, with just the right casual touch: 'Oh, I'm in movies, you know.'

While Stig played it cool, Wildie was prowling the place, annoyed because some guy in his forties and his two teenage boys were hogging the Frogger machine. Wildie had played some pool, but now he wanted to mash electronic frogs on the road. The guy and his kids had moved on to Galaga on the same tabletop machine and the guy was good, playing for ages. The Wild Man sulked and attacked his third beer.

'So I haven't seen you around here before,' the chick behind the bar said to Stig. 'What do you do?'

'Oh, you know. I'm sort of in the movie business.'

And he was away. That'd get her and every girl like her asking questions, appraising this tall guy – lean but with that kind of sinewy muscle that you know is from real work, not just ego-driven bodybuilding. Wondering if he was for real. And usually he could swing it; he was constantly amazed at how many people would just swallow a story. Stig would have to start lying, or at least get hazy about the details, pretty quickly – but they'd go with him, wanting to believe that they were hanging out with the Australian equivalent of a Hollywood heavyweight. It was pathetically easy.

In fact, Stig Anderson had exactly one movie credit to his name. It was in a film made on the Gold Coast a few years back called *Cairns Means Muscle*. A shit title for a shit film – so bad, in fact, that it only briefly made video release, dropping into the two-dollar per week category in most stores after about a month, and kept on drifting right out the back door of every video outlet in Australia after that. You couldn't give it away.

The film starred a guy called Warren Clayton, an Australian Rules football has-been who was still something of a pretty boy and fancied he had a movie career just waiting for him. At least that was what his agent kept telling him. The only problem from a director's point of view was that this guy couldn't act, work a fight scene or even stay sober for more than two days in a row. Clayton was afraid of heights, too, which caused big problems on set as there was a pivotal scene where the hero showed another guy how tough and cool he was by hanging a piss clean off the side of a twenty-storey-high rock cliff. Clayton said no way, that wasn't in the contract; they could shove the safety net, securing ropes, whatever, where the sun wouldn't see them. He wasn't doing it.

It was about then that somebody noticed that Stig, who was working as a day-labour scaffolder on the set, bore a vague resemblance to the altitudinally challenged Clayton. Stig's build was less beefcake but, in the hero's matching denim-shirt-and-jeans outfit, from a medium-to-long-range shot, they could get away with it. So Stig got to stand on top of this cliff, feet arrogantly apart, ropes tied to his ankles, hand hovering in front of his groin holding a little balloon full of water, while the director fooled around with about nine different angles. When it was finally all lined up, camera rolling, Stig thought he might as well make the most of the moment. He tossed the balloon over the cliff's edge, unzipped and let fly with a golden stream of real piss, arcing off into space. The director almost died.

You had to watch for it but, right at the end of the film, about two-thirds of the way through the credits scroll, was: 'Stunt Urinater – Stig Anderson'.

His mother – the drunken, wasting woman he'd left in Footscray, Victoria all those years ago, the bitch who'd inexplicably named him Stig in honour of the manager of the Swedish band, Abba – would have been proud of him.

Stig was mid-stories at the Tramway, just getting to the one about how he was once at the same party as Keanu Reeves, when the Wild Man finished yet another beer and stalked over to the video-gamers, sweeping a hand through the pile of two-dollar coins on the tabletop.

'You're done, mate. You and your kids. Well played but fuck off. It's my turn.'

The kids sat frozen as the guy, not in bad shape but clearly a good judge of a situation, stood and said quietly, 'Steady, mate. My kids are here.'

'Fuck you and fuck your kids. Fuck off.'

'Charming,' said the guy, but he moved past Wildie without pushing the point. 'Come on, boys. Let's leave him to it, hey?'

And they did, walking out, the man muttering to the still-shaken younger boy about manners.

The Wild Man didn't miss it. He stormed to the pub's door and yelled down the street, 'MANNERS? I'LL SHOW YOU SOME FUCKING MANNERS, YOU WEAK PRICK!'

Which had the barmaid looking at Stig in a whole different way, Hollywood stardust dissolving. Stig was forced onto the street, steering the Wild Man to the car to keep him from chasing the father and his boys; Stig no longer a movie star in the Tramway's eyes, and Wildie not very Fitzroy at all.

CHAPTER 3
GHOSTS AND DREAMS

He had the dream again that night. It was his wedding day and he was in black tie. But instead of being at the church where Marcia was waiting, he and 'Flipper' Dolfin were approaching the wedding car from opposite sides, the car's white finish flashing blue and red as it reflected the flashing lights on the roof. The headlights were on high beam to dazzle anybody looking back from inside the vehicle in front. Just like they were taught at the academy.

In the dream, Laver and Flipper were constables again, Laver's wedding suit tight under the arms like he'd always remembered his cadet uniform being, the memory vivid even though it had been fourteen years since he'd felt that discomfort.

Flipper started to say, 'Please come out with your hands in front and empty,' and out of the corner of his eye Laver saw the guy moving, just as he always did in the dream, even though it had been so different in reality. In the dream, Laver was swinging around, gazing down the straight of his revolver, feeling his breath catch with fear as Wesley Coleman loomed in front of him, wild hair flying and flannelette shirt billowing in the strong northerly, dull metal in his hand. Laver thinking simply: 'Jesus, he's got a gun.'

Laver always noticed how dirty the guy's jeans were, like it was a detail that mattered instead of something that could be solved in a laundrette, and he was wondering if the stains were what they looked like – which was smeared shit – when Coleman started screaming at him, really screaming, calling him a fucking cop maggot. Laver heard his own voice, like he was removed from it, asking Wasted Wes to drop the weapon, to please drop the weapon and stay calm, while Coleman was looking ever crazier and raising his pistol.

It was all in slow motion, just like it had felt in real life. Laver, heart thumping, asking him yet again to drop the weapon. Where was Flipper – did he know what was happening? Laver watching in disbelief as the flame burst out of Coleman's gun for what must be the hundredth time since the actual shooting. Feeling the hot breeze of the bullet sear again past his ear, and only then tightening the pressure on the index finger of his right hand to pull the trigger. Feeling the gun recoil, and seeing the dream Coleman's shirt implode, the red starting to spread as he stood there, swaying and looking down at his chest. Marcia now next to Laver, in her wedding dress, arms crossed, sighing. And Laver shooting Coleman again and again and again.

Laver taking the shallowest of breaths as the guy finally fell to his knees and then toppled forward onto his face in the gutter, and only then could he hear some girl screaming, so loud and so long and so high and so endless as he stood there with his gun pointing on a forty-five-degree angle to the ground, the involuntary shaking just starting to grip his body. Laver taking a couple of steps and vomiting savagely onto the nature strip.

Finally looking around, expecting to see Marcia, eyes full of hate – but instead finding Callum standing on the other side of the road, silently watching the whole thing. Laver staring at him dumbly, vomit-mouthed, shaky, blood-splattered. Guilty.

And then the final image of the dream: Coleman's bloody back, a red puddle oozing from beneath his body, his face visible in profile. One dead eye staring sideways at the gutter like it couldn't believe what had just happened. Which put it on a par with Laver.

And then Coleman's corpse grinned.

Laver jerking awake in horror. As he always did.

That fucking dream. Laver lay in bed, tangled in a twisted sheet, until he got his bearings, returned to reality, then untangled himself and stood, heart still pounding. He padded to the kitchen for a glass of water.

Standing in the lounge was Wesley Coleman, still with the blood all over his chest, swaying slightly. Laver regarded him and sipped his water. Looked away and looked back to find the ghost still there, just staring.

'I know you're not real. I know my brain is fucking with me,' he said to the ghost.

Coleman stared at him and swayed.

Laver regarded it for a few moments.

'Fuck you,' he said to Coleman. And then went back to bed, where he would not sleep at all for the rest of the night.

If Laver wasn't such a big tough cop, he would have considered going to see the police psychologist for counselling. He wondered if everybody went through this after they'd killed somebody for the first time – or whether he was soft when it came to the crunch, whether that was why he was doomed to spend the rest of his life among pedal-powered rookies.

'Just let me sleep, Coleman, you bastard,' he said to the empty room. 'How does stopping me sleep help anything? You're still dead, you career crim fuck.'

The ghost didn't say anything in return. What was there to say?

* * *

It was Thursday and Jake's heart was pumping, adrenalin levels deep in the red. He had arrived later than usual at the Fitzroy pool, just before 8 am, and now, about forty minutes later, he was hurtling up and down the pool in an adrenalin-charged frenzy.

There she went, sliding past his right shoulder on at least her twentieth lap – and Jake would have grinned happily if he hadn't been mid-stroke. The Legs had appeared in the fast lane right on five minutes to eight and Jake had almost crashed headfirst into the tiles.

Today was the day and he was bursting with nerves and excitement.

For the past couple of days, he had made a point of coughing quietly, as though to himself, whenever Barry was around. He had gradually wound the cough up until yesterday he impressed even himself, exploding with a racking, from-the-gut runaway hack halfway through a meeting to finalise the details of the next month's stocktake. Barry's secretary, Wendy, had asked with real concern in her voice if he was okay. Jake put up his hand to say he was fine as he reached for a glass of water. Barry was looking right at him, and Jake should have won an Oscar for the way he looked his boss squarely in the eye, smiled bravely yet with a certain fragility, and replied that he thought he was okay – although, shit, he might be coming down with something.

Today it had been a snap to ring Barry at home at about 7.30 am and croak that he thought he'd better have a day in bed to try and kick whatever it was. Barry hadn't sounded too thrilled, but bought the story – and now Jake had the whole morning to finally see what the Legs looked like out of the water and in real clothes.

Here came the wall again with some resting legs in sight. Hairy, thick calves. Definitely not hers. Tap, turn, right hand, left hand, away Jake went again. His thinking was that she would be a blonde. Not with dark roots and a perm or anything, but a genuine blonde, maybe with a slight wave going through her shoulder-length hair. She'd probably wear a knee-length dress, some Country Road kind of thing, as she came home for dinner at his house. She'd even love his mother, although she'd whisper between courses, taking his hand under the table, that she thought they should escape back to her place after.

Jake had been dreaming about this day all week, and had been lucky not to ruin the sheets before he woke that morning. The dream where she was on top was his favourite, kind of familiar, and this morning he had finally realised he was reworking one of the sex scenes from that TV series, *True Blood*. Sookie Stackhouse turned into the Legs and he, lucky Bill the vampire, was lying back and enjoying the show. Jake pictured the Legs as a middle-class queen with a bad girl underneath, all style and poise but not hung up with the kind of snobbery that would look down on an honest, hard-working career like, say, for example, assistant supermarket manager.

It was time to get ready. He had to be dry and dressed before she was so that he'd be ready to spot her when she did the same. Jake practically launched himself out of the pool and within ten minutes was cold-showered and dressed in jeans and a white T-shirt – cool and absolutely fashion-safe. Nobody could take offence at that outfit. He kind of wished he hadn't gone with his usual running shoes. He should have gone with his Blundstone boots, even if they were shiny and hardly worn. Too late now.

Jake sauntered out of the men's dressing room to check she was still in the pool. There she was, gliding down the lane, so he ducked back into the men's and got some gel in his hair. He combed it back so that the slightly too-long dark-brown wave was pushed back, but free to fall, just so, over his forehead once it dried.

Now he walked out for real, his eyes drawn to the fast lane.

Which was empty.

Jake froze. What if she'd just thrown on a tracksuit or something and headed straight home? What if she lived so near that she showered at her place?

What if he'd missed her?

The clock said it was 8.37 am. He should have been at work by now but here he was, staring at an empty pool.

Jake, struggling not to run, hurried onto the street where he tried to look in every direction at once. Okay, she wasn't walking towards Brunswick Street. She wasn't heading towards Smith. She wasn't in the car park set into the wide median strip on Alexandra Parade. She couldn't have crossed the street already, with two separate sets of pedestrian lights to navigate. She hadn't had time for anything like that.

She wasn't at the bike rack, which only contained a couple of state-of-the-art road bikes and an old, battered purple bike that looked about a century old – the equivalent of a biplane to a space shuttle when compared with the other two-wheelers sharing the rack.

Jake took a deep breath and almost relaxed. She was still inside. She had to be, unless – holy crap! – he'd forgotten about the other exit, near the baby pool on the other side, near the park.

Now Jake looked like a hostage let loose on the green line in Beirut. He didn't know which way to run. Leaving the entrance was risky but if he didn't, there would be absolutely no doubt she was heading away from the other exit. Jake took a last look at the pool's front door and bolted back through the pool's main area to the grassy expanse to the east where you could see the small park. Apart from a guy throwing a ball for his dog, some kind of terrier, there was nobody there.

Jake was on the run again, his damp hair banging on his forehead as he came back to the pool's main entrance. 'She couldn't have left that quickly,' he told himself, heart pounding. He was shaking. It had taken him – what – two minutes, maybe three, to gel and comb his hair. There was no way she could have left the pool, dried and dressed herself even superficially in that time and disappeared. She had to still be in there. Just relax.

He walked down the steps onto Alexandra Parade and moved the twenty or so metres east to a place where he could also keep an eye on the opposite exit through the park.

Blonde wavy hair like hers would require some nurturing. She was probably busy right now, applying her lipstick or blush or something. Maybe singing to herself. Sighing at being alone, wondering when she was going to meet Mr Right.

Jake kept an eye on the main door to the pool. An old couple, at least in their eighties, eased down the stairs, his receding hair immaculately combed across his scalp, her blue-rinse perm unaffected by the swim thanks to the miracle of the modern swimming cap. Now a guy about Jake's age came belting through the doors, sweating from the exercise, warm water, hot shower and the fact that he was late for work. Jake knew that feeling – Barry went off his head if Jake was at work two seconds after 8.30, the inflexible prick. Nobody ever came into the supermarket until about 9.30 anyway.

He'd missed her. He was sure of it. If he took another day off work tomorrow, he would have to get a doctor's certificate. Why hadn't she come high-heeling out those doors yet? Here he was. Ready for her to come walking over, lips spreading into an inviting, warm smile of recognition as she put her arms around his neck and said, 'I was wondering when you would finally wait for me.'

A punk came slinking out of the pool. Jake assumed it was female; it was always hard to tell. White-and-black hair with streaks of green and purple in the fringe cascaded from a purple ribbon on the right-hand side of its scalp, falling raggedly to the shoulders of a torn, full-length red-and-blue dress. Jake squinted. The dress looked crocheted. Jesus. Had he shared a pool with that? Did chlorine kill skin diseases?

Jake's eyes flicked between the sad, empty exit and the punk unlocking the padlock that had chained the old purple bike. It looked like the punk had a nice figure under that abysmal dress somewhere, but it was hard to tell, what with the green stockings jarring against the rest of the outfit. She was wearing Dunlop Volley shoes that looked like they'd walked to Perth and back.

Still the Legs failed to come walking out from the pool. His agitation growing, Jake found himself taking it out on the punk. He had her pegged as a Brunswick Street wanker by now. He'd be willing to bet she hung out in Atomica Café all day writing shit poetry and spending her dole cheque on coffee.

The bike was freed and the wanker punk hitched her dress clear of the chain before she glanced his way. Grey grey grey eyes looked straight and deep into Jake's. One of the Legs pressed firmly on a pedal as she came straight at him and then past.

And she was gone.

Jake recovered just in time to run through the park to his car as she headed off up Napier Street, moving south towards the city. He prayed the entire small block to Westgarth Street and then left at the roundabout onto Napier that she hadn't turned off – and there she was, still cruising along about two hundred metres ahead, crossing Kerr Street. It wasn't easy to make a slightly grimy, battered white Mazda 323 hatchback look inconspicuous driving along at the speed of a leisurely ridden pushbike, and the punk wasn't in any hurry. Jake just hoped she didn't look around and she didn't, finally turning left onto Johnston Street.

Now it was harder, in traffic, to crawl, so Jake passed her, drove a hundred metres or so and parked, copping some horns from behind as he pretended to take a phone call on his mobile and watched those legs pedalling ever closer in his side mirror. As she went past him, she was approaching Smith Street and neatly picked a gap in traffic to move into the right-hand-turn lane. Jake gunned the 323 back into the flow and was one car back from her by Smith, waiting for the light to turn amber or the Carlton-bound traffic to ease. The punk stood up on her pedals, calves flexing before, in one smooth movement, she plunged neatly to the right, cutting off a four-wheel drive and a bus trundling up Johnston, its air brakes hissing furiously and its driver yelling abuse as she sailed serenely south on Smith, middle finger raised behind her.

The light turned amber and the car in front of Jake hesitated, waiting for the bus to run the red light as it got going again.

The Smith Street traffic was already moving. Jake was staring at brake lights, stuck on Johnston, helpless.

She was gone.

CHAPTER 4
LIFE IN THE
SADDLE

Laver arrived on Wellington Street, Collingwood, for day two of his new job, parking his silver Pajero in the visitors' car park.

The day before, he had sat in the Mobile Public Interaction Squad's bunker within the giant old clothing warehouse–turned–Victoria Police garages and watched the slick tar dance with rare summer rain.

'Are you going to join us?' asked Ashley McGregor, one of the youngest and keenest rookies on the bike squad, as he strapped on his helmet. He was already wearing his fluorescent green police-issue rain jacket.

'What do you reckon?' said Laver, eyes not moving from the window.

McGregor gave a nervous laugh, as though he was hoping there was a joke buried somewhere in Laver's response. Then he'd decided there probably wasn't, and fled.

There were twelve other officers on the squad, led by a dry, no-bullshit cop called Henry Slattery. Word had it that Slattery had been one of the best cops on the street ten or fifteen years ago – before he had children, decided he wanted to live to see them grow up, and lost his nerve. It had obviously been a good decision to step out of the firing line. Now he looked younger than his age, even looked respectable wearing riding shorts, and his job stress amounted to making sure none of his rookies got lost in the Fitzroy Gardens.

Their initial meeting hadn't been encouraging, Laver walking in, a backpack slung over one shoulder, carrying a cardboard box with a few bits and pieces in it and gazing at the man with lycra-clad legs walking back to his desk, cup of instant coffee in hand.

'Tony Laver reporting for duty. Which desk is mine?' Looking pointedly at Slattery's legs, he added, 'And do I have to wear shorts like yours?'

Slattery had sat and leaned back, putting his hands behind his head. Gazed at Laver for a long moment. Finally saying, 'Tony. I'm sorry to hear about your bit of strife.'

Laver noted the 'your': nothing to do with us, mate.

'Shit happens,' he said.

'That's not all I'm sorry about.'

'Oh?'

'No. I'm even sorrier you've been sent down here for isolation. You must be pretty down on the world right now, and I'd prefer it if the kids you're going to be partnered with didn't take that attitude on board, if you know what I mean.'

Laver gave him a look. Slattery returned his gaze, calm and unblinking.

Laver shrugged. 'Yeah, fair enough. I'll try not to kick any dogs unless I know I'm alone.'

Slattery gestured towards an empty desk. Laver went over and started dumping the contents of his box in the top drawer. He carefully fixed his prized original 1960s Mr Potato Head figurine to the top of the computer monitor with Blu Tack. He and the Spud had come a long way, up and down, together. Lately, mostly down.

Slattery was still watching him. Taking in his lean shape – more a boxer's physique than that of a gym junkie. A surfer's shoulders maybe. Probably in his mid-thirties, standing about 180 centimetres – average height for a cop – and with laugh lines around the eyes, softening that slightly haggard, hard-edged look veteran cops couldn't help but get. But mostly, Slattery noticed Laver's eyes. They had that undefinable some-thing that marked a man as somebody who had killed. It was a look Slattery had worked hard to drum out of his own face, to drain from his own eyes, by taking on this softer job three years ago. A look he hoped his kids would never notice.

'What rank were you in the majors, Laver? I assume you were a D, but what flavour?'

'Senior sergeant. I got promoted about eighteen months ago.'

'And you're still on full pay. That means you're on more than me, you prick.'

'Yeah, but you look like you get more sleep, mate.'

'True. You married, Tony?'

'Nup. I've got a fiancée. I think.'

'You think? Just starting up or just hanging on?'

'What do you reckon?'

Slattery's chuckle was a wheezy, rattling sound within his chest. Former smoker, thought Laver instantly.

'Shit, you are kicking goals, Tony.'

'Like I said, shit happens.'

Slattery stood and picked up his helmet, walked over to Laver's desk. 'Listen, I want us to understand each other, because then I hope we can get on well. I'm happy not to interfere too much in your life if you'll stay out of mine. Just clock on and clock off regularly enough not to attract interest from head office. Take a bike, ride around, keep your eyes open, help people where you can. Obviously this branch is more public relations than hard-core criminal justice, so go with the flow. Broadbent's been on the phone and I promised to give you some elbow room while you get your head around what's going on. All I ask in return is that you don't open the window on too much baggage. The kids are impressionable.'

Laver nodded. 'Fair enough. Thanks. I'll try to stay out of trouble.' He put out his hand. 'If you like, you can call me Rocket.'

Slattery took his hand and shook it. 'Slatts. With all the originality of the police force.'

Laver watched Slattery getting his riding stuff together. Gloves, a utility belt with a baton, handcuffs – the usual. He was surprised to see a holster.

'We carry guns here?'

'Yes. No. Well … you don't.' Slattery grinned apologetically. 'Orders from on high.'

Laver stared at him. 'You're kidding.'

'Gun free. It'll make you lighter in the saddle.'

'And so when some crazed maniac stumbles onto the road in front of me, shooting randomly, I … ?'

'Ring your bike bell at him. And try not to be so melodramatic. You want to know how many times bike cops have found themselves involved in a shootout?'

'I'm guessing never. Which only makes the order more pointed.'

'Take it as you like,' Slatts replied, holding out a peace offering. 'Here, have a banana.'

'You cyclists prefer bananas to morning coffee?'

'Not really, but you'll need something for your holster.' Slattery headed for the door, then turned. 'By the way, what sort of bike do you want?'

'What?' Laver was still lost in the humiliation of not being trusted with a gun.

'You get to choose. We have a deal with Kona, so a lot of the rookies go for that brand – but you can get whatever you like as long as it's within reason when it comes to price. Four grand is usually the upper limit. The only rule is it has to have a minimum of XT gearing. And most opt for XT drivetrain, SLX hydraulic disc brakes and an ST or Mavic Crosstrail wheelset.'

'Like I said: what?'

Slattery grinned at him. 'Another language, isn't it? The bikes are bought out of a special police trust fund: believe it or not, the official budget won't spring for them. Let me know what you want and I'll try to organise it within the week. Ride our spare bike until then. It's a Kula Deluxe, an off-roader modified for the street. It's a beauty.'

Laver stared out the window at the yellow bike on the rack. 'Slatts, when I get my own bike, can I get those little flowers in the spokes?'

That was yesterday. Today the sun was shining so Laver had no excuse. He found himself riding the borrowed bike alongside Constable Matthew Standish, a twenty-two-year-old with the height, muscle and meathead attitude of a key-position football player.

'The thing I find, Senior Constable Laver, is that if you ride with the right attitude, the dirtbag element straighten up before you even know they're there. If I ride around looking like a mountain-bike courier, I'll get treated like one. But if I make sure my uniform is perfect, my bike is shining and my back is straight at all times, I find the respect is there before I even need it. We learned about positive passive aggression in Cadets.'

'You're serious, aren't you,' said Laver.

A couple of kilometres out from the garage, in East Melbourne and heading for Bridge Road, Richmond, they pulled up at a red light and Laver fiddled a bit with the handlebars of his bike.

'Do you ever have trouble with these gripshift gear things?' he asked.

'No mate, I haven't got them.'

'What do you mean you haven't got them? Every brochure I looked through yesterday, every bike had them.'

Standish gave him what was supposed to be a dismissive gaze. 'I stayed away from the *brochures*.' Putting an edge on the word. 'I chose my own bike and had the boys in the lab make a few alterations, to my specifications.'

'The boys in the lab, huh? You're good friends with them?'

'They understand how seriously I take my job, yes. I like to feel that my transport is good enough for any situation that may arise.'

'You just never know when a traffic light might break down and you'd find yourself directing traffic, hey?'

'Listen, Senior Constable, this role might be a step down for a big-time gunslinger like yourself, but I happen to believe the Mobile Public Interaction Squad does important work. I was also taught at the academy to be prepared for any situation at all times. So if I do come across some nutter or some dickhead driver, I want to have a bike that can at least make an attempt to keep up.'

'To be clear and make sure I'm not misunderstanding you, you plan on chasing runaway cars on a bike?'

'In city traffic. Yes.'

'So, what have you changed?'

Standish glanced towards the cogs on his back wheel. 'I've updated to XTR Hydraulic brakes with a few of my own modifications, Maxxis CrossMark Exception 26 by 2.1 Kevlar tyres, a RaceFace Deus XC stem and the Fox 32 F80 RLC 80 mill forks – I mean, the standard ones on this model are shit. And the gears are quick-fire Shimano XTR, hooking into the XTR Shadow system … It's pretty much the racing model now, but street-ready. The whole bike was pretty much custom built once I finished working on it. Six grand in modifications, all up.'

'No flamethrower?'

'What?'

'Exocet not standard? The boys in the alleged lab are losing their touch.'

Standish stared. 'What the fuck are you talking about?'

'Nothing.' Laver nodded to some umbrellas on the sidewalk a couple of blocks ahead. 'C'mon, let's decamp in a southerly direction and apprehend a coffee.'

'I don't drink on the job, Laver.'

'Well, okay, you can be on the lookout for potential serial killer motorists while I do.'

'I am not going into that café, Senior Constable.'

'Fine. See you back at the station this arvo.'

'We're not supposed to separate,' Standish huffed. 'There must be at least two officers, travelling together, at all times.'

'Excellent. Good to follow the rules, meaning you do have to wait while I get a coffee. Is it against regulations to sit at separate tables?'

Standish muttered under his breath, but Laver was already pedalling towards the café.

* * *

Stig slouched on the couch, smoking and watching the Wild Man play Xbox. It had pretty much been like this for two days.

'Have you even been to the toilet since we got here?'

Wildie's eyes didn't leave the screen. 'Yeah. Why? You want to watch? Didn't think you were like that.'

'You haven't stopped playing that thing for hours.'

'Haven't seen this game before. It's good. You can shoot soldiers in the head from close range. Watch … boom.'

'Wildie, we've got things to do.'

'In a bit. She'll be right. I want to take this al-Qaeda base first.'

Stig contemplated the Wild Man, orange hair everywhere, beard untamed, powerful shoulders revealed by his blue wife-beater singlet. Thinking of how they'd met, as drug mules for an Asian syndicate between Bali and Rockhampton – home to the airport with the laxest and most easily bought security in Queensland. After they got through, they'd driven the long way south to the Gold Coast, pumped up on adrenalin, laughing stupidly with relief that they'd made it. Everything the Wild Man did then seemed hilarious: whether he was throwing full beer cans at road signs at speed, listening behind the car for the explosion if he managed a hit; or whether he was groping and occasionally managing to even screw one of the bored young waitresses in a small-town café in exchange for a tiny packet of the product they were trucking, yelling through the bathroom door to Stig, mid-fuck, if he wanted a go once he was finished. No morals at all. Or whether he was wiping a sandwich he wasn't happy with on the glass windows of a roadhouse, daring even the truckies to take him on. The Wild Man was psycho and fucking fearless, but was also surprisingly smart. Somewhere in his dubious past he had managed an education. When it came to doing business, he could be sharp. Which made him a good guy to have along on this trip.

But shit, he could be lazy – happy to coast and let Stig lead.

'Mate, I organised this house. I did the shopping. I got rid of the car.'

'You want a fucking medal, Stig? Keep your shirt on.'

'We need a car. We need to go see people about the merchandise.'

'That's what we're calling it now? "Merchandise"?'

'Well, I find it's better than saying "stolen drugs", in case people are listening or a room happens to be bugged.'

The Wild Man flinched as his on-screen self took a hit. 'How can this place be bugged? You say your mate hasn't even lived here for a few months.'

'No, well, he hasn't had much choice about that. Good behaviour might see him out in a year.'

'Crap house too, just quietly.'

Stig sighed. 'Well, excuse me for not putting you up at the Hilton.'

'Good pub on the corner though.'

'Wildie, we have things to do.'

'Oh for fuck's sake, you old woman. Chill. Take a tiny percentage off the merchandise and help your brain party for a few minutes, instead of fucking worrying all the time.'

'We didn't take it to use, Wildie. I need to think straight to get this done.'

'Well, then think straight somewhere else. This is your home town, isn't it? Haven't you got any old girlfriends you can annoy or something?'

Actually, thought Stig, that wasn't a bad idea.

* * *

Laver and Standish returned to the garage for lunch and Laver quietly pulled Slatts aside and suggested that, for their deal to stand, it might be best if he and Standish – or 'Nazi Bob', as Laver called him – were separated.

Slatts grinned. 'Yep, Standish is one of the reasons it was felt best that you weren't allowed to carry a gun.'

So in the afternoon, Laver rode with a kid, Ollerton, who he had pegged as Standish Lite. Ollerton looked at his reflection in shop windows far too often and took himself and the job far too seriously – but otherwise, he was not actually offensive. So far.

Laver tried to play nice as they pedalled along. To his credit, Ollerton actually did the job, directing tourists, moving along double-parked cars, phoning in an abandoned and almost certainly stolen car in a lane behind Brunswick Street. At one stage, he pulled up a bike courier, a big guy with a massive gingerish beard, for riding on the tram tracks on Swanston Street, which Laver thought was a little harsh, given they had also been riding along the tram tracks at the time.

'We're cops, he's not. For him, it's an offence,' Ollerton shrugged. 'He didn't have a bell on his bike either. Another fine. You let those bastards get away with one thing, and they take the piss forever.' Laver was unconvinced, watching the courier curse and mutter as he rode away, but decided it was his second day and he should just concentrate on enjoying the sunshine.

Otherwise, things went well until about 4 pm. Laver and Ollerton were riding along Lygon Street, Carlton, when their radios burst into life.

During his career, Laver's police radio had sent him flying to murder scenes, crazed gunmen, sieges, interrupted burglaries – known as 'hot burgs' – rapes and attempted rapes, arsons, desperate suicides trying to take others with them and political demonstrations turned ugly. Today, as a dutiful member of the Mobile Public Interaction Squad, he listened to the tiny speaker hanging on his chest squawk: 'MPI 5, MPI 17, please attend domestic disturbance at 129 Station Street, Carlton. That's 129 Station. Copy?'

Ollerton, all business, already had his microphone in his hand. 'MPI 5 reads you. Situation update?'

Laver had to hide his grin.

Slattery sounded tired over the speaker. 'Domestic disturbance, Wayne. An old lady's had a fall and hurt her arm. She's a bit spun out and she won't get in the ambulance. She's screaming assault and wants the police to arrest the ambulance drivers. Can you guys just humour her until they can lock her in the back? Copy?'

'Roger that, Sergeant Slattery. MPI 5 and MPI 17 acknowledge and are actioning that request now,' Ollerton said, already starting to ride.

Laver pressed his transmitter and added, 'This is MPI 17, Laver, responding. I can confirm that action and add that we're decamping in a northerly direction now, Sergeant Slattery, sir.'

'Thanks Tony,' said Slatts drily. 'Remember our deal.'

Laver caught up to his partner and yelled, 'Vamoose! We ride!'

Ollerton didn't laugh. In fact, he rode straight back past Laver, legs like pistons, pumping remorselessly as he pedalled hard. He turned to look back at Laver, who was struggling to keep pace, and there was no mistaking the note of contempt in his voice as he said, 'It's not my fault you didn't cut it in the Major Crime Squad, Senior Constable Laver.'

Laver rode a few moments in silence, wondering whether it was worth it, but finally couldn't help himself. 'I did cut it, mate. I cut it a little too well. That was my problem.'

'You've got more problems than that,' Ollerton said, confident that the older cop couldn't catch him if he tried. They rode in silence for the rest of the trip, Laver thinking his generation at the police academy would have shot themselves before showing such obvious disrespect to senior police. Damn youths.

The scene at Station Street was chaos. Laver could hear the woman's shrieks before he and Ollerton had finished leaning their bikes on the wrought-iron fence outside the sagging Victorian terrace house. Two other cop bikes were already there, along with a gathering of neighbours and passers-by standing around outside.

'Don't you use that tone with me, young lady! I'll give you more than you bargained for if you try to give me any more of your lip!' a shrill voice carried through the open door of the house out into the street, the hint of an English accent.

A young, exasperated female voice responded, slowly and loudly for greater clarity: 'Mrs Davies. We're just trying to help you. C'mon, love, let us pick you up off the floor.'

A scream pierced the air, startling the gathered onlookers.

'Don't you lay a hand on me, you little slut! I want the police! This is assault! I know my rights!'

'C'mon Mary,' pleaded another voice.

'You won't get nowhere being that way. I'm not putting up with your insolence. I want the police!'

'Mary, I AM the police.'

'Like hell you are, you little tramp.'

The crowd parted so Ollerton and Laver could pass. Laver spotted a kid, maybe eleven years old, leaning on a Razor scooter, school bag over his shoulder. Laver pulled him aside. 'Keep an eye on my bike and I'll let you blow the siren after.'

'Your bike has a siren?'

'Don't touch it while I'm inside or I'll have to arrest you.'

The kid's eyes went wide like saucers.

The interior of the house had clearly gone unchanged for fifty years.

'God, the smell,' said Ollerton, gagging.

Laver sniffed, unconcerned. 'You ever been in a house with a decom?'

'A what?'

'A dead body, decomposing. Usually they're an oldie who's keeled over and nobody has noticed for days or weeks. Or a lonely suicide. During the height of summer is the worst. Trust me, you smell that and this is like perfume.'

'Jesus.'

They walked down a dark, badly wallpapered corridor, past a couple of bedrooms, into the main lounge room. There was another door on the opposite side of the room, promising access to the back of the house where Laver could bet there was a basic bathroom, a kitchen with a dangerously old gas burner and a back door leading to the outhouse.

The lounge room was crowded. Two ambulance officers stood near the door, hands behind their backs so there could be no chance of an accidental blow, while one of the other bike cops, McGregor, watched on.

'We were only a block away,' he explained, eyes on Laver. 'We heard your call but didn't have anything on and we were closer.'

Laver shrugged. 'Mate, is this a turf war? Relax.'

McGregor's partner, Constable Aimee Ratten, a cute twenty-something Laver had only met briefly on his first day, was crouching beside the old lady who was on the floor, her back supported by the timber legs of a lounge chair. The old lady was holding her arm and rocking slightly, her eyes flying wildly around the room, looking up at all the uniformed youths.

'There are two sides to every story,' the old lady was yelling. 'Come in, all of you outside. Come in and see what they're doing to me. It's assault. Police!'

'We are the police, Mary,' Ratten said. 'We're trying to help you. Calm down and let us get you to the ambulance.'

'Don't you touch me, you little bitch,' Mary hissed, waving her good arm at Ratten. 'I know what you're planning, and you won't get me that easy. I won't stand for it, you hear!' Her voice suddenly escalated. 'Don't touch me!'

Ratten stood and saw Laver and Ollerton. She rolled her eyes and came over.

'What's the situation, Constable?' Ollerton asked.

'Apparently she's been like this for almost an hour,' Ratten said quietly. 'A neighbour found her on the floor about 3 pm and called an ambulance. They tried to move her for about half an hour before they called us. She hasn't shut up ever since, screaming assault and that she wants police protection the whole time.'

One of the ambulance officers bent down, getting on the old woman's level but keeping his distance. He smiled and she recoiled. 'Demon! You stay away! Don't you touch me!'

Ollerton shook his head with contempt. 'She should be in a bloody home.'

'She is, mate. Hers,' said Laver.

Ollerton barely even glanced at him. 'This is hardly the time to get fucking soppy. McGregor, you get ready to grab her good arm and I'll try to get her around the waist on the side with the broken arm.'

Ratten said, 'You can't—'

'Well, how else are we going to move her?' Ollerton cut her off. 'It's for her own good. She'll be doped up, in hospital, at the taxpayer's expense, before she knows it.'

Laver, reassessing the 'Lite' part of 'Standish Lite', took one short step forward to stand directly in front of Ollerton and leaned in close.

'Listen carefully, Moose. I want you to understand the situation exactly. If you lay one finger on her, she's going to scream assault and I'm going to ride straight back to Slattery and tell him that her charge is justified. You go near her broken arm and I'll ride my fucking bike to Darwin and back if necessary to appear as a witness for the prosecution. You'll be a car-parking attendant before the year is out. What do you think, Constable Ratten?'

She took a moment to look at Ollerton and Laver, toe to toe even though Ollerton was half a head taller than the older man and about twice as broad, all muscle.

She made a choice. 'Yeah, I reckon you've got no right to go near her if she doesn't want you to, Wayne.'

Ollerton gave Laver a long look. Laver stared straight back, his eyes dull. The two ambulance men stood and stared. Even old Mary seemed to have gone quiet.

Finally, Ollerton turned his head and bumped Laver hard with his shoulder as he headed for the door. 'Fine. You deal with it, smartarse. You're probably fucking the old bitch on the side.'

Laver watched him go, then shot a grin at Ratten. 'He's a keeper! I don't know how Slattery finds them.'

He brushed past the ambulance duo to the opposite side of the room to Mary and sat down, cross-legged, facing the old woman. They gazed at one another over the stained floral rug and he gave her his most disarming smile.

'G'day, Mary. You having a bad day, love?'

She eyed him warily. 'Who are you?'

'I'm a police officer. My name's Tony Laver.'

She eyed his shorts. 'You're not dressed like a police officer.'

'No, that's true. They make us dress like this so we look as stupid as possible in other people's lounge rooms.'

Ratten giggled. Mary shot her a glance.

'Are you with that young hussy?'

'Yeah, I'm afraid so, but don't you worry. I'll make sure the Chief Inspector knows exactly what she's been putting you through. She won't know what's hit her.'

'Good. Finally, somebody who sees my side of it.' She nodded at the ambulance officers. 'Don't forget to mention those two, either.'

'Ah, they're okay. They were just following orders, Mary. It's all her fault.' He jerked his head backwards towards Ratten, who stared open-mouthed. 'So what's going on with you, Mary? What are you doing on the floor?'

'I've been here since seven o'clock this morning,' the old woman confided.

'Since seven! That's terrible.'

'Oh, I know,' she agreed. 'It's been a terrible day.'

'You look like you could do with a cuppa. I know I could. You going to offer me one?'

She looked down at her arm, which she was still holding tight with her good hand. 'I can't offer you anything, love. I'm afraid I've done something to my arm.'

Laver appeared to notice her arm for the first time. 'Yeah? What do you reckon's wrong?'

'I'm not sure. It's gone kind of numb, around the elbow.'

'Oh dear. Anywhere else hurting? How's your hip?'

'That's sore as buggery too, love. That's why I haven't been able to get up.'

Laver crossed his arms and rocked slightly. 'You poor thing. What do you reckon we should do?'

'I—I'm not sure.'

'Well, I think you should probably see a doctor, Mary. That arm could be nasty.'

She looked down at it, looking tired and old, all her fight gone. 'I don't want to leave my house. They'll put me in one of them homes where I'll be stuck in a bed. That'll be the end of me.'

'Mary, look at me.'

She lifted her head to meet Laver's eyes.

'Mary, I guarantee that unless there's something really wrong with you, you'll be home within a couple of days. The doctors'll want you to remain independent. They'll fix you up and maybe keep you in hospital for a night or so to make sure you're okay. That's it.' He noticed Mary was sweating. 'Are you in pain, love?'

She nodded, starting to cry. 'My arm's not so numb anymore. It's killing me.'

Laver unfolded his legs, crawled over to her and put his arm carefully around her shoulders. 'C'mon, Mary, let's get you into the ambulance and on your way.'

'I can't get up.'

Laver jerked his head at the ambulance pair. 'I'll help you. So will these two. They're going to be nice to you from now on. Look how handsome they are, Mary. All these young men sweeping you to your feet. You got any children, Mary?'

'I've got a daughter. She's married. She lives in Geelong.'

'Where's her number, Mary? We'll give her a call so she can meet you at the hospital.'

'On the wall by the fridge. Thank you.' The ambos helped Mary lie down and started moving a stretcher into place. Laver stood back to give them some room but stayed within her sight.

'So I'm the bad guy, huh?' muttered Ratten quietly from alongside.

'It's okay,' Laver said under his breath, 'I won't really tell Slatts you were trying to beat Mary up.'

She gave him a look and decided he was joking.

When they got outside, Ollerton and his bike were gone.

'You sure know how to make friends in the squad, Tony,' McGregor said.

'At least you're still talking to me. What is it with Ollerton? And Standish? It's like the Hitler Youth reborn.'

McGregor smiled. 'You know what they say about drugs in the Tour de France. Standish and Ollerton act like they've got roid rage. They ride Beach Road with the Hell Riders every weekend and pump iron like you can't believe.'

'And I got them both on my first day in the saddle. So much for Slatts giving me an easy ride.'

Ratten gave him a look but Laver beat her to it, saying, 'Pun intended.'

CHAPTER 5
FRIENDS OF THE PLANET

Jake was so busy wallowing in self-pity that he almost missed the bike. It was four hours since he'd lost her as she rode away from the pool, and his seventh cruise along Smith Street as his 'sick day' ticked hopelessly away. He'd battled the peak-hour traffic in his Mazda for a while, towards and then away from the city, but this time he walked, bewildered by the variety of restaurants, bakeries, two-dollar shops, seconds fashion outlets, art galleries full of what looked like the same graffiti that was on the walls down every lane, and a bar called Kent St, which made no sense given its address was Smith Street. Bikes were everywhere, locked to every pole and bike rack. Jake took it all in, wondering if he shouldn't buy a bike, on the off chance he saw her riding along and they could some-how bond by pedal.

He only saw the bike because he was looking down one of the side streets, frowning and wondering if the Legs lived some-where just off Smith Street, maybe in the old Foy & Gibson clothing warehouses turned into apartments. But, hell, for all he knew she lived or worked in Chadstone or St Kilda, miles from here. There was no reason to think she had any connec-tion with this grungy street full of rumoured drug deals, very real beggars, crazy street-walkers mumbling and occasionally ranting, alcoholic derros and occasional clusters of Indigenous locals. Not that he had a clue about this world. He felt a long way from his mum's house in safe, middle-class Kew, even though it was less than five kilometres away.

But geez, she'd fit right in, dressed like she was. And if she lived or worked somewhere else, why would she be at the Fitzroy Pool every day? And how far could she be going if she was on a battered old purple bike?

Which he was stunned to find he was staring right at; it was chained to a pole down the side street. He walked down and inspected it more closely. It was covered in stickers relating to whales and Kyoto and woodchips and abortion and other causes, as well as one calling the Liberal Party dickheads. One big purple sticker was for Friends of the Planet, which rang a bell somewhere in Jake's overwhelmed brain.

He backtracked to Smith Street and realised which shop he was standing in front of, a double-fronted, glass-windowed grocer–cum–café–cum–clothes store. The Friends of the Planet.

He checked his reflection in the window of the empty shop next door, the 'For Lease' sign cutting his face in half. He looked a little strained and sweaty, and a lump of hair was standing up over his right ear – no, it was his left in the reflection – but he looked okay. He was glad he'd gone with a white T-shirt today; any other colour would have shown sweat-rings ballooning out from under the arms by now. She'd only notice the sweat if they hugged, he thought, and then he chuckled. That was hoping for too much but, heck, there was nothing wrong with dreaming.

Jake pushed the glass door open, prompting the three large bells mounted above it to swing into space before they came crashing, clanging and bouncing back against the frame. Jake fought his way through a curtain of multi-coloured beads and took in the shelves of tie-dyed clothing, handmade candles, animal harm–free running shoes and other paraphernalia cluttering the shop. A café area of tables and chairs filled the right-hand side of the front of the store. He spied a kitchen door further back, the blackboard above it offering what appeared to be exclusively lentil dishes. Crystals hung from fishing-line along the front window, sending rainbow shafts of light onto the opposite wall, revealing swirling dust within their beams. From the ceiling hung dozens of T-shirts with slogans about everything and anything. Moving further inside, Jake took in the organic foods on offer in the grocery section.

Somewhere deep in the bowels of the shop bells started to chime, softly at first but growing steadily, coming closer all the time. Finally a woman appeared in the kitchen doorway behind the café counter and the source of the bell-frenzy became clear.

Her hair was a frizzy mass of red curls erupting magnificently skywards, adding at least a foot to her otherwise below-average height. She was wearing a puffy bright-purple jumpsuit, as though she had just dropped her parachute in the other room before coming out to smile what was clearly supposed to be a beatific, calming smile of welcome in Jake's direction. The woman had a Greenpeace badge pinned to the scarf that fought desperately to keep her hair off her temple, and her earrings were giant silver circles with crosses connected to their bottoms. It was her feet that were ringing; she must have had small bells on her anklets or sandals although Jake couldn't see them. The parachute suit was unbuttoned at the front, revealing a T-shirt that said something about women and the night, but Jake, trying not to be caught staring at her chest, didn't read it too closely.

That smile, radiating inexplicably intense warmth, peace and love, was still fixed on him and Jake fidgeted, wondering if he should just keep pretending to look at the junk on display or whether he should say something – ask about the Legs? What would he say?

'Hi. Just looking,' he stammered and immediately took an intense interest in a book about how to make your own dream-catcher. But he needn't have worried because the bells were slamming against the frame of the door again and the woman behind the counter instantly forgot that Jake even existed.

Jake saw the look on her face before he half-turned to glance at who had entered the shop. He saw a tall, broad, deeply tanned man in a Rip Curl singlet, camouflage cargo shorts and green thongs. At least half a head taller than Jake and a few years older, the man was wearing a baseball cap with 'Dreamworld' on the front. He had a goatee and a large tattoo of what appeared to be a flying tiger curled around his left bicep. The guy glanced briefly and dismissively in Jake's direction and then shoved past him, the curl of a smile appearing on his lips.

The enduring image for Jake, when he later thought about the first time he ever saw Stig, was of the hard, dark eyes that fixed on the woman and stopped her, like headlights closing in on a startled and horrified rabbit.

'Oh, it's you,' said the rabbit, finding her breath.

* * *

Stig smiled, glad to finally be out of the house, away from Wildie's endless video games, back in his old hood, and obviously remembered. He was enjoying the woman's distress. 'Hello Bindi. It's been a while. You don't look too thrilled to see me.'

'You just took me by surprise, that's all,' she shifted uncomfortably, eyes darting. 'I thought you were interstate.'

'Yeah, I was. But now I'm back. I couldn't live without all my brothers and sisters in the Melbourne greenie movement. How have things been around here?'

Bindi treated the question like it was a landmine. 'Umm, not too bad. About the same, you know. Nothing much has been happening.'

'Yeah? What about my little Louie?' Stig asked, leaning in.

Bindi stiffened a little, steeling herself. 'I don't know that Lou wants to see you, Stig. I think it would be better if you left.'

Stig gave Bindi a wide grin. 'Aw, come on, Bins. What kind of a way is that to treat an old mate? I drop by to have a cup of carob-chino with a former lover I'm still very fond of and you try to turn me away? Whatever happened to peace and goodwill to your fellow man and all that?'

Bindi was stiff as a board now. 'Our philosophies don't mean we have to be civil to people who use us and our good intentions for the kind of means you did, Stig. Life around here is a lot happier since you've been gone.'

'Is that right, Bins? Is that right? Everybody's got nice, calm auras, have they?' Stig was absentmindedly holding the tail of a dreamcatcher with his right hand. 'Everybody's chakras are radiating positive vibes into the atmosphere, huh? The moonbeams are generating love and harmony?'

He jerked his arm and the dreamcatcher snapped in half. Bindi physically recoiled.

In a trembling voice, she muttered, 'I think you should go.'

Stig took half a step closer to the counter and leaned forward so that his face was only a few inches away from the quivering rabbit with the high hairdo.

'Guess what, Bindi,' Stig said softly. 'I don't give a flying fuck what you think, you stupid bitch. If I want to see Louie, I'll see her. Because guess what? I don't have to pretend I'm into all this peace and lentils and shit anymore. Now, where the fuck is Louie?'

'Not here,' said the rabbit. 'She doesn't work here anymore.'

'Really? Gone back to the 'burbs, has she? Seen the error of her bullshit hippie ways and gone back to silvertail luxury?'

'Just leave, Stig.'

Stig smirked at her, the attempt at defiance, and said, 'You're bullshitting me. I bet she is still working here.'

'She's not here,' Bindi said miserably.

'Well, you tell Louie I'll be seeing her very soon and I'm looking forward to seeing a lot of her, if you know what I mean.'

'You are disgusting,' Bindi spat with terrified venom, but Stig responded with a cheerful wink. He turned and walked out, slamming the door so hard the bells sounded as though they were announcing the apocalypse.

Bindi leaned hard against the counter, put both hands to her mouth and began doing an exaggerated breathing exercise, body quivering, until a female voice from somewhere out the back of the door where Bindi had first appeared called, 'Bindi love, is that you breaking the door? Have we got customers?'

'No Lou. It's all good. I've got it,' Bindi said, and closed her eyes, taking several more careful deep breaths while placing her hands together out in front, palms up as though to receive something. Then she suddenly opened her eyes to catch Jake staring.

'What?' she asked. 'What do you want?'

Jake was already edging towards the door. 'Nothing thanks, just looking.'

And then he was gone.

CHAPTER 6
RIDING WITH ROCKET

Laver liked Constable Cecilia Valencia immediately, the pair deciding to start off the day by heading towards Carlton. It was his third day in the saddle, and his arse hurt as soon as it hit the seat.

'So, you drive a Pajero,' Cecilia said as they left the garage. 'Strange choice for a bike cop.'

'Why?' Laver asked, puzzled by the comment.

Well,' she said, 'somebody devoted to police work and saving the environment by cycling gets in his car at the end of the day and all but personally clubs baby seals to death with carbon monoxide?'

'I'm unconvinced about the science of that statement,' Laver replied. 'Anyway, let the record show that I have been known to load the Pajero with surfboards, scuba-diving gear and camping gear. It's huge, and not that reliable, but it's useful.'

'You're a camper,' she said, an eyebrow raised in his direction, black hair whipping back in the wind as she pedalled.

'I've been known to camp, yes.' Laver wished his legs would warm up or at least loosen up enough to stop the cramping.

'When did you last camp? In the bush.'

Laver had to think. 'About two years ago. But it wasn't in a tent, if that's what you mean.'

'A cabin? That's not camping.'

'No,' smiled Laver. 'Not like that. We were performing surveillance on a suspected terrorist cell near Macedon. Had to lie flat on our stomachs, guns ready, wearing camo gear and night-vision glasses, taking photos and trying not to need to piss or crap for the best part of thirty-six hours.'

'You serious?'

'Sure. We thought they were al-Qaeda, planning to blow up the Supreme Court.'

Cecy, whose entire police experience so far had been giving fines to motorists and dealing with minor street-level offences, was impressed. 'So what happened?'

'Nothing. They were all talk. We ended up rumbling their farm – busted them for growing some pot, gave them a few gentle taps to remind them they shouldn't move beyond pub boasting, and packed it up.'

Cecy decided he might be serious and wondered what 'a few gentle taps' entailed. The scenario he described wasn't like anything she'd read in the thick police work manuals in her training. They rode in silence for a while.

'Who've you been out with so far?' she finally asked, as they cruised side by side along Johnston Street.

'The first time, I rode with Standish and Ollerton.'

Slatts hadn't done the new guy any favours. 'Oh Jesus. The terrible two. You guys bond? Talk about guy stuff?'

'Sure. You know Standish ... couldn't stop chatting.'

'Like about what?'

'Oh, everything and anything. Correct depilation techniques. The fact he sleeps upside down, like a bat, in gravity boots. His secret collection of Barbie dolls. His love of poodles.'

'Okay, you're kidding. Right?'

'Ask him.'

'You are kidding. I know you're kidding,' Cecy stared hard at Laver. 'Right?'

Laver just grinned.

'Okay,' she said, suddenly sure. 'You're lying. You called him "Standish". If you were that close, you'd be on first-name terms.'

'It's a guy thing,' Laver said dismissively. 'Goes back to army days.'

'You were in the army?' Who *was* this guy?

'God no. Worse. I was SOG. Anyway, does a gorilla like him even have a first name?'

Good point, thought Cecy.

Over coffee at Tiamo, Cecy told Laver a lot about herself. There was something disarming about him, this veteran cop who clearly didn't give a shit; something that made you feel like you could talk – something she didn't normally do with work colleagues. She didn't spill everything, though – not by a long shot.

She told him that her parents had come from Colombia in the 70s. She'd visited there a few times, struggling to digest the fact that close relatives lived in poverty while the Australian Valencias were in comparative working-class luxury in the western suburbs of Sydney. She told him she missed living up north, but she'd joined the Victorian police two years ago, while chasing a boy, and she loved her job. The boy, on the other hand – a TV actor – she now listed as a bad mistake.

She didn't tell Laver that the actor dickhead was only the latest in a long line of mistakes, and far from the worst. Didn't reveal that she'd joined the police force in an attempt to iron out her life when it seriously needed some ironing out, that she'd moved as far away as she could from a loose, lawless and dangerous crowd that was close to unravelling her. Of course she didn't explain, to Laver of all people, that she clung sometimes desperately to the order and rules of the law she now enforced; that she loved them for giving her ground rules and a foundation.

Instead she talked about family – the good thing in her life. About how she mostly missed her sister and her brood of nieces and nephews. Said that she still got up there, to Sydney, a few times a year. She told him how last time she'd visited, she'd seen the *duende*: three little nodding goblin-like creatures that sit by bedroom windows and try to coax people outside.

Realised she couldn't believe she was telling him this stuff but pleased at his reaction, not greeting the *duende* with scorn but with genuine curiosity.

'What happens if you go outside?' he asked.

'When?'

'When the little nodding guys are around.'

'You die. Well, you disappear.'

'They kill you?'

She frowned at that and had to think. 'No, they take you away. Children, actually. They take the children away.'

'Where to?'

'To their world.'

'How big are these guys?'

'That's not the point. They're spirits.'

'And you saw them?'

'I saw their shadows, all nodding right outside the windowsill.'

'What did you do?'

'Burrowed into the bed, closed my eyes. They can't come in.'

'Why not?'

She shrugged. 'They just can't.'

Laver sat up and leaned closer. 'You Colombians have anything on finding a dead bird in your house?'

'A dead bird?'

'Yeah. Not long after I shot the guy, I got home and found a dead pigeon in my lounge room.'

'It had flown in?'

'That's the thing. All the windows and doors were closed. I double checked.'

Cecy frowned. 'I can't think of anything but I'll ask around.' Maybe her parents would know something.

There was a lull in the conversation. Cecy scanned Laver's face and decided to go for it, ask what everyone in the squad wanted to know but was too chicken to ask: 'So what's it like to shoot someone?'

Laver smiled, acknowledging her bravery. Then frowned, looking for words. 'It's … surreal,' he finally managed. 'It's one of those moments that you can't believe is happening, even as it is. Like you're watching a movie but you know you're not. It's real. But your brain can't quite compute that reality.'

She took it in. Was back seven years, telling her older sister, hearing herself say the words, that their grandmother was lying dead in the bedroom. 'Yes, that makes sense.'

Laver suddenly stood, stretched and then grinned down at her. 'I'll bet your nickname is OJ. You know, like the orange juice.'

What? Grasping for the conversational change of gear, she stared at him.

'Valencia orange juice? No?'

She rolled her eyes, getting it now, and laughed. 'Oh god. You men and your nicknames.'

As the morning progressed, Cecy felt more and more conflicted. Go-by-the-book recovery Cecy was struggling with her partner's often complete disregard for the job – but there was another part of her, that other part, that couldn't get enough of hitting the road with Laver. At lunch, she asked Slatts if she could have more shifts with the newbie, and watched her boss put his head in his hands.

'What's wrong?' he asked. 'Your caffeine intake been down? Life getting too comfortable so you need a grenade thrown into the mix?'

'I just find his approach to police work ... interesting.'

'That's what worries me.'

'What do you mean?'

Slattery sighed. 'Cecy, I've watched you develop as a police officer with great potential, doing everything by the book, cutting no corners, exceeding all KPIs. And now you want to join our five-minute freak show?'

'It's hard to explain. You know I love the job, the rules. But it's fascinating to see a cop with so many years on the road, knowing what's worth pressing and what isn't.'

'I don't want him to take you down with him, Cecy.'

'Well, how about we're partnered semi-permanently rather than permanently?'

Slatts sighed again. 'For the nanosecond he survives here. Look, I'll give you a few shifts together. It'll help keep Laver away from Standish and Ollerton. They might kill him if I let them get their hands on him.'

'Thanks, boss.'

'Your funeral.'

'I'm a big enough girl to take the risk. Either way, it won't be boring,' she smiled.

Slattery had to admit she was right about that.

So Cecy rode out with Laver from that afternoon, getting to watch him first hand – someone with more than a decade's experience as a cop in the murkiest end of the criminal pool. She knew enough to give him space when his face darkened and he got silent, but loved it when he broke free of whatever was consuming him and started to talk.

He told her the story of how inhumanely tough the selection process for the Special Operations Group had been, how he'd known he was in for a hard time the moment he finished climbing one of Victoria's steeper mountains only to find makeshift hospital tents and drips waiting for them – the day not even half over. Candidate after candidate had ended up on those drips; one was even hospitalised from being pushed far too hard for far too long. Laver had been close to delirious, not even sure how he survived it, his body operating on memory by the end. He watched a mate crumple next to him, a mate who had remorselessly trained physically for three years for this one test.

Telling her how, once he got into that squad, he'd been king of the world. Cecy open-mouthed as he sipped coffee and recalled the stories.

Like him and his mate Dolfin drinking in a King Street nightclub at about 11 pm, partying hard on a day off, when Dolfin got a call that there was a siege, a gunman in a house, and they needed to get there. Dolfin explaining to the dispatcher that they were rostered off, nowhere near the standby roster, but told firmly that there was a lot going on – multiple events requiring the SOG, a once-in-a-decade line-up of events – so get your arses to this siege.

Laver and Dolfin driving there in Laver's car, running red lights and getting changed into their Kevlar, Laver finally saying to Dolfin: 'Mate, I'm pissed.'

Dolfin, assembling a semi-automatic rifle, replying: 'Me too. This is fucking nuts.'

Cecy, unable to help herself, needing clarification. 'You're saying you were actually carrying guns and heading to the scene, knowing you were inebriated?'

Laver shrugging. 'Yep. That's the point of the story. Thanks, Mum.' Remembering the pair of them crawling along a lane behind the house, unable to stop laughing at being pissed and armed – then shocked by a shotgun blast taking out the timber over their heads. Dolfin and Laver sniggering, wide-eyed, like schoolkids, plastering themselves flat to the bluestone bricks. Laughing even more when a TV reporter, trying to climb a fence to get nearer to the scene, fell and hung upside-down by his suit pant cuffs. Only stopping laughing when they realised, from the toys strewn around the backyard, that there was a kid in the house. Hearing another gunshot. Moving fast. Bursting through the door, guns ready. But finding the gunman dead. He'd killed himself in a bedroom.

Cecy with no idea how to respond to a story like that. It was partly because of the matter-of-fact way Laver mentioned the dead gunman, like it was just a loose end in the story. Cecy thought to herself that there was no way that story could be true – but also knew instinctively that Laver wasn't the type to big-note or lie.

Every day was a new sideshow. She liked watching public interaction, Laver-style. Here, flatly pointing puzzled tourists with maps to the information centre at Federation Square, saying, 'What am I? A meter maid?' Or there, telling a German guy, 'If you take one more photo of me in this cycling gear, you're going to be physically merged with your camera.' Cecy thinking the police PR department would be having a fit.

Or Laver about to ride down a Richmond street but instead stopping to front a construction worker, who looked startled until it turned out Laver just wanted to ask about the Glad Wrap circling the man's calf. The worker explaining that the new tattoo was drawn free-hand, a steampunk design. Laver enthusiastic; Cecy wondering if this was yet another thing she didn't know about Tony Laver. That he had tattoos hidden on his body, somewhere under the bike uniform.

One day, riding through Docklands, in the wasteland of Melbourne's shiny new Harbourtown precinct. Laver saying he hadn't been there for years, since his uniform days when he'd stood guard at the police tape as at least five bodies were fished out of the nearby water. Organised crime along the docks and a mafia power struggle at the nearby wholesale fruit and vegetable market had kept the fish fed for years.

Now marvelling at the eclectic shopping centre and a big grey building called the Icehouse, brand new and billed as Australia's Winter Olympic training facility.

'Meaning what?' Laver asked Cecy.

'No idea,' Cecy replied.

Laver went and fetched a brochure. 'Figure skating, speed skating, ice hockey. Australia plays ice hockey? Hilarious.'

Or the day they had to stop for coffee with Rags, a stringy-looking guy, lined face and oily, ratty hair. Tatts on both arms, where the sleeves of his hoodie were pushed up. Rags and Laver swapping small talk, talking about the prospects for their footy teams in the coming season, bands and how the guy's job as a chef was going. Cecy sitting quietly, trying to work out the energy.

Then after, asking Laver who the guy was. Laver explaining that Rags was one of the better cat burglars in Melbourne, able to climb anything but currently believed to be on the straight and narrow. A guy who knew pretty much everybody in Melbourne's underworld and was worth occasionally buying a coffee for.

Cecy said, 'You are the most interesting person I've ever met.'

'Thank you,' replied Laver.

They sat in silence for a while before he added, 'But, if that's true, you should get out more.'

* * *

For the third day straight, Jake visited Friends of the Planet at lunchtime. He'd been buying ever more bizarre groceries from Bindi at the register near the organic food section. He was seriously wishing he drank coffee because it would be much easier to loiter in the café section – he could pretend to read some of the leaflets and anarchist newspapers scattered around while he waited for the Legs to appear.

So it came as a shock when Jake walked in and there she was, sitting at the counter in Bindi's usual position, reading a magazine article. Her hair was orange, purple and green today, and she had a black singlet on, with 'The Alley' scrawled on it in white lettering, at least three bra or singlet straps emerging from underneath. Jake's breathing became ragged. He still had trouble reconciling this woman with the swimmer he broke his neck trying to watch every morning.

She looked up quickly, something like apprehension crossing her face, but then relaxed, those grey eyes looking right at him. Jake wandered to the far wall as he waited for his heart to stop pounding, feigning interest in a rack of oils until he realised with a start that the shelf's label listed them as 'Gentle body oils, designed for sexual lubrication'.

She called from behind the counter: 'Can I help you?'

'Umm, just looking around, checking things out,' Jake stammered, moving on quickly.

The girl looked amused, then squinted. 'Have I seen you before?' Her voice had a kind of throaty gruffness about it.

Jake swallowed hard. 'Umm, dunno,' he said, staring pointlessly at the tea towel reading 'Jabiluka Mine: All washed up' that was pinned to the wall, cursing his inability to put words together.

He tried again. Deep breath. Sweaty palms. 'Now you mention it, you do look kind of familiar. I guess you'd be hard to forget with that hair and all.'

Her brow crinkled. 'What? The colours? You don't like them?'

'Yeah, yeah. I do. They look great. They, umm, really suit you.'

She looked at him sceptically. 'You don't look like the kind of guy that would be into this kind of hairstyle.'

He was at the counter now, reading a sticker that said, 'No sweatshops. Global warming is bad enough.'

'Well, you know. I'm into a lot of this … kind of stuff.' His arm gestured pointlessly around the room. 'I can't go with a, umm,' he pointed at his own head, 'a dyed hairstyle myself because of my job but if I had half a chance, you know, I'd love to. I've always thought I'd love to dye my hair blue.'

'Blue?' She was openly laughing now. 'Yeah, that would look good. Like Superman in the comics with that cool blue-black. Where do you work, mate?'

Jake had never been called 'mate' by a woman before. 'Umm, at the Heidelberg Groc-o-Mart. I'm assistant manager there.'

'Good for you.'

The door of interest slamming shut.

'Yeah, it's just a job, you know. I want to move on to bigger, better, more worthwhile things but I just think you have to start somewhere. Make a difference where you can.'

Losing her attention, if he ever had it. She opened her magazine again.

Jake watched her start to read and was on the verge of feeling completely lost when it hit him. The single greatest, most original and most timely brainwave he had ever experienced. He almost yelled in surprise.

He stared vacantly at some bottles, summing the idea up, turning it around and looking for holes in it before he tried to make it float. But it just kept getting better, looking more solid with every moment.

He turned to the counter and she glanced up, the grey eyes right there in front of him, looking doubtful.

'Excuse me, but I'll tell you the truth. I didn't just wander in here by chance,' Jake said with new confidence.

'You didn't?' she said.

'No. I actually wanted to talk to somebody who works at Friends of the Planet about an idea I've got which I think could be really great for the environmental cause, your organisation and my store.'

'Is that right?' She was a long way from hooked.

'Yes. The thing is, the only people who come into this store are those who already believe. You're preaching to the converted. We need to take the Friends of the Planet philosophies out to the people who need to hear them most, in the suburbs. Like Heidelberg.'

Her eyebrow was raised, almost comically. 'We.'

'Please, bear with me, umm … what was your name?'

'Lou,' she said. She was Lou. He knew her name.

'Lou? Jake.'

He put out his hand and she shook it. They touched. Her skin was soft, her grip almost floppy, putting no effort into the awkward handshake. Her grey eyes were laughing at him.

The silence broke when she prompted, 'An idea you said.'

'Oh, yeah. Listen, I really want to run this idea past you. The reason I came here was to see if, together, we could set up a promotion for the Heidelberg Groc-o-Mart where we clearly label truly environmentally friendly products with Friends of the Planet stickers.'

She was listening now. Despite herself.

'A lot of products like to say they are environmentally friendly, produced in all the right ways, but it's not always the case. In fact, just about anybody can slap that on their label and nobody does a thing. The laws are pathetic and you have everything but CFC-riddled sulphuric acid claiming to be green all the way.' Jake hoped with his entire soul that this was true.

'That's true,' she said. 'We've been campaigning for years to have the label system changed to truly reflect the environmental sympathetico of various companies and products. You've probably seen our slogan: "Get Real, Get Green".'

Jake had never heard of the campaign, or the word 'sympathetico'. 'Well, yeah, of course. That's why I came to you.'

'So what's your idea?'

'To have you come to the store and help me define which are genuinely environmentally friendly, so we can label those products.'

'There are books about that stuff,' she shrugged, nodding her head towards the bookshelves.

'But that requires people to be pro-active, to buy the books and read them. I'm talking about putting the info right in front of them when they shop. We could put some pamphlets advertising Friends of the Planet, the store and your philosophies, on the racks and actually try to reach suburbia at its very heart – which is its stomach.'

He couldn't believe what was coming out of his mouth, or that she was staring at him with such interest.

'It's actually not a bad idea,' she said, unable to keep the surprise out of her voice.

'I know. I've been working on it for a while.'

'You should probably talk to Rachel about it. She's the boss here.'

'Umm, listen, to tell you the truth, I'd rather keep this between us at the moment, you know.' He leaned against the counter with what he hoped was a certain nonchalant cool. 'Even though I've been working on this for months, I'm a little out of my depth at your end of things and I don't want to officially propose the plan until I'm certain of all the loose ends, so that it won't be dismissed by somebody like – Rachel did you say?'

'Yep, Rachel. She's lovely. I'm sure she'd give you a good hearing, umm – what was your name again?'

'Jake! Jake Murphy.' He took a deep breath, hoping he wasn't pushing it too hard. 'Listen, I'd love to talk to Rachel, Lou, but would you mind if the two of us just had a coffee or something first? Just to swap thoughts before I go to her? I think I'd like the idea of working alongside you.'

There, he had said it. He couldn't believe it.

She gave him a long look and said, 'Okay. We'll have a coffee and a talk.'

'Great,' he said, allowing himself to drown in those grey eyes. He lost track of time.

'Not *now*,' Lou finally clarified. 'I'm the only one in charge of the shop.'

'Oh right, of course. When do you finish?'

'I have Bikram yoga after work.'

Jake looked confused.

'Hot yoga. Forty-three-degree heat.'

'Don't you fry?'

'You don't wear much clothing.'

Jake gulped. 'When can we meet then?' he managed.

'Let me think about it,' she said.

'Um, okay. I'll drop by in a day or two.'

'Sure,' she said.

Not 'don't'.

Or 'I can't wait'.

Just 'sure'.

Jake was smart enough to get out of there without saying another word.

* * *

Cecy and Laver were sitting beneath the yellow umbrellas of Retro, on Brunswick Street, next to their bikes, enjoying the sun. Laver suddenly nudged Cecy and nodded silently to an overweight girl in a green hoodie and leggings. Her hair was tied back, face obscured with sunglasses, as she walked very deliberately along the line of parked cars. Cecy was confused as to why Laver had pointed her out until the girl approached a red BMW with a tinted sunroof and pulled out what looked like a tube of indelible lip-gloss. Glanced both ways and started writing on the windscreen with it. Cecy began to move, already listing four or five criminal charges in her head, but stopped when she felt Laver's hand on her arm. They watched as the girl stopped writing then walked off, eyes straight ahead, desperately trying not to look furtive. They walked to the car and read the damage: 'I am a wanka'.

Laver was casual as he strolled around the corner, but picked up speed until he caught up to the girl a block away.

'Let me guess,' he said loudly as he was just behind her. 'An ex-boyfriend? Didn't end well?'

The girl paled as she turned to face the two police, knowing she was gone. Suddenly she raised her chin, unrepentant. 'He fucked my best friend and then lied to my face when I asked him straight out.'

Laver replied, 'You misspelt "wanker".'

The girl frowned. 'I did?'

'Hey wait,' Laver said. 'I've got a better one. What about this: "Penis substitute sports car"?'

The girl smiled, but still had the fear of being arrested in her eyes. 'I like it.'

'C'mon, that's a great line. Go write it on his car and we'll keep an eye out for the police,' Laver cajoled.

The girl stared at him. 'But you *are* the police!'

Laver made a dismissive gesture. 'I mean the real cops. We're just drinking coffee.'

Cecy crossed her arms. 'You have got to be joking ...'

Laver grinned at her. 'You're on his side?'

'Of course not, but—'

'Prick's got it coming.' And so they wandered in the other direction as the girl headed back to the windscreen to do the job properly.

'You didn't feel any need to enforce the law with regard to damage of property back there?' Cecy said, incredulous.

'What?' Laver laughed. 'Assault with lip-gloss? Bastard sounds like he got off lightly.'

Cecy shook her head. She wondered if this was just his way of coping with the boredom of his new beat.

But he couldn't really be that bored. She'd noticed that he didn't seem to be in such a hurry to get back to the garage at the end of a shift now. Starting to get a feel for the pedals, even if he complained endlessly about his sore legs and butt. He'd actually mentioned that he was starting to enjoy being on the bike, out and about, especially when not partnered with that prick, Standish. Once, in a particularly contemplative mood, he'd said he felt like he was re-emerging into the light after years of being locked in the hard-core dungeon of police work.

And it was true. Laver noticing things on the bike that he'd never seen before, when he was dressed in Kevlar and driving Holden Commodores around the city. Like some of the gorgeous old buildings around town – beautiful Gold Rush Victorian architecture – plus Melbourne's alleys, weird shops, hidden bars and even the street art. Finding himself marvelling at the stencils and airbrush work in the city's lanes, while shaking his head in disgust at the mindless tagging, saying, 'This tagging your initials is just shit, pure vandalism, but this other stuff is really creative.'

Cecy, Ms By The Book, responding, 'As of April, it's an on-the-spot fine of five hundred and fifty dollars. Imprisonment of up to two years for the big ones.'

'That's crap. Look how much skill goes into the good ones. It must be really hard to perfect.'

Laver pulling out his mobile to take a photo of the art.

So Cecy just knew she was in for a show when they rode their bikes down a back alley, off Hardware Lane in the city, and came across a guy in a khaki jacket, ultra-baggy jeans and a beanie, his face covered in a paint mask, spraying an image of an orange woman in a string bikini onto a brick wall that made up the foundations of an office building. The guy seeing them way too late and tossing down his spray can, saying, 'Ah crap.' He looked resigned.

Cecy watching the dude's face, mask now pulled down, as Laver said, hands on hips, gazing at the half-finished artwork, 'How about I do you a deal? We can arrest you or you can let me buy you a coffee and ask you how it's done and how you got into it.'

'I don't drink coffee.'

Laver looked at him. 'The coffee isn't the important part. Pay attention. I'll buy you a Coke or a creamy soda if you like. What I want to know is more about this whole street art thing. It rocks.'

And so they spent an hour with the guy. He called himself Monkey, and he said he was sometimes paid commissions to decorate walls in houses or offices. He'd inked the outdoor section of St Jerome's, a cool bar that recently closed down on Caledonian Lane, and was part-owner of the shop next door that sold T-shirts with his and other art on them. Laver said he'd drop by and check it out, when he had a chance. They parted ways, Monkey waving goodbye, smart enough not to head back towards his artwork just yet.

Later that shift, over yet another coffee for Laver (Cecy having moved to orange juice), Cecy asked whether he planned on making any arrests or landing any fines at all while on the squad. Laver grinned, shrugged and said, 'What? You think we should have quotas like the grey ghosts? Let the parking officers be the pinheads of the street. The way I see it, we're around if any real crime happens. That's enough.'

And it was. The next day, on Smith Street, Cecy felt the adrenalin surge as a woman waved them down, a scarlet splash of blood staining her temple and dripping into her eye. The woman quivering in shock as she told them she'd just had her bag snatched, offering a good description of the thief and pointing to where he'd run a minute or so earlier. Laver unexpectedly pleased, telling Cecy that it was enough time for the thief to have turned around and seen he wasn't being chased, which would have made him relax – almost certainly a junkie after quick cash for a hit. And, sure enough, moments later finding him, on his haunches in a lane near the Union Club Hotel, going through the bag's contents. Laver, wearing a new, hard face Cecy hadn't seen before, suddenly pumping his legs on the bike pedals and landing on the guy before he had taken more than two steps in an attempt to run. Laver planting the thief's head into the rough tarmac of the lane, twisting the guy's arm sharply behind his back, Laver's full weight on him. 'Good luck finding a score in the detention centre, you arsehole,' Laver hissed.

When the cops in the wagon arrived, one said to Laver, 'Rocket, you're losing your touch. You didn't kill him.'

Cecy could tell that Laver had to work hard to smile and tell them, 'You guys are hilarious.'

Laver quiet as they rode away.

'Do you think you can make it, away from Major Crime and copping shit from other cops like that?' Cecy asked.

'As long as I stick to coffee and don't start noticing all the good pubs around here, yeah,' he replied. Then he gave her a grin, saying, 'Besides, I could have a worse life than getting paid to tone my legs and hang out with you, right?'

Cecy thought it wasn't quite a come on, but not far off.

CHAPTER 7
CAR SHOPPING WITH THE WILD MAN

Brian Salter had been selling cars for twenty-three years.
From the early Kingswoods to the latest science fiction–inspired
Holden Special Vehicles, he had sold them all – even through
the global economic meltdown that had made even Holden a
shaky brand. The tiny lot he had set up on his own fifteen years
ago – just one corner block on the Nepean Highway, halfway to
Brighton from the city – had expanded to take in more than an
acre of frontage. Secondary dealerships with other players in
the auto market, like Daiwoo, Hyundai, and even Skoda, had
kept Salter's Special Auto Stadium – he always dressed his lot
in sporting themes – in respectable shape.

This morning, Salter was checking that the early morning
kids had done a thorough job of hosing the cars along the street
frontage. A couple of the Commodores were a little streaky
with dust and pollution – the price of being on the southern
suburbs' main artery to the city – and so he yelled at Angelo, the
lot foreman, to have them re-hosed.

Angelo shook his head, raised his arms as though to ask,
'What can you do?' and started yelling at one of the kids who
hadn't taken off yet.

Salter was heading back to his office when he saw a tall
bearded man, wearing sunglasses and a beanie pulled hard
over his head, bending over to look inside one of the new
Series Five Holdens. Years of experience instantly told Salter
that there was no way this guy could buy the $60,000 vehicle.
But Salter was proud of his ability to guide customers towards
their true level of car and price-range. He was sure he could
find something for this gentleman.

He straightened his tie, squared his shoulders and switched
on the salesman's grin as he strode across the lot.

The Wild Man watched the salesman through a reflection in
the car's side window: fat around the middle, thinning on top,
in a dark-blue suit that fit badly and a loud red-and-yellow tie.
Looking older and fatter than the version of him on the giant

billboard overlooking the yard, Salter with a giant pencil on the advert, along with the words, 'Pencil in a visit to Salter's Special Auto Stadium today!' He was walking with an idiotic grin on his face, like the Wild Man was a long-lost son. The Wild Man straightened enough to regard the approaching dealer with disdain.

Salter bounced past a second-hand Datsun and gave the Wild Man a wave.

'Hello, hello, hello. What a wonderful morning, eh? Straight out of the box. I love it when the morning sun sparkles off the cars. Makes me feel like I'm in the right business, eh? How are you, sir? Can I help you?'

'I'm just looking.' The Wild Man wandered away, past a couple of cars, glancing through the windows at the dashboards. Salter took in the broad shoulders bulging beneath the dirty white T-shirt that was scrawled with a motif for something called 'Spiderbait'.

'Well, that's fine. You look as much as you like. Are you after any particular kind of car? We have several individual dealerships for new cars but also an extensive range of potentially more affordable used cars …'

'No. I'm just looking.' The Wild Man gave Salter a lingering look, as though to emphasise his point, and Salter felt a slight chill. The guy was tall as well as muscled, and impressively suntanned – the sort of tan Salter spent hours trying to achieve, either under a UV lamp during the Melbourne winter or on his annual mid-winter sojourn at his timeshare townhouse at Noosa.

'You from around here, mate?' he asked, still walking fast to try and keep pace with the man who remained a potential customer, slightly threatening or not.

'No.' The Wild Man bent to examine a late-90s Subaru.

'Ah, beautiful little car, that. Four cylinders with the power of a six. Very straight body. Low kilometres. Great sound system.'

The Wild Man straightened, his back to Salter, and turned slowly. 'I've got an idea. Why don't you fuck off and let me look at cars? Okay?'

Salter drew himself up to his full height – about half a metre shorter than the other man. 'Well, hey, there's no need to use that sort of language, young man. I happen to own this lot and I'd thank you to remain civil.'

The Wild Man faced him fully now, then looked over to the massive billboard of Salter and the giant pencil. 'Civil, eh? How 'bout I shove that giant pencil of yours up your arse and then twist it? Would that be civil enough for you?'

'Now, hey.' Salter looked around, trying to spot Angelo. 'There's just no need for that.'

The Wild Man smirked at him and gestured at a nearby four-wheel drive. 'How much is the Subaru, big guy?'

'What?' Salter stopped in his tracks.

'How much is the fucking car?'

'Twenty-seven thousand, nine hundred and ninety-nine dollars. You want to buy it?'

'You're fucking kidding. It's not worth half that.'

Salter started to chuckle nervously, looking again for Angelo. He was way down the other end of the yard, supervising a kid with a hose, not looking Salter's way once. Salter fiddled with his tie. 'Now, look, I really don't think you understand the car you're looking at. Maybe I should get one of my senior salesman to come and—'

'You got the keys? I want a test drive.'

'Well, the keys are in our reception office. I'll have a salesman fetch them if you're serious about the car, but clearly we wouldn't go below twenty-five thousand.'

'Listen dickwit. You're the boss of the lot. You have skeleton keys to fit any car here. Hand over the key for the Subaru. Now.' The Wild Man loomed over Salter, blocking out the early morning sun.

'Umm, no, I haven't got keys like that, certainly not on me.' Salter's right hand involuntarily drifted towards his pants pocket. He tried to adopt a firm tone. 'I think maybe it might be better if you just left, thank you. I don't think Salter's Special Auto Stadium actually wants to do business with a man such as yourself. There are plenty of other lots along this road. So move along, please son. Thank you.'

The Wild Man took one fast step forward and ripped a short, sharp left uppercut into Salter's ample stomach. The salesman didn't even see it, only found himself trying desperately, unexpectedly, to breathe. His lungs couldn't find any air as he bent double, arms futilely trying to protect his gut after the damage was done. The Wild Man glanced around, then hit Salter twice in the face: once on the right temple and then flush on the nose. There was a breaking sound from within the nose and blood started to flow instantly. Salter went down, making a low moaning sound, his shoulder sliding against the door of a Corolla station wagon, and the Wild Man kicked him three times in the chest, breaking ribs, before lifting Salter up by the tie and giving him a last, heavy punch to the face. Salter gurgled a little as he sank back onto the bitumen.

The Wild Man crouched, dug into Salter's right-hand pants pocket and grabbed the substantial bunch of keys he found there. He expertly flicked through them until he found the ones he wanted: a Subaru key and the single Lockwood padlock key on the bunch. Straightening, he walked fast around the bonnet of the Subaru and unlocked the padlock holding the metal chain that acted as a fence for the lot.

About two hundred metres south, a caryard worker yelled, 'Hey!' and started moving in the Wild Man's direction.

The Wild Man waved a single finger in the guy's direction then ducked back around the car, kicked the inert Salter in the kidneys, and slid into the Subaru's driver's seat.

The guy yelled 'Hey!' more loudly and broke into a run as the Wild Man fired the engine, slammed the gearstick into first and planted his foot, erupting onto the Nepean Highway in a wide-arcing left-hand turn that had several cars veering wildly to avoid him, horns blasting.

The Wild Man raced up to ninety kilometres per hour, screaming the gears through second and into third, before swinging left again and then right down a side street. This ring of skeleton keys is pure fucking gold, he thought to himself, grinning madly. Driving more sedately, he cruised along until he spotted a white Commodore parked outside a row of single-fronted shops. He parked the Subaru, got out, walked calmly but quickly up to the Commodore, inserted the appropriate key and managed to pull out without anybody noticing.

He wove his way back to the Nepean Highway and headed for the city, pulling off his beanie and glancing at Salter's Special Auto Stadium just long enough to register the group of people huddled around a blue-suited form, one blonde girl talking furiously into a mobile phone.

The Wild Man flicked on the radio and winced when talk-back voices filled the car. He punched buttons until he found Triple J. That was more like it.

The Wild Man cranked the volume and enjoyed the drive.

* * *

'Well, Stig, this is a surprise.' The voice of Andrew Wo, one of Melbourne's rising drug stars, came calmly through the phone. 'I'd heard some bad news about you, mate. You seem healthier than the Queensland authorities would have the world believe.'

'Alive and well and loving the Darwin weather. But let's keep all those facts between us, hey, Andrew?'

Stig hoping that some profitable dealings with Wo before he went north would count for something.

'You can't seriously be trying to go behind Jenssen's back?' Wo said.

'Once in a lifetime opportunity, Andrew, and top secret so nobody will even know. You in?'

There was silence. Then Wo said, 'You're insane. I want no part of it.'

'Why?' Stig was genuinely shocked. 'I can get the gear down to Melbourne within a day. What do you owe Jenssen?'

'Nothing, Stig. It's about staying alive. I owe the man nothing, but I also have no wish to find myself at war with him.'

'For Christ's sake. I'd heard you were the new muscle here.'

'Do you mean Melbourne or Darwin?' Stig winced at his slip, but luckily Andrew didn't wait for a response. 'I am a rising star, Stig – mostly because I conduct smart business. It's time we wrapped this up. Now.'

'Okay. Sure. I respect that,' Stig said. 'Andrew?'

'What?'

'Just because you don't want in doesn't mean you have to fuck me, does it?'

'What can you possibly mean by that?'

'Can we keep the fact that I'm alive between us?'

'Of course, Stig. I'm not entirely amoral, you know.'

'I'm sorry, Andrew. You're right, I shouldn't have raised it. Just nervous, I guess. Better safe than sorry, hey?'

Andrew Wo chuckled quietly. 'Better safe than sorry? Better safe than fucking sorry? My friend, you left that behind forever the moment you took this path. Good luck, but please do not contact me again.'

CHAPTER 8
LANCE ARMSTRONG

Another night of being tormented by Wesley Coleman's ghost.
It was standing mutely at the end of the bed when Laver woke
from what might be called sleep. Laver rolled over and growled
at it to piss off. The ghost was still there forty-five minutes later
when he woke yet again – Laver had serious words with it at
that point – but then it was gone half an hour after that.

Now he lay on his back, groggy and as tired as before he'd
tried to sleep. Said to the room: 'You shot at me first, you prick.
Go to hell.'

Laver staggered out of bed and winced at his stiff legs –
which seemed like his biggest problem, until he sat down for
breakfast and almost yelped at how tender his buttocks were.

'Who is the bastard who invented the bike seat?' he mused
aloud to the empty flat. 'Coleman, wherever you are? Got an
answer to that?'

Driving to Collingwood, he frowned at the rain lashing the
windscreen. The only sure way to end Melbourne's endless
drought – the cause of catastrophic bushfires and dangerously
low water levels in the dam, the reason the cricket ovals were
bone-dry and trees across the city were wilting – was to send
Laver out on a pushbike so the gods could pour buckets of rain
on his sorry head.

It was just like when Melbourne and Sydney staged the
biggest charity concerts ever, for the bushfire appeal, and it had
bucketed rain in both cities all day. Laver had long ago come
to the conclusion that God, or nature or whatever you wanted
to call it, had a perverse sense of humour.

At the Mobile Public Interaction Squad's office, Slattery took
one look at Laver and didn't pair him up with anybody. Cecy
headed off with Ratten, giving him a small wave as she left.
Laver donned his ridiculously luminous green rain jacket with
'POLICE' in black letters on the back, rode the two blocks from
Wellington Street to Brunswick Street, rain trickling down his
neck the whole time, and hobbled to one of the bench seats,

which required less leg-bending, in the window at Mario's, wondering if his arse would hurt less if he sat on a folded newspaper. Instead, he took off the glowing green jacket and sat on that.

Now that he was off the road, the rain backed off noticeably. Cruel as well as perverse.

As he sipped his coffee, Laver's thoughts turned to his fiancée. Marcia had hardly been in touch. Told him she was going to the theatre with a friend one night; too tired to come over, another. Giving him that distracted 'uh huh, uh huh' on the phone that she only did when she was actually working on her computer, or surfing Facebook, or doing something else while pretending to listen to him. When Laver tried to bring her up to speed on the worrying lack of an actual inquiry date, Marcia was barely concealing yawns down the phone.

'You don't give a shit about this stuff?' he asked her straight out.

'It's just part of the game, isn't it? You look contrite, they tell you off. "Bad boy, Tony. Don't shoot anybody else, okay?" You say, "Sure, sorry again." Then you head back out when it's done, gun packed, until the next one. Why should I get worked up about it?'

'Babe, I killed a man.'

'I know. Got a tattoo marking the occasion yet?'

'Fuck, Marcia.'

'Fuck what? I know how you cowboys work.'

You cowboys. Not him, her fiancé. Not her Tony. You cowboys.

Laver knew a lot of cop marriages gone wrong. Christ, he'd already had one of his own. Being married to a cop was a tough gig that took a certain sort of person, and a woman who showed little to no empathy when her partner killed somebody was not off to a good start.

Laver wondered where she was, not just physically but mentally. Why wouldn't Marcia have rallied to be with him, to support him, now of all times? Her future husband's career was destroyed; he'd been dragged out of Major Crime onto a fucking pushbike. How could she stand by, watching him lose everything, even the ability to sleep? Well, actually, not watching that at all because she simply wasn't there. Laver wondered how long this slide, this distance between them, had been brewing. How had he missed it?

She'd said often enough that he was already married to the job when he'd raised the issue of when they might actually get hitched. Maybe she'd meant it. Maybe he had been. He needed to talk to her.

He was on his second coffee when he saw the silver Commodore shuffling south towards the city, stuck behind a tram and the usual snarled traffic. Laver sighed as he saw the familiar faces recognise him and break into grins. The light had just gone red on Johnston Street, so the car would be there for a couple of minutes. Laver creaked to his feet, signalled to the waiter that he'd be back and wandered out to the middle of the road to say hello.

'Well, well, well. If it isn't Lance fucking Armstrong,' said Steve 'Beer With' Duncan, a Major Crime detective.

'Jealous yet, desk bunnies?' asked Laver. 'Squid, imagine how good you'd look in this gear.'

Evelyn Calomoulous looked unconvinced. 'I'd certainly carry it off better in the legs, Rocket. You look hobbled. Is that from riding bikes or should I be impressed by Marcia's abilities?'

'Only if you mean her ability to kick kneecaps. Forget any bedroom stuff, even if I was capable of it right now.'

'Oh dear,' she said, wincing sympathetically. 'Life doesn't look so bad though! How's the coffee?'

'It's good. In fact this whole new job is nothing but exceptional coffee, suntans, beautiful pedestrians, gorgeous tourists wanting personal service, and the deep satisfaction of being a serving member of Australia's finest police force.'

'Hating it, huh?' said Duncan.

'I'm going insane. Some if it is fun but shit, it's like going back to primary school.'

'Decent teammates?' Evelyn asked.

'Some great kids, others totally dickwads. You know how it is.'

She looked deliberately at Laver and then at Duncan before she said, deadpan, 'Yes. I know exactly how it is.'

'We're not supposed to be talking to you, you know,' said Duncan.

'Yeah, funny.'

'Dead set,' Duncan insisted. 'The boss made it very clear. No contact. You're in deep, deep Siberia.'

Laver stared at him. 'Siberia? Broadbent said that?'

'Well, it felt like he was the messenger, the way he said it,' Beer With grinned. 'Anyway, doesn't mean we listened to him, mate. So what's the plan?'

'The plan? Jesus, I don't know. Mountain biking is an Olympic event now. I could still make the next ones.'

'You coming back to Major?'

'You tell me. Depends on the pollies mostly. The deep Siberia bit is a worry. You heard anything on my post mortem?'

Duncan grinned. 'Inquiry, Rocket. It's an inquiry. A post mortem is what they had to do on that poor bastard you plugged.'

'The one that shot at me first. You heard anything?'

'You kidding? Down in our little mushroom patch?'

Laver glanced up at the light: still red. 'What are you two up to?'

'Wild goose chase,' said Beer With. 'We've been investigating a supermarket in the inner north as a potential drug distribution centre, but it seems unlikely.'

'How far in are you?'

'Not far. Just having a look, digging some records. Paperwork, Rocket, remember that?'

'Thing of the past.'

The light turned green but traffic remained jammed on Johnston Street, three cars caught across the intersection so that the Brunswick Street traffic couldn't move in either direction. A chorus of horns started up.

'Shouldn't you be on to that, officer?' Evelyn said, nodding towards the confusion. 'That looks like a challenging job for a member of the Elite Public Mobile Interaction Squad.'

Laver regarded the chaos. One of the drivers blocking the intersection on Johnston was giving the finger to the drivers at the front of the Brunswick Street queue. They leaned harder on their horns in response.

'Hmm, looks a little heavy. I don't think I'm up to dealing with aggression yet. I'm working my way up from lost tourists.'

Finally, the cars shifted and traffic began to move. Rocket stood and jogged painfully back to the parked cars on the Mario's side of the street.

'See you, Rocket,' called Evelyn. 'On the other side of Siberia. Maybe even the Christmas party.' Rocket looked back at them as Duncan shrugged and started to drive.

The sun was starting to come out but Laver went back to his window seat at Mario's and ordered a third coffee, guaranteeing himself a headache.

* * *

It was lunchtime, and Jake's battered Mazda was making the increasingly familiar journey back to Smith Street. He grabbed a park on the north side of Johnston, among all the brand-name seconds shops that seemed to have more expensive sports gear than most retail shops, and walked past the picture framers and the bead shop, a gallery and a pawn broker. The walk was good for him. He'd been avoiding the pool for days now, not wanting Lou to recognise him in Speedos and wet hair, panting from doing laps – at least not at this delicate stage of their courtship. He felt the usual thrill as he got closer to her shop.

But Lou was nowhere to be seen in Friends of the Planet. A small man, balding and with a neatly trimmed beard, was behind the desk of the grocery section, reading a book with an ominous black cover entitled '2012'. He smiled at Jake as he came in, then went back to his pages. The café area was busy, all sorts of Smith Street wildlife chowing down on salads, curries or lentil burgers. Jake wandered towards the merchandise stands and poked around among the T-shirts and cruelty-free shoes for a while, keeping an eye on his watch and hoping Lou would turn up.

Eventually he drifted into the clothing section and found himself in front of a mirror, taking stock.

Jake was wearing his standard work-wear: grey business pants and a collared white shirt he'd bought at Myer. As he studied his black business shoes, Jake realised with a start that his everyday work-wear was almost identical to his old school uniform. Just add a red-and-green tie with the school crest, and he was back in year 12. His hair was a little longer now, and his face had lost some of its puppy fat, but he could still be looking at a dodgy school profile pic, those ones taken in front of a smoky-blue curtain every February and sold in packets of different-sized images. Even if you'd blinked mid-shot, as Jake had a rare talent for doing.

And here he stood, in this shop of colour and passionate causes and belief in a better world, wearing his corporate uniform. Jake thought about Lou and her crazy hair and even crazier fashion sense. He saw himself at the edge of something, a new awakening, a potential new *him*, and wondered if this shift was something to be pursued.

At that exact moment, he saw the hat. It was an oversized, baggy green, red and yellow cap, like a mutated cross between a French beret and a baseball cap. There was a large green leaf sewn into the left-hand side of it, above the short brim. Jake had no idea what kind of leaf it was. It looked vaguely like a thin oak leaf, but spiky on the edges.

He checked to make sure nobody was paying much attention before he tried on the hat. It swam in colour on his dark hair and made a mockery of the sweat-stained white business shirt. Jake went back to the racks of T-shirts and looked through the mediums. He disregarded all the white shirts and went for colour. There was a black one emblazoned with the words, 'Is that the truth or did you read it in the *Herald Sun*?' A blue one had a picture of a whale with the slogan, 'Not having a whale of the time in the Southern Ocean' and a logo for some organisation or something called the Sea Shepherd. A green one said 'Economic Rationalism Isn't', which made no sense at all, while a purple one had a bright picture of a nuclear sign with a black handprint over it, surrounded by the words, 'No weapons. No uranium. No war. Reclaim the future.'

Jake briefly considered an orange T-shirt with a picture of a cartoon chicken and the words 'Nice chicks don't murder for dinner'. But then read the tag inside, which said, 'For Vegans Only'; he'd never been into Star Trek.

In the end, Jake went for a Sound Relief T-shirt from the big charity concert. It was black, but with a swirl of colour as fire met water. Jake hadn't gone to the concert, but he remembered the event. And now the shirt was on sale.

At the counter, Jake almost lost his nerve when the bald man sneered at him after he'd replied 'Yes' when asked if he'd like a plastic bag. But Jake held firm. He liked whatever was stirring inside.

He bought the T-shirt. And the beret.

'See you around, Marley,' said the man.

Jake had no idea what he was talking about.

* * *

'I seriously never thought I'd say this, but in Queensland the crims have got more fucking class than in Melbourne.' The Wild Man sat in the driver's seat, arms folded, staring at the tacky fast food outlet they were parked in front of. 'I'm not going in there. If their tough guys are going to lounge around at the outside tables, I'm going to as well.'

'So you're my "tough guy"?'

Stig grinned at his partner until the Wild Man replied, 'I'd fucking want to be or you'd be utterly screwed. Just remember for once that you're supposed to be the smart guy and get the deal done.'

Wildie ended up not even getting out of the car, just dangling a lit cigarette out the window from his right hand and gazing insolently at the beefy white guys trying to pose just so. They were wannabe made men decked out in summer fashion, all singlets, groomed hair and gold chains: straight from central casting for *The Sopranos*. Wildie wondered how many of them would last five minutes in Sydney's Long Bay Jail, where he'd done most of his time.

Stig was inside, at one of only two occupied tables, sipping a thickshake and talking to a haggard-looking, unshaven man in a dark blazer but with a gaudy Ed Hardy T-shirt underneath. The man an ex-boxer and a very large player in the Melbourne underworld. The other occupied table was his right-hand man, looking bored and reading a tabloid. The fast food outlet's staff made the occasional crashing or banging noise out the back, in the kitchen.

'I was very sorry to hear about your brother,' Stig said.

'Which one?' The ex-boxer stared at him, sizing him up.

'Both of them. And your uncle.'

The man almost smiled. 'Which one?'

'Yeah, the war sounds like it was like that. Fucked up,' Stig said, shaking his head.

'Whose side were you on, Mr Smith? I can't recall.'

'I was Switzerland. Unaligned. I wasn't involved in, umm, merchandise at all at that point.'

The man sipped on a cola. 'Fair enough. So why are we meeting, Mr Smith?'

'As per my email. You're still in business?'

'Always in business, Mr Smith. With considerably fewer rivals than I used to have to worry about.'

'But only a minor role in the *Underbelly* TV series. You must have been gutted about that.'

Stig worried he may have overstepped, but the man smiled. 'They got my name wrong, too. Blessing really. Otherwise I'd be signing autographs when all I really want to do is make a quiet point or do a deal.'

'Well, speaking of deals, the pipes I have to offer are of the highest quality,' Stig said. 'Best materials, from the north. Only because of over-ordering that they're even available at this price.'

'Easy mistake to make, given the speed with which the Global Crisis hit,' the man said. 'The housing market is a rollercoaster.'

'I can pretty much have them in Melbourne within a day if you're interested.'

'Depends on the price, Mr Smith. I'm not short on pipes. This would be an investment, need storage. Depends on ware-house space.'

'The price can move around a bit but my boss would want at least two hundred and fifty.'

'How many pipes are we talking again?'

'Twenty or thirty tonne. High quality, like I said.'

'Still, two hundred and fifty is a lot for spare pipes. I might just buy some local pipes as I need them.'

'You'd regret that,' Stig said.

The man was instantly hostile. 'Would I, Mr Smith? And why would I regret that?'

A table away, the right-hand man looked up from his paper.

'Not like that,' Stig said, backpedalling. 'We're all friends. I'm just saying that once you tried one of these northern pipes, you'd appreciate what you were paying for.'

The man's face was an impassive mask again. 'Craftsmanship, Mr Smith?'

'Exactly. Quality craftsmanship.'

'When would I need to let you know?'

'Sooner the better. I won't offer them elsewhere until I hear.'

'I'd appreciate that, Mr Smith.'

'However, waiting on your reply does put me in something of a position, so I'd appreciate an answer either way as soon as you're able.'

The man's face was unreadable. The right-hand man stood and walked over to the door, a full three seconds before his boss stood and headed towards that exit. It was clear the meeting was over, but then the ex-boxer stopped and turned. 'Mr Smith, there wouldn't be any problem with me making a few phone calls to the north to check the authenticity of these pipes, would there?'

'I'd appreciate it if you didn't. Not everybody in head office knows that we're offloading them at these kinds of prices.'

'Is that right,' the man said.

'In fact, extreme discretion would be much appreciated,' Stig said.

The man looked at him steadily and then nodded. 'You have my word, for now. But pipes can be a dangerous business. Call me tomorrow.'

CHAPTER 9
LAVER'S DAY OFF

The sleep thing was becoming a problem, Laver decided, as the alarm went off forty minutes after he'd dropped into his first deep sleep of the night. He woke with his arm splayed out across the empty side of the bed. Marcia's side. Cold. Laver felt the heaviness and stared at the sheets for a long moment. Then looked around and was relieved to see that bastard Coleman had disappeared again.

He finally staggered out into the lounge room and stared at his police bike, propped up against the wall near the door. He'd optimistically brought it home in the backseat of his car last night, with the idea of going for a decent, leg-building ride after such a slack day at work. Two whiskies in, he'd admitted that wasn't going to happen.

This morning, he didn't even bother hacking across to Collingwood or phoning. Just emailed Slattery, with the subject line: 'Sore arse'.

He wandered down to the local café for breakfast. Over eggs, he read the paper and was stunned to feel his eyes swim when he came across an article about police culture with a giant graphic of a gun pointing straight out of the page. He read the first two paragraphs and was smart enough to stop right there. Laver reached for the sports pages and wished the footy was on, so he could get really interested. Cricket only engaged him to a certain level. It wasn't a passion like AFL – but it was enough to offer a distraction for blurred eyes.

Laver tried to remember the last time he had actually cried. When his grandmother died, about five years ago? No. He'd been sad, desperately sad, but hadn't cried. He'd been the rock for his aunties as they cried their eyes out.

When his dog had died, when he was a teenager? He'd bawled then. He remembered lying on his bed, wondering if he was going to throw up from crying so hard.

And the Callum thing. Talia's ruthless exit. Losing his wife and his son. He'd unravelled back then, no doubt. Could that really be the last time he'd cried? Man.

Walking home, he assessed his state of mind. He felt frayed. Like he was losing his grip and didn't know what to hold on to, which move to make. He was in this ridiculous holding pattern, his career possibly ruined, and there was nothing he could do. Nobody he could convince that he was the same cop, the same detective who had never put a foot wrong in all those years.

And then there was Marcia. For a time, they had soared. She hadn't minded the long hours, the sudden disappearances, the stuff he couldn't talk about upon his return. She'd found all that exciting and liked her independence. Made Laver believe again. Laver tuned in often enough to start to feel his walls descending at last; feeling the lonely, bitter years that followed the sudden brutal departure of Talia, and Callum, falling away at last.

He'd meant it when he said they should get married – but then, that side of his life sorted, he'd gotten back to work. And was slightly annoyed by all Marcia's questions about the actual wedding plans, the details. Not realising until now that she hadn't even asked for a while. Realising with a jolt, he wasn't sure if she was still wearing the ring.

Laver went to the gym. Maybe riding the bike around wasn't making him as tired as he thought and his body needed to be more exhausted so it could rest and shut out his mind – his dreams of dead birds in his house. Coleman's ghost.

Even with police shiftwork, Laver rarely found himself at the gym on a weekday morning. It was full of women who'd presumably managed to ditch the kids for a few hours and lowlife types that Laver pegged as waiters or maybe musicians. Which reminded him that Damian was coming around tonight, pre-gig. It was lucky he had the bike at home. Damian would love it.

Laver lifted some free weights, sweating, grunting and crashing them to the floor, despite the frowns from the mother's club, who were working more gently on the various fitness machines. It still wasn't enough. A converted squash court upstairs housed a boxing set-up, but when Laver arrived he found it already occupied by one of the resident personal trainers who was egging a woman in her fifties through arm-shaking push-ups.

'Okay if I hit the bags?' Laver asked and the guy nodded, while never stopping a monologue: 'That's great, Margie. Keep it going. That's three, love. Lower yourself slowly, hold it for a breath and now come on, you can do it. Push, push, push. Fantastic. That's four!'

Laver wrapped the tape over and under his hands, through the fingers to protect the knuckles, and around the wrist. Then pulled on his gloves and stretched his arms behind him.

Margie, having completed five push-ups, staggered to her feet and reached for a water bottle.

Laver started on the floor-to-ceiling bag, ducking and weaving while drumming out combinations, his left jab flicking and catching the waving bag every time, the elastic that held it to the roof and floor snapping and stretching. A right hook or jab occasionally straightened the bag back out as it floated past his face.

Then it was the heavy bag and Laver didn't hold back. Deep rips to the body, thundering hooks. Straight rights and lefts that shook the entire bag, its metal chains clanging and jolting as Laver's frustration flowed down his arms, all the way from his set legs – knees slightly bent, toes turning in with the punch. The onslaught lasting for several minutes.

Laver stood back, gulping for air, his arms jelly.

Margie, now gently tapping a lighter bag, looked slightly stunned.

The trainer gave him an amused raised eyebrow. 'Family, girlfriend or work?'

'At least two out of three,' Laver gasped.

A sauna and shower took him up to lunchtime, and he felt slightly better. Perhaps he should have gone to work after all. Laver hadn't had time off in Melbourne in years, and was unsure what to do. The answer, when it came to him, was obvious but deflating.

Of course he knew what to do. It was a step up from visiting his mother's grave, but not much of one.

His father lived in a semi-detached house in Hawthorn with neat roses in the front yard and a clipped lawn. Neither of which would be the work of Laver's dad.

Bill Laver was sitting in his chair as usual as Laver kissed his step-mum, Daisy, and came through the front door.

'Well, look who the cat dragged in,' Laver's dad said, putting down the crossword. He adjusted his glasses to better frown at his son, while adjusting the gut that spilt over the edge of his recliner chair, bad comb-over as reliably in place as ever. His face all harsh lines and deep wrinkles from endless scowling at the world. 'Shot anybody today, Clint Eastwood?'

'Great to see you too, Dad. Don't get up. No need for a hug.'

'I wasn't going to get up.'

'I know, Dad.'

'So. Haven't you made a name for yourself, hey, boy? Feeling famous yet?'

Laver sat on the couch, the safety of a coffee table and a vase of fresh flowers between him and his father. He wondered if Bill had even noticed Daisy's flower arrangement. If he ever did. 'Not any kind of famous I asked for, Dad. He shot at me first. Almost got me.'

'Almost. Pfft.' Laver watched his father try to toss his head and shake it in disgust at the same time. Why the hell had he thought coming here would be a good idea?

Daisy walked back into the room with a tray. Coffee for Laver, tea for her and Bill. Biscuits. Possibly shortbreads, by the look of them – pre-Christmas baking. Laver noticed how tired Daisy looked. How haggard from living with this man. But not going anywhere.

His father was pointing a finger at him now.

'I thought you were the one kid who might not be a fuck-up. I was only saying to Daisy the other day that her kid, Jackie—'

'It's Johnnie,' she snapped.

'Johnnie then.'

'He always gets that wrong,' she said to Laver, giving him a look.

Bill spoke over top of her, 'The woman's got three kids and none of them are mine, so what does she want from me ...?'

'God, give me strength,' Daisy said. 'We're married for fifteen years and your loser of a father still needs blessed nametags.'

Laver wondered if, with all his practice lately, he could finish his coffee within a minute and get out of there.

* * *

Jake looked around to see if anybody in the Groc-o-Mart car park was watching, decided they weren't, and awkwardly pulled his business shirt over his head, bashing an arm into the roof of the Mazda. He pulled on his new T-shirt and then put the red-yellow-and-green beret on, staring in amazement at himself in the rear-vision mirror before starting the car up and heading towards the city on Heidelberg Road.

He took a while to find a park on Smith Street and walked self-consciously back a couple of blocks to Friends of the Planet, forcing himself not to look into the various bars and cafés to see if anybody was laughing at his new look. Occasionally he let himself sneak a glance at his reflection in shop windows, and couldn't help grinning. He looked so unlike the usual him.

Bindi was behind the counter – Jake was relieved it wasn't the bald guy again. But no Lou anywhere in sight. How often could he try to come here twice a day on the slight hope of bumping into her? Maybe he should start swimming again, just to ensure they crossed paths in some capacity, even soggy and out of breath?

Jake bought something called 'carob', which he assumed was some kind of chocolate, and headed back onto Smith Street. He stood outside in the afternoon sun, watching the colourful local population drift past and the peak-hour traffic crawl along. It occurred to him that he should buy a bicycle. He could ride in from Kew, to keep fit – and he would have a better chance of bumping into Lou in the bike lanes that seemed to be placed randomly around Collingwood and Fitzroy.

He peered back in the window of Friends of the Planet, but there was only Bindi.

Jake headed home. His mum would be cooking dinner. Best not to be late.

CHAPTER 10
THE DEVIL'S MOCKERY

Laver checked his email while waiting for Damian to show up. Broadbent's secretary, Linda, had sent one two hours ago, asking him to phone, so he did.

'He's not here now,' Linda told him. 'He wanted you to come in but we couldn't reach you. According to Slatts at the mountain bike squad, you forgot to take your mobile with you today on the bike.'

'That's right,' Laver said. 'You hang out with rookies, you start making rookie errors, huh?' Slattery was a good bloke.

'Well, Neil's gone for the day but he said I could pass on the message. The inquiry is probably set for April. He'll let you know an exact date nearer the time.'

There was a long pause.

'Constable Laver?'

'April.'

'"Maybe May but probably April" is what he said.'

'That's months. What am I supposed to do between now and April?'

'Neil said you should ride your bike.'

'Did he?'

'And keep your head down. Low down.'

Laver didn't say anything.

'He emphasised that, Rocket.'

'I'll bet he did.'

Out of respect for his gym session, Laver didn't have a whisky or even a beer. He drank dry ginger until his doorbell went off. Looking into the security camera from the block's front door, he saw the grainy sepia image of an emo youth with jet-black hair, dark eyeliner and highlighted lips on whiter-than-white skin.

He pressed the 'talk' button. 'No thanks. Whatever you're selling.'

'Rocket, it's me. Damian.'

'What the hell?' Laver buzzed him in.

Damian Minack, veteran of the Melbourne pub-music circuit and long-time mountain-biking enthusiast, trudged wearily up the stairs to Laver's front door, sounding heavy-legged in large Doc Marten boots. His black T-shirt had a grey skull printed on it, between the deliberate rips, and was half-covered by what looked like a black spiderweb draped over his shoulder.

'Don't say a word,' he warned Laver.

'You've just been featured in *Alice Cooper's Eye for the Straight Guy*?'

'I said don't say a word. Just give me a beer.'

'Do emos drink beer?'

'No, emos drink vodka-raspberry coolers because none of them are mature enough to handle actual alcohol. I drink beer.'

'So, you going to explain or what?'

'As is patently obvious, we have set up an emo band. A few of us put on black wigs and mascara every Wednesday afternoon at a pub near Monash Uni and play for a couple of hours as classes finish. You know my mate Tommy from that punk band, Kitten Sex Frenzy? And Clive from the Freeballing Astronauts?'

'If Clive's the one I'm thinking of – the bass guitarist? – I cannot see him doing the emo thing.'

'He's a sight,' Damian agreed. 'But it's a solid earner.'

'Are they actual Doc Martens?'

'Vintage,' Damian nodded. 'Depressingly easy to find, all these years later. Hey! The bike!'

Laver handed Emo Damian a beer as he stood appraising the police bike as though it were a painting.

'Do I even want to know what the band's called?' Laver asked from the couch.

Damian looked at him sideways, grinned and raised his stubbie. 'The Devil's Mockery.'

Laver had to nod, despite himself. 'Yeah, okay. That's good.'

'Thanks. Have you heard about the new emo website?'

'Nope,' said Laver.

'Look it up. It's www dot emo dot com slash wrists.'

Laver tried to laugh. 'That's pathetic.'

'Slays 'em in the aisles at Monash. You know, I'm fast becoming one of the emo headliners. I could pull all the emo chicks I'd want if emo chicks put out. But I think they're too busy moaning about the world to consider pub-toilet knee-shakers.'

'I'm convinced you can do better. What happened to Jenny?'

Damian shrugged. 'Her band's on tour. Playing Brisbane tonight.'

'What are they called again?' Laver could never keep track of the dozens of bands Damian was either in, moving between or mates with. 'The Vegetarians?'

'The Dirty Vegans.'

'Oh yeah, that's right. So what do you think of my new steed?'

'Mate, it's a fucking beauty. I can tell without even riding it. They just gave this to you?'

'It's a loaner. But it looks like I'm stuck there for months so, yeah, they'll let me choose my own bike. It will be better than this, apparently. This is the ageing spare.'

'Better than this? Holy crap. This makes my bike look like an old dragster from the 70s – and my bike's worth about three grand.'

'Really?' Laver was genuinely surprised.

'Hell yeah. Those disc brakes are top of the range. See the front forks? They're quality. I'm pretty sure ...' Damian lifted the frame with one hand. 'Yep, it's a lightweight titanium frame. If you didn't have all that Batman–utility belt cop crap all over it, it would be light as a feather.'

'We love our utility belts.'

'Clearly. So you're hating every minute of riding this baby around, huh?'

'Well, the bosses have ordered that I'm frozen out by my old squad. As in, police-ona non grata. And this bike thing is kind of a comedown from where I was.'

'Yeah, I guess. Must be shit. Not getting shot at. Less internal politics. Fresh air. Sunshine. Getting paid to keep fit. Babes in bike shorts … I'll bet there are babes in the squad.'

Laver had to grin. 'One or two. Mostly it's mini-Hitlers behind the handlebars.'

'Well, let's face it. They are fucking cops.'

Damian swigged his beer with distaste. Even with Laver, a best mate since school and a career cop for fourteen years now, he still maintained the musician's hatred of the uniforms who broke up perfectly good parties and occasionally searched you for drugs.

Laver respected that. It was rock and roll.

* * *

Stig was going mad, waiting for one of the locals to ring him back. It had never occurred to him that it would be this hard to move the merchandise. He figured they'd be in Melbourne for a couple of days at the most, then gone. But he was still here and going nowhere.

Maybe it was that frustration – or perhaps it was just because he couldn't believe the Wild Man really was that fucking stupid – that found him standing over Wildie, in ever-reliable Xbox-playing mode on the couch, and waving the newspaper at him.

'The description could not be any clearer if they'd taken a bloody picture of you, Wildie. I said go and get a car, not make page nine of the biggest-selling tabloid in town, you dumb prick.'

Wildie barely looked up from the game, fingers moving confidently among the buttons.

'Mate, it was two days ago. He gave me some shit so I gave him a little tap. Big deal.'

'A little tap.' Stig read through the reported injuries again. Induced coma. Swelling on the brain. Fractured ribs. Grave words from the doctor in Emergency. 'Mate, we're trying to fly under the radar here. You might remember a large Queensland crime syndicate that may or may not be wondering where we are? And you make the paper, beating up used-car salesmen.'

'Why would they be looking for us? We're dead, remember.'

'I know we're dead but Jenssen might decide to double check. He might be keeping an eye out.'

'So what you're saying, dickhead, is that Jenssen is sitting up there on the Gold Coast, reading a Melbourne newspaper. Then thinking, "Shit. I reckon a used-car salesman I've never heard of way down in Melbourne, Victoria, might have been beaten up by the zombie corpse of one of my dead ex-employees."'

'He has people in this town too, Wildie, for Christ's sake.' Stig was reading and frowning. 'The article even says the car was found nearby where another was taken. A perfect description of the car right outside this house, Wildie. Now we have to get rid of it and get a new one.'

The Wild Man winced slightly as he died on-screen. 'It'll give us something to do. You didn't tell me this would be such a boring process.'

'I didn't know it would take this long – but it's all the more reason why we have to lay low, mate.'

The Wild Man sat patiently as another digital hero appeared on the TV screen, ready for battle. Stig sighed.

'Wildie, can you try to stay off the nightly news for me? Just for a day or so? Could you do that for me, mate? Please? … Fuck!'

The next time Wildie failed a level they got out of there, just to see daylight and feel air on their faces – and to get a new car that wasn't the subject of an assault inquiry. The Wild Man drove and they headed to Northland shopping centre, finding a decent silver Commodore near the back of the multi-level parking bay.

'Perfect,' Stig said. 'The four A's. Anonymous, Air condition-ing. Air bags and A bit of grunt.'

Wildie had the car revving inside of thirty seconds. Stig, jittery, got in, taking the first toke on a joint. Offered some to Wildie, who shook his head. 'I thought you were keeping your head clear for this deal.'

'Yeah, but the waiting is shitting me. Need to stay calm.'

'Don't get too calm,' Wildie said. 'I want my cut fast and I want out of this city.'

As they drove back, they detoured to Fitzroy and grabbed hamburgers at a place Stig didn't remember from before, called Grill'd. Good burgers that beat McDonald's all ends up.

Back in the car, Stig drove and took a quick detour into Gore Street. About a hundred metres along, he drove slowly past a double-storey terrace with Buddhist peace flags flutter-ing across the front and a few old bikes scattered around the porch. The house was completely dark.

'Looking for a root, mate?' asked Wildie.

'Something like that.'

'Is this place a brothel? I've noticed a few in Fitzroy.'

'No, it's not a brothel. Old girlfriend.'

'Even better. Comes for free. We could always hit a singles night down on King Street.'

'We're facing enough danger already, mate, without getting suicidal,' Stig said.

They headed back onto Brunswick Street and turned north, Wildie unusually quiet – not attempting to put on the usual hip hop CD, just staring out the window – until he said, 'You know how you said Jenssen had people in town.'

'Yeah?'

'Why don't we offer the stuff to them?'

Stig drove for a while. 'Offer the gear to Jenssen? Is that what you're actually suggesting?'

'No, fuckwad. Offer the gear to Jenssen's bloke in Melbourne. As a side deal. It's a different thing.'

Now Stig was thinking about it. 'But if he makes the call north, we're dead and buried.'

'But if he doesn't, the gear goes into the usual distribution channels, we get paid and he gets a larger cut than usual because he doesn't have to send any of it north.'

Stig shook his head slowly. 'It's bloody risky.'

'And which part of this wasn't, since we left the bodies in the car?'

Stig had to think about that. The Wild Man had a point.

* * *

Stig was ringing from a payphone – nothing that could be easily traced. Almost two states away to the north, the phone rang. He could see it: one of those old white Telstra-issue handsets sitting next to the sunny window that looked out on a panoramic sweep along the coast, including the headland of Byron Bay.

She answered on the fifth ring.

'It's me,' he said.

'Oh my God.'

'Can you talk?'

'Of course. God. I couldn't believe you were really dead. Where are you?'

'Perth,' Stig answered.

'Should I come to you?'

'Not yet. I have a few things to do first. Has Jenssen been in touch?'

'Of course. He rang to say he was sorry you were dead but after that, there wasn't much to say.'

'So he bought it?'

'Sure. Why wouldn't he? We all did. Even me, you bastard.'

She sounded as though she was on the brink of crying.

'Babe, I'm sorry. I couldn't tell you. The less who know, the better. I promise I'll make it up to you. In a big way.'

'I'm so glad you're alive. I'm just glad you're alive.'

'And kicking, Sophie. Listen, just sit tight. Wildie and I weren't the only thing that got out of that car in one piece. Let me make the most of that and when I can, I'll send for you, okay? It goes without saying that you don't say a fucking word in the meantime.'

'How dumb do you think I am? Jenssen would have my arse too, Stig.'

'Yes, he would. I'll be in touch, okay?'

'Sure ...'

Silence stretched down the line until she said, 'Jesus, babe.'

'I know. I'm sorry. But it will be worth it. I promise. Love you.'

'Love you too, honey,' she said.

Stig hung up.

And so did Sophie.

Sitting in the sunshine, wrapped in a towel, gazing down on Byron and smoking a home-made rollie, the scent of marijuana drifting through the room, Karl Jenssen said: 'Where is he?'

'Melbourne,' Sophie said, reaching for the joint. 'I heard a tram in the background, the stupid fuck.'

CHAPTER 11
SHOWDOWN AT THE SOUL FOOD CAFÉ

The Friends of the Planet door clanged as usual. Jake could never get used to those bells that hung off it, crashing into the glass. It took him a moment of steadying them with his hand before he looked around – and there she was, sitting behind the counter, watching him with one thin eyebrow raised over those amazing grey eyes.

'Nice entrance, Jeff,' Lou said.

'Jake.'

'Oh sorry. Jake. I've always been crap with names.'

'It's okay. We hardly know each other,' he said, feeling himself blushing for no apparent reason. 'I really like that T-shirt,' he stammered to divert her attention, pointing randomly at the shirts hanging over her head.

Lou turned and gazed at the shirt before reading, deadpan: '"Abortion is murder. Hang them high." Really? You love that one?'

'Umm, the one next to it,' Jake said weakly. '"Vegan future. Valid future."'

'You're a vegan?'

'You bet,' Jake said, thinking he might have been wrong about the Star Trek connection. He'd really better look up that term. 'So, um, we were talking about a coffee to discuss my idea. Is there a day that would be good, you know, for you and everything?'

Lou stood up and swung her arms behind her head, her chest straining against her shirt before his eyes as she stretched and yawned. 'What about now?'

'Now?' Jake was trying to look anywhere but at the two undone buttons of her shirt. He'd taken a late lunch break to come here, hoping to catch her when she wasn't busy – but this he hadn't expected.

'Yeah, I've got cabin fever. Warren is in the back somewhere. He can keep an eye on things. HEY WAZZA? CAN YOU MIND THE DESK FOR A BIT?'

'Sure,' came a voice from the kitchen area.

Jake looked at all the empty tables and chairs in the café section at the front of the shop. 'You don't want to just grab a coffee here?'

Lou was already at the front door. 'Nah, I need to get out.' Then she leaned in, smelling of something Jake couldn't quite grasp – soap? sandalwood? – and whispered, her breath thrilling his neck, 'Plus the organic coffee they serve in here is nothing but weak mud.'

What she didn't mention was the guy who worked behind the counter at Soul Food, a café just down the street on the other side of the road. He and Lou had been appraising one another for a while. Turning up with another man, even one as dodgy as this supermarket geek, would keep counter boy guessing.

Blissfully ignorant of all this, Jake walked tall down Smith Street in his kick-arse hat, his cool T-shirt and streetwise jeans, accompanied by the hottest hippie chick on the planet. His heart soared. When one of the ever-present Smith Street desperados shuffled up, yelling that she needed three dollars for a fare to Ballarat, Jake gave the woman a five-dollar note. He was living large.

They managed to avoid being killed by a tram as they crossed the street and headed for the Soul Food Café: All organic. All the time.

* * *

Stig stopped to check out some vintage footy jumpers in the window of a collectables shop. One looked a lot like the guernsey he had worn as a junior playing for Yarraville in the Western Region Football League, just after the club fell out of the VFA. The Mighty Villains, as the club had once been known. Now he'd heard they were the Eagles, combined with bloody Seddon. Footy wasn't the same.

The Wild Man was checking out the shop assistant in a clothes shop: spectacular legs ruined by leggings cut off at the calves, which seemed to be the fashion in Melbourne, but made no sense to a Queenslander. Either wear leggings or let bare legs do their thing. The girl caught Wildie looking and gave him a stare, then grimaced when the Wild Man slowly grabbed his crotch and thrust in her direction.

They continued along Smith Street, Stig planning to scope Friends of the Planet in search of his old girlfriend. But then, shit: there she was, right in front of him, weaving through the traffic and hurrying to get out of the way of a tram, maybe a hundred metres down the street. Stig took a half-step into a doorway to look at her. Damn, did she do justice to his memories. She still had that body, even if she insisted on wrapping it in tie-dyed dresses and mottled stockings, her hair held back by what looked like a crocheted headband. No doubt about those tits though, swinging under a half-buttoned shirt. And the legs had lost nothing in his time away. Stig had a lot of fond memories of being tangled amongst those legs. And still well groomed, under the hippie façade, he'd bet. Louie's shocking secret: she hadn't fully bought into the hairy, unwashed greenie scene. But you had to make it to her bed to find out.

What Stig couldn't believe was the dweeb she was walking with. Some nerd in a ridiculous hat, kind of shuffling to keep up with her, and wearing black business shoes with jeans. He was saying something and she laughed, but politely, not with much enthusiasm. And then they were gone, stepping through the door of the Soul Food Café.

'Hey Wildie,' Stig said. 'You want to meet my girlfriend?'

'Isn't she your ex-girlfriend?' The Wild Man replied.

'Only until she sees me again. Come and meet Louie.'

* * *

'Admit it,' Cecy said. 'You're enjoying yourself.'

'That's a big call,' Laver replied as they cruised east along Gertrude Street.

'You know you are.' Cecy just behind his shoulder as they rode. 'The sun's out, you've had some good coffee, you spent half an hour checking out some industrial design shops, you got to read the paper cover to cover.'

'I call it quality police work.'

'You even look like riding isn't such an ordeal anymore.'

'I have to admit, my arse is only hurting me badly today, not absolutely killing me.'

'Thanks for sharing,' she said.

'And my legs are feeling better. The sun helps. But I'm not sure I'd go all the way to "enjoying myself".'

'Keep telling yourself that. Be so much more fun sitting at a desk at St Kilda Road, drinking instant coffee, sleep-deprived, trawling paper records, looking for white-collar crime.'

'Is that what you think my life used to be like?' he said, swinging around in the saddle to look at her – and then almost running into a door swung open by an oblivious woman getting out of her car.

Heart pounding, he concentrated on where he was riding for a bit but then admitted, 'Actually, that was a fair chunk of most days. I'd be gagging to be out in the sunshine on a day like this.'

'Well, there you go.' Cecy sounding dangerously close to smug.

'Except for the pointless and futile nature of the work,' he added.

'Jesus,' she said, shaking her head. 'The example you set.'

They turned left onto Smith Street and Cecy said, 'I had the weirdest dream last night.'

'You were a real cop who got to ride around in cars?'

'No, I was at a rock concert and I had to fight my way to the stage because my band was on.'

'What was the band called?'

'The Theatre of Cruelty.'

'Good name,' Laver said. 'Is that an actual band?'

'No idea. It was just in my head.'

Laver, thinking he'd have to mention it to Damian, continued: 'So then what? You played the gig?'

'No, I realised that I had to arrest the lead singer. I had to arrest him for a whole bunch of minor offences, the sort you learn at the academy by the hour but in the real world, they don't matter at all.'

Laver laughed. 'Attagal. The Chief Commissioner would be proud of you. So did you make the arrest?'

'No. The lead singer turned out to be a giant, some kind of South American gangster about twice my size. He sort of waddled towards me and the crowd was chanting for me to give him a head job on stage. I could either arrest him or go down on him, and I couldn't work out which I should do.'

'Jesus, Cecy.' Laver had no idea how to respond to that, instead turning his attention to check whether the usual gang of crazies were behaving themselves in front of the Woolworths. He wasn't in the mood to tackle hobos or drunks.

Cecy was right beside him. 'I'm sorry. Did I shock you? What sort of dreams do you have, Rocket?'

'Takes more than that to shock me, unfortunately, after some of the human behaviour I've seen over the years, including my own.'

'Do you dream?'

'I actually have the same one, over and over. An old police friend of mine, Flipper, and I are in the Soggies and the guy I shot, Coleman, is shooting at us. I'm yelling at him to stop, that I don't want to kill him again but he just keeps firing.'

'So what happens?'

'He keeps shooting so I kill him.'

They were past the Woolworths. All quiet.

'Wow,' Cecy said. 'Then you wake up?'

'No,' Laver said, pulling off the road and swinging a creaking leg over the bar of his bike. 'I used to, after his dead body opened its eyes and looked straight at me. But now he keeps on firing and kills me as well. The dream's not over until we're both dead.'

Wondering if he should mention the ghostly form of Coleman in his apartment most nights. Deciding against it. 'Want a drink?'

'We just had a coffee.'

'We've ridden at least two hundred metres since then. I want a water.'

'Where's your water bottle?'

'Those things look unhygienic. I prefer pure water from plastic bottles.'

Cecy sighed. 'No wonder I barely work up a sweat when I ride with you.'

He thought about crossing the road to the 7-Eleven, but then wondered if they'd have water in the Soul Food Café.

* * *

No sign of the hot waiter, Lou realised as they came through the door. There was the chick with the shaved head and the nose ring, and the other waitress Lou was pretty sure she'd seen playing in a band at the Tote a few weeks ago. She was in stripey stockings and a T-shirt, looking sexy. Lou smiled to herself at Jake's reaction, his eyes almost falling out of his head at how the T-shirt barely covered the waitress's butt.

They got a table by the wall, Lou sitting on the bench seat and Jake taking a chair, his back to the coffee machine. Jake fascinated by the guy at the next table, with a twirly moustache and a red jacket like Michael Jackson used to wear. He looked like he was out of a circus. The café wall had flowers painted on it and a huge woman's face painted in yellow on the ceiling. The room ran deep, with lamps and couches and maybe a bar down the back. There were no cafés like this in Kew, that was for sure.

The waitress with the shaved head came over, and Lou noticed she had a tattoo of flowers snaking from the back of her neck to under her ear; the big new thing in town. It looked okay. Lou ordered a strong latte. Jake went for a hot chocolate.

'How's that whole vegan thing going for you?' Lou asked.

'Good,' Jake said. 'Why?'

'You just ordered a hot chocolate.'

'Yeah.' Jake was still checking out the people at the other tables like he was in a zoo.

'Never mind. So, these stickers?'

'Yep,' said Jake, tuning back in and looking slightly startled.

'You've been working on this idea for a while, huh?'

'Oh months,' he said. 'It's frustrating watching people grab the brands that are so bad for the environment and not do anything about it.'

'Like which brands?'

'Huh?'

'Which brands are you thinking of specifically?'

Jake waved a hand. 'Oh, you know … some of the washing powders. Detergents. That tissue company that is right into wood-chipping the Otway forest.'

She nodded. 'OzSoft.'

'Yeah, that one,' he said, leaning to his right as the waitress delivered his hot chocolate and placed a latte in front of Lou, who was still weighing up whether this guy, middle class and largely clueless, was for real.

'So, how serious are you about this idea of yours, Jake?'

'Oh, very. I really want to do it. If I don't try to make a difference where I can, I hate myself. Anyway, mine's a pretty meaningless job if you don't look for worthwhile aspects, and this is one.'

Lou made her decision. 'I think you should put the whole thing down on paper – recycled paper too, Jake. Don't mess this up with Rachel through clumsiness.'

'Who's Rachel?' he said, looking confused.

'The manager of Friends of the Planet. Pay attention. I'll have a read of the proposal first, to see if it's in language and a format that she'd like, and then maybe we could present it together.'

'You'd do that? Present it with me?'

'Sure. I deliberately left the suburbs behind because I couldn't handle how apathetic, how uncaring your average person out there was about the environment. So many plants and fauna and species going out of existence every day, the rainforests still being mowed down in Brazil and elsewhere, and bastard companies still testing cosmetics and shit like that on animals. It makes me sick. And the thought of getting something going in the heart of a middle-class suburb like Heidelberg is very exciting – if you can convince your boss to do it.'

'Oh, I'm sure I can. Don't even think about that.' Jake's eyes darted nervously. 'It will be totally fine.'

Lou sipped her coffee. 'So, what's the wording on the stickers going to be?'

'I wanted to talk to you about that.' He leaned forward. 'Do you have any ideas?'

'Oh, plenty,' she said, glancing up as the café door opened. And then forgot all about stickers.

At first the two tall, tanned men were framed by the bright sunshine outside. But now she could see them. One with bright-orange hair, a thick beard and thick, blocky tattoos; a circus freak, but huge. The other, buff and tanned in a singlet, somebody she recognised in an instant, just by the way he moved. Somebody who'd thrilled her and then disappeared literally overnight. Somebody who even now gave the bad-girl side of her a surge, at the same moment that the loyal Friends of the Planet employee felt pure rage.

Jake, seeing her face change, turned to look at who she was looking at. Physically startling as he saw the big redhead but then, worse, realising the other guy in the singlet was the one who'd scared Bindi at the Friends of the Planet. Who was now smiling at Lou like a cat that's found the mouse out of its hole.

A predatory smile was Jake's first thought.

Lou's arms folded across her chest as Stig said, 'Well, look who it is. Louie, Louie.'

Louie not saying a word, just staring at him and past him to Wildie.

'This wild man is a friend of mine,' Stig said. 'A buddy from up north. I thought he might like to meet you.'

'I've got nothing to say to you,' she said.

'Oh babe, don't be like that. We're lovers, remember.'

Watching the pudgy-faced kid she was with digest that and trying not to laugh. Stig slid onto the bench, sidling right up to Louie's hip so she could feel his heat, as Wildie took a chair from another table and sat down next to the kid, staring straight at him.

'Mind if we join you? Catch up for old time's sake.' Stig gave her a big smile. 'You're still looking fantastic, Louie, although I'm not sure about the new hair.'

'I don't want to talk to you. You should be across the road, talking to Rachel about those funds that mysteriously disappeared about the same time you left Friends of the Planet.'

'Now don't be like that. I haven't seen you for ages, and you go straight to unsubstantiated rumours.'

Wildie moved in his seat and grinned. 'Mate, something you didn't tell me about?'

'Nothing to tell. A misunderstanding, I guess.'

'Bullshit,' said Louie, arms still tight across that great chest of hers.

'Why don't you play nice, hottie?' Wildie said. 'We're a lot more fun to be around if you're not so hostile.'

'And your new best friend threatens strangers. Charming.' Louie's voice rising.

'Oh geez, babe, relax,' Stig said. 'I didn't remember you being this uptight.' Now looking at the guy sitting across from her, dwarfed by the Wild Man – physically and in sheer presence. He was sitting frozen, staring at his cooling mug of hot chocolate.

'Who's your little buddy, Louie?' Stig asked. 'You got a new boyfriend?'

'None of your business,' Louie said. The kid looking at her in surprise as she didn't deny it.

Leaving Stig to ask the kid directly, 'Where do you fit in, fella?'

But the kid only looked at him and swallowed, as though contemplating speech and failing. Jesus, thought Stig. Louie has dropped her standards.

He was about to suggest that Wildie and this kid, whoever he was, go for a wander, leaving him and Louie for a few minutes so they could get reacquainted, when Wildie, looking towards the door, hissed 'Stig' and he saw the look on Wildie's face.

Lou did too, watching Stig and the big guy turn to stone, their faces turning insolent and blank, as a cop dressed in cycling gear materialised from the blinding sun of the café door. Lou thinking the guy looked slightly ridiculous in lycra shorts and shirt. He had the wrong haircut and somehow the wrong face for the look.

The cop had his back to them as he asked if he could buy bottled water there. Then asked if, in that case, he could maybe trouble them for a glass of tap water? Thanking the chick behind the counter.

* * *

It's funny how a glance is all you need, Laver thought. You just had to relax and let your brain remember the details. Four people. Three men and a girl with coloured hair. No read on the girl, but the guy opposite her, a guy who didn't fit, looking scared. The other two giving Laver the look only criminals give police. One, bearded and orange hair. The other, tan and lean. Both big. Both thirty, give or take.

Laver's spider sense going haywire from the moment he heard a word whispered as he came through the door. Was it 'Cig?' The two men stiffening. He was feeling eyes on his back now. Who were they and what was going on? A drug deal? The other two at the table didn't feel right for that.

Laver sipped his water and turned around.

The guy against the wall was looking at him and now looked away, doing it at a careful pace. The bigger guy, with orange hair, like fairy floss on his head, hunched, turning his back to Laver.

He wandered over to the table. They were all staring at him, except orange-hair who very deliberately wasn't. The kid next to orange-hair pale. The girl not much better.

'How you all doing?' Laver said. 'Great day out there.'

Silence.

'Everything okay here, people?'

'Why wouldn't it be?' It was the guy against the wall, in the singlet. Who Laver now knew was the leader.

'Just making conversation. You nervous?'

'Why would I be?' That dead-eyed stare. Laver wondering, do they have classes among crooks to learn it?

'No idea. What's your name, son?'

Laver seeing his eyes burn on the word 'son', but the guy holding it together. Saying, 'Do you mind, officer? I just hit town and I'm trying to catch up with my girlfriend here.'

'Good for you,' Laver said happily. 'Is that right, Miss?'

The girl nodding. Looking at her coffee.

Laver saying to the guy, 'You didn't give me your name.'

'No, I didn't.'

Laver giving him his own dead-eye cop stare before glancing to the younger guy with the silly hat down the end of the table. 'How are you, mate? All good?'

The kid swallowing and nodding. The girl still staring at her coffee. Now taking a sip.

Laver taking his time. 'Mind if I pull up a chair? I've been riding for hours.'

'You're fucking kidding, aren't ya?' said orange-hair, finally giving Laver a glance, but getting a harsh look from his mate.

Laver saying to orange-hair, 'They prison tatts, buddy?'

The other guy getting up, saying, 'We're actually on our way, so you can have the table. Catch you later, Louie. I'll drop by.'

'How about you don't?' said the girl.

Orange-hair was on his feet as well. Big, now he was standing. Very big. Laver sipping his water as they left. Noticing the dweeby guy exhale. Watching how the girl gave it a few moments before she said, 'Let's talk about this later, Jake,' went to the counter and paid the bill. She asked if she could borrow a pen, scribbled something and walked back over to their table, handing a slip of paper to Jake. 'My number. For the project.'

Then she was at the door, checking the street before she left.

Laver and the dweeb now alone. Laver saying, 'Who were those guys, Jake?'

Jake, staring at the magical piece of paper in his hand, saying, 'I have no idea. I think they're hippies.'

'Hippies? They didn't look or act much like hippies. You don't know their names?'

Jake shook his head. 'Nope. And I'm happy if it stays that way.'

Laver finishing his water and thinking, well, that makes one of us.

He headed into the sunshine, where Cecy was staring off down the street.

CHAPTER 12
SPIDER SENSES

'Eleven ball. Corner pocket.'

Laver missed the shot and cursed – but not too loudly. The pub was almost empty, with only a few diehard early drinkers nursing their glasses.

Mitchell Dolfin scowled and tilted his head as he surveyed the table, then leaned over his cue and doubled the four ball into the middle pocket.

Laver nodded his admiration and sipped his beer.

'Flipper, how big a role do you think intuition plays in police work?'

'I thought we'd agreed we weren't going to talk work, especially with me not supposed to even speak to you at all.'

'I'm not sure playing pool can lead to a suspension.'

'Don't bet on it, the way the Force is going.' Dolfin missed a length-of-the-table attempt at the six ball and wandered over to his beer. 'So, intuition,' he said.

'Yeah. Once you've done it for as long as we have, how much do you work by knowledge of laws and procedures as against your gut?'

'Clearly, this is a loaded question.'

'Yeah, I guess it is.'

Flipper munched on a chip. 'So why the loaded question?'

'I saw two guys yesterday. In Smith Street. My spider senses went nuts.'

'Who were they?'

'I don't know. They were heavying some greenie chick and a nerd.'

'Yep, they sound like major criminals. Your shot.'

Laver assessed the angle on the blue ball and the corner pocket. 'No, you don't get it. The moment I saw them, I *knew*. They were the real thing. Bad guys, Flipper. Genuine bad guys.'

'So what did you do?'

'Went over and said hello.'

'And?'

'One of them, the one who seemed to be in charge, said he had just arrived in town and was catching up with his girlfriend.'

'What did she say?'

'She confirmed it but seemed glad to get out of there.'

'Jesus, not exactly Tony Mokbel in his prime, mate.'

Laver had bent to play the shot but then stood again, looking at his mate. 'Flipper, I told you. This is about your gut. It wouldn't have mattered if they were shopping for flowers. I knew who these bastards were. The leader is shifty and criminal. The other guy is big and dangerous. Prison tattoos. He's definitely violent. And they're out there now.'

'Rocket, working on the Noble Taskforce has brought home to me exactly how many potentially violent arseholes are walking around Melbourne at any given time, whether they're officially underworld or not. There's hundreds of crims or potential perps out there. Big deal.'

Laver finally bent and hit the blue ball. Click. It dropped. He addressed the orange ball, saying, 'Because these guys might actually be new in town. You're right; cops usually have a working knowledge of every perpetrator going around. But I reckon these guys are fresh off the boat.'

Flipper sighed. 'Mate, you know full well that all you have to do is keep your head down for a while. Ride your bike.'

'What does that mean?'

'You've been out there pedalling for five minutes and the Major Crime cop in you is looking for *Underbelly 6*.'

Laver stepped away from the table to sip his beer. 'I'm saying that my cop senses haven't vanished overnight just because some dickhead in head office has planted me in lycra. And my cop senses didn't like these two at all. Would it kill you to ask around?'

Dolfin almost snorted his beer as he drank. 'Did you get their full names and addresses? Maybe their licence or passport details? Ask them to ink some fingerprints?'

'I think the violent one called the other guy Cig.'

'Cig? As in "cigarette"?'

'Maybe. It sounded like it.'

Dolfin laughed out loud now. 'Mate, you're fucking losing it.'

'Could you ask around?'

'Has anybody heard about a mad smoking criminal genius hanging around Fitzroy, possibly saying hi to his hippie girl-friend? Sure. It's your shot.'

Laver circled the table, looking for any sort of angle. Dolfin watched him and said, 'I'll keep an ear out. How's that?'

'All I can ask.'

'Fucking right it is. Moving on, how's Marcia?'

'Who?'

'Your almost-fiancée.'

'Oh, her.'

'Like that, huh?'

'Yep. Crisis dinner tomorrow night.'

'You're kicking nothing but goals at the moment, buddy.' Flipper sipped his beer. 'Where?'

'She's nominated Brunswick Street, like I haven't been seeing enough of that strip lately. Some place called the Vegie Bar.'

'Vegetarian,' Dolfin grinned. 'Sounds an unlikely place for a cold-blooded killer like yourself.'

'Well, I probably won't be armed, so the lettuce should be safe.' Laver leaned over his cue. 'Thirteen ball. Side pocket.'

Click.

'Damn!'

* * *

Jake's boss, Barry, had always spent a lot of time on the phone – but now he seemed to have it grafted to his ear. More than that, he spent the majority of his time with his office door closed. If the door happened to be open, Barry was giving you a furtive glance every time you walked past, looking like you'd caught him in the middle of something sordid. None of it encouraged Jake to go in there and raise the idea of putting political stickers on half the products in the supermarket below.

Jake walked the aisles, peering at labels and trying to work out how to tell if something was genuinely environmentally friendly, rather than just packaged in green with a sunflower on the front of the box. Picking up a box of washing powder, Jake read: 'Ingredients include surfactants (anionic and nonionic) and enzymes.' He had no idea.

He'd waited until yesterday, the day after their attempted meeting at the Soul Food Café, to use the phone number he couldn't believe she had given him, texting Lou to ask how she was. She had replied, all business, with the news that she had left a book for him at the front counter of Friends of the Planet: a book that had done all the legwork, digging into the ownership of companies making everything from breakfast cereals and toilet rolls to eggs, and looking at the manufacturing process. He'd picked up the book yesterday, and was surprised by what he read. Jake hadn't realised a farm could label their eggs as 'free range' just by letting the battery hens stagger around a pen measuring about a metre squared for a few minutes once a day. He never knew that a lot of wine was created using animal products; the wine 'fined' or filtered through egg white, milk powder or even isinglass, which apparently came from the swim bladder of a fish. Jake had a whole new understanding of how artificial fragrances in products were often made from petroleum that wouldn't degrade and could cause problems for animals and fish after being trashed.

Jake was looking at the Heidelberg Groc-o-Mart in a whole new way.

But Lou was getting antsy. They'd texted a few times today, with Lou all business, asking if he was reading the book and when could they timetable the placement of the stickers, finally sending him a text reading 'Bar Open. Brunswick Street. Tonight.' He needed an answer, now, so he finally took a deep breath and headed for Barry's office.

The door was closed and Jake stopped in his tracks. He wasn't about to interrupt whatever his boss was up to. Briefly, Jake found himself wondering if Barry was addicted to online pornography. Then realised how badly he didn't want to know if he was.

Behind the door, he heard his boss's voice say, 'Christ, it's a long way to Heidelberg from there.'

Another man's voice said, 'Our mate's not stupid. Don't ever forget that, Barry. Not ever.'

The door opened and the man came out, looking slightly startled as he almost walked straight into Jake, but then recovering and walking straight past. Jake only seeing a stocky man in a bomber jacket, maybe suit pants. European-looking. Italian? Greying hair and a hard face. Gone.

Jake knocked on the half-open door and could have sworn Barry jumped in his seat.

'Jake. How long have you been standing there for?'

'At your door? I haven't been.'

'You're there now.'

'I just arrived.'

'Good, good.' Barry was fidgeting, a hand lurking near the phone as if he was dying to pick it up. 'All going well in the store?'

'I guess so. I haven't heard any complaints.'

'I need you to be on top of things down there, Jake. I've got a lot of management issues going on. Franchise issues. Head office stuff. I can't be worrying about expiration dates on dairy products or the strawberries going off. I need you to be right on top of your game just now.'

'Sure, Barry. I'll "Go go Gadget" hard.'

Barry stared at him.

'That was a TV show.' Jake cleared his throat. 'Well, a cartoon.'

'I have some calls to make, Jake. Off you go, boy.'

'Um, Barry, can I ask you something?'

Barry sighed. 'What?'

'Um, a friend of mine, well, actually me. I had an idea that might be fun, to put some stickers on a couple, well, quite a few products as a kind of—'

'Mate, I haven't got time. We'll have to talk about it later. Off you go. Shoo.'

Barry actually waved him away with a hand and then picked up the phone and started dialling. Jake stood awkwardly until Barry turned his back on him, his balding head visible over the back of his office chair.

Jake skulked back to his own desk. What would the new Jake do? Wait until Barry had time for him or be bold?

Maybe Barry would have time later this afternoon.

* * *

All the waiting was driving Stig crazy. Coming face-to-face with a cop, even a bike cop, didn't mean anything, he told himself, but it had somehow unnerved him, to the point that they'd barely left the house for two days. Wildie didn't seem to care. Wildie could play the Xbox for hours, completely still except for the movement of his wrists and thumbs on the controllers. Stig couldn't work out how the bastard managed to stay so lean and fit when he was immobile for so much of the time. Meanwhile, Stig prowled the house and wondered what was happening out there. Who else he should call. Whether Melbourne dealers were giving him the thumbs up or down. Whether he should seriously consider the Wild Man's crazy plan to directly approach Jenssen's man in Melbourne.

Stig had had six cups of instant coffee. They were out of milk. He'd done push-ups and sit-ups. He'd had a wank. There wasn't a decent book in the house. He was out of rollies papers, which was probably a good thing, going by the bloodshot red of the eyes staring back at him in the mirror.

Stig decided to go for a run, even though it looked like it might rain. It had been almost a fortnight since he'd last run along the Byron beach and his body needed action.

From Thornbury, he headed south into Northcote and followed Separation Street to Fairfield, then realised where he was and thought, it's only another couple of kilometres to Heidelberg, feeling great now his muscles were warmed up.

Stig stopped at the edge of the car park, sweating heavily but pulling his Dreamworld baseball cap down further over his eyes. The Groc-o-Mart was as he remembered it, a barn of a place with specials posters on the glass doors and trolleys scattered around the car park. Barry Paxton's office was on the first floor, but the blind was down so Stig couldn't see anything. It also meant Paxton couldn't see him.

But then, shit, Paxton emerged from the sliding doors, talking to a younger guy in a white shirt and dark pants, the young guy almost chasing his boss as Paxton walked fast. They got to a car where Paxton beeped open the door and got in.

Barry waving his arm, and Stig close enough to hear him yell, 'I haven't got time for bloody marketing plans. Write me a memo or an email or a proposal on floral paper. I don't care. Just piss off.'

Really giving it to the younger guy who Stig thought looked vaguely familiar but had no idea where he'd seen him before.

And then realised.

The young guy was walking back towards the Groc-o-Mart as Paxton's car was starting to move.

Stig realised he was standing near an exit.

He got out of there.

* * *

Jake watched Barry's car disappear towards Upper Heidelberg Road and sighed deeply. If he waited until Barry gave him a hearing, Lou would be long gone, planting stickers and falling in love with the assistant manager at some other supermarket in Coburg or even Collingwood. Jake considered letting New Jake have his head. The upside was that bloody Barry was so distracted at the moment he probably wouldn't even notice if Jake and Lou painted Friends of the Planet slogans in red paint all over the walls of the mart.

Jake was almost back at the store's front door when the sensation crept up on him, as though from the side of his brain. Two men sitting in a white car, off to the southern end of the car park. Was he imagining things? He turned and looked at the car – it was empty. Jake wondered if he was losing it.

CHAPTER 13
A NASTY ACCIDENT

As far as rallies go, it was pretty pathetic. Laver had taken a while to work out what the motley crew of sixty or so were complaining about. He was pretty sure it was something to do with the G20 summit, but since Obama had been elected anti-American sentiment was a lot harder to whip up. Laver ticked them off his list of clichés: the guy with a goatee and a crocheted beanie carrying the obligatory anti-nuke sign, tick; the guy in a full black body stocking with an effigy of somebody in a suit, carrying a briefcase, tick; the militant feminists, tick; the Aboriginal flags – black and red behind a large yellow sun, tick; a woman waving a 'Get Out of Afghanistan!' sign, tick. All these random elements, thought Laver, arms folded as he watched them half-heartedly chant and hand-clap their way towards Federation Square along the Birrarung Marr grasslands by the river.

Laver had two major concerns. The first was that the sky was loaded with rain-threatening clouds and he couldn't bear to wear the luminous green police raincoat that made his ridiculous bike-cop uniform even more humiliating. The second was that, in a rare scheduling mishap, he was paired with Standish, now sneering at the protestors as though they'd personally affronted him. No coffees and laughter with Cecy today but that was okay. Enduring Standish was more in line with Laver's mood. He was feeling extra snaky after being snubbed by a cop from the drug squad when he'd gone to the supermarket after playing pool with Flipper yesterday. His Siberian status was obviously still in place, but not many cops were actually rude enough to follow through with it away from the office. Of course, the ghosts of Wesley Coleman and a dead pigeon had circled Laver's bedroom for the majority of the night. Marcia again was nowhere and their crisis meeting loomed. True sleep had only come about half an hour before the alarm sounded, which was always the way. And now he was watching the world's feeblest protestors and wondering if he would be concerned or entertained if his fascist partner shot one of them, which wasn't entirely off the cards.

'You've got to be kidding,' said Standish now, looking past the protestors.

Laver peered in that direction and saw a man and woman in uniform, also on bikes. But not cops. Laver recognised the markings of ambulance officers on their lycra shirts.

He turned to Standish in surprise. 'Cycling ambos? Really? How long have they had those?'

'They're a fucking joke,' Standish sniffed.

'Why?'

'Ambos on bikes? Are you kidding?'

'As opposed to police pedalling after criminals?'

Standish glared at him. 'Oh, excuse us, Mr Major Crime.'

Laver couldn't help but notice he didn't get a lot of respect as a senior cop from guys like Standish.

The ambos cycled over and nodded hello. Laver nodded back while Standish stared at them with undisguised scorn.

'G'day,' said Laver. 'Tony Laver. Nice to meet you. How much equipment can you guys carry on those things?'

'Enough,' said the ambo guy, who introduced himself as Shaun. 'We can handle the preliminaries of a heart attack, o.d., epileptic fit, stuff like that.'

'At a rally like this, the biggest danger is exposure to bad poetry,' said the ambo chick, name-tagged Sally.

'Not exactly the hundred thousand that marched against Kennett, is it,' Laver commented.

Sally frowned. 'Against who?'

Laver realised for the first time that she was young.

'Jeff Kennett. Former Premier. Pre-Bracks. Never mind.'

Standish leaned over his handlebars and said very deliberately, 'I don't mean to be rude, but would you two frauds move away and maybe stand near the St John's volunteers where you belong so we can get on with policing?'

Shaun gave Laver a look. Laver caught it.

'I'm not sure you're giving these two the respect they deserve, partner,' Laver said.

'Whose side are you on?' Standish asked, genuinely shocked.

'Why are there "sides"? We're all in the business of helping the public, aren't we? These guys help people who faint. Only this morning, you helped that nice tourist from China find the Eureka Tower.'

'Fuck you, Laver.'

'Jesus,' said Sally. 'Are you bike cops always like this?'

'Only Standish,' said Laver. 'But you have to understand, he's the best of the best.'

'Is that right?' said Shaun.

'Oh yeah, he's the bomb.' Laver nodded towards where the grass of Birrarung Marr became very steep, leading down from the Exhibition Street extension to the river. 'A rookie bike cop like me, I can barely ride along Swanston Street. But Standish here, he could ride straight down that steep hill, no sweat, in full kit.'

'So could I,' said Shaun. 'Easy.'

'Bullshit,' said Standish.

'I fucking could. Look, the hill's only about sixty degrees. I could do it without dropping a Band-Aid.'

'That's crap,' Standish snorted.

'So you're saying it can't be done? I guess not, for a cop like yourself.'

Standish glared. 'I could do it blindfolded. You pussies with your kit bags full of toiletries wouldn't have a prayer.'

'Geez mate, big talk,' said Laver. 'I don't know if I could manage it. Are you sure you should be putting us up on this riding pedestal?'

'You saying I couldn't do it?' said Standish.

Laver gave it some thought. 'Yeah, I think maybe I am. Shaun, do you think he could?'

'No fucking way. I'll put a fifty on it.'

Eyes burning with scorn, Standish strapped on his helmet. 'Watch and learn, wannabes.'

He rode his bike hard up the gentler slope leading to the top of the sharp hill. Laver, Sally and Shaun watched.

'I suspect the term you're looking for is "Cock With Ears",' Laver said into the silence.

'You got that right. You have to work with this knob?' Shaun said.

'Not often, thankfully.'

'You look familiar,' Sally said. 'Do I know you? Have you been on the tellie or something?'

'Nope,' Laver said flatly.

Standish was at the top of the hill, about to ride.

Sally was already pointing her iPhone camera.

CHAPTER 14
QUESTIONS WITHOUT ANSWERS

Laver arrived back at Mobile Public Interaction Squad HQ,
threw his helmet on his desk, then wandered over to the water
fountain. Slattery watched him every step of the way.

Finally the boss said, 'Precautionary scans.'

'They don't think he'll be in overnight,' Laver said.

'Concussion.'

'And abrasions. Poor guy.'

'Standish doesn't often fall off his bike, Senior Constable
Laver.'

'Lesson for us all, Slatts. Lucky there were a couple of ambos
on hand, really.'

Slattery continued to give him the stare but Laver couldn't
care less. Cecy had also been watching, the beginning of a smile
on her face, and said, 'Do I even want to know?'

'Nope,' Laver said, trying not to grin.

He picked up the phone and dialled Flipper's work number.
The phone at the other end had that strange metallic ring that
he only ever heard at the St Kilda Road police headquarters.
Laver felt a pang of homesickness.

'Dolfin.'

'Flip? It's Rocket.'

'Sorry, bad line. I can't hear you, whoever you are.'

'Flipper, stop arsing about. Did you find out anything?'

'Nope, sorry ... basically static. Is that you, Detective Laver?
If it is, I'm not allowed to converse with you, especially about
police matters.'

'Flipper. What the fuck? You think your phone is tapped?
You're getting paranoid on me now?'

'Gotta go. If that's you, Mum, I'll call tonight after work.'

'Flipper!'

'Love you.'

Flipper was gone. Laver cursed quietly but vigorously,
then picked up the phone and dialled a new number. And

not the obvious mobile number. Instead, Dolfin's little-known second mobile.

Dolfin's voice said, almost whispering: 'Oh, Rocket, for fuck's sake. Fuck off.'

'Eloquent. I won't keep you a second.'

'What part of "I can't talk now" are you having trouble with, dickhead?'

'Yes or no? Did you chase up that name for me? Cig? I think it's Cig.'

'Mate, that's about nineteenth on my list of priorities right now.'

'Flipper! You said you would.'

'Said I'd *try*, not *would*. Siberia is in full force, orders of some pollie called Strickland. Over and out.'

'Strickland? He's the one who started Siberia? Why Strickland?'

'No clue. Sorry. Bye.'

Dolfin hung up, leaving Laver with an ear full of nothing. Strickland. The out-of-Perth wannabe politician with the bad moustache. Screwing up his life by pulling strings from Parliament House in Spring Street. Life got stranger. And worse.

Laver cursed, with even more feeling. He could feel Cecy watching him, no smile now.

He dialled again. Listened to the metallic ring.

'Reference library,' said a female voice. 'This is Carla speaking. How can I help you?'

'Carla, this is Detective Senior Sergeant Laver. I'm chasing a record check on a suspect.'

'Just one moment, Detective. I'm just clearing another search off the computer. Now, what's the suspect's name or names?'

'I've only got a few details. The first name is believed to be Cig, Charlie India Golf, but I don't know his last name. I've got a solid description.'

Laver heard buttons being tapped and then there was a silence at the other end of the phone.

Laver said: 'Hello?'

'I'm sorry, Senior Constable, I'm afraid I'm not authorised to conduct any searches on your behalf while you are suspended from the Major Crime Squad.'

Laver felt a hot flush creeping up his neck. 'Did it say that? On the computer?'

'I can't comment any more to you, officer, until you are reinstated. I'm sorry.'

'But Carla, this is just a routine check—'

'Good day, Constable Laver.'

'Carla, it's a mistake. Check with Assistant Commissioner Broadbent.'

The phone was dead. Again.

* * *

It looked like Wildie hadn't moved for the entire afternoon. Stig had completed his run, had a shower, headed out to do some shopping, come back and had two beers and three cigarettes before finally telling Wildie what he'd seen in Heidelberg. The Wild Man didn't even take his eyes off the screen, Xbox controller jerking in his fingers as he mowed down untold numbers of virtual soldiers. But he'd listened and now asked Stig, 'So when you were with this Louie chick back then, you never mentioned Jenssen or the Groc-o-Mart? Or the bloke who runs the supermarket?'

'I told you, I didn't,' Stig rolling a joint now. Needing one. 'I didn't even know Jenssen's name. I was way down the food chain then. I only went to the Groc-o-Mart a couple of times, to get the gear or drop the cash. They didn't encourage us to hang out there. It was in and out, fast.'

'But you know what the manager looks like.'

'Yeah, he was the one I dealt with. He's a bit older but the same bloke.'

'But Louie wouldn't know him?'

'For fuck's sake, Wildie, I just said—'

'Yeah, but what you didn't say is why she'd be hanging out with a bloke who works there. You don't think that's strange?'

'It's bloody strange, but I honestly can't see the connection.'

Wildie couldn't help but look at Stig: tight-faced, bags under red eyes, drawing hard on a joint. Wildie's character was promptly blown away on-screen. 'Are you fucking kidding? You don't think maybe you're the connection?'

'But the kid didn't know who I was when we met in the café.'

'We thought he was scared, right? Maybe he was just surprised.'

'No, he was scared shitless. And clueless. There's a difference between that and surprised.'

Wildie looked at his on-screen avatar, in full khakis, huge and with a giant orange mohawk. Personally designed by Wildie, who was quite pleased with the mohawk. He hit the button to restart the stage but then hit pause. 'Stig, your ex-girlfriend is hanging out with a guy who works for the Melbourne end of Jenssen's operation. At the exact moment we may or may not be deceased and a large shipment of Jenssen's property is missing and potentially for sale somewhere in Australia. And where better than your old home town? Mate, join the fucking dots.'

Stig shook his head, took a drag on the joint. 'I hear what you're saying but it doesn't smell right. That kid is not a player in this.'

'Easy to find out,' Wildie said, back to clicking buttons, mohawked soldier running through virtual sand to a computerised Middle Eastern town.

'Not yet, mate. Let me think about this a bit first.'

'Yeah, because your thinking has been brilliant so far.'

'Mate, you're not helping.' Stig getting pissed off.

Wildie unflappable as explosions began to light up the television screen. 'And you haven't sold anything yet.'

* * *

Jake was heading out to meet Lou at Bar Open, which he assumed was a bar, on Brunswick Street. Heart pounding, he donned his trusty 'Sound Relief' T-shirt and baggy beret and told his mother he might not be home until late. He was going to an environmental meeting.

'What about your dinner?' she asked, couch-bound in front of *Home and Away*.

'I'm trying to save the world, Mum.'

'Even Gandhi needed to eat.'

'If you say so, Mum.' He got out of there, nursing the Mazda through Kew Junction, over the hill with the great view of the city and down into Collingwood. The road became Johnston Street and a traffic jam at about the same time and Jake edged along, listening to a public radio station, PBS, that Lou had mentioned at one point. He'd found it was a bit of a lottery as to what the station would be playing at any particular time, and right now it was in hillbilly mode. Jake inched across Hoddle Street, wondering what he was more scared about: doing the sticker plan behind Barry's back, or those guys Lou knew turning up again.

Lost in his thoughts, Jake crossed Smith Street and headed towards Brunswick Street. He never once noticed the silver Honda that had followed him all the way.

CHAPTER 15
THE VEGIE BAR

The Vegie Bar was packed with the full assortment of Fitzroy wildlife. Laver and Marcia had a drink in the courtyard, waiting for a couple of seats to free up in the restaurant. It was actually a nice courtyard, peaceful after the chaos of the dining hall and with a decent list of wine and spirits. Knowing Marcia's eyes were on him, Laver dodged the whisky and ordered a light beer.

She had white wine and talked about her work, about this funny new guy who had recently moved down from Brisbane, about how much she was enjoying running at the moment – was even thinking of training up for a half-marathon with some of the crew from her office – and about some of the better stuff she'd seen on Facebook lately.

Marcia never once asking about the shooting inquiry, Laver's new job or why he looked so tired.

In the end, a waiter in a kilt and singlet came to get them and they agreed to two stools in the window, overlooking the street. It actually wasn't bad, with their backs to the human bedlam that filled every corner of the restaurant.

Marcia was no longer even trying to keep the one-way conversation going, as Laver waited for any kind of question to come his way. But no, instead she checked her iPhone and tapped texts as their wines arrived, Marcia silent, right up until the burrito and gado gado arrived.

'So Marcia,' he finally said, 'I'm aware that there have been times my job has appeared to have priority over us.' Marcia snorted into her wine – not exactly the response he'd been hoping for.

He tried to find another way in. 'I'm going through a really hard time at the moment, and it's made me realise how important you are to me, and how much I need you.'

Her phone beeped with a text, but Marcia had the decency to ignore it.

'We've been together a while but I feel that, right now, we're not really together. I'm wondering what we can do to change that, to be, you know, more to one another.'

He was sounding like a bad movie. Marcia folded her arms.

'I'm seeing this whole thing, moving to a mountain bike, being out of Major Crime, as a chance to assess my priorities and for us to look at how we can take things to the next level where, you know, my job isn't such a roadblock, where we can truly consider the word "family".'

Marcia's phone chirped again and this time she said, 'Sorry, I'll just answer this quickly.'

Which almost made Laver put the phone through the fucking window, but he held himself – just.

Instead, jaw clenched and trying to breathe, he distracted himself by watching the tide of people passing outside the window. Across the road, couples were eating ice-cream on the stools outside Trampoline. Marcia was smiling slightly as she tapped the screen on her phone. Laver, breathing slowly, concentrated again on the view. Hey, wow, the second-hand bookshop looked like somewhere he should visit next time he rode through there, killing another work day.

He found himself wondering about the speech he'd just given. Was it even true? Laver hearing the words come out of his mouth about family taking priority and wondering: was he only telling Marcia what she wanted to hear because he didn't want to lose her? Or was he really ready to step back from Major Crime? From serious, time-consuming police work? He didn't want to lose her. But was he prepared to ride a bike around for the rest of his career? Or leave the force altogether?

He kept watching the street and a guy in a full-length leather coat, with a big black cowboy hat and a long beard and moustache, caught his eye. He was handing out flyers, giving one to a kid in a T-shirt and a colourful floppy beret that didn't suit him at all. Laver thought he'd seen a hat like that before, and then realised with a jolt that he was looking at the kid from the Soul Food Café.

Barely registering that fact before seeing a balding man in a suit, slightly overweight and looking entirely out of place on Brunswick Street, never taking his eyes off the kid ten metres in front of him. Both headed south towards the city, the kid oblivious that he was being followed.

Laver found himself sliding off his stool, only barely aware of Marcia's voice, behind his back, saying: 'Honey? Tony? Where are you ...? What the hell?'

Laver thinking, as he moved to the door, 'So now you look up from your phone.'

The guy in the suit was about a block ahead when Laver made it outside and he moved onto the road, jogging along the bike lane to catch up and then get ahead, hoping the guy didn't look to his left. He didn't. Laver picked a gap in the traffic and made it to the pavement just as the kid got to Bar Open, looked at his watch, peered through the door of the bar and then walked a few doors further up to the Brunswick Street Bookstore, and wandered inside.

Laver followed him and came around the other side of the central display to loom over the kid's shoulder as he flicked through a book of great superhero comic covers.

'Don't look around,' Laver murmured in his best ventriloquist impression, almost feeling the kid jump. 'I'm the cop from the Soul Food Café the other day, off duty. Don't look at me or respond in any way.'

Laver picked up a book at random, appearing to read the back cover. 'You're being followed,' he said quietly, 'but I don't know who by. What's your name again?'

'Jake,' the kid whispered, his voice high, standing frozen as though Laver had a gun to his back.

'Okay, Jake, here's what I want you to do: keep walking up Brunswick Street, towards the city, like you don't have a care in the world. Do not look behind you. Check out some shop windows, free as a bird. Cross Johnston Street and walk a couple of blocks, then turn and saunter, very easy, very casual, back here, to the bookshop. Wait for me here. Don't nod or say yes. If you understand me, just go.'

To his credit, the kid turned without a sound and headed for the door. Laver hung back and then followed, watching the guy in the suit, who'd been fascinated by the menu in the window of the restaurant next door, begin to move after him.

Laver picking up his pace and, when they got to the next side street, grabbing the man's right elbow hard and guiding him into the off–Brunswick Street gloom.

'Hey.' The man pulling against Laver's grip. 'What do you think you're doing?'

'Having a chat.'

'How dare you! I'll call the police.'

'I am the police.'

The man looking, wide-eyed and panting, at Laver in his T-shirt, jeans and cowboy boots. 'Like hell you are.'

'Off duty. If you promise not to run while I reach into my pocket, I'll even show you a badge.'

The man nodded warily but stood there as Laver reached for his wallet and showed his police ID.

'I'll be filing a formal complaint,' the man said.

'Good for you. Why are you following that kid?'

'I have no idea what you're talking about.'

'I just watched you tail that kid, and not very well, for two blocks. Why?'

'Nope, no idea. This is outrageous. You'll be hearing about this.' The man was straightening his jacket, starting to breathe again. He had nicotine-stained teeth and Laver could smell old sweat. Laver put him in his mid-fifties.

'Fine. Let's go get the kid. He can ID you and then he can lay charges for harassment.'

'What harassment? That charge would never stick.'

Laver shrugged. 'It doesn't really matter whether it does or not. By the time it's heard you will have spent at least one night in the cells. You been to the Remand Centre? It's not a lot of fun.'

The man sagged. 'Listen, it doesn't have to come to that.'

'I agree. Who are you? What's going on?'

'I'm a private investigator. I'm working for a client.'

Laver crossed his arms. 'Okay, then it's my turn to promise not to run while you show me some ID.'

The man dug around in his jacket and it occurred to Laver, far too late, that he might be reaching for a gun. He was losing his edge in Siberia. But the man just pulled out a thin plastic folder and handed it to Laver, who tried not to show his relief or the fact he was cursing himself for being so sloppy.

The ID said that Jack Thirsk was licensed in the state of Victoria to practise as a private investigator, operating in conjunction with the Privacy Act and under the regulations administered by the Private Agents Register.

'Fine,' Laver said, handing it back. 'Why are you tailing the kid, Mr Thirsk?'

Thirsk looked almost smug. 'I'm not at liberty to say.'

'Oh, give me a break. Don't try to be Sam Fucking Spade with me, okay?'

'I'm sorry, officer. Client confidentiality.'

Laver sighed. 'Fine. Then I am officially telling you, as an officer of the law, that the man you are following is part of a wider Victoria Police investigation and if you are considered to be deliberately hampering that investigation or withholding potentially important evidence, your arse will be in a lot more trouble than Remand for one night.'

Thirsk was looking shifty, trying to process information on the fly, which Laver suspected was a struggle.

'What's the investigation?' Thirsk asked.

'Yeah, right. Why are you following this bloke?'

Thirsk shook his head, so Laver dug out his mobile phone. 'Fair enough, I'll call a wagon. Let's hope your cellmate uses condoms.'

'No.' Thirsk sagged, sighed and dug around inside his coat again. The whiff of old sweat was stronger as his jacket opened. Laver felt slightly queasy. Finally, Thirsk pulled out a photo of a schoolgirl. She was pretty, with strawberry-blonde hair that was set off nicely by her green checked private-school uniform. Her hands were clasped in her lap and she was smiling. Laver had a moment of thinking she looked familiar.

'Who's she?'

'My link to the man I was following. I can't say any more than that.'

'Not even her name?'

'No.'

'Who is your client?'

'Please, officer. You know I don't have to tell you that.'

'Is the girl missing?'

'No.'

'Then what's the issue?'

'Really, officer …'

'Call me Detective Laver. What's the issue?'

Thirsk paused then said, 'The company she might be keeping.'

'A guy called Cig?'

'Huh?' said Thirsk, looking confused.

'Never mind. Good girl goes bad, huh?'

'Eloise isn't necessarily bad.'

'Eloise.'

Thirsk's face was priceless as he mentally kicked himself.

Laver said, 'For what it's worth, the guy you're following is about as dangerous as a kitten.'

'If I could do my job, detective, I might be able to ascertain that.'

'Don't get sniffy, Thirsk. I'm more interested in looking after the kid than your income.'

'Can I go now?'

Laver took a moment, thinking, then said, 'One more question. Is your client a local?'

Thirsk looked genuinely surprised. 'Yes. Why?'

'No reason. Why don't you have an early night, huh? The kid might want some privacy.'

Thirsk looked like he wanted to argue, but the Remand Centre threat was still in the air so he let Laver walk him back to Brunswick Street, headed north and kept going. Laver watched until he was sure and then wandered into the Brunswick Street Bookstore. The kid was deep in the store, behind stands of greeting cards, near the crime books, nervously sneaking glances at the doorway, but still took a moment to realise Laver was coming towards him. Laver remembered he hadn't looked back when they'd spoken earlier.

'Yeah, I'm the guy. My name's Detective Tony Laver. We met at the Soul Food Café, yeah? You okay?'

The kid nodded, but unconvincingly. 'Who was following me?'

'Nobody you need to worry about. He's a private detective who's on the wrong track. We had a chat and he's gone home.'

'But why me?'

'No idea. Did you say your name was Jake?'

'Jake Murphy.' He actually put out his hand, so Laver shook it, Jake's hand moist with sweat.

'You're having a rough few days, Jake. Might be keeping the wrong sort of company.'

'I'm thinking the same thing myself.'

'Who were those guys the other day? Did you find out anything?'

'No. Lou, that girl I was with, works at Friends of the Planet, a shop on Smith Street, and one of them is her ex-boyfriend or something, from there. I don't know anything about the other guy. When you said I was being followed, I was really scared it was one of them.'

'Why would it be?'

Jake shook his head miserably. 'I don't know.'

'You'll be okay but keep your head down, okay? Where were you heading to tonight?'

'Bar Open, just down the street.'

'I'll walk you down there. I have to be getting back.'

As they walked, Laver pulled out his wallet and gave Jake a card. 'I'm not actually in Major Crime at the moment but the mobile number hasn't changed. You call me if you need to. Especially if you see those two from the other day.'

'Sure. Thanks.' Jake was reading the card, still sweating. 'You know, I thought I saw a couple of men in the car park at work today.'

'The ones from the café?'

'God, no.'

'Then what made you notice them?'

'I don't know really. They were in a white car. A sedan. I wasn't even sure they weren't just customers. Maybe I'm jumping at shadows.'

'Can you describe them?'

'Big. In suits, like cops in cop shows. Just the sense that they were watching. I might be imagining the whole thing.'

'The guy tonight was real and those two in the café were very real.' Laver was thinking as he spoke. 'I reckon tonight's was a loner. Didn't seem the sort to have a partner and if he does, the partner was nowhere tonight. You've got my card. If you see anything weird at work, call me, okay? Even if it seems dumb. I don't mind.'

Jake looked very young as he said, 'I don't get why I'm being followed. I don't understand any of it.'

'Then it's probably nothing to do with you, Jake. Come on, we're here.'

They were at Bar Open and Laver saw the hippie chick, standing by the bar. His immediate thought was that she was way out of Jake's league.

'Hey Jake, one last thing before your hot date.' A blush appeared on Jake's neck. 'Those two at the café. Do you know their names? I thought I heard one call the other Cig.'

Jake screwed up his face, remembering. 'Lou's ex said his mate was a wild man, I think. And then the big red-haired one said something when you walked in. I thought it was "Stig".'

Stig. That's why 'Cig' had been annoying him ever since, his cop instincts knowing it was not quite right.

But, really? Stig?

The hippie chick was gazing steadily at them, sizing him up, as Jake said goodbye and wandered in.

CHAPTER 16
THE MUTANT CHILDREN OF OSSIE OSTRICH

Laver got back to the Vegie Bar to find that, of course, Marcia was gone. Oh Christ, he was going to pay for that.

He called, but got her phone's message bank, inviting him to leave a message. He did, asking her to call him back, but decided not to hold his breath.

He badly needed a drink and, now he thought about it, noise. Escape. He thought about ringing Flipper, to see if he'd talk outside work hours. But what was the point?

In a sudden moment of inspiration, Laver made another phone call instead and, leaving his car where it was, headed towards Johnston Street and then down to Wellington, to the Tote Hotel: one of the last bastions of live pub rock in Melbourne.

Nathan Funnal arrived about half an hour after Laver, as Damian's band was setting up in the wake of a band that was a wannabe Nirvana or Oasis – Laver couldn't decide.

Funnal bought the first beers and they found a corner where the noise from the sound check wasn't too bad.

'So, how's life in the saddle?'

'Up and down, pun intended. It's so weird not being in Major.'

'Do you actually turn up? Go out on the bike?'

'Yeah, mostly. I have to sign on and off so I'd only be sitting at a desk. May as well get some fresh air. The actual bike bit isn't too bad, it's just the fact that the work is so … juvenile. Tourists and parking tickets, you know?'

'Can't imagine.' Funnal sipped his beer. 'Look at the bright side, you're not involved in some of the shit going on.'

'Like what?'

'You know that underworld taskforce?'

'Noble?'

'Yep. Did you hear about the Italian connection?'

Laver felt like crying, he was so in love with having an actual non-Siberian cop talk, even if Funnal was a Soggie. He leaned in. 'Go on.'

Funnal was trying to speak quietly but also yell over the drums being tested. 'They had this guy in their sights for the hit on that bloke outside the gym. Remember the one in Bentleigh?'

Laver was nodding. 'Sure. Part of the Williams–Moran thing.'

'Yep. The Noble ones thought they had the shooter cold. They'd bugged pretty much every object in his house short of the dunny – and maybe that, too. They had him on tape saying to his girlfriend, in Italian, according to Victoria Police's finest translators: "I shot him in the head. It was beautiful."'

'Nice.'

'Off go the Noble boys to northern Italy where the alleged hitman now resides, having made the smart decision that it might be in his best interests to leave Victoria for a while. The Noble detectives have full cooperation from the local constabulary so they have a getting-to-know-you session before they head up to said alleged hitman's remote villa. Of course, they proudly play the tape. At which point the Italian cops all start looking at each other and grinning.'

Laver waited for it. Funnal swigged his beer and leaned closer to Laver's ear.

'One of them says, "Who translated this?" The Noble guys say it was the Melbourne translator. "What Italian does he or she speak? Northern or southern?" Noble guy says, "Fucked if I know … he speaks Italian." Locals laughing openly now. Turns out in the local dialect, which is what the hitman happens to speak, the tape has him saying to his girlfriend, "You give great head. That's beautiful!"'

'No!'

'Yes.'

'Halfway around the world.'

'On taxpayers' money.'

'Explains why the girlfriend didn't say much on the tape?'

'Very much so.'

'Oh Jesus. That's hilarious.' The two cops now with their shoulders quaking. 'No wonder Flipper has been in such a foul mood.'

'He was one degree of separation from the surveillance, lucky for him.'

Laver went and got more beers. As he sat down again, he said, 'Spider, I've got a problem. Nobody will listen and I've spotted some potentially nasty stuff about to happen.'

Funnal looked serious. 'Rocket, you know I can't get involved.'

'You're a Soggie, Spider. You're the guys who famously don't give a shit.'

'The squeaky-clean demands currently washing through the Force haven't missed us, Rocket. You know that. You think you're the only one being looked at? No wonder the assistant commissioners are all shitting themselves, given the number of skeletons out there – literally in some cases. This new chief has the right head for the job and he's brave, even braver than the last one was. Rest her soul with the bushfire commission.'

'Mate, all I want you to do—'

'Nope. Flat no. He's already looking at the bodies below him. Four separate shooting investigations, corruption charges looming against senior uniforms, that potential murder charge against the ex-vice bloke. It's heads-down time. Mushroom city. Cliché of your choice that means "stay within the lines".'

'I get all of that, but I'm talking street level. I'm out there and I've seen some bad heads. New ones too, as far as I can tell. You know my instincts … I'm sure this is noteworthy.'

Funnal shrugged. 'I'm not doubting that. But if I lifted a finger to help you I'd be on the Malvern Star two bike racks down from yours.'

'You can't run some names for me?'

'Rocket, think about it. I'm a Soggie. They point us in a direction and we break down doors. Why would I be running fucking names?'

'You don't know what it's like, Spider. It's like they've just cut off my balls. Like all my years of knowing who to watch and who to ignore have been wiped by that prick Strickland from the ombudsman.'

'And Broadbent, but mate, just sit tight. All going well, it's not permanent.'

'But these dickheads are out there right now. They're not waiting for the Coleman inquiry to run its bloody course. And people might get hurt.'

'If they do, they do. You don't have to catch them all, mate.'

'Are you serious?'

'Deadly.' Funnal leaned in and pointed a finger at Laver's chest.

'Listen, when you are saddled up where you belong, in Major Crime, you do great work, Rocket. You put nasty people behind bars. You protect the public if you want to get all holy about it. But right now, you aren't in that chair, so relax.'

'That's what everybody says. Relax. Get a suntan. Fuck.'

'So do it.'

'Spider, I'm a cop. I'm not a bike courier. I've never taken my fully allotted holidays. I've worked the crazy hours and chased the half-arsed leads, because it's the job. I think I'm on the brink of losing my second serious relationship because of my work. I'm a cop.'

'Only just, Rocket. Remember that. And if you keep sticking your head up, it could be gone forever.'

'What does that mean? Is that a threat?'

'Oh for fuck's sake. It's a mate giving you advice, dickhead.'

Laver took a deep breath. 'Sorry mate. Truly. I'm not coping well with this.'

Funnal gave him a look. 'Gee, you think?'

Laver swigged his beer to the bottom and stalked off to get some more. When he came back Damian was on stage, wearing jeans, a green T-shirt, a full-length fur coat and a Fender Stratocaster guitar.

'Hey y'all,' he said, voice booming out of a speaker to Laver's left. 'Welcome to the Tote. We're The Mutant Children of Ossie Ostrich and we're going to rock this place! In honour of a friend of mine who's in the audience, we might even go all Mixtures on your ass and play "The Pushbike Song". You ready? Boys – pedal to the metal!'

As the band fired up, Laver raised a single middle finger in the stage's direction.

'Mate,' Laver went to shout to Funnal, but the Soggie raised a hand.

'No Rocket. No. Let's just get pissed and listen to your mate's latest shit band.'

So they did.

CHAPTER 17
LOST IN SIBERIA

Jake swam but there was no sign of Lou. He'd finally returned to the pool because he was worried about losing his fitness, plus he missed the routine of swimming and, even more so – if he was totally honest – he missed seeing her in that bathing suit.

Their meeting at Bar Open the night before had been a trip. Jake had been shaken by the whole thing with the cop and the guy following him but hadn't mentioned any of it to Lou. Part of him was dying to tell her, to show what a potentially dangerous, mysterious cat he was under his supermarket assistant-manager disguise. But then he'd thought of Lou's ex-boyfriend and his mate and realised he had a way to go when it came to being dangerous.

In the end, he'd decided not to mention it – he didn't want her thinking he was getting paranoid or was about to get cold feet about the sticker plan, which she wanted to do, sooner rather than later. So he'd ordered a light beer and they got to talking, which wasn't easy over the thrash band playing at the back of the room.

Lou had brought a tiny booklet with her: 'The guide to ethical supermarket shopping'. The Earth in a shopping basket on the cover.

It claimed to be the bible of which companies were genuinely environmentally friendly, actually organic or really cruelty-free when it came to the treatment of animals. Jake had been surprised flicking through it. Some major brands were firmly in the 'Avoid where possible' and 'Boycott!' categories, while others had question marks over them. He couldn't help thinking that anybody who lived by that book would have trouble walking down any aisle of the Heidelberg Groc-o-Mart.

Lou had said they should meet the day after tomorrow, at night, to plant the stickers, which she was organising. Jake swam, knowing he had a date: a guaranteed night-time rendezvous with Lou.

He was still thinking about it when he arrived at work, hair damp from the pool. The car park was mostly empty. Barry's car was in its usual spot, there was a delivery truck at the loading bay, and there was a white sedan over in the back corner, almost hidden behind the industrial bins and a bush that was getting seriously overgrown. Jake felt his heart jump. He worked hard not to look directly at the car, but he instantly registered that it was a Ford. And there were two people sitting in the front seats.

Jake hustled into work, sweating straight through his after-swim shower and deodorant. The cop's card was in his wallet. But it was 8.27 the morning after he gave it to him. Jake would look like an idiot if he was on the phone that quickly. He decided to wait and see if the car was still there in a few hours.

* * *

Head pounding, Laver caught a taxi to Brunswick Street and found his car with three tickets already fluttering on the windscreen. The first one, from when Brunswick Street was a morning peak-hour clearway, was $400. Laver reflected that Siberia probably meant nobody would even make the bastards disappear. As though in protest at having been abandoned the night before, the car refused to start until the third try, something that was happening often enough that Laver thought he should probably get it looked at.

It had been an expensive night in lots of ways. He had taken a taxi home from the Tote, with a long detour to Marcia's apartment block in Toorak, where she didn't answer the buzzer. Either she ignored him or she wasn't there. She must have been pissed off or upset, so maybe she'd stayed at a girlfriend's place? Should he send flowers to her work? Flowers and a fluffy toy? Have the Botanical Gardens sent there? Would anything help at this point? God, his head hurt.

As Laver finally walked in the door of the Mobile Public Interaction Squad headquarters, holding two takeaway coffees, Slattery tilted his head, smiled and said, 'An hour late. That's coming off your pay.'

Just the two of them in the room, everybody else already having ridden into the day.

'Fair enough,' Laver said. 'If it involves a memo, don't type it too loudly.'

'Actually all is forgiven if one of those coffees is for me.'

Laver winced at the fluoro lighting as he removed his sunglasses. 'Actually, they're both for me. Medical emergency.'

'Second strike,' Slattery said, shaking his head.

'Oh okay, have one. With the extra entertainment of watching me suffer.'

Laver pulled up a chair on the other side of Slattery's desk. They both sipped coffee.

'Slatts, I've got a name I'd like to run through the database, if you could help me out as senior officer.'

'Someone you woke up with this morning?'

'I wish. A potential perp that Officer Valencia and I encountered recently on our rounds.'

'If you didn't look like such shit, I might actually believe you.'

'Ask Cecy,' Laver said.

'See, that statement worries me all on its own. What are you getting Cecy involved with?'

'I believe the technical term is "police work", which I know is generally frowned upon around here. All I want is to run some profiles.'

Slattery leaned forward. 'You know you don't have privileges. To anything at St Kilda Road.'

'What if Cecy asked?'

'I want Cecy out of this.'

'Jesus, Slatts. What language am I speaking? Klingon? This is a straight police matter.'

Slattery gazed at him. 'I'll consider it. But I don't want Cecy getting dragged into whatever shit you have going on.'

'Man, if you have something to say, just say it, Slatts.'

Slatts almost smiled, leaned back. 'You want to go home? You look terrible.'

'Nope, ready for duty, even if a little dusty. Never once missed a day because of a hangover. And, yes, there have been hangovers. Biblical hangovers.'

'An old-time cop.' Slattery grinned.

'Tell the kids; even Standish, when he's up and about. I need their respect for something.'

* * *

Laver was onto his third Gatorade, pondering the enzymes or whatever those things are in sport drinks that are supposed to rehydrate you.

He and Constable Aimee Ratten had cruised through the city and out the other side, riding to the Shrine and patrolling the Tan, Melbourne's favourite inner-city running track – which was no hardship for Laver, as a parade of women in lycra jogged past.

They were taking their Gatorade break on St Kilda Road, close enough to police headquarters that Laver could see cops coming and going, feeling pangs of something resembling homesickness, as well as anger that he was on the outside looking in. Now watching a silver Statesman pull up out front, so that Laver saw a slim man with thinning red hair climb out of the back seat in an impeccable navy-blue suit, talking on a mobile phone.

'Laver?' Ratten asked, but he was already moving across St Kilda Road, walking fast to get out of the way of a tram *ding ding ding*ing as it rushed towards him. Giving the driver the bird but making it alive to the footpath outside Police

Headquarters, Laver catching up to the man at the top of the stairs, just before the revolving door.

Strickland studied Laver in his lycra uniform, raising an eyebrow but not attempting to go through the door. He finished his call and carefully pressed the red 'hang up' button before putting the phone in an inside pocket of his suit coat.

'Senior Constable Laver. What a pleasant surprise. The outdoorsy life looks as though it's agreeing with you.'

'Why am I in Siberia, Strickland?'

Strickland sighed. 'It's extremely juvenile to ignore titles, Senior Constable. You don't do yourself any favours.'

'Excuse me for being juvenile, Mr Strickland.'

'Actually, in police terms, I am by far your superior, Senior Constable.'

'Good for you. I'm more interested in real life, and anyway my understanding is that you're not a policeman anymore, in any capacity, certainly to go by your actions lately.'

'And what exactly does that mean, Senior Constable?'

'Freezing me out, for starters. Smells much more like a politician at work than a policeman.'

'You insolent prick. I've done more than my share of years in uniform and on the streets.'

'Well, those years certainly didn't scar you with anything resembling empathy for working cops.'

Strickland turned towards the revolving door. 'As lovely to see you as I would have expected, Constable.'

'You haven't answered my question, Mr Strickland, sir. Why would you possibly have invoked Siberia on me?'

Strickland swung back to face him. 'Because you're the subject of a serious police inquiry into a fatal shooting. I would have thought that was reasonably obvious for an officer of your experience.'

'My experience doesn't seem to carry much stock when I report potentially dangerous perpetrators in my current status.'

'Because you're in Siberia,' Strickland smiled pleasantly. Laver wanted to punch him.

But didn't. Instead he said, 'So if I was to tell you that I believe a major crime might be in the works?'

'And what sort of major crime would that be, Constable?'

Shit, Laver thought, considering the evidence he actually had, now it came down to it: two dodgy guys in a café giving him dead-eye stares. He hadn't actually thought about what they might be up to, beyond being generic criminals.

Strickland was waiting, so he said, 'Drugs, sir. I think there's a good chance a major drug deal is going down.'

'Then I'd say the government and the ombudsman's office share full confidence that our highly accomplished and professional serving police officers – who are *not* under investigation for reckless shootings – will discover any such deal and catch those responsible.'

'Other officers can't be told about it because I'm in Siberia.'

'Well, it is unfortunate that you appear to be the only source and you don't currently exist.'

'Because you seem to be the one insisting on it. Shouldn't it be my direct superior, Assistant Commissioner Broadbent, who tells other officers whether to cooperate or not?'

Strickland frowned, either in annoyance or anger – Laver couldn't tell. His voice remained infuriatingly level.

'You seem to have a rare ability to look for divisions within the Force, Laver. We're all actually in this together. Remember? Good guys versus bad guys. Maybe Assistant Commissioner Broadbent hasn't become involved because he liked and respected you and you're fast becoming an embarrassment to him.'

Laver didn't miss the past tense in 'liked' and 'respected'.

'So, just to help a constable along, are you representing the good guys or the bad guys by being the government PR spinner in all this and by freezing me out?'

'Being a smart-arse isn't exactly helpful to your situation, Senior Constable.' Strickland leaned in close, and now a grade of steel found its way into the civility of his voice. 'You're on ice so thin that a single snowflake might cause a crack. I'd worry less about who put you in Siberia and worry more about whether you'll ever get out. Your apparent refusal to actually keep your head down and ride your bike is an encouraging start for those who'd like you off the Force.'

'That would be you.'

Strickland shrugged. 'I don't think a trigger-happy cowboy with bad manners would be a great loss to Victoria Police. The government has a wider view than you do from your bike saddle.'

'Trigger-happy? He shot at me first.'

'That's for the inquiry to examine, Senior Constable. And now I'm late for a meeting with the commissioner and his assistants – including your old friend Broadbent, as it happens. I'll send him your best.'

'Please do. He certainly doesn't return my phone calls.'

Strickland gave him that same smug smile Laver desperately wanted to punch and said happily, 'Well, why would he?'

And walked through the revolving door into headquarters. Leaving Tony Laver outside.

* * *

Lou felt his presence before she saw him. Heard the bells on the door jangle as she dug around under the desk for a paper bag and somehow just knew. She finally lifted her head and felt her body jump. There he was, hair shaved into a mohawk style now, looming behind the woman with the pram. Lou placing the organic-oatmeal Anzac cookies in the bag and composing her face, handing them to the customer.

Watching him fail to stand back and give more room as the woman struggled to negotiate the pram into reverse and out the door. Now watching him approach, just the counter between them.

'Louie, Louie,' he said. That punched-in-the-throat voice. 'Oh boy. I say. Away I go.'

Lou not saying a word, registering body odour.

'Stig was right about you,' he said, looking her slowly up and down. 'You're a package.'

'I don't think I have anything to say to you.' Louie involuntarily crossing her arms across her chest, aware of the sinewed muscle in his shoulders, of the tattoos emerging from where the singlet covered his chest. Of the faded tattoos on his arms. Jail tattoos. Of other customers also sneaking worried looks.

'Why not?' He looked genuinely surprised. 'We're friends of a friend. Isn't that a good enough reason to share a friendly coffee in Melbourne?'

'Not when the only time we've met you were threatening me.'

'How was I threatening you? I was playing.'

'Well, you and I have a different idea of the word "play".'

The tall man grinned at her. 'I'm not so sure about that, Louie. I reckon we could find some common ground you might enjoy.'

Lou gave him a level look, determined not to show fear, and said, 'What's your name again, friend of Stig's?'

'You can call me Wildie.'

'Okay. Then I do have something to say to you, Wildie. Fuck off.'

He laughed and picked a stick of Tasmanian gluten-free liquorice from the open box on the desk. He chomped on it and smirked.

'Come on, Louie. We could be great friends. Very close. Just like you and your little boyfriend the other day.'

'He's not my boyfriend,' she said and cursed inwardly the moment the words left her mouth.

'Really?' Wildie's eyebrows shot up in mock surprise. 'So there's room for a tall stranger in your life then? Excellent news. But what I'm really wondering is who the non-boyfriend is, if he's not a boyfriend?'

Lou's arms were still crossed, tight. She frowned at him but remained silent.

'Stig's kind of interested in who his girl is hanging out with, so I'd love to put his mind at rest.'

'Good for you. And I'm not Stig's girl.'

'Stig's concerned this guy might not be a friend.'

'If Stig keeps hanging around with you, that would be true of pretty much everybody.'

Wildie laughed again, a genuine laugh, loud as he threw his head back. Customers who hadn't been staring now stared.

'That's good. You're funny. Stig always said you were funny. I think he mentioned passionate and flexible and tasty as well.'

'Wildie,' Lou said sweetly, working hard to keep a tremble out of her voice, 'fuck off or I'm calling the police.'

Wildie stopped smiling. 'All I want to know is who the dweeb was.'

'All I want to know is why you can't take a hint and use the door.' Anger replacing fear.

Wildie shrugged. 'You're playing this wrong. If you don't tell me about him, I'm going to have to talk to the non-boyfriend directly.'

Lou didn't say anything. Wildie pointed a finger at her, like a gun. And fired it.

Lou leaned forward. 'Wildie. Next time, tell Stig I'd rather talk to the organ-grinder, not the monkey.'

She felt her mouth dry up as his eyes hardened. The rules of engagement had shifted. To somewhere she didn't know, or like at all.

'Careful babe,' he said softly. 'Being highly fuckable only gets you so many "Get out of jail free" cards.'

And then he was leaving, the Smith Street wildlife in the shop peeling out of his way by instinct. Darwinism has always worked in its truest form on the street.

CHAPTER 18
THE GREVILLEA WING

It took forty-five minutes to ride back to bike-cop HQ. Ratten was heroic in not pointing out how many times she'd had to wait for her clearly labouring partner to catch up.

It hadn't helped that, on top of his hangover and his run-in with Strickland, he'd tried five times throughout the morning to contact Marcia. After the two messages to her work phone, on top of a trifecta of voicemail on her mobile, he figured she knew by now that he wanted to grovel.

Laver was hardly stunned to find his work email and phone were both message free; it wasn't just Marcia giving him the silent treatment. There was no response to his attempts at information from official sources. No calls from mates within the Force. No flowers from Broadbent. Clearly, Strickland hadn't been moved to a dramatic change of heart by their talk.

Mixing Berocca into a glass of water, he felt Cecy approach and saw her grin spread as she took in his face.

'Looking sharp, Laver.'

'Ever heard of respect for a senior officer, OJ?'

'At this exact moment, we're ranked the same, so sit and spin,' she returned. 'And keep calling me OJ and see what happens to you.'

'Can't believe nobody here has taken it and run with it.' Laver chugged his fizzy drink, grimacing as it burned his throat. 'The Force isn't what it used to be.'

'Thank God. You look like you're moving slowly today.'

'Which is a shame because Victoria Police has endless demands for my talents, right?'

'Man up,' she shrugged and, with another dazzling smile, was gone.

He was still watching her walk away when his mobile went off. He felt an unexpected flush of shame, as though Marcia had caught him scoping his young colleague's lycra-clad shape. Glancing at his phone, he realised it wasn't her number. It was a 9497 prefix. Where the hell was that? Fairfield?

'Laver.'

'Umm, Mr Laver? It's Jake Murphy, from last night.'

* * *

Stig found a quiet corner of the internet café. He and Wildie drew enough looks without people getting a close look at his web search.

He couldn't believe Wikipedia had an entry for Her Majesty's Prison Barwon. Home to Victoria's worst prisoners, along with the usual lightweights, it was in a depressingly bland series of buildings on the Bacchus Marsh Road in Lara, a nothing suburb in the wastelands near Geelong, to Melbourne's west. Only a few kilometres further west than Stig's origins, which struck him as no coincidence.

The Acacia wing of Barwon Prison was even listed, where the Who's Who would be found. The Hoddle Street shooter Julian Knight, now studying law and annoying the attorney-general with legal questions for all these years. The Russell Street bombers. A host of creepy criminal lowlifes, from serial rapists to disturbing killers – like the murderer who spear-gunned his wife and kid a few years before – often in high security to protect them from outraged fellow inmates, many of whom were the fathers of daughters and had plenty of in-built anger looking for direction.

Also working quietly on their empires from within Barwon, and of more interest to Stig, were the few gangsters and drug lords still breathing after the much-celebrated underworld gang war.

But looking at the prison's description, they might be in the Grevillea wing – some government nuff nuff thinking a maximum-security division would be less brutal on everybody if named after a flower.

He clicked on one of the gangland figure's names and found even more detailed Wikipedia entries existed for the individual criminals. Who filled in this stuff? The crim? Those weird crime groupies you saw outside the court when somebody got sentenced? The entry said Stig's man was housed inside Grevillea. Thank you, Wiki.

What Wikipedia didn't tell him was the requirements of a potential visitor to either of these sections. Stig's fake driver's licence – Steve Anderson from Clovelly Beach, a suburb of Perth; nice to meet you; yes, I do miss the weather – was good, but Barwon security would surely be better.

Stig was aware that he was no genius when it came to surfing the net; computers had never been a major part of his life. He squinted and scrolled through the page and then found a link to a reference site. Department of Justice. He felt dirty even clicking on the link, but now he was at the official page for Barwon – and the navigation bar had a 'Visiting Prisoners' section.

Stig clicked and waited impatiently as the café's slow internet took forever to load the page.

Arranging to visit a prisoner

You will need to write to the prisoner (care of Corrections Victoria) and ask him or her to have you placed on their approved Visitors List.

In your letter, you should include your full name, date of birth and address. It is then up to the prisoner to make the arrangements for you to be able to visit them.

Write to:

(prisoner's full name)

C/- Corrections Victoria

GPO Box 123

Melbourne VIC 3001

Your letter will be forwarded to the prisoner.

If you have been previously convicted of an offence you will have to get permission to enter a prison. You will need to write a letter to the general manager of the prison that you wish to visit, providing your CRN and the name of the prisoner you wish to visit, and requesting permission to visit.

Fuck that, thought Stig. Not going to be doing the business face to face with anybody in Barwon. He was about to close the page when he realised somebody was behind him.

'Do you want another half-hour?' The Asian girl, probably a uni student, from behind the counter. Straight-faced and wide-eyed. Who me?

'Maybe. I don't know. My mother's in a bit of trouble.' Why was he bothering to come up with a story for this chick?

She was gazing at him. 'Your mother is in Barwon Prison?'

'No. I mean, she works there. Listen, you could piss off and stop reading over the shoulders of customers, you nosy bitch.'

'There's no need to be like that, sir. I was just asking.'

'Give me five minutes.' Stig clicked back to Google.

Her shadow still behind him on the screen's reflection.

'We only sell thirty-minute blocks.'

Stig turned slowly and gazed her. Then said, 'You must have misheard me the first time, so I'll say it more slowly. Fuck. Off.'

She turned and got out of there.

Stig checked his email. Not a word from Sophie, out the back of Byron. He ached for that house. Ached for her. But never again. Unless she could meet him overseas, later. If she would.

There was a hard rapping on the window of the internet café. Heads bobbed up from screens and gazed impassively at the rangy man in a singlet with a bushy beard and orange mohawk, spreading two huge arms in a universally recognised 'what the?' gesture.

Stig yanked the power cord out of his computer, thinking that would clear the web memory. That would do it, wouldn't it?

He left without paying. The nosy bitch stayed behind her desk and didn't say a word.

'You took your bloody time,' said Wildie, walking fast, edgy. Stig wondering if he'd taken something or if it was just the usual Wild Man volcano building.

'You think I'd be a fast typist? What do I look like, a geek?'

'You really want me to answer that?' Wildie giving him a sly grin so that Stig relaxed, realising his mate was in control. They arrived at a brand-new Ford Territory SUV, crimson red. Stig regarding it.

'This our wheels?'

'You bet. I thought you'd enjoy a family wagon. Mate, it's hilarious. In the city car parks, they have car cleaning while you're gone ... just leave your keys. For us, it's like an all-you-can-eat buffet. I was going to go for a brand new BMW sports.'

'Nah, this is a better call, Wildie. Less obvious. To go with your new mohawk. What's say we cruise over to Heidelberg. Think about some shopping?'

Wildie starting the car. 'We need groceries?'

'Maybe. Can't hurt to check some out.'

CHAPTER 19
DOING THE
KEW CONGA

The little Greek man was already getting up from his cluttered antique desk in the back room of the deserted café, beaming a smile of welcome, arms outstretched, as Laver, in jeans and a T-shirt, approached.

'Mr Rocket! It's been a long time. *Yassou*, my friend.'

'Sammy. You haven't changed! Although is that grey hair in the moustache?'

The man's face collapsed in exaggerated self-pity and sadness. 'There might be a sprinkle. When you live a hard life like me, this is going to happen, my friend.'

'You down to your last million?'

'Laugh it up, Mr Rocket Man. Do I see you down here at five am in the morning every day before the sun, no sleep from your aching back, or not? No, I don't.'

'I know how hard you work, Sammy. That's never in question. Business okay?'

Sammy shrugged expansively. 'What can I say? There's a global crisis.'

'I wasn't aware it had crept all the way to authentic Greek restaurants.'

'It's hitting everybody, my friend.' Sammy, serious now, leaning in. 'More than half the restaurants on Sydney Road are losing money, you know.'

Laver was genuinely shocked. 'Is that new? I assumed that was the norm and they were all tax write-offs.'

Sammy waved him off. 'You know so much about it, Mr Big Shot.' He leaned in again and said quietly, 'I haven't seen you for so long. I thought maybe you might have gone straight.'

Laver grinned. 'Not yet, Sammy. It remains a world of opportunity.'

It had always suited Laver to have Sammy think he was some minor criminal. Meant he asked a lot fewer questions than if he'd known Laver was a cop and, anyway, it was sort of fun to have somebody in Melbourne who believed he was on the other side of the fence. Laver had never spelled it out either way. It was Sammy who had come to the conclusion that a man paying handsomely for the use of his café's white van for irregular periods must be up to something.

He asked Sammy, 'Can you do without the old girl for a few hours?'

'It is yours, my friend. It is lovely to see you. The price can even remain the same, despite a percentage rise, because of the time being completely reasonable.'

'Stop it, Sammy. I'm getting misty-eyed.'

Laver found the van was as tinny as ever but it drove well enough as he battled traffic, heading east towards Preston, then across towards Ivanhoe. He even realised his hangover had lifted enough that his head felt clear, so he turned on the radio, searching for music.

The idea had first occurred to him when he was living in a rented flat around the corner from Sammy's café, about seven years ago. Whoever thought that trailing people in a black sedan, the driver in forbidding dark glasses, was a good idea hadn't thought far beyond Hollywood reality. Even a Commodore or Fairlane sedan, the usual unmarked police option for surveillance, was pretty obvious if somebody checked their rear-view mirror more than a couple of times. Plus, if you found yourself behind them or beside their car at a red light, your face was right there in their line of vision.

Laver had been walking past Sammy's café and saw the white van, magnificent in its nondescript anonymity. The archetypal courier van, who knew how many thousands of which were endlessly circulating on Melbourne's roads, delivering anything from mail to seafood. Sitting in one of these, he'd be higher than a driver's eye level, unless they were in a four-wheel drive. And he'd be just another delivery van. Even if they saw the van a dozen times in a trip, most criminals wouldn't register it.

On a whim, he'd wandered in, shaken hands and asked Sammy if he could borrow that van, no questions asked, for a small cash donation. Sammy had turned out to be perfectly up for some side business, especially as he only drove the van about three times a week, pre-dawn, to get fruit and vegetable supplies for the café. An agreement, with a lot of unspoken assumptions, was reached – and, over the years, friendship had blossomed.

Laver cruised through the commercial FM stations on the van's factory radio, wondering if the static or the DJs were the worse noise pollution. He eventually left it on Triple R, a local community station, which was on one of its jazz trips. Hopefully something else would kick in at the turn of the hour.

He pulled into the Heidelberg Groc-o-Mart car park just after 4.40 pm, the car park about two-thirds full and chaotic, with kids running in all directions as mothers grabbed some last-minute dinner provisions on their after-school runs. Laver nursed the van to a parking spot near the exit onto Upper Heidelberg Road but within sight of the supermarket's front door and the other car-park exits. He was glad to see Sammy hadn't indulged in an unexpected cleaning spree in the time since he'd last used the van. As usual, his clipboard was jammed behind the passenger seat. Laver picked it up and pretended to be going down some sort of list, true to his disguise. Even such a small detail could be all you needed to make anybody sussing you shrug and turn away.

As he checked the empty list against his fictional delivery, he scoped the parking lot. The white Ford was about forty metres away, the two men sitting comfortably. It was an hour since Jake had called Laver, so they'd been there for at least that long. It obviously didn't bother the two men that they might look suspicious, not leaving their car. One with a hand holding a cigarette out the open window. So they didn't really mind if they were seen.

Or it hadn't occurred to them that anybody might be looking.

Laver's eyes kept roving and landed on a red Territory with two guys in it. He had to work hard not to jump as he realised he was looking at the two men from the Soul Food Café. The guy who might be called Stig and the other big one. What were they doing there in the car park, their SUV facing towards the Waterdale Road exit?

He fished in a pocket for his mobile phone and SMSed Jake, asking what time he was knocking off.

The reply beeped: 5 min :)

Laver spent the intervening time contemplating why Jake would add a smiley-face emoticon to a text to a cop who was watching his back against people who might want to hurt him. Was Laver getting old, falling off the back of the Twitter generation? Or was Jake maybe just an idiot?

Laver typed into his mobile: get in car. drive home. cat normal.

Then cursed the predictive spelling he hadn't yet worked out how to turn off on his phone and backtracked to change 'cat' to 'act'. And sent it.

And then cursed again, and SMSed a final time, asking Jake for his home address, which was beeped back, emoticon free. Laver put aside the clipboard and studied the Melways street map for Jake's house.

To his credit, when Jake emerged, he did a pretty good job of not looking scared to death. He wandered out of the main sliding door, went to his car, got in and drove off without obviously looking in any direction apart from checking for moving cars.

Laver watched Jake's left indicator blink on as he waited for a gap in traffic so he could turn left onto Heidelberg Road. Laver watched the red Territory cruise slowly in that direction. The white Ford stayed where it was.

Jake turned into the traffic, and the Territory was right behind him. Laver was still watching the Ford, wondering if he could get the licence plate before following the Territory, when a silver Honda shot past him, going too fast for the car park, and caused a car to jam on its brakes, honking, as the Honda lurched out into traffic in front of it.

Laver grinned as he recognised the sweaty profile of the private detective, Thirsk, through the Honda's window. Amateur hour.

Laver was going to have to follow or risk losing them and leaving Jake to Stig and his mate. But just as he started the van, the Ford began to move and glided smoothly to the exit and out onto Heidelberg Road.

Laver was two cars back and one lane over from the Ford as they headed down the hill from Ivanhoe towards Alphington. By the time they turned right at the bottom of the hill, straightening up towards the city, the Ford was cruising a full five cars back from Thirsk, who was right on the Territory's hammer. Jake sailed along, three cars further ahead, and now turning left onto the Chandler Highway towards Kew.

Across the Eastern Freeway overpass and the Ford was still hanging back, a calm and distant tail but one that was worrying Laver in case he and the Ford missed a vital traffic light, as he battled along behind the entire caravan. He was glad he'd checked Jake's address. But then they were lucky in getting through an amber light at Princes Street and were still within range as Jake, then the Territory, then Thirsk's Honda turned left at the next roundabout.

Laver was able to slow now, because he'd done the Melways homework. Jake would turn at Barnard Grove, the second street, where his mother's house was about nine along on the left-hand side. Instead of following the others down the narrow one-way street, he would be able to watch from the intersection. This little pocket of houses, jammed next to the walls of the freeway where the traffic rushed in early peak-hour frenzy metres away, was like a small suburban air pocket. Any cars that went down Jake's street had to loop back out and come straight past Laver again to return to the main roads.

Laver planned to watch the others from the intersection of Barnard Grove and Willsmere, the street they were all now on – but the men in the white Ford had the same idea, so he hung back even more, stopping fifty metres behind, then hanging a U-turn while he had the opportunity so he was ready to pick them all up on their way back out. The whole plan banking on the hope nobody would actually follow Jake into his house. If Stig didn't re-appear in a reasonable time, Laver's plan got sketchy. Charge in on the white horse, gun-free? It wasn't as though he could call the police. Or maybe he could? As Mr John Citizen? A career cop forced to phone in an anonymous tip – thanks again, Strickland, you politician bastard.

It took a few minutes, but the red Territory emerged from Grandview Terrace, the loop road, with a long arm and a single middle finger greeting the motorist who blasted the Territory for pulling out in front of it. That would be them, thought Laver. The Ford now needed to turn, apparently caught by surprise that the Territory had come back out a street behind them. Traffic meant they were stuck and Laver had a decision to make.

Clearly, they were trying to turn, wanting to go with the Territory, not stay on Jake. Thirsk wasn't to be seen, but he didn't matter.

Laver was very interested in the two in the Territory. He went with them.

The Territory swung right then left onto the feeder ramp to the freeway, and Laver smiled that the men in the Ford were screwed now if they hadn't been close enough to spot that. Even if they were, they needed to get back on the pace before the freeway ended a couple of kilometres later. Traffic was lighter heading towards the CBD so they wouldn't know if the car had turned south for anywhere in the city, or north, or straight ahead to Carlton and the west.

CHAPTER 20
SEWER LIFE

'Well, that was a fucking waste of time.'

The Wild Man was perched back in front of the Xbox, clearly ecstatic to be driving a virtual car in *Grand Theft Auto* rather than a real car in the real world. Stig making a cup of instant coffee in the kitchen, feeling his jangly nerves, considering another dip into the merchandise to calm things down. Again.

But tried to focus on the here and now as he said, 'You think? We found out where the kid lives.'

'Yet we didn't sort him out, then and there.'

'Because of that Honda, whoever that is.'

'And yet we didn't sort him out either, then and there.'

Stig poured the boiling water, being careful with the kettle. 'You're not much of a one for forward planning, are you, Wildie.'

'We're not supposed to be in Melbourne long enough for planning, remember? We were going to be in and out of here in about twenty-four hours and the fuck out of the country. I think you're planning to be here to collect superannuation.'

'That's fair,' admitted Stig, coming into the lounge room. 'It's taking way longer than I'd planned. I'm pushing it as hard as I can.'

'How? Drinking coffee in your tracksuit pants? Consuming the majority of the stash before we can sell it?'

Stig let that one go. Pondered what else he could do. He couldn't believe how the drug underworld had changed in such a short time. A few years and everybody was dead, in jail or appearing as a celebrity criminal, riding the *Underbelly* wave. Not at the level Stig dealt with, but at the top. It was surreal.

He stood and opened the blinds a crack, gazed at a white courier van parked across the road and two houses down. Why would a courier be in Thornbury? Maybe the bloke lived in the street? Was there somebody in it?

Stig went to the front door and out to the yard, standing with his coffee and staring, directly, at the van. There was a guy in it. Wearing dark glasses and staring right back at him. What the fuck?

Stig took a deep breath, wished again for some of the product, and told himself to stay calm. Looked around in general, not a care in the world, and then wandered back into the house.

'Wildie,' he said. 'I think we have a visitor. Feel like seeing if you can tear a courier van into pieces, or is your muscle strictly virtual these days?'

The Wild Man was on his feet. 'No, mate. Action is what I need. Who is it?'

'No idea.'

'Giddyup.'

Wildie moved fast to the front door and onto the veranda, heading for the lawn. But then stopped dead.

'What van?'

Stig followed him to the yard. The street was empty. The van was gone.

'That's not good,' he said. He sipped his coffee. 'Wildie, there's no way Jenssen could have tracked us already, could he? It's not possible.'

'If he had, we'd be dead,' Wildie shrugged. It was a statement of fact. 'We might have to check out that silver Honda after all.'

The Wild Man looked at his partner, pondered again why Stig always thought he was the brains. 'Who was following the dweeb, Stig, from the Groc-o-Mart. The dweeb is the key.'

'Maybe both,' Stig said.

'Maybe three, including your little Louie, who seems to be very bloody matey with this guy, whoever he is.'

Stig sighed. 'Come on, let's pack up. We should get out of this house for good.'

'Thank Christ,' Wildie said. 'And once we've moved, I say we hit the town. I want to let off some steam.'

'I might have things to do. If you do go out, no headlines tonight, okay?'

'What are you,' Wildie asked, 'my mum?'

'Just a guy trying to stay alive,' Stig said.

'Then sell the shit and get us out of here.'

* * *

Laver dropped off the van and headed back to Collingwood, remembering he had left his stuff at his desk and hadn't officially signed off for the day. Marvelling that he even still remembered such a detail with his career so far down the toilet.

He was coming through Carlton when his mobile buzzed. An SMS from Marcia.

The text read: Last chance. Same place. Same time. Be there. Or don't.

That gave him an hour and a half. Shit.

At the Mobile Public Interaction Squad headquarters everybody had gone, apart from Ashley McGregor, on late shift. They nodded to each other, McGregor taking the sensible approach of only engaging with Laver if it was absolutely unavoidable. A cop who would go far, Laver decided. Good judge of character and good instincts.

One of the computer terminals was still active, Ollerton having forgotten to log out. Gold. Laver grinned.

He sat and moved into criminal records. Typed the word 'STIG'.

The computer offered five.

Four were recent, crims known for carjacking and joy-riding who had adopted the moniker of The Stig, the mystery racer on *Top Gear*, a popular TV show.

But one was from eight years ago: a minor assault charge. ANDERSON, Stig Sebastian, of Footscray. Just a boy.

Laver clicked for detail. The accused had been outside the Sun theatre in Yarraville at 3 am and became involved in an altercation with two drunks. The police had happened to be driving past in time to break it up and the accused took off, decamping in a westerly direction to the train station. He was arrested mysteriously close to where a small pile of white pills was also found in the scrub, but he denied all knowledge and there were no fingerprints. He got a good behaviour bond for the fight.

That was it.

Laver sat and stared at the blinking cursor on the screen. Thornbury, he thought. Time to head into The Sewer.

Moving to the underground wire required shifting databases, and a pop-up screen demanded Ollerton's password. Laver cursed and logged out, logging in again under his own username and password. His Siberian status meant he could not input info or access the major databases, but he could surf the wire.

He tapped some more keys and started scrolling. Narrowed his search results to the previous fortnight.

The underground wire is like a cop blog. It's known among police as The Sewer because it is where all the undiluted shit of the city flows and ferments. It's where members lodge incidents and observations that may not have led to formal charges or aren't officially investigated. Also outstanding crimes that might have loose leads or new evidence and could use help from another unknown cop's knowledge. The Sewer is a virtual scrapbook of what is happening at street level and who's roaming. As he browsed, Laver couldn't help but reflect it was the computerised version of exactly the discussion he'd been trying to have with every police officer he knew since seeing those two guys on Smith Street.

The Sewer can be daunting, a mess of random activity and notes, but if you know what you're looking for, it can suddenly take shape. Laver could see his target moving across Melbourne like a cyclone, heading north/north-west. A car salesman assaulted south of the city by a large, violent man with orange hair. A woman complaining that a man with strange-coloured hair and a beard, very tall, had sexually taunted her in St Kilda. Two men, one tall and with bright red hair maybe, threatening a man and his two teenage sons in a Fitzroy North hotel. A minor traffic accident where one of the drivers, appearing to be a giant man in his twenties, orange hair, beard, yelled an obscenity and then left the scene of the accident. A dog kicked savagely in Thornbury two days ago, the owner too scared to press charges. No description offered. Just that the attacker was 'very big, very frightening. Tattooed'.

Laver wished he had an actual name to call up. There was no way this guy wasn't on a police computer somewhere, in Victoria or elsewhere.

Laver looked at his watch. It was getting tight but he grabbed a phone and dialled Flipper's mobile. Message bank, dammit.

'Mate, it's Rocket. Those two guys I keep talking about? They're in The Sewer, more than once, clear as day. And there's a few new bodies as well, in the mix. You heard of a private snoop called Thirsk? Very amateur but somehow involved. And two blokes I don't know yet. Call me. This is brewing.'

He printed all the noted incidents, bundled them and left the office. If he wasn't on time for Marcia, the world would shake.

CHAPTER 21
THE NAKED KOALA

Lou was enjoying the thrill of being nude in the middle of Brunswick Street. She never tired of it, walking stark naked under the loose fur of the giant koala suit, complete with cartoonish stuffed animal–style head with mesh in the eyes. It was always hot in the suit and she was usually out there for several hours at a time, collecting change in a white bucket for the Wilderness Society. A month ago, she'd thought: why not? Stripped completely and donned the suit. It was liberating, like anonymously streaking across the Melbourne Cricket Ground. In full view but seen by no one. She even smiled as group of guys after group of guys fobbed her off. If only they knew what was going on under the suit. All they saw was a slightly tattered human koala.

The suit was sweaty and claustrophobic and Lou wished she could get some fresh air. The night was warm and her vision was being hampered by sweat in her eyes, as well as the black mesh. She stopped for a moment, leaning against a traffic light in front of Polyester Records.

Found her mind drifting, thinking of a cool shower, and of hands on her. Stig's hands, which disturbed her and excited her in equal parts. The ex-boyfriend from hell, who had ripped off her not-for-profit workplace, and vanished without a decent goodbye, and now showed up with a Neanderthal mate, involved in who knew what? And yet … and yet … God, she hated the way her heart had started pounding, her physical reaction, when he'd appeared in the Soul Food Café. Even as the anger kicked in, she couldn't deny that rivers were running underneath. And he'd known it, too, the bastard. She could sense it. She'd have to be careful if he showed up again. He'd surprised her last time, that was all. Next time, she'd have her walls up.

She tried to shake it off, starting to walk again, rattling her bucket at passers-by. Lou saw the couple walking on the other side of the road and peered through the eye-holes, trying to work out how she knew the guy. She was so crap with names, but better with faces. It struck her – he was the cop who had walked into the Soul Food Café and sent Stig packing. Out of uniform, he was the guy who had been with Jake when Jake had arrived at the bar last night. Tonight the cop was walking with a woman, hands in his pockets and taking in the crowd. The woman had her arms folded across her chest and was walking slightly ahead of him. She was in a business suit with a medium-length skirt. High heels. Corporate. He was in a T-shirt and jeans.

Lou watched him catch up to the woman and then ahead, so he got to the door of the Vegie Bar in time to open it for her. Chivalry, Lou thought, smiling. They were gone and she flicked sweat out of her left eye. Could feel a line of perspiration crawling down the slope of her breast, gathering on her nipple then falling, somewhere south in the suit. She shook the white bucket and got back to work.

* * *

Jake had driven home in a state of confusion. The texts from the cop had said 'get in your car and go', so he had. A normal drive home, nothing out of the ordinary. He'd hurried from his car in the driveway into the house, just in case, but hadn't noticed anything apart from a couple of cars drifting past his house. A red SUV and a smaller car. But late afternoon sun hitting the car windows meant he couldn't see in and anyway, they'd kept going. It wasn't a white Ford with the guys from the car park at his work. He eventually got another text from Detective Laver, checking he was home safely and he'd replied, 'sure :)'.

It was the American sitcom *Two and a Half Men* that got Jake back out of the house. A week ago, he would have settled in and enjoyed the show. Tonight he looked at his mum glued to the TV, laughing at Charlie Sheen, and Jake couldn't do it, his head full of the wonders and wildlife of Fitzroy.

'But *The Bill*'s about to start,' his mother said as he reached for his keys, tonight wearing a brand new T-shirt with 'Red Hot Chilli Peppers' on the front, red on black.

'Tell me what happens later,' he said, and headed for his car.

Now he was parking in a side street, off Brunswick Street, thinking he might just walk up and down, or maybe get a light beer in the hotel on the corner near the Fitz Café. Look at some books. This time tomorrow night, he and Lou would be in the Groc-o-Mart, placing their stickers. He was surprised to realise he was more excited than nervous. New Jake was in full flight.

As he locked the car door and wandered towards the lights, he was blissfully unaware of the car that had followed him all the way from Kew, now illegally parked with its headlights off.

Or the silver Honda that had pulled up right behind him.

The two occupants of the first car found themselves caught, watching the kid walk away but wondering about the dishevelled-looking man getting out of the silver Honda and fumbling with his keys. The kid not waiting for him, not even seeming to be aware of him.

The same guy who'd also followed the kid home.

A man who kept turning up.

CHAPTER 22
THE VEGIE BAR, TAKE TWO

It hadn't started well. Laver and Marcia were still waiting to be given a table at the Vegie Bar when Laver spotted Andrew Wo sitting in a dark corner, near the door.

'Excuse me for one second,' he said to Marcia.

'Where are you going?'

'Say hello to somebody.'

'Wow,' she said, pulling out her iPhone and starting to tap the screen.

Wo was sitting with a beautiful woman. Laver registered long blonde hair, stylish but simple clothing; pegged her as maybe in her early thirties, sitting very straight in her chair. Great posture. Laver forced himself to keep his eyes mostly on Wo as he approached.

'Detective Laver. What a pleasant surprise,' Wo said in his precise English.

'I feel the same way, Andrew. How's business?'

Wo smiled without warmth. 'The trucking industry is always a tough one, Detective. Fuel excises, driver fatigue, government regulations on loads. It's an endless headache.'

'I'm sure,' Laver said, taking in Wo's companion.

'This is my wife, Charlotte. I don't believe you've met.'

'No, we haven't. A pleasure,' Laver said and meant it. She held out a hand and he shook it. The skin was cold.

Laver turned back to Wo. 'Andrew, I was wondering if you might have heard about anybody new in town?'

'In what sense, Detective? Another trucking company?'

'Possibly – maybe an importer. Somebody who might be a competitor who's turned up unexpectedly from interstate.'

Wo's face was a pleasant mask, not the least bit offended or worried by the question – possibly slightly bored. 'I really wouldn't know what you were talking about, Detective. There are so many cowboys with their own trucks and big ideas these days.'

'Just a long shot, I guess,' said Laver. 'Better get back. Take care of yourself, Andrew.'

'You too, Detective. I hope you get over your, ah, troubles.'

Perfectly delivered, without any chance of a comeback. Laver gave him a nod, offered another to Charlotte, and walked to the bench seats in the window where Marcia was now sitting, putting her phone away and glaring in Wo's direction.

'Who was that?'

'Andrew Wo.'

'A friend of yours?' she asked. 'A cop?'

'One of Melbourne's bigger drug dealers. On the rise.'

Marcia looked shocked. 'And you went over and said hello, like he's an old footy teammate?'

'Best to stay on good terms where you can.'

'The man's a drug dealer.' Slightly too loudly for Laver's liking.

He leaned in and said quietly, 'Unproven.'

She hesitated. 'So he might not be?'

'Oh no, he is. Worth millions already.' Laver still keeping his voice low. 'He's got some of the best distribution channels in the country.'

'But you exchange pleasantries, then sit here, both having dinner in the same restaurant.'

'Marcia, a guy like him, you don't throw him across a table and fish a bag of cocaine out of his pocket. It takes years to build a case and to swoop at exactly the right moment.'

'So there are police working on it?'

'Absolutely. I just don't happen to be one of them.'

A waiter arrived with two glasses of wine. They sat in awkward silence until he was gone.

Marcia said, 'So why say hello? Why dignify his presence?'

'Because he might know things I need to know.'

Laver noticed she hadn't clinked glasses before taking her first sip.

Instead she said, 'Did he?'

'No,' Laver admitted. 'Well, if he did, he wasn't saying.'

Marcia shook her head in exasperation. 'So this is tonight's trick. As opposed to last night, where I think you might have been discussing us being together forever, with your work no longer coming between us, at the exact moment you got up to chase some suspect and left me sitting in this restaurant, never to return.'

And so it begins, thought Laver. 'I did return. You were gone.'

'Why wouldn't I be?'

'When I did try to talk about us being together forever, you chose instead to sends texts to whoever is on the end of that phone.'

'I have friends that aren't you, Tony. Outside your world.'

Laver wondered what that meant. 'Outside my world. Which is different to yours?'

She shrugged. Reached for her wine.

'Marcia, I'm sorry about last night. There's a lot going on.'

'When isn't there a lot going on?'

'I'm not an accountant. I don't work nine to five, deliver a pay cheque and a foot massage at the end of the day. You know that. You even liked that about me at the start.'

Again, a shrug.

'Marcia, I killed a man and it's been messing with me. I'm not the cowboy you seem to have decided I am. My career is flushed down the toilet. I can't sleep for shit. I'm seeing a ghost. Really. I've had things on my mind.'

'Well, this is the first I've heard about it.'

'Because you haven't been around. Not answering your phone, or at the theatre, out for another run with the gang from work.'

'I have a life.'

'But not with me, right now. When I need you.'

'So suddenly you need me. To help prop you up in your little cop world until you get your slap on the wrist, tut, tut, Tony, and are allowed to disappear back into the murk.'

'You don't think it's reasonable that I'm upset I killed a man?'

'Well, you clearly didn't when you murdered him.'

Murdered him. Christ.

Laver was contemplating how to answer that when he looked out the window and couldn't believe his eyes. There was the kid, Jake, walking towards the city on the other side of the road. In baggy jeans and a black T-shirt, the usual silly hat on. But look who was ten metres behind him: the big guy with the orange hair, now, ridiculously, shaved into a mohawk. Tattooed arms swinging as he walked. Wanting the whole world to see him, the footpath traffic parting before him. His eyes firmly on Jake's back.

Laver was already somehow on his feet when he heard Marcia's voice, with a note he hadn't heard before, truly shocked, say: 'Tony! Don't you even think about it.'

He stopped and looked at her, this woman he loved, was sure he loved, and said desperately, 'I'm sorry. I am truly sorry. But I have to go. Just for a few minutes. I will be back.'

Her face was icy calm as she said through thin lips, 'I won't be here.'

'A life might be in danger.'

'When isn't it, hero cop?'

He had nothing to say to that. He headed onto the street, Laver the cop in the ascendant even as he hit the footpath, moving fast. For better or for worse.

* * *

Enough with the Xbox. Enough with the fucking Xbox. Enough with sitting around the house with a finger up his arse. The Wild Man was on the move.

Stig knew some guy, yet another friend, who had got them into a house on Rathdowne Street, Carlton. Stig full of all sorts of helpful friends, unless it came to actually selling the drugs they needed to get rid of. Once they'd shifted in, two backpacks and some groceries, mostly beer, Stig had made a few phone calls, run into a few more brick walls in his supposed network of Melbourne criminal contacts, and had slumped back onto the couch, sinking stubbies, smoking away their profit margin, stewing yet again over all the contacts who still hadn't rung him back, wondering about Barry at Heidelberg, getting spooked that Jenssen might be doubting their car-crash deaths by now. All jittery over whether this bloke hanging out with Louie was a threat. Stig frozen, stoned and useless.

And suddenly the Wild Man had had enough. Told Stig he could choose to sit around while this entire plan went to shit but Wildie wasn't going to. As of tomorrow, once Stig straightened out, they were going to do this properly. Front the nerd Louie had been hanging out with, grill Louie if it came down to it. Contact the Groc-o-Mart manager if necessary. Sort shit out.

Stig stared at him, stupidly, nodding vaguely. Wildie couldn't stay in the house. He grabbed the car keys and headed into the night. He needed to let off steam, and the only options were sex or violence.

King Street, in the city, was the place for violence, but instead he let his dick win out, driving to Fitzroy, thinking there should be a band playing at one of the pubs there, or at least people – women – getting drunk in the many bars. He was horny as hell.

But Wildie had barely arrived on Brunswick Street when, shit, he saw the kid from the supermarket emerging from a side street. Wearing his silly hat and looking in shop windows.

Wildie barely able to believe it, thinking of Stig prone on the couch and deciding, fuck it, this was the perfect time to handle things his way.

The kid walked up towards Johnston Street and into a bookshop as Wildie crossed the road, wishing he knew the alleys better so he'd know which one to drag him down. Now he was standing slightly behind the statue of some clown in a side street that led to a pool hall Wildie wouldn't mind checking out, the Red Triangle.

Wildie making plans in his head, thinking on his feet, and all while watching some idiot in a furry giant koala suit on the other side of the road, shaking a bucket for loose change.

* * *

Lou almost said hi to Jake as he walked past her, oblivious and muttering that he didn't have any change. She wondered how he, of all people, would react to knowing it was her – naked – beneath the suit?

It wasn't exactly difficult to see that Jake had the hots for her, like that was ever going to happen, but she wanted to let him down gently – and not until after tomorrow night, when the stickers had been planted. She wondered briefly how the stickers were coming along. That was the problem with trusting the job to an anarchist. How smoothly could a printing factory operate and still be considered anarchic? He'd said they'd be ready for tomorrow.

She watched Jake walk away, tonight wearing a Red Hot Chilli Peppers T-shirt, which surprised her. A change from the Sound Relief shirt. He still had the ridiculous hat on though, his longish hair plastered underneath.

And then she saw Wildie. Stig's scary friend, with his eyes unwaveringly on Jake's back as the crowd parted to let him through. Lou drifting against the wall as he passed, smelling his body odour even through the mask's mesh, and seeing him watch Jake go into the Brunswick Street Bookstore. Wildie hovering briefly then heading into the cars, walking across the road and letting them stop for him. On the other side now, lurking and sneaking glances at the bookshop.

Lou looking to her left and seeing the cop, no longer in the Vegie Bar, and coming this way.

* * *

Wildie saw the koala look his way again. A third time. Wildie staring back, wondering what the hell it was looking at. Not about to be unsettled by a fucking koala.

Then seeing a guy in a T-shirt and jeans walk past the koala to the bookshop door, hesitating like he might go in. Wildie almost jumping out of his skin as the guy instead turned and looked straight at him and, shit, started to cross the road. Wildie telling himself to be cool, it might be a coincidence. But the guy walking right up to him, staring Wildie in the eye, even from half a head shorter, looking oddly familiar, and saying: 'How you doing? Don't the drug deals usually happen over on Smith, near the Safeway? Or is it a Woolworths now?'

Wildie, spooked but aiming for a cool, unhurried stare, mumbling that he didn't know what the guy was talking about.

'No? Well, I'm going near Thornbury if you need a lift.'

Wildie finally realising where he had seen this guy before: in uniform at the café the day he'd met Louie. The same cop stare.

Wildie wasn't the type to walk away from a situation. A few years ago he'd taken on five bikies – fully patched members of the Comancheros, no less – in a pub near Pambula on the southern New South Wales coast, and walked out of there no more damaged than they were afterwards. Which, to be fair, was a lot. Prior to that, he'd been to jail and had learned, the hard way, how to spot the truly dangerous men, as against those trying to bluff it. During his drug-running career for Jenssen, he had found himself staring down the barrel of a gun twice, confident both times, as he looked into the would-be gangsters' eyes, that they didn't have the nerve to shoot.

And yet, looking into this man's eyes, this man dressed casually on a trendy Melbourne street, Wildie was stunned to realise he actually felt scared. Those eyes had seen things, been places. Places Wildie also knew and had no wish to revisit. An emptiness.

And the cop had mentioned Thornbury. And the cop, almost certainly unarmed, off duty, was in his face in a way that people simply did not get in the Wild Man's face.

He hadn't really looked at this cop in the café, but now he did, tried to turn it into a long, defiant look, and started to walk. When he was around the corner, off Brunswick Street, he walked faster. He forced himself not to run, but Wildie got the fuck out of there.

Laver watched him leave, wishing he could follow, but decided to stay close to Jake.

When the orange mohawk was out of sight, Laver picked a gap in the shuffling cars and crossed back to the bookstore.

On the footpath, he said to a baggy suit of grey fur, 'You seem awfully curious for a koala.'

'Just enjoying the show,' an unexpectedly female voice said to him, slightly muffled.

'You get hot in that suit?' Laver asked.

'You have no idea,' the koala replied.

Laver, with his hands on his hips, appraising her. 'How do you keep cool?'

'You have even less idea,' the koala replied.

CHAPTER 23
CODE 33

Laver woke to his phone ringing, and fumbled for his mobile.

Marcia. The name flashed immediately into his waking brain.

Still little more than half-asleep, it took him a moment to realise it wasn't even the phone in his hand that was ringing. In fact, it was more of a buzzing sound.

The security for the front door.

That meant standing and, oh boy, realising the severity of the hangover as his senses started to kick in. Palm to temple, wincing, he staggered into the lounge room and pressed the intercom.

'Wha—?'

'It's Flipper.'

'Tennis is tomorrow, you dickhead. Tomorrow.'

'Rocket—'

'And not this fucking early. What time is it?'

'Rocket. This is work.'

Laver's brain was staggering. Cogs not meshing. 'Work?'

'Will you let me in, for Christ's sake?'

Laver did. He was on his second large glass of water, three Panadols down, when Flipper walked through the front door, only a one-day growth on his chin and wearing a dark-blue suit.

Laver squinted at him and said, 'The fuck are you dressed like that for?'

'You might have forgotten that this is how detectives dress, dickhead.' Flipper tilted his head, staring at a haggard version of his mate: hair everywhere, in a faded Hoodoo Gurus T-shirt and fitted boxers that looked slightly saggy. 'Shit, you look good.'

'I'm supposed to be asleep. For another five or six hours.' Laver winced and put his hand across his face, groaning.

'Like that, huh? Let me guess. It was the last beer that did the damage.'

'It always is, mate. Only in my case, it was the last six whiskies after pissing Marcia off for probably the last time.'

'Oh.'

'Yeah, oh's right. Flipper, what's going on?'

'You need to come with me. There's a crime scene I think you might want to attend.'

Laver was squinting, as though trying to see out of his left eye. 'I'm allowed?'

'I haven't asked. Come on. Get dressed. It's cold out.'

'That's because the sun is hours away, you fuck.'

'Get ready or I'm leaving without you.'

'Why would I care?'

'You'll care. Plus this is your first chance in a while to stop playing Captain Lycra.'

Laver dropped the c-bomb in his mate's direction once or twice, but then said, 'I'll be one minute.'

Jeans. Caterpillar-brand work boots so he didn't have to negotiate laces. A jumper over the T-shirt. A leather jacket. A return to the bedroom for a beanie.

Then one luxuriously long piss and a final large glass of water and he was out the door, Flipper muttering about whenever he was ready, maybe sometime this year.

They drove straight at the city but veered onto Batman Avenue and then the freeway, towards the West Gate before Flipper looped off onto the tollway over the Bolte Bridge, aka the Goalposts, and pointed north.

Flipper driving fast and expertly through the almost empty roads, sitting twenty or thirty kilometres per hour above the speed limit the whole time, but occasionally glancing to see if Laver was awake or about to throw up. He seemed okay, blinking and frowning at a faint glow on the horizon that might be the beginnings of the sunrise.

Laver mumbled, 'Want to tell me what this is about?'

'You'll see.'

'Even where?'

'Near the airport.'

'So it's a Code 33.'

'Yep.'

'Not a 69?' The difference in code between 'body found' and 'murder'. Cop humour.

'Probably. You know how it is.'

'Yeah. Three knives in the back, headless and set on fire. Might be self-inflicted.'

Flipper almost grinned. 'Good detectives don't assume anything, Constable.'

'Senior Constable, cockless. Do you know who it is?'

'Not confirmed. That's where I'm hoping you can help.'

Laver yawned, but the mention of a body had sliced into his hangover and lack of sleep. He could feel his blood starting to pump, like it hadn't for a while.

'You want to talk about the Marcia thing?' asked Flipper.

'Nope. Let's just say it was an epic fail.'

'If you're going to fail ...'

'... may as well be epic,' Laver finished. 'I also saw one of those guys.'

'Which guys?'

'The ones I keep talking about. The bad guys.'

'Oh yeah?'

'He was about to assault a civilian. That kid from the café the first day I saw them, if you remember.'

'So this guy was about to assault the kid?'

'I dissuaded him.'

Flipper actually laughed. 'Dissuaded. Good word: you're waking up. So he didn't assault some Joe. Just might have.'

Laver didn't say anything.

'We can add "failed to assault a member of the public" to "possibly being named after a cigarette" and the other mythical charges,' said Flipper.

'Maybe. Or maybe I actually do miraculously still have cop instincts. It was actually the other guy, not Stig. I'm pretty sure his name is Stig, not Cig, by the way.'

'Jesus,' Flipper muttered. 'I feel like Doctor Watson in the presence of genius.'

'As you should. And anyway, if everything I'm saying is so full of shit, why am I in your car right now?'

'We'll see soon enough,' Dolfin said.

They were quiet for a while, driving north, until Laver said, 'It must have been good to be a cop in the old days. You know, a hundred years ago. All the bodies would have been down city alleys, convenient nearby lanes. These days, every bastard gets topped on the outskirts and we have to hack miles to get there.'

Dolfin flexing his shoulders, hands loose on the wheel. 'Who says today's was topped?'

'So you woke me up because an old bird died in her sleep?'

'Fair call. But in the old days, they didn't have forensics. To help find the bad guys.'

'Or decent cars.'

'Or comfortable uniforms.'

'Or titanium-framed mountain bikes.'

'Or cute female constables in lycra shorts. Now you're apparently single again.'

'Oh stop,' Laver said. 'It's too early in every sense.'

Melrose Drive leaves the freeway just after the turn at Essendon Airport, and then runs in a straight line to Tullamarine, where Melbourne's major airport sprawls across the suburb-sized space. Just near the runways, the buildings become sparse and there's a large block of bush behind a wire fence and a sign, proclaiming the property to be the 'Tullamarine Flying Club'.

'This mob must have great club meetings with 747s taking off twenty feet above their heads,' Laver said as they drove through the gate, a uniformed cop nodding at Flipper as they passed.

Dawn still hadn't fully kicked in, so the giant fluoro lights on stands brought their usual artificial daylight to the scene. Police tape was unfurled in a wide arc, an area the size of a couple of tennis courts cordoned off. As they parked, Laver asked, 'Is there just the one body? Why have they taped the entire suburb?'

Flipper shrugged. 'Looks like it's a property with no passers-by and no houses, apart from the flying club HQ. Plenty of room. May as well give the forensic boys and the meat truck some elbow room.'

Laver hit the fresh air and breathed it in, fully awake now, hangover put aside. Wishing to Christ they had grabbed a take-away coffee on the way, but feeling alive. He had wondered if he'd ever be at a crime scene like this again, and wondered if this little moment of recognition was actually just a way of avoiding whatever reason it was Flipper had brought him here. It suddenly occurred to him that he hadn't seen a body since Coleman.

The scene looked the way they always do. A couple of clusters of cops, some in uniform protecting the scene, some in suits even at this hour. A white van for forensics and a guy and woman in lab coats poking around while two detectives stand to one side, drinking coffee out of takeaway cardboard cups. Damn them.

They regarded Flipper and Rocket.

'What is he doing here?' said the taller of the two, looking hard at Laver.

'Reckon he might know the bloke lying over there.'

'Wrong tense,' said the shorter of the homicide cops.

'Huh?'

'You reckon he *knew* him. When he was alive. Which isn't now.'

'Christ, a wordsmith,' said Flipper. 'At this time of the morning.'

A car pulled up next to Flipper's and the police photographer, a guy named Melican, got out and nodded to the group.

'Nobody ever dies at four in the fucking afternoon,' he grumbled. 'Why can't somebody die just after lunch?'

Nobody bothered to answer so he went to the boot to get his gear. Laver left them to it, took another deep breath, and then walked over to where the white coats were fossicking around. He looked at the body. It was lying face down, legs in a small stream that had saturated the body below the waist. One arm was flung out to the side, and one was underneath the torso.

It wasn't Jake.

And it wasn't Stig or his mate.

He was pretty sure who it was.

Flipper appeared beside him, hands on hips, not looking remotely cold in his suit.

'You know him?'

'I think so. If I can see his face, I'll be sure.'

'That might be difficult.'

'Because forensics can't roll it over yet?'

'Because we don't think he has a face. Back of the head. Executed. Unofficial, of course.'

'Of course. Easy to confuse that cause of death with a heart attack.' Laver turned to Flipper. 'Did you find any ID?'

'Yep.'

'Licence?'

'Yep.'

'Then what do you need me for?'

'Good to be sure.' Flipper shrugged.

'Name of Thirsk?'

'Bingo. As in the same bloke you mentioned recently? See, I have been listening. Part of your Super Case for the Ages.'

'The sarcasm isn't helping,' Laver said. 'But yeah, it looks the right size and shape to be him. Drives – drove a silver Honda.'

Flipper looked interested. 'Really?'

'I've got the rego written down somewhere.'

Flipper looked even more interested. 'Okay, that is good. I'll let them know.' He clapped Laver on the shoulder. 'Who knew you could still be useful? Try not to shoot him, just in case he's not dead yet.'

'I'll do my best.'

Dolfin wandered off, talked to some colleagues. Came back to where Laver was standing, still staring at the corpse.

'He doesn't have to be dead,' Laver said.

'What does that mean?'

Laver looked at his mate. 'Flipper, I know who did this. And I've been trying to tell you and every other bastard for days that this was going to happen.'

'You have absolutely no doubt in your mind who the killer is.'

'Killers. No.'

'You woke up less than an hour ago, took one look at the body and solved the case. Eat your heart out, Poirot.'

'Mate, you know what I've been telling you and you got me here for a reason. You already ID'd the corpse. I've seen him following this kid, Jake. I've seen these two perps following Jake and Thirsk. And then Thirsk turns up dead. That alone isn't worth pulling them in for a yarn?'

Dolfin looked at him, made up his mind, then sighed. 'Okay. We need to talk to them.'

'I even know where they live,' Laver said. 'The biggest problem, they aren't the kind of guys to welcome being pulled in.'

'We're not going to Rambo our way into some house on the basis of wanting to ask some questions.'

'Your call. It's only just dawn. Maybe we can catch them in the sack, guard down.'

CHAPTER 24
STIG COPS A BULLET

The bullet struck Stig just above the heart, probably catching a lung. The impact swung him around, left arm flying as his face creased into a silent scream of agony. His legs held briefly but then the second bullet caught him flush in the stomach. A look of confusion joined the pain on his face as his knees buckled and he landed on them, as though praying, holding what was left of his stomach. Then slid sideways to the rug over the timber floorboards, eyes open and staring in death.

Louie, sitting up in bed, her perfect breasts visible above the sheet, applauded.

Stig, naked, rolled onto his stomach and did five push-ups, hoping Louie could appreciate his shoulders working, before rising to his feet and returning to the bed.

'Man, you're in even better shape than before,' Louie said. 'Being in Perth has agreed with you.'

'Gotta keep fit, babe. And I'm not alone; you look amazing. You still swimming?'

'And yoga,' she said, feeling his lips, gentle against her nipple.

'You're every bit as hot as I remember you.' He slid under the sheet, his mouth nuzzling the neat shave of her pubic hair. 'From head to toe.'

'Enough,' she said, pushing his head away. 'I'm sore. You're killing me.'

'It's been a while,' he said, emerging. 'And I'd forgotten how good we are together.'

'You'd forgotten?' she asked indignantly. He sat up in bed and she snuggled into him, fitting neatly under his left arm, his hand cupping her left breast.

'No, I hadn't forgotten. That was a total lie.'

He'd been waiting for her at her front gate when she'd gotten back, sweaty and smelly from koala duty. Emerging from the darkness and briefly scaring her half to death.

'How long have you been waiting here?' she'd asked.

'About an hour,' he'd said. 'I wanted to see you. To check you were okay.'

'Why wouldn't I be?'

'No reason. Never know who might be visiting you these days, you know. Anyway, seeing you the other day in the café was too brief.'

'It was certainly unexpected,' she'd said, arms crossed. Thinking she should tell him she saw his idiot mate tonight, and the cop from the café. But not wanting to get into it.

Stig saying, 'You going to invite me in?'

Louie appraising him. As handsome as ever, even with a few more years on his face. Eyes very wide. Nowhere near as scary, now he didn't have his thug with him, and looking strangely vulnerable; a little ragged, in ways he hadn't before. Not exactly appearing to be the sharp, heartless opportunist she'd painted him as in her mind after his disappearance and all the questions from her workmates and her boss. It had been a couple of months before they'd relaxed and realised she honestly wasn't in touch with him, wasn't in on it, didn't know a thing about the money. By which time she'd joined them in hating him, and had rewritten history so that Stig was always a heartless, self-serving prick who'd used her as well as the shop.

But now he was here, and that image didn't suit the man standing in front of her. Looking like he was in need of a hug, which she knew she would be very unwise to offer. And yet. His body lean and muscled, the T-shirt tight in all the right ways, and he was dark in the gloom, more tanned than she remembered. Despite herself, she felt the old strong stirrings. What was it about this guy, despite his many and appalling failings?

Maybe it was his smell. She sniffed and then said, 'Can I smell pot? Are you stoned?'

'A bit,' Stig admitted. 'I hit it hard earlier tonight.'

'Did you bring some with you?'

'A bit.'

'Okay, one drink, if you roll me a joint,' she'd said, opening the door to the terrace house. 'But first I need a shower.'

'Sure,' he'd said. And had let the water run for a full minute before he joined her.

Now it was the next morning and she was asking him, 'So where did you learn to die?'

'It was part of the acting classes I took when I first got there. We workshopped dying, and fake fights, and stage kisses and having babies. It was hilarious; even us men had to go through labour. I was looking around, thinking, surely they're taking the piss?'

Louie's voice coming from where she was nestled against his chest, 'You were pretty serious about acting then?'

'I had ideas,' Stig admitted. 'Had visions of going to Sydney or the Gold Coast, trying to land roles in blockbusters being shot at Fox Studios or Movie World. But it didn't happen, apart from this one film where I was a stunt pisser.'

She raised her head to look at him. 'A what?'

And he told her the story and they laughed.

She smelled fantastic. Stig could feel himself getting hard. They'd only done it four times. He hoped she was up for at least one more time. But first there was something he wanted to know.

'So babe,' he said. 'Who was that guy you were with in the café?'

Louie groaned and moved away from him, sliding to the other side of the bed, pulling the sheet with a fist to ensure it covered her. 'Jesus Stig, what is it with you guys and Jake?'

'Jake,' he noted.

'Yes, his name is Jake and he's nobody. Just leave him alone.'

'I was only asking who he was.'

'And sending your gorilla down to heavy me about him at the store.'

'Wildie visited you at the store?' Stig looked genuinely surprised.

'Like you weren't behind it,' she scowled. 'I don't want him anywhere near me, Stig, I mean it. There's a screw loose or something.'

'He's serving a purpose right now.'

'If that's the case, I hate to think of what you're involved in these days.'

Stig smiled. 'Baby, you're getting it all wrong. I'm not "into" anything. He's just a travelling partner, that's all.'

Lou thinking he'd want to act better than that to make it through the gate at Fox Studios.

'So, this Jake,' he said.

Louie shook her head. 'Look, he's a fucking guy who wants to be an environmentalist, all right? We're talking about putting stickers on some products. That's it. I barely know him. It's a Friends of the Planet campaign. End of story. Happy?'

'What products?'

'At a supermarket where he works.'

'He works in a supermarket, huh?'

'Yes. That's the point. We're going to attempt an environmental campaign in his supermarket.'

'Has he asked anything about me?'

Louie gave him a look. 'Why would he ask about you? He doesn't even know you.'

'Saw me the other day though. He must have said something after.'

'He was scared. Like me, he was probably wondering why you were hanging out with the Missing Link. You happy now? Yes, he wanted to know who you were. I said you were my ex-boyfriend. He looked rightly shocked. I felt the same way.'

Stig reached an arm, all muscle, across the bed to her face and stroked her cheek. 'But not now, Louie.'

'Keep asking about my friends and, trust me, it will be right back there.'

'So he's a friend now.'

'Fuck, Stig. I'm going to have a shower.'

He reached for her arm as she started to move. Missed it.

'Louie, one more time. It's still early.'

'Are you on Viagra?' She turned and looked at him in disbelief. 'There's a box of tissues. Why don't you take care of it yourself?'

She headed for the bathroom, Stig enjoying her in all her naked glory until she disappeared.

* * *

In the end, Flipper caved and rang 'Spider' Funnal. He and three other SOG guys drove to the address and beat Laver and Flipper there. You had to hand it to the Soggies; when they decided to act, they didn't muck around. Or they had run out of decent DVDs at the dawn end of the overnight shift and were bored enough to mobilise fast.

They all parked two houses down from the Thornbury house and the Soggies positioned themselves, Spider and another guy flanking the front of the house, shotguns ready, the other two silently disappearing into nearby yards. Flipper and Laver waiting until Spider received confirmation via his earpiece that they were in place at the back door.

Spider giving Flipper the signal. Dolfin hammering the front door.

'Police. Open up.'

Silence.

'This is Detective Senior Sergeant Dolfin of the Victoria Police. Please open the door immediately.'

Dolfin pounding the door one more time before the Soggies kicked it in, the lock falling away under the heavy-tread boot as though it was paper.

Inside, the house was not only empty – it was deserted. They were gone.

Laver annoyed, but still with a lead. The Soggies tagging along as Dolfin made contact with the head of Friends of the Planet. Asking the woman, Rachel, if she had a home address for a female employee. Rachel giving Dolfin some attitude, beginning a rant about the police state, until Flipper explained that the employee, who he believed was named Lou, might be in considerable danger. Rachel finally offering up an address.

And then they were on the road, two carloads of cops heading to Fitzroy. Laver telling Dolfin and Funnal that Lou might be able to give them some clues about the perps' other contacts.

Walking up to the house at the exact moment that, shit, one of the guys they're looking for walks out the front door of her house.

Laver saying, 'It's the guy. The one in charge.'

Dolfin, dubious, saying, 'That's him?'

'One of them, yeah.'

Dolfin stepping in front of Laver to say, 'Excuse me, sir. Police. Stay where you are and keep your hands where we can see them.'

The Soggies not even out of their car yet.

But the guy seeing them and their gear over Dolfin's shoulder and not moving a muscle, instead saying, 'What's this about, officer?'

'My name is Detective Senior Sergeant Dolfin. We'd like you to accompany us to the St Kilda Road Police Headquarters to answer some questions.'

'About what?'

'I'm not at liberty to say until we get there.'

Stig making himself breathe, just like he was taught in the acting classes. Slowly in, chest expanding; relaxing his muscles as the breath came back out. Willing himself to be cool, to find out what they had, if anything.

Saying, 'I think you have me confused with somebody else.'

The detective saying, 'We can find out if that's the case once you come with us.'

'I don't think so.'

The cop standing next to the one talking, in casual street clothes, looking sort of familiar, shaking his head and saying, 'This is bullshit. Let's just cuff the prick and drag him out of here.'

His partner saying, 'Steady. Sir, I'd ask you again to come with us voluntarily.'

Dolfin watching the guy slowly raise his arms now, Dolfin feeling the Soggies mobilising behind him, but the guy only putting his hands on his head, biceps flexing under his T-shirt sleeves. The man smiling faintly.

'Can I ask, who do you think I am?'

The first cop giving the cop next to him a look. That cop, who looked familiar, saying, 'Stig, say your full name please.'

Stunned the cop knew his first name. Blurting, 'Why don't you?' and realising his question had been met by silence.

Stig starting to smile. 'You don't know my name? You turn up at my girlfriend's house, two carloads of cops with guns, harassing an innocent civilian without even knowing his name? I'm so going to sue for harassment. This is priceless.'

Dolfin becoming aware of a woman watching all this from the front door. Multi-coloured hair, pale eyes. In an oversized T-shirt and maybe nothing else. Also noticing a couple of neighbours peering out their windows. Dolfin starting to feel sick.

'We would appreciate it if you would come with us, sir. I'm sure this can all be sorted out if we can just have some time with you at the station.'

'I'm not going anywhere, officer. If you want to arrest me for something, then do it. You don't even know who I am. While we're on names, what was your name again, and your mate's there, so I get it right when I speak to the Police Ombudsman?'

'Detective Senior Sergeant Dolfin. With an F.' Flipper not about to be bounced that easily. 'And Detective Tony Laver. What was your name? So I'll know which complaint it is. We have so many it's hard to keep track.'

'I don't believe I legally have to provide my name. Should I call a lawyer? Are you planning to charge somebody you don't even know with a crime you won't mention?'

Dolfin giving the guy next to him, Detective Laver, an even sharper look. Stig, trying not to grin, thinking they'd be having words in the car.

Dolfin finally saying, 'Maybe we could just ask you now: what were your movements last night?'

'I don't have to tell you, you realise. But if it puts this lunacy to bed, I was here all evening. My girlfriend can verify it.'

Dolfin looking past him to the door and saying, 'Miss, can you confirm this man was with you all evening?'

The girl nodding. 'Everything except the part about me being his girlfriend.'

'From what time, please, Miss?'

'I'm not sure. Quite early.'

Stig wanting to kiss her.

'And your name, please, Miss.'

'If he's not giving you his name, I'm not either. This is total harassment. You're just a heavy-handed tool of the machine.'

Dolfin taken aback. 'The machine?'

'Yeah. The government. The whole G20 conspiracy.'

Laver, now saying to Stig, 'And what about your mate?'

'Which mate?'

'The big guy. Orange hair. Beard. Jail tatts.'

'No idea who you're talking about.'

'The one who was spotted with you in a Collingwood café and has been seen driving with you in a red Ford Territory.'

'I don't have a red Ford Territory. I think your information is wrong.' Breathing hard.

'I saw you in the café and in a red Ford Territory, with the orange-hair guy.'

Stig realising now that shit, he was the bike cop, from the café. But saying, 'Nope. No idea what you're talking about.'

'Can I see your licence please, sir?'

'No.'

'I can legally ask to see your licence.'

Stig sneering. 'I'm not driving. Why would I have a licence on me?'

The bike cop turning to Dolfin, 'Maybe we can get him on one of the new terror suspect laws?'

At which point, Dolfin let out the deepest sigh, saying, 'For Christ's sake, Laver. This is over.' Then saying to Stig, 'I'm extremely sorry to have inconvenienced you, sir. My apologies.'

The other cops standing awkwardly as Dolfin headed back towards his car, Stig saying loudly, 'I'll be suing for harassment. You'll be a witness, won't you, babe?'

The girl at the door staying silent.

The bike cop, Laver, not having moved; just staring at Stig with a dead-eye cop stare. Plenty of heat behind the eyes.

'What are you looking at? See you in court, Detective Laver.' Really emphasising the surname. Stig floating on air now as he turned and walked back to the front door. The bike cop finally heading towards Dolfin's car. Stig's beaming smile lasting all the way until he saw the look on Louie's face.

'Like fuck you're coming back inside my house.' Louie standing with her arms clamped across her chest.

Stig pleading, 'Louie, just until they're gone.'

'What is all this about?'

'I honestly have no idea. You saw. They were just flying kites. Let's have a cup of tea. Maybe go back to bed.'

Louie hissing, 'This was a major mistake, Stig. Stay the fuck away from me. I mean it.'

CHAPTER 25
NIGHTMARE SCENARIO

'**Well, in one sense, it's bloody impressive. I have to give** you that. I thought you were already in the maximum amount of shit possible for a cop to be in, short of literally holding the chief commissioner at gunpoint and rubbing your genitals against his wife. But no, Tony Laver has managed to find an even higher level of shit.'

'Even I didn't know about this one. It's like a secret bonus stage,' replied Laver.

He and Damian were sitting in his lounge room, playing PS3 and drinking beer at 11 am. Breaking all the rules. Well, all Laver's rules. Drinking hours were a little more flexible in Damo's world.

Slattery had phoned at 7.30 am, politely suggesting Laver take a few days off. Sounding more tired than Laver, which was an achievement. Clearly the debacle of his half-arsed murder investigation had done the rounds. Laver was just praying he didn't get a call from Broadbent. Hated to think of the expression that would be on Strickland's face right now.

'Did you play last night?' he asked Damian, who was looking seedy and enjoying the early beer just a little too much.

'At the Espy. Quiet crowd.'

'Which band?'

'Helping out a mate's band. Nightmare Scenario.'

'Good name!'

'And appropriate, given how bad the drummer was. I'll get you a T-shirt.' He fell silent as he finished off the level, fingers a blur on the controller. Sighed contentedly and sipped his beer. 'So what happens now?'

'Dunno,' Laver shrugged. 'Slattery suggested I not turn up until I actually want to ride the bike around. That means I'm technically not working, which might throw the whole "suspended from Major Crime but on full pay" thing out the window. Flipper won't talk to me, because the attempt to apprehend the hippie's boyfriend was such a Hall of Fame fuckfest. And, even more than before, nobody will listen to a word I say regarding potential crimes.'

'I believe you've redefined clusterfuck.'

'Oh, without a doubt.' Laver's head was pounding, and it wasn't the early beer.

Damo said, 'So Flipper isn't talking to you at all?'

'Well, he rang to say CCTV at the airport had picked up two men wandering to the taxi rank from outside the airport – as in, from the direction of where the private detective was murdered. Smart way to leave a scene, actually … walk to the airport and join the throng heading in all directions. They just didn't realise the security cameras watch the surrounds as well, from before the long-term car-park exits.'

Damian hit the button to start the next stage of his game. 'What does that all mean?'

'It means there's a very good chance, in Flipper's eyes anyway, that the big gorilla with the orange mohawk wasn't remotely involved in Thirsk's death.'

'The gorilla only being a figment of your imagination anyway as far as the other police are concerned.'

Laver gave his mate a look. 'Are you helping?'

'Sorry. Just trying to lay out the reality for my own understanding.'

'It's pretty simple,' said Laver. 'I'm fucked.'

The security buzzer from downstairs interrupted. Laver wandered over and pressed the button. 'Hello?'

'It's Cecy.'

Laver raised his eyebrows to Damian and said, 'Come up.'

'I'll just lock up my bike,' she replied, and the speaker went silent.

Damian was grinning faintly. 'So, Marcia is officially history then?'

'This is a work colleague, Damo. Keep it in your pants.'

'You can talk. Maybe you should play this rogue cop thing all the way?'

'She's young, Damo. And untarnished by the life, so far. And likes to play it by the book.'

Damian shrugged and reached for his stubby. 'Turning up at your place, unannounced. Off duty. Very professional behaviour.'

Laver found himself wondering.

In the end, a strange thing happened. Cecy gave Laver a hug, meaning it. Then they sat around, Laver in his own world, just letting the conversation drift by him as Cecy and Damian yarned easily about music, talking about bands Cecy liked that Laver had never heard of. Bliss n Eso. Drapht. The Herd, and that band's alternate-reality incarnation, Horror Show. The Hilltop Hoods. He might have heard of that last one on Triple J. Turned out Cecy and Damian had both been at the concert where Tim Rogers from You Am I, Josh Pyke and others covered The Beatles' *White Album*.

Damian, inspired, put on some music as they talked. Cecy, on a day off, drank a beer from the stubby, laughing her barking laugh at Damian's rock 'n' roll stories. Laver, still quiet but feeling himself coming out of his funk, wondered when he had last heard genuine laughter in his living room. It felt strange, with Cecy in his home and Marcia gone in a puff of smoke. He briefly wished for a joint but, thinking it might send him into a downward spiral, stuck to sipping beer. Contemplated how few of his police colleagues over the years had ever been to his house, or vice versa, beyond an all-in barbeque. And here was this rookie cycling cop ...

And then Damian, all traces of his hangover gone, was leaping to his feet.

'We've been sitting around too long.' He pointed at Laver. 'What you need is sunshine and exercise.'

'You're kidding, aren't you?' Laver asked, horizontal, one arm dangling to the floor where he was clutching a beer. Looking like he may never move again.

'No. He's totally right,' Cecy said, getting to her feet. 'You need to move.'

'You're outvoted, Rocket,' Damo said. 'Move your arse.'

Laver didn't have it in him to argue and so they hit the road on their bikes, Damo in front on his city cruiser, Cecy and Laver on their cop bikes but not carrying all the usual kit. Laver muttering, but Cecy just laughing at him.

They headed away from the city, following Damo as he hooked into a bike trail, and suddenly they were on the banks of the Yarra, cruising along the river, gazing at the astonishing houses that sprawled on the other side of the river and dodging the occasional walkers and joggers. Laver realised after a while that his butt wasn't even particularly sore.

'You look like you're getting some riding legs, Rocket,' said Damo, cruising effortlessly beside him.

Cecy, just behind them, called, 'Why do they call you Rocket?'

Damo turned and said, 'That's a disgrace. You're un-Australian! Do you really not know why anybody with the name Laver would be called Rocket?'

'Um, no.'

'Give her a break, mate,' Laver panted. 'She's Colombian, for Christ's sake. How many Colombian tennis players can you name?'

'Well, none,' conceded Damo. 'But then again, no Colombian has won a Grand Slam. Twice.'

'It was a while ago. Have you noticed Cecy is a bit younger than us?'

The suburb of Richmond turned into Hawthorn on the other side of the Yarra, as they swung west towards Collingwood. Damian took them to the Abbotsford Convent, an old complex that was saved from developers and instead transformed into a collection of cafés and artist's spaces; freelance writers huddled in what used to be the nuns' chambers. At Handsome Steve's House of Refreshment they sat on a balcony, enjoying the sun, and then cruised back to Laver's apartment block.

Laver couldn't believe it. He felt clear-headed, sweaty in a good way and in love with cycling.

'That's a minor miracle,' he said.

'We'll have you bush-bashing before you know it,' said Damo, before waving and riding off to get ready for that night's gig.

Laver was still feeling great, right up until he arrived home and checked his message bank.

'Tony, this is Marcia. Your stuff is in a suitcase on the nature strip outside my block. If you want it before it's stolen, you had better get moving. And I won't be here so don't bother knocking.'

'I need a drink,' Laver announced.

'Is Marcia your girlfriend?' Cecy was loitering near the door.

'I think the tense would now officially be past,' he said, rooting around in the fridge. Heard the words leaving his mouth. 'My ex. Beer?'

'Not for me,' Cecy said. 'Best not to drink too much and ride.'

'Who breathalyses a bike rider?'

'It can happen.'

'Not if you're on a cop bike.'

'That's not really the point though, is it? We're supposed to set an example.'

Laver shrugged, opened a beer for himself and toasted her. Then poured her a glass of water.

'I think my example-setting days might be as dead as my engagement.'

'Oh wow, engagement! I'm sorry.'

Laver swigged. 'Me too. It's all gone to hell. Maybe it already was before the shooting, but it feels like the relationship died with Coleman. It's hard to explain.'

'You don't have to. It's private.'

He looked at her and she was not meeting his eye, sipping her water and suddenly looking awkward. A single woman in a single man's house.

'Hey Cecy?'

'What?' Apprehension in her voice.

'Don't take this the wrong way, okay. I think you are very beautiful and fun and you rock in just about every way but we're workmates and there's an age difference and I really don't think I'm a person anybody wants to be in a relationship with right now.'

'Tony … Rocket … It's not like—'

'Mates, okay?'

He raised his beer and she suddenly smiled and clinked her glass, sitting down beside him on the couch. 'We were always mates, dickhead. Now, if we're making speeches, it's my turn.'

'Uh oh.'

'In all your howling at the moon, especially about how nobody will listen to you now you're in Siberia, or whatever you call it, you've forgotten one thing. I saw those guys as well, in Smith Street. I was outside the café. I saw them come out. I heard the big one, with the orange hair, say, "That cop was trouble." You've never considered this, but I have an antenna as well. And mine was going crazy too.'

'I sort of promised Slattery I'd keep you out of it.'

'Why? Who says you have the right to stop me doing my job?'

'Jesus, Cecy.'

'Let me finish. All I'm saying is that I want to keep an eye on those two as well. I'll help – and not as a favour to you, because we're mates and all, but because we should. It's our job. All your precious senior cop friends, the ones who are wiping you at the moment, they haven't seen these two. I'm only new and haven't dealt with many criminals yet, but I've seen you work. I trust your instincts. And I trust mine.'

'Cecy, politically—'

'Fuck "politically", Tony. All I'm saying is that if we can get a name or if you see them again, I'll help. From what you've said, they're definitely up to something.'

She sat back, speech over. Looking spent. 'Jesus, give me a beer after all.'

Rocket went to the fridge and threw her a stubby. Clinked beers and meant it. 'Well, cheers. It means a lot to me. More than it probably should to a tough-guy career cop, but the goalposts have moved. Just keep it on the quiet with Slattery, all right?'

'Sure. I'm not career-suicidal, you know.'

They drank in silence until she said, 'Standish says he's in, as well, by the way. Will do anything you ask.'

'Now I *know* you're bullshitting.'

She laughed, the sound exploding into the room as she threw her head back.

Cecy drank some beer, frowned and said, 'Now all we need is a name.'

'We might have "Stig".'

'Oh please. That can't be real.'

Laver sighed. 'Who knows what the hell "real" means anymore?'

CHAPTER 26
IN THE DARK

Jake's wet dream: alone in a dark room with Lou. Except that the room was the main floor of the Groc-o-Mart, cavernous at night, aisles stretching into the gloom.

Lou was on her knees yanking boxes of dishwashing detergent off a low shelf, then peeling the stickers and carefully placing them above the brand name on each box.

Jake loomed over her to see which sticker she was placing. Was it 'This product is truly green' or 'Not as green as they'd have you believe'? Both in wattle-green lettering on a subtle yellow background.

From here, he could see down her shirt to the curve of a pale breast: the line of a bra. Lace.

But the worst thing would be to get caught looking. He focussed on the label she was sticking onto the box.

It was blood-red lettering on a black background and read: 'Buying this? Why not just drown the polar bears yourself?'

Jake read it again.

'What's that sticker?'

'It's one I thought up after we'd talked about it.'

'You can't put that on a box.'

'Why not?'

'Because, crap. Barry will have my balls.'

Lou looked up at him and he worked extra hard to keep his gaze from her shirt.

'Jake,' she said matter-of-factly. 'You were always going to cop it for this. We may as well make it count.'

'But it's one thing to tell people if a product is environmentally friendly. It's a whole other thing to rip into it, like this.'

Lou shrugged and went back to the label, a curl of green hair flopping down to meet her chin.

'It's just a matter of wording. This will catch people's attention.'

'But Lou,' he protested.

Lou looked at him again and her face was set, eyes shining.

'We're at war, Jake. The future of the world is at stake. Don't get squeamish on me now. I thought you were this totally committed environmental warrior.'

'I am,' he said weakly.

'Then walk the walk, soldier.'

He stood up, dry mouthed. 'I'm going to keep putting on the stickers we agreed.'

'Good for you,' Lou said, concentrating on her work. There was a long pause. 'Hey Jake.' Her voice softer now. 'I'll buy you a drink after.'

'You will?' He winced as he heard his voice rise.

'Definitely.'

And then they heard a car pull up outside.

'Fuck!' she said. 'You said there was no security.'

'There isn't,' Jake whispered. 'Not until 5 am. Quick, follow me.'

They pushed the stickers under the shelf and ran, crouching, towards the front, where the registers were.

'Not the back?' Lou hissed.

'Nowhere to hide,' Jake whispered urgently. 'Trust me.'

The car's engine had stopped, but another car was approaching.

'Oh shit, gotta be the cops,' Lou said quietly.

Jake didn't answer. He took her hand – took her hand! – and led her into the small storeroom to the side of the registers, where the cigarettes, flowers and papers were kept.

They heard a key in the lock of the front entrance.

'Get down,' he whispered.

Lou did, crouching behind some wilting bunches of flowers. Bizarrely, she found herself enjoying their fragrance.

Jake was listening to somebody entering the Groc-o-Mart, charting the footsteps to the security panel and then hearing four beeps as the security code was entered. Another beep was supposed to turn off the system, but instead it turned on.

'What the fuck?' said Barry's voice. Jake's heart lurched.

Five more beeps re-entered the pin and turned off the system. Then there was silence.

'Hello?' Barry raised his voice. 'Anybody there?'

Lou and Jake looked at each other, big-eyed in the tiny dark room.

They heard Barry sigh. 'Fucking security. May as well just leave the door open while they're at it. Jesus.'

'Clear?' said a new voice.

'Yeah. The alarm hadn't been turned on. Probably since security checked the place a couple of hours ago. I don't know why I pay the bastards.'

'Fascinating. Barry, you know who we are?'

Lou's eyes widened even further. She pulled Jake down so his ear was next to her mouth and breathed more than said, 'Stig.'

Jake's heart pounded so loudly that he thought it might be heard.

'Yeah, I know who you are,' Barry was saying. 'I can't believe you'd contact me. You want to get me killed as well as you?'

'Nobody has to be killed. I'm offering you an opportunity.'

'Jenssen offers me plenty of opportunities already. Why would I piss in that nest?'

'Because Jenssen will never know. And you could make a lot of money without having to funnel any of it back to Queensland.'

They could hear the faint crinkle of packaging being opened.

'Tell your mate to stop stealing cigarettes.'

'Mate, please. This is a business meeting.' Stig's voice was exasperated.

They heard a dismissive snort.

'Okay, tell me,' Barry said.

'It's simple.' Stig's voice was confident. 'You buy our stuff off us now, for cash, and bury it for a while. I'm guessing nobody among your distributors knows how often shipments arrive. In six months or maybe a year, you slide an extra batch out there and when the proceeds come back, they're all yours.'

'Why in six months?'

'Because that will put distance between us going missing and the extra turning up on the street.'

'Why does that matter if nobody's looking? I thought Jenssen would never know.'

'Just because Jenssen doesn't know doesn't mean he isn't keeping an eye on things. I'm treating him with respect, as you should with me.'

'Some opportunity. Work my arse off not to get killed.'

Now Stig sighed. 'No, make *a lot* of extra money very easily. Barry, I'm saying that if you're careful, as you should be and as you've proven for years now that you are, you'll be okay. Why do you think we're meeting now, after midnight, instead of during office hours?'

Jake's leg was cramping as he crouched but he didn't dare shift his weight. Lou was looking at the floor, listening intensely.

Barry's voice said, 'What do you two get out of all this?'

'Payment up front. At a cheaper rate because we're not waiting for returns.'

'So I'm buying outright? Taking all the risk?'

'Shit, Barry. You think we haven't absorbed some risk over the past week?'

'How do I know the cargo is legit?'

'Oh for Christ's sake,' said a guttural new voice loudly. Lou and Jake's eyes met as they thought the same thing: the Wild Man.

Stig's voice overrode the interruption. 'Because we're not about to do what we're doing on a phoney run. This is a once-only stunt by us, Barry. You know that. Nobody will be seeing us again.'

'I want to think about it,' Barry said.

'Fair enough. But not for long. I do have other potential buyers.'

'Sure you do. Which is why you're standing here, exposed, in front of Jenssen's local guy.'

There was a silence before Stig spoke again.

'That's a calculated risk, Barry. And if we feel the risk was ill-conceived, we can rectify it.'

'So you're threatening me now, as well.'

'Just letting you know this is life and death. For all of us. I know you're a smart businessman and I'm offering you a free spin of the wheel, as far as sending the usual profits north goes. It seemed like a simpler way of moving the cargo than putting it on eBay.'

'Okay. That is attractive. Let me think about it.'

'We can trust you not to pick up the phone as soon as we walk out of here?'

'Yeah, of course. I've known a dozen like your mate here. I'm not suicidal.'

'Good. Then we understand one another.'

Jake's leg was screaming underneath him.

'Yeah we do,' Barry replied. 'How do I contact you? I don't want my voice or number on any phone you're caught carrying.'

'There are still a couple of phone boxes left in Melbourne. I'll call you tomorrow afternoon. About four.'

'Fair enough. Now go. You head out and I'll get the alarm.'

'Cool. Thanks for meeting. I know it's a weird situation.' Stig's voice getting fainter as he spoke.

Jake and Lou listened to Barry's footsteps shuffling. Five beeps on the security system.

'Do not move a muscle,' Jake whispered.

The door closed and was locked. Two cars started and moved away, their sounds becoming distant.

Lou stared at Jake, his face sweaty in the dark. Her eyes huge. He slowly unfolded himself, wincing as he straightened his left leg.

'Oh crap, that was hurting.' He flexed the leg a few times, swinging it gently in the air, bending the knee. 'Wow. Okay, once I leave this room, the motion sensors kick in and I have twenty seconds to turn it off,' he said. 'Don't blink until you hear the fifth beep.'

Lou nodded slightly and held her breath as he limped out of the room. As he passed the registers, she heard beeps start, soft but regular, as the alarm registered the movement. She'd counted twelve beeps when she heard the louder sound of the security system's buttons being pushed. And then Jake's voice saying: 'It's off.'

Lou stood up, cramped legs groaning. Took a few steps out of the storeroom and found that she was shaky.

'God, my heart is pounding,' she said.

The adventure was gone out of the night.

Jake, standing near the entrance, said, 'That was your boyfriend? The guy from the café?'

'Ex-boyfriend,' she said. 'Very ex.' She almost laughed at the relieved look that crossed Jake's face.

'And his psycho mate,' Jake said, almost to himself. 'With Barry.'

'What was it about? I can't believe Stig would be pushing drugs.'

'You think they were talking about drugs?' Jake looked shocked. 'I only heard them say "cargo". I thought it must be a container off a ship or something.'

Lou stared at him. 'For real? Contraband groceries?'

'Maybe,' he said defensively.

'You don't sneak around at one a.m. discussing groceries, Jake.'

'You and I were before they arrived,' he said, suddenly smiling.

'Yeah, we were,' she agreed, and started sniggering. 'Maybe they're planning their own sticker run and we beat them to it?'

And then they were both laughing so hard that it hurt, high on adrenalin and the pure relief of not being caught.

'Oh God, I almost pissed when they arrived.'

'You did?' Jake looked shocked.

'Not literally, Jake.'

They started giggling again, shoulders quaking.

Until finally Jake said, 'I think we should go.'

'Then again,' Lou had a look in her eye as she put a hand on his chest, Jake's heart finding a new level of pounding right underneath her touch. 'We're never going to want to be here again now we know how scary it would be to be caught.'

Jake looked at her. Confused.

'So we should make it count,' Lou said.

He barely dared to say it: 'You want to have sex in the Groc-o-Mart?'

She stepped back and frowned at him. 'Ewww. Umm, no, Jake, I don't.'

'Oh,' he said. 'I get it. You want to get back to the stickers.'

She gave Jake a grin. 'There any alcohol in this place?'

CHAPTER 27
IT WAS PROBABLY NOTHING

'Cecy? Rocket.'

'Hey,' her voice came down the phone. 'You coming in today or is that now a redundant question?'

'Possibly, later in the week. Is everybody missing me?'

'Let's just say life is quieter without you.'

'I'll take that. Can you do me a favour?'

'Sure. Shoot.'

'I need you to look at the missing person logs. A girl called Eloise.'

'Any other info? Age? Address?'

'Um, no.'

Cecy laughed that laugh of hers. He could see her head thrown back. 'You love challenges, huh?'

'Cec. This is how it works when you finally get your arse off that bike saddle and move into detective work. The tiniest of threads may be important.'

'Christ. You sound like one of the lecturers at the academy.'

Laver was genuinely alarmed. 'Do I? Jesus.'

'It's okay, sweets. I think we can both assume it was a rare lapse. I'll see what I can do.'

After hanging up, Laver was surprised to find himself looking across the lounge room at his bike, seriously considering it as an alternative to his car. But since he actually had no idea how far he'd be travelling, the car won out. It even started on the second try, in appreciation of his loyalty.

White Pages Online had listed Thirsk's office, 'Ace Investigations', as an office block in Camberwell. Laver fought his way along Bridge Road and then Burwood Road, inevitably caught behind a tram until he could turn and shunt his way through to Camberwell Junction.

He was only a couple of blocks from where Thirsk's office would be when he saw her. Marcia's animated walk unmistakable as she left a café and dodged a couple of pedestrians coming the other way, swinging her hips. Wearing her scarlet high-collared shirt and a short black skirt; shorter than she'd normally choose. With a man in a silver-grey suit who said something that made her laugh, really laugh. Laver's stomach clenching as the man put a hand on her arm, no big deal, and said something, speaking softly into her ear, which had her smiling. The prick with blond hair, possibly blow-dried, Laver noticed. Now blipping a remote to unlock a white Lexus sedan and stepping onto the road, coming around the back of the car to the driver's door as Marcia opened the passenger door and climbed in.

The car behind Laver honked loudly and he realised the traffic had moved, who knew when, and he needed to accelerate, leaving them behind. He put everything he had into paying attention to the brake lights in front of him and the movement of the traffic. There was a good possibility he'd rear-end the car in front of him if he didn't focus.

It had only been a hand on an arm. He probably did that himself, to Cecy, to Ratten, to other women, a dozen times a day without even realising. The guy had been telling a joke. It was nothing.

Laver scored a park within a block of the address and forced himself to sit in the driver's seat, eyes closed, breathing for a few moments – what he thought of as his Jedi mind trick. A discipline that had taken him years of cop work to achieve; turning everything off when he was about to go into work mode. Opening his eyes only when he was certain he was not the guy wondering who the fuck had just been talking to his fiancée with such familiarity, but Laver, the detective. Double-checking his emotions to make sure and then finally opening his door. He had work to do.

Thirsk's building turned out to be an 80s block, all glass and metal and completely devoid of any soul. Rent-an-office on all six floors, with small-timers trying to present a professional face while sharing one nineteen-year-old receptionist to answer phones.

Laver was glad he'd actually bothered to wear a collared shirt instead of his usual T-shirt. And boots instead of runners. He gave himself half a chance of passing for a cop.

He flashed his badge at the teenage receptionist and said he was a follow-up from the Homicide Forensic Squad that had already been through.

'They were here all day yesterday,' she said. 'So many of them.'

'We're very thorough,' Laver nodded. 'Just a couple of loose ends today so it's only me.'

She frowned. 'But they said they were coming back to pick up the boxes and the computer at 4 pm.'

'Oh, sure,' Laver said. 'That's right. But things move fast in a murder case so I want to check a couple of things before the forensic boys clean the place out.' He pointed at her massive switchboard phone. 'Why don't we phone head office and you can double check?'

On cue, the phone started to ring, line one's button flashing. She chewed her lip. Then line two started ringing.

'You want me to call?' Laver said.

'No, it's all right, I guess. I saw your badge.'

She'd handed over the key. And now he was pulling on disposable rubber gloves, opening the door to Thirsk's dogbox office, ducking under the police tape across the doorway, locking the door behind him and then standing in the silence. It was habit, more than anything, to stand at the edge of a scene, taking everything in, before he entered the space. A desk. A couch covered in stacks of paper. A couple of lamps. Two bad prints of nondescript Australian rainforest. A coffee table with three or four dirty cups and a plate with a crusty dirty knife. Fingerprint dust on its handle. A shopping list on a notepad. The items of a person who left with no idea he was never going to return. A giant fake fish on the wall which, when Laver finally took a step into the room, suddenly burst into a tinny electronic version of 'The Chicken Dance', scaring the living shit out of Laver. How had Forensics not turned that bastard off? He so wanted to, but knew he couldn't change a single element in the room.

Which reminded him that the sniffer dogs would be back in five hours, to clear the place out. Without a solid suspect, Thirsk's case notes, diary and contacts would be vital in the initial trawl. He was slightly surprised they hadn't loaded everything up within an hour of the body being identified.

He stepped over to the computer, sparking another chicken dance, and noted the angle of the chair before he sat down.

It was too much to hope that the computer would be turned on, logged in, fully accessible – and it wasn't. But Laver was able to boot it up and open a browser. He got onto Google and typed in the letter 'a'.

Automatic memory kicked in, with a drop list of words starting with 'a' that had been searched appearing below the search box. Alan, Armadale, ABC news, Australian Open tennis, anal … Laver had seen enough.

He deleted the 'a' and typed 'b'.

Bali, Blackburn, back pain, Bananas in pyjamas, blonde, boobs, bukkake, Brighton, Brisbane, Brunton Avenue, Bunnings, Bundoora, Burwood, butt, butt plug. And so it went.

Forcing himself not to go directly to 'e'. Noting each letter's findings. But finally getting there and watching the search results unfold.

eBay. Essendon football club. Eaglemont. EzyDVD. Easter show. Elastic. English.

Eloise Stanek.

There it was. Laver looked at Thirsk's files. Packed in boxes, looped with police crime-scene tape. One of which would contain a file that he knew would be for Stanek, E. But it was impossible to search them without waking up tomorrow with Ethical Standards cops pointing guns at him from every side of his bed, or whatever the pen-pusher's equivalent of a gun was. Pointing Bibles at him, maybe? Throwing rocks from the moral high ground?

Laver stood and readjusted the chair to how it had been. Exactly. Even though the forensics had already dusted for prints and he was wearing gloves, he used a handkerchief to wipe the keyboard and the door, enduring the fishy chicken dance three more times before he finally got clear of the office. He gave back the key, reminded the desk girl that his name was Detective Terry Porpoise, drove home and logged onto his laptop.

He opened the internet browser, called up Google and typed in 'Eloise Stanek'. Three listings for generic 'find a name' databases came up. Otherwise nothing.

Facebook had two Elise Staneks, no Eloises, and the Elises had no info, so he didn't even know if they were Australian.

He wasn't yet desperate enough to attempt MySpace.

Instead, he went the old-school police way, showing his rich cop heritage by clicking into whitepages.com.au, residential section. Tapped in 'Stanek' and found seventy-one hits Australia wide, which was a blessing.

He stood and wandered into the kitchen, pondering why the ghost of Coleman never materialised during the day, even though it was daylight when he shot him. Laver stared mindlessly for a few moments, then shrugged and made himself an instant coffee, silently thanking Holmes, the patron saint of investigators, that he wasn't chasing Eloise Smith.

He returned to his laptop and narrowed the search to the state of Victoria and now had fifteen Staneks, mostly in the Mitcham/Vermont area, east of the city.

But they weren't the right ones. He found it on the twelfth call, to P Stanek, Brighton.

The phone rang nine times before a woman answered.

'Hello?'

'Mrs Stanek?'

'Ms Stanek.'

'I'm sorry. My mistake. This is Detective Senior Sergeant Tony Laver from the Victoria Police.'

The woman uttered a faint 'Oh!' and the line went dead.

* * *

Stig Anderson was on the phone, at the third phone box he'd tried; this one finally worked. He'd already had two strike-outs for sales. And Barry wasn't answering his phone.

There was one more matter to take care of, Stig making one final call to a number he hadn't used in ages. Surprise at the other end, some small talk. Stig making up whatever crap he could think of regarding what it was like to work in the mines near Broome. Old classmates discussed and laughed at.

Stig all friendly banter as he said, 'Mate, yeah, big favour to ask, although I know it's out of order. You still got the old access to the database at your work? You have? Sweet. A friend of mine recently had a lot of help from one of your fellow officers. Yeah, yeah. Was close to being mugged by a druggie on Smith Street and this bloke stepped in at exactly the right time. She wanted to send him a bottle of something, to say thanks, but I told her that if she sends it to the office it'll be gone before he ever lays eyes on it. She wants to send it to his home address, to make sure he gets it.

'I know. I know, but it's touching, huh? And listen, you might be doing him a major service, between you and me. She's quite a party girl and if he's really lucky, she'll drop it off in person, and let him know in other ways how grateful she is. She's very tidy, just quietly.

'His name's Tony Laver. A bike cop, bless him … Yeah, I can wait. She'll really appreciate this.'

The line went quiet while Stig's old schoolmate searched the database.

Wildie had told Stig about this Laver guy fronting him in Brunswick Street. The night before he'd turned up at Louie's. Time for the hunter to become the hunted.

* * *

Laver hit Punt Road and drove south, cursing the traffic build-up through Prahran but finally clearing St Kilda, driving too fast through Elsternwick and making it to Brighton inside of forty minutes.

Her street was blue-ribbon Brighton, just off St Andrews Street, one block back from the bay. A place where traditional money, Portsea holiday houses and pearl necklaces met nouveau riche modern mansions, mostly built by real estate agents or bankers before the global financial crisis. But Brighton was rich enough to mostly withstand a global recession, so the For Sale signs were only occasional blights on the otherwise manicured landscape.

Laver felt slightly grungy, parking his dirt-splattered Pajero in the street.

He walked carefully along the pebble path between the perfect lawn and the strictly controlled flowerbeds. Curtains moved as he approached the front door. The house was single-level, white with a lot of glass. Probably from the 50s or 60s. Tennis court out the back, he'd bet what was left of his wage.

He knocked on the door and wondered if she would try to wait him out, but she didn't. The door opened and he was facing a woman in her mid to late sixties, immaculately dressed in a pink jumper with a white blouse underneath. A grey skirt. And yes, pearls.

Along with a face that hadn't seen sleep for a long time.

Laver held up his badge so she could examine it. 'Ma'am, I'm Detective Senior Sergeant Laver. We spoke on the phone. Well, I did.'

'I'm sorry I hung up on you,' she said. 'Why don't you come in?'

She seated Laver in one of those living rooms that is for anything but: cold and spotless and completely without character, from the expensive but emotionless artwork to the cream lounge suite and rug.

She seemed resigned, and exhausted, as she asked if he'd like a cup of tea.

'Why not?' he said, thinking it would give her time to regain her poise. Once she left the room, he sat watching stirred dust swirl in the sunlight through the window, idly wondering if she ever actually clutched her pearl necklace, like the cliché. If anybody did.

She came back with a tray, handed him his tea and placed hers carefully on the coffee table before finally perching on the very edge of her armchair, hands folded one on top of the other in her lap. Looking like the queen on a day off.

Laver nursed his cup of tea, wondering how much the china was worth, and said, 'I want to reassure you that as far as I know, nothing bad has happened to Eloise.'

She looked surprised. 'Oh. I thought you were here because I killed that private detective.'

That had Laver staring. And pulling out a notebook and pen.

'We'd better start again, Ms … I'm sorry, what is your name?'

'Pamela,' she said. One hand moving over the other in her lap. Too many lines on her face.

'Thanks, Pamela. Now, you'd better talk me through what you just said. About killing the detective.'

'Well, that's how it feels. I hired him and then I read in *The Age* – not even in that tabloid the *Herald-Sun*, but in *The Age*! – that his body has been found. You can imagine. I haven't dared go outside.'

'You think he died because of the job you hired him for?'

Pamela shrugged, a picture of misery. 'I don't know what to think.' One hand crept to her chin. So close to the pearls.

'Why would somebody connected to you want to kill this man, Thirsk?'

She looked at him sharply. 'Nobody who knows *me*. Somebody who knows Eloise is what I was thinking.'

'Ms Stanek – I mean, Pamela – I met Thirsk a few days ago. Our paths crossed professionally. He told me he was following leads to do with Eloise's circle of friends. Is that why you hired him?'

'I was worried about the sort of company she keeps. Oh, I lost track of her a long time ago. She moved out the moment she turned sixteen and was legally able. Still went to school, and a very good school too, but chose to live at her friend Erica's house. It was an unusual situation, but I knew she was safe with them, and Erica's parents didn't seem to mind. My husband paid them for her board after a while.'

'Pamela—'

'Do not ask what you're about to ask,' she said, with steel in her voice. 'Why Eloise felt she needed to move out is no longer relevant, and any grubby theories you might be contemplating would be disrespectful to my late husband. The point is that once she finished her schooling, she moved to the other side of the river and became involved in a crowd I did not like at all. In fact, I told her that I'd brook no truck with the clothes she was wearing, the haircuts she wore. It was embarrassing.'

The hand had moved from her chin to actually stroking her throat.

'The youth of today, hey?' he said, deadpan.

Pamela snorted. The hand moved back to her lap. Damn.

'Exactly. They have no idea. She claimed she was passionate about saving the world. All I could think was, no Brighton Grammar boy is ever going to go near you looking like that, young lady.'

'So she stopped coming home for visits?'

'Yes, after about a year of us fighting, not to mention Len – that's my husband – having his say. She would only call every now and then. We were in despair. On the TV news once, we saw her at a rally outside Parliament House, for goodness sake, fighting police officers. Actually slapping a policeman.' She suddenly gasped and her hand involuntarily reached up to clutch her pearls. 'Oh, you're not going to charge her for that, are you, now I've told you?'

Laver only just won a brief but immense internal battle not to cheer and said, 'No, I think we can keep that one between us.'

'Well, thank you. I can assure you that we were mortified. Len tried to talk to her and found she was seeing a very unsavoury young man, somebody who also was involved with the shopfront she frequented in Collingwood.'

'She works in a shop?' Laver asked.

'I'm sad to say that the answer is yes. Some ridiculous shopfront run by unwashed greenies.'

Laver blinked. 'Do you mean the Friends of the Planet?'

'That's the one. Bunch of criminals and dole-bludgers. I can't believe Len and I put so much work into trying to create a young lady, only to see her turn, well, turn feral.'

'When exactly did she "turn feral", Pamela?'

'Oh, at least two years ago. Maybe three.'

'But you only recently hired the private detective, Thirsk …'

'It was stupid, I suppose. Len died last year and Eloise is my only family, ridiculous hairstyle or not. I suppose I wanted to just quietly see if she was all right, who she was spending her time with, whether she'd started to grow up in the last few years.' She shrugged wearily. 'A mother can hope.'

'When did you hire this man, Pamela?'

'A couple of weeks ago. I gave him some school photos of Eloise and details of her known addresses, and that shopfront. He was due to report back soon. But then ...' Her voice suddenly choked.

'Pamela, please listen to me. Mr Thirsk's death is being investigated. At this stage, there is absolutely no reason to think that you, or Eloise, are involved in any way. I give you my word.'

The woman looked at him, her eyes swimming.

'It's true, Pamela. Thirsk was murdered but not in any way that puts Eloise in the frame.'

'Do you promise me that, officer?'

Laver shook his head. 'Not promise. The investigation has only just begun. The killers haven't been caught. But as it stands, there are no paths back to you. The homicide squad might want to talk to you, as I have today, but that's just them being thorough.'

She looked confused. 'If you're not with the homicide squad, who are you?'

'I'll be honest. I'm actually investigating an entirely different matter, but I wanted to check Thirsk's employment as part of my case. Which is why I wanted to ask you about the Eloise connection. Speaking of which, would you have any photos of your daughter?'

'Speaking of *whom*,' she said, standing up. 'Not speaking of which, speaking of *whom*.'

'My mistake,' he said. 'Clearly not brought up around here. I apologise.'

'It's not where you come from. It's where you're going that matters,' she said, handing him a royal-blue photo album. 'That's what worries me about my daughter.'

The photos were all school shots, apart from a few from family weddings or maybe an eighteenth birthday. None of them looked recent. But the birthday shots were what he needed. By then, she'd put black streaks through her blonde hair and had thick black liner under her eyes.

Pamela Stanek called her daughter Eloise. Jake had told Laver her name was Lou.

'One last question, Pamela, and I'll leave you alone. You mentioned she was seeing a young man from the Friends of the Planet. When Len dropped around.'

Pamela was back in her chair, back stiff as a board, her mouth thin with displeasure. 'A particularly cocky and nasty young man, from Yarraville, would you believe. Over near Footscray. You know the sort of people over there.'

'I barely know where to start. Do you remember his name?'

'Of course, because that was ridiculous as well. Do you know what he called himself? Stig! Isn't that the most ludicrous name you've ever heard in your life? I'll never forget it. Stig Anderson.'

CHAPTER 28
A SOCIAL CALL

Jake could feel the sweat stains forming under his arms. He looked at his hands: still trembling. He used his hankie to wipe his face and wished he could blame the office's dodgy air conditioning for his perspiration. On the CCTV, he watched Barry walk along aisle 6, talking to Kevin, one of the shelf-stackers.

Peering at the grainy black-and-white image wasn't good enough. Jake thought he may as well face the music in person now Barry was on the shop floor: the moment Jake had dreaded the entire day. He got up and wondered if he should put his things in a cardboard box, ready to go, but then just put on his suit jacket to hide the ballooning wet patches under his arms and headed downstairs.

Barry was standing in Home & Gardens, arms folded, discussing something with Kevin, as Jake entered the aisle. Right next to Barry's head, on the front of a can of insect spray, was a red-and-black sticker reading: 'You want to kill a fly? Shit, why not poison the whole planet?'

'Ah Jake,' Barry said as he saw Jake approach. 'Just the man I was looking for.'

Jake's bowels almost releasing. 'Yeah, boss?'

'We've got a bit of a problem.'

'We do?'

'Yes. Eggs. Kevin here has a good idea about eggs. If we evenly distribute eggs from expired punnets into fresher punnets, we could move the older stock without anybody wising up. One or two bad eggs in a dozen isn't worth coming back to complain about.'

Jake blinked. Barry hadn't noticed the stickers? He took a moment before responding, 'Are we allowed to do that?'

'Of course we're not, you dickhead. But we'd need to be caught to get in trouble. If only the three of us know about it, she'll be apples.'

'What if somebody gets sick off one of the old eggs?'

Barry looked at Kevin, shaking his head. 'Sounds like a problem at the distributor end, don't you think, Kev?'

'Definitely,' said Kevin, his grin baring a mouth of crooked and occasionally black teeth. 'Who have they got packing these eggs at the farm? Retards?'

'Well, it's got merit,' Jake said, in the mood to agree with putting broken glass in the cereal if the stickers would remain unnoticed. 'Everything good down here otherwise, Barry?'

His boss gave him a look. 'Yeah, Jake. Shouldn't it be?'

'Yeah, of course not; I mean, of course. No. I'll be upstairs … Paperwork.'

'Good on you.'

Jake could feel their eyes boring into his back as he walked away, or maybe he was just imagining it. He strode down aisle 9 and watched a mother reach over the toddler in her pusher to grab two packs of a coffee brand that Lou's sticker clearly identified as connected with an environmentally damaging cola brand. Another aisle over, a woman in her thirties didn't hesitate as she selected a toothbrush from a brand that Lou's sticker, plastered clearly to the shelf, suggested was almost single-handedly responsible for wiping out the world's rain-forests. In Medical Needs, a husband and wife loaded up on at least four products from a multi-national drug chain that was clearly stickered as boycott worthy.

No wonder Barry hadn't noticed. Nobody noticed. Or if they did, nobody seemed to care. Jake was very glad Lou wasn't there to see the indifference to their campaign, how so many bright, in-your-face stickers could be invisible in the face of ingrained grocery habits.

He wandered outside to see if a breeze would calm his nerves and stop him sweating. He had barely walked out the door when he saw a white Ford pull into the car park. As Jake stared, the two men opened their doors and got out. One in a suit, one in a bomber jacket. Jake spun on his heel, went back inside and up the stairs two at a time into his office.

He shuffled through spreadsheet printouts and other debris on his desk and found his mobile. He searched through his recent contacts, found Laver's number, and dialled.

As it rang, he could hear Barry coming up the stairs outside his office, hissing: 'What are you doing here? We can't be seen here.'

Laver finally answering, a miracle, and saying: 'Spooky. I'm on my way to see you.'

Jake overlooking the weirdness of a cop saying 'spooky' in his surprise and relief. 'Where are you?'

'A few blocks away. A couple of minutes.'

'I'll meet you in the car park,' Jake said, and darted down the hall past Barry's closed door.

In the car park, Jake saw the white Ford was empty now.

Watching Laver appear a few minutes later. The cop out of uniform, driving a beat-up-looking silver Pajero and parking near the giant bins.

Getting out of his car just as Jake saw a green Jeep pull into the car park, the driver shaved bald, except for a strip of orange hair. The guy next to him, rangy in a singlet. Stig.

Jake saying, 'Laver,' and nodding his head in the Jeep's direction so that the cop also watched as the two in the Jeep noticed them. A brief stare-off. After which Laver started walking straight at their car, Jake unable to believe the bravado of this guy, but then hearing the Jeep engine rev and watching the car start to move.

Laver watching them leave, fast, and walking back to Jake who was breathless and saying, 'Wow, you scared them off. They're terrified of you.'

'For now,' Laver said. 'I was actually just being a cowboy, which is very dumb. What's wrong with me?'

But then replaying the scene in his head and seeing Stig looking towards the Groc-o-Mart entrance in the moment before their car started, whacking his mate on the shoulder. Laver looking over there now and seeing two men talking to a man in a white business shirt and a grey tie.

'Who's that?'

'My boss. Barry.'

'And the two mystery men? Who apparently know your boss?'

'They're the ones from the white Ford.'

'Oh yeah,' Laver said. 'I'd only seen them huddled in their car, driving. They're who spooked Stig, not me.'

Watching the two men leave, one saying something earnestly to Barry as they started to move away, Barry not looking happy. The men climbing into the Ford and moving towards the exit.

Jake asking, 'Are you going to follow them?'

'No, not now. I reckon I might follow you home. It could be a good night to stay in and have a quiet one, Jake. And don't answer the door.'

'Really? Do you think I'm in danger?'

'Let's hope not. But best to be cautious.'

'Mr Laver,' Jake said urgently, 'something is going on here. Last night, I was here in the middle of the night with my friend, Lou—'

'The hippie chick? You were spending the night with her?' Laver's respect for the nerdy kid found new legs.

Jake blushed furiously, from his throat to his face. 'Not like that. We were putting stickers on the shelves, an environmental campaign, and then Barry showed up and we had to hide. He met some guys and Lou said it was Stig's voice. They were talking about a deal. Lou thought it was drugs.'

'Did you see any faces you could identify?'

'No, we were in a storeroom, listening.'

'Do you remember the exact conversation?'

'Not really. I was terrified.'

'They didn't get a whiff that you were there? That you heard this?'

'No. Barry turned the alarm back on and they left. They definitely didn't see us.'

Laver thought for a while. 'Okay. I'll try to talk to some of my people. Now grab your stuff and I'll wait for you. And if you see those guys near your home, ring me immediately, okay?'

* * *

Laver was making a stir-fry for dinner, only just having hung up after talking to Cecy and hearing about her findings. As usual, nobody else in the Victorian police force, including Dolfin, was taking his calls, even if he had much stronger evidence of crimes brewing. Now the phone rang and he was briefly hopeful, but no, it was Mrs Macleod saying it was only her, from downstairs.

Laver cradled the receiver between his ear and his shoulder as he cooked. 'How are you, Lucy?'

'Oh, I'm okay Tony dear, thank you, and I'm sorry to phone at tea time, but there's a young man who I don't like the look of and he's just outside. I don't like the look of him at all.'

'Outside your flat?'

'Yes, dear, he was hanging around the security door, I think waiting for somebody to go in or out, but now he's back on the street.'

'Can you describe him to me?'

'Quite tall, suntanned and very mean looking. A strange hairstyle – and *orange* hair, if you don't mind – and very unshaven. I'm sorry to say he has several tattoos.'

'I'll take care of it, Lucy.'

'Thank you, pet. Tony dear, is somebody nasty looking for you?'

'I'm afraid that's likely, Mrs Macleod. Sorry about this.'

'Well, it's not your fault. It's the uniform, love. I'm sure if they knew you, they'd know you're a lovely young man. But everybody hates the cops and that's all there is to it.'

'Umm.'

'I suppose this is probably some friend of the young man you slaughtered recently.'

Slaughtered, thought Laver. Jesus. 'You knew about that, Mrs Macleod?'

'Oh yes. I didn't think the photo of you in the paper was very flattering.'

'I was only a cadet when it was taken.'

'Much more handsome now, love.'

'Thanks, Lucy.'

'You've grown into your face well. You're a man now, love.'

'Sometimes more than others.'

'Oh, so you say. How is that young lady of yours?'

'Gone, I'm afraid.'

'Oh dear. Again. Oh well. And your boy?'

'Haven't seen him for a while either. Listen, I'd better go and say hello to our friend, hey?'

'Of course, Tony. Toodles.'

* * *

The Wild Man had given up on the security door.

He wandered back out and turned into the side street, where a ramp led down to the apartments' underground car park.

The Wild Man hoisted himself onto the brick wall to the left of the ramp and then carefully picked his way along the edge of a fern garden, the ramp ever further below him so that he wouldn't have wanted to overbalance and take the three-metre drop.

But now he was able to jump the low brick wall and he was in the lobby, on the residents' side of the security door. Finally in good shape to get the jump on this prick, to meet on the Wild Man's terms. Wildie moved along the side of the building, checking there was nobody in the pool or in the gardens that filled the centre of the complex. Noting the numbers on the doors and heading up the stairs, to the second floor.

And finding the cop sitting on an old green couch on the landing outside one of the apartment doors, holding two beers, apparently having watched Wildie from the moment he'd arrived on the stair landing. The cop in a singlet, showing muscle, and shorts. Holding out a stubbie and saying, 'Here. You want one? The uniforms are still a couple of minutes away.'

Wildie still surprised but managing to keep his hard stare going, saying, 'I might keep moving. But good to know where you live.'

The cop saying, 'You only had to ask. Buzz 2-3-0 and the key button next time. Save you the climb.'

Laver enjoying watching the struggle behind the man's face as he tried to regain the upper hand.

Wildie wondering how this kept happening with this fucking cop. Finally saying, 'You might want to watch your back while you're riding that bike of yours around, pig.'

'You threatening me? I thought you only took on defence-less dogs, road ragers and used-car salesmen. Why wait until I'm riding? I'm right here.'

'Now is not the time. But it will happen.'

'What I don't get,' Laver said, 'is why you're even bothering to be here. You saw those guys at the supermarket this afternoon and bolted. You were more scared of them than you are of me.'

'I'm not scared of you. I'm not scared of anything,' the Wild Man snarled. 'You'd do fucking well to remember that, pig.

I only came here to say why don't you just pull your head in, and your little grocery mate too. I don't give a shit if you are a cop. You'd do well not to keep crossing my path.'

'Or what?'

'You don't want to know the answer to that question.'

'Hmm, threatening a police officer. A charge all on its own, along with trespass and the rest,' Laver cocking his head stagily. 'Last chance for a beer if you want one. I'm pretty sure I can hear the sirens.'

Wildie hated himself for it but he got out of there. Again.

* * *

Stig was on Smith Street, watching the front of the shop. He was waiting for Rachel, the manager, to disappear. No sense being forced to go over the potentially unpleasant details of those missing funds from when he left Friends of the Planet.

He had enough on his mind, still trying not to panic at the thought of Brunetti and Wilson, definitely Jenssen men, talking to Barry at the supermarket. Unable to believe Paxton had sold them out within a day and wondering if – shit – maybe it wasn't him, maybe it was the dweeb who worked for him and kept hanging around Lou?

Finally, Rachel disappeared out the side door and then reappeared in a Toyota Prius, turning left into Smith and heading towards the city. Stig crossed the road and bought a coffee, sitting at one of the tables near the front of the shop as he looked around for Louie.

She finally came down the stairs from the first floor, Stig watching those legs of hers in stripey stockings, a purple miniskirt over the top. She saw him and visibly sagged, but walked over and sat down.

'You shouldn't be anywhere near this place. What are you doing here?'

'Came to see you,' he said. 'I was beginning to think you weren't here.'

'I was upstairs. A meeting about protesting the bay dredge is taking forever. Stig, I don't want to talk to you.'

'You did the other night. More than talk.'

'I told you. A mistake. And then a bunch of pigs turned up.'

'They weren't accusing me of anything. I'm here, aren't I? It was nothing.'

'There was a murder in the paper that day. Some bloke out at Tullamarine.'

'Which I know nothing about. Jesus, Louie. You think I'm a killer these days?'

'I have no idea what you are, Stig. That's the problem.'

'Who's this kid you've been hanging around with?'

'That again? What is it with you guys and Jake?'

'Jake. That's him. Hanging out with cops last time I saw him.'

'When? You were watching Jake?'

'At his little supermarket. Looking very cosy with a cop.'

'What were you doing at the supermarket, Stig? I didn't think the sort of thing you sell could be bought in aisle 3.'

Regretting it the moment she said it.

'What the fuck is that supposed to mean, Louie? What do you know about anything I might be trying to sell?'

She shut up.

'Did little lover boy tell you about that? A bit of pillow talk from the Groc-o-Mart?'

'No.'

'Sorry, babe? What was that?'

'It's nothing to do with Jake.'

'Louie, I think we should get out of here and have a little talk. You clearly know things that I need to know.'

'I'm not going anywhere with you, Stig. Piss off or I'll be the one calling the cops. You can watch me chat with them, seeing as that's apparently your new thing. Watching my friends.'

Stig had a look on his face she hadn't seen before and Louie wondered if she should run, if she'd have any hope of getting away, but the noise from upstairs saved her. The twenty people from the bay dredge meeting clattering down the stairs, finishing several conversations, but then seeing her and asking if she felt like a drink. A wind-down beer after the meeting?

And Lou was relieved to say, absolutely, let's go right now, to the astonishment and delight of the several male activists who had dreamed of this moment for some time. They were so pleased, they barely even noticed the eyes of the man Lou was leaving behind at the table.

But Lou did.

Stig just watched her go.

CHAPTER 29
THE WALLET

Laver fought his first instinct: to phone Dolfin and report that Stig and his mate knew where he lived. Flipper probably wouldn't take his call anyway. Laver thinking he needed to somehow take the initiative in this situation, not sit at home wondering who they were and when they might turn up again. But without resources, without ideas.

Laver not used to feeling alone and vulnerable, and not coping too well now the thug had gone and his adrenalin had ebbed. He tried watching television but couldn't. He poured a whisky. He tried reading, but quit after two pages of reading repeatedly but without any memory. He dug through his vinyl collection and put on a new LP by the Black Keys. He wondered where Marcia was right now. He ate the stir-fry he'd made. He felt it welling up inside him. He wondered how he and Marcia had unravelled so fast. He had another whisky. He sat on the couch and stared at the night. He thought about ringing Cecy or Damian or somebody who might actually take his call. He wondered where Coleman's ghost was. Saw his bullet hit the man again, for the thousandth time.

He could feel it approaching, rising through his throat.

A text message chimed onto his mobile phone and as always, every time his phone rang or a text arrived, his breath caught: Marcia! But, as always, it wasn't. It was his gym enthusing that he should sign up five friends. Laver deleted the message while wondering if he even had that many friends.

Marcia. He was marvelling at how many red Mazda 323s were on the road, so that he thought he saw Marcia driving past every time he set foot outside his apartment. Having to check the number plates before he could relax. Haunted by Mazdas. It was getting closer. He thought about that man's hand on her arm, the familiarity of it. Cop instincts telling him to stop bullshitting himself, that he *knew*, even if he had no proof. He thought about how much he'd love to be able to talk to his mother right now, given his dad would be something worse than useless.

His brain, the bastard, drifting back, to before Marcia. Not fair, so not fair. His brain not on his side at all. Needing to have his shit together in case Stig's mate came back. But he couldn't stop himself from thinking the single word: Callum.

And that was it. Laver was suddenly crying violently, uncontrollably, explosively, as though something had snapped inside of him and the ghost of Wesley Coleman, his lost son, his ruined career, Marcia and every other hurt he'd been carrying around for so long came gushing out in a vomit of tears.

Laver curled up on the couch and cried and cried and cried: huge sobs from his stomach that surprised him in their savagery and rage and pain. He was close to retching while crying, the physical reaction was so intense. Snot poured from his nose, his eyes stung, but he didn't fight it. Didn't fight at all. Drowned in his tears. He let himself cry. He let himself fall into abject misery. Surrendered to it.

He had no idea how long it lasted. All he knew was that the sobs would finally lessen and then subside so that he lay there, breathing shakily, trying to regain himself – and then he'd start uncontrollably sobbing again. He was helpless, exhausted, either shaking with grief or recovering before the next onslaught.

Finally, he rose from the couch, blew his nose, had a large glass of water and sat down at the table between the kitchenette and the living area. He blew his nose again and briefly shook with sobs but fought them down.

The sobbing was over, but the empty feeling remained and Laver suddenly knew he could not stay in his flat. He needed to connect with someone, anyone. He needed noise and light. Anything to distract him from where he was right now.

He SMSed Damian: 'Which pub? What time?'

And received a reply by the time he was out of the shower. 'Corner Hotel. 10.'

Bless, thought Laver. The Corner Hotel was only a couple of kilometres away, in Richmond.

It was raining out, so he drove, despite the whiskies he'd consumed pre-tears. He felt horribly sober. The kind of sober that cannot possibly be softened. A cold, hard light that shone on his life – no chance of denial. He didn't know if it was Marcia or the shooting or the humiliation of Siberia or maybe just his age, but something had died in him – and he feared it would never come back.

Best not to think about it really. He parked in front of the Dimmey's department store, walked down to the rail pass and dived headlong, with thankfulness, into the sweaty noise of the crowd at the Corner.

Damian, tonight lead guitar for Senor Retardo, was already on stage, wailing away on one of the band's two decent songs. Laver had to wait three back at the bar, deafened by the music, until he could finally order a beer. Gazing around the room, he felt a jolt of recognition and then smiled for the first time in hours. Just what he needed. He forced his way through the crush of people to a small table where a man about his age, jockey-sized, was sitting, wearing an old-school brown hat with a feather in it, his arm around a tired-looking blonde in a push-up bra barely hidden by a singlet that was at least two sizes too small.

'Oh, Jesus,' the little man said, seeing him.

'No, just me,' Laver shouted back over the music, moving into the table's spare seat. 'How are you, Stavros?'

'Nose clean, thank you, Detective.'

'Call me Tony. I'm off duty, as I'm sure are you.'

'I'm not in the habit of calling cops by their first name, Detective. No offence.'

'None taken, I suppose. What about your lady friend?'

'Denise definitely doesn't talk to pigs. Do you, love?'

'Fuckin' A,' said the blonde.

'Charmed, I'm sure. So how's the pickpocket business?'

Stavros stared ahead at the stage, acting as though he hadn't heard the question.

'I'm serious, Stavros. Relax, I'm off duty. I'm just curious. Has the global crisis, talk of recession and all that been good or bad for you guys?'

Stavros gave him a look, and shook his head. 'I'm not biting, prick. You want to question me, arrest me.'

'You're not much of a drinking buddy, Stavros.'

'That's because we're not drinking buddies, Detective. Now can I be left alone please?'

Laver shrugged and stood up again, to see Damian mid-solo. He was lying his guitar on the stage in front of him, not even holding it, and sort of jabbing at the strings with his right hand. Then he somehow got his left hand's fingers to the neck in time for some complicated notes, and picked the guitar back up, in position, without losing the solo at any point. Laver would have to ask him how he did that next chance he got.

The crowd was going nuts, whooping as Damian brought it home, but one corner of the dance floor had a different energy: the unmistakable feel of conflict, with people making room, turning to watch and trying to stay out of it. Laver saw a shaved head with an orange mohawk somewhere on the other side of the jostling crowd. Words were being exchanged.

Laver ducked back down and tapped Stavros on the shoulder.

'Oh, for fuck's sake,' said the small man.

'Stavros, you're not going to believe me but I have a job for you. I'm not kidding. There's money in it.'

* * *

The Wild Man had thought the guy was going to throw a punch, wanting him to, a big footballer by the look of him, plenty of muscle. The Wild Man eager for the physicality, still disconcerted that he'd been forced to retreat yet again by that cop. Sick of Stig's inactivity. Freaked by Jenssen men in the Heidelberg car park. In other words, totally up for the satisfying jar down the forearm that he'd feel landing a decent punch. Dying to see the blood explode from this footballer's face. Legs itching to sink boots into ribs to feel them break and give.

But then the guy had thought better of it, a very smart decision, and let his mates drag him out of reach. Wildie was disappointed, snarling until the guy was on the other side of the room, but still finding he had a circle of space that nobody else seemed to want to enter.

Until he was bumped into from behind. He turned from the waist and found a smallish man, only just maybe reaching Wildie's shoulder, even in his hat, and looking very pissed.

'Shorry, mate,' said the drunk. 'She pushed me, the bitch.' The man waved generically at the crowd behind him.

'Fucking watch yourself,' Wildie growled.

'I will, buddy. I will,' nodded the drunk. 'Mate. Mate! I'm really shorry. Give us a hug.'

And lurched into Wildie, front on now, to try and wrap him in a drunken bear hug.

Wildie got a hand between them and pushed hard, sending the pissed idiot flying.

'What is it with this place?' he spat at the woman next to him, who was giving him worried looks. 'Can't a bloke watch a fucking band in peace?'

She edged a metre or so away, the packed dance floor somehow finding even more room for Wildie. He looked around, but the small drunk had been swallowed by the crowd.

* * *

In the men's toilets, Stavros stood outside the closed door of a cubicle and said, 'You owe me one, Laver, you bastard. That guy could have killed me.'

Sitting on the closed lid of the toilet, Laver was going through the wallet. A Quiksilver one, very worn. Laver marvelling that somebody could have no credit cards: just $300 in cash. He dug through pockets but there was no pot of gold, like a driver's licence. There was a blurry photo of a parrot, sitting on what looked like a couch. A condom packet, promising pink fluoro strawberry bubblegum–flavoured fun. Jesus. A Dr Who Official Fan Club discount card. And finally a membership card for a video shop in Narrabeen, NSW, in the name of Colin Wilde. Member number 000356.

It wasn't much but it was something. Laver pocketed the card, emerged from the cubicle and handed the wallet to the pickpocket.

'Stavros, you've done really well. The cash is yours if you want it. But keep in mind who you're dealing with. If he realises it's missing, you might want to be several suburbs away.'

'Don't worry, I'm gone. This band is shit anyway.'

'Hey, that's a mate of mine on stage. Careful.' The noise of the band rose as the door to the toilets swung open. They both pretended to wash their hands as a guy wandered into the cubicle Laver had left, closing the toilet door and fumbling with a lock that didn't work. Laver handed Stavros some notes and said quietly, 'Here's the two hundred we agreed, anyway. The bad news is I need you to return the wallet.'

'You're kidding.'

'Giving a wallet back must be easier than taking it.'

Stavros looking sniffy. 'What would you know about my art?'

'Art.'

'Absolutely it's an art, Detective. Just because it isn't legal doesn't mean it's not a skill.'

Laver thought about that, and nodded. 'Fair enough. I don't really give a shit. Just don't let him know his wallet was lifted.'

Stavros looked genuinely pained. 'How am I supposed to do that?'

'Dunno. You're the *artist*. If you don't, I'm going to tell him you stole it.'

'Bloody coppers.'

In the end, it wasn't that hard. Denise danced right up next to the big man, looked at the floor, squealed, bent, wiggling her butt, showing plenty of g-string and came up holding a wallet.

'Look what I found on the floor,' she said to him. 'Is this yours?'

The Wild Man felt his pocket and yelled back, 'Yeah, it is. Shit, thanks.'

He was looking hard at her push-up bra, exploding from within her tiny singlet, Denise grooving in front of him, an eyebrow raised.

'Wanna dance?' he said.

'We just did,' she replied.

Three songs later, the band finished and Wildie staggered out of the pub, feeling the beers he'd put away. There'd been a few. He walked straight past the queue waiting for a taxi and took the first one, giving a glare to anybody thinking about arguing.

He gave the cabbie the address and closed his eyes, which was a mistake because the world started to spin. He'd only had eight beers. He was getting soft from all this sitting around. Melbourne was boring him rigid and it was time to move on. He'd have to talk to Stig once he sobered up, maybe tomorrow. Let him know that if they weren't going to sell the stuff right now, he was going without it. Pull a robbery of some kind for cash and blow.

The taxi pulled up outside the house in Rathdowne Street, Carlton. Wildie even paid the driver, under orders from Stig to not attract any more pointless attention from the police or neighbours. It was a double-fronted brick house and Wildie didn't have a front door key so he lurched around the side, fumbling with the gate and finding his way to bed through the unlocked back door.

Laver, in his Pajero, watched until Colin Wilde was out of sight and the lights went off in the house. Then he drove home, actually hoping he could conjure up the ghost of Coleman to rant against tonight, to keep his mind off where else that silver-suited bastard's hands were roaming over the body of his ex-fiancée.

CHAPTER 30
ONE MINUTE
TO MIDNIGHT

Stig chose a phone box near the Carlton Library, across the road from La Porchetta pizza. He glanced up and down the street, adjusted his sunglasses in the weak morning sunshine, slotted the coin, checked the number on the torn piece of paper and dialled.

'Barry Paxton.'

'You've sold us out, you prick.'

'What? Stig? What are you saying?'

'You were seen yesterday. Speaking long and hard with two of Jenssen's enforcers. You've sold us out.'

Barry's breathing came down the phone. 'Oh Christ, you gave me a heart attack. Bloody hell, Stig.'

'You're a dead man, Paxton.'

'Shut it, will you. I haven't sold anybody out, you dumb bastard. The deal is sweet.'

Now it was Stig's turn to breathe into the receiver. 'Explain.'

'Of course they came to see me. Jenssen has worked out the car crash was a fake. He knows you've run, with the gear. He's putting feelers out everywhere. I had to see them. What would it have said if I hadn't met them?'

Stig found himself glancing sideways, trying to look everywhere at once. Half-expecting to see a white Ford right there, and two men walking his way. 'Where are they now?'

'No idea. Probably heading to Adelaide. Jenssen has already checked Sydney and Brisbane. They put in more time here because it's your home town.'

'So we need to move. What's your answer, Barry?'

'It's on. I'm going to have to sit on the shipment for a long time, now Jenssen's looking. I want a discount.'

'A discount? What is this? The Boxing Day sales?'

'Call it danger money then. Or just leave it. I don't need this grief either.'

'No, but you like the idea of a royalty-free collect, hey, Barry?'

'As long as you disappear, as you've promised, after.'

'Oh, we'll be gone. Don't worry. The Wild Man is very antsy as it is. When should we meet?'

'Your place? What's your address?'

'Yeah, right, Barry. And you won't cum in my mouth. How about midnight tonight, in the Groc-o-Mart car park?'

'Yeah, that's fine. I'll have to get the money though.'

'Fucking make sure you do, Barry. I'll phone this afternoon to check. This needs to happen now.'

'Just you and me tonight,' Barry said. 'Keep that gorilla mate of yours clear.'

'I'm not turning up alone, but he can sit in the car. And Barry?'

'Yeah?'

'If one nasal hair of mine smells something that's not kosher, you're very dead.'

'You're a lovely guy to do business with, Stig.'

'I'm a careful guy. Speaking of which, do not say a word about anything to do with Queensland in front of that helper of yours.'

'What helper?'

'Jake.'

'Jake Murphy?' Barry's voice was pure confusion. 'What the fuck has he got to do with anything?'

'Just keep an eye on him and remember silence is golden. I'll confirm you've got the money sorted later this afternoon and then see you tonight.' Stig hung up and walked fast away from the phone box, still looking around the street, jittery as hell. He should probably get some breakfast but God, what he really needed was a joint.

In Heidelberg, Barry Paxton loosened his tie slightly and dialled a new number.

A voice said, 'Yep.'

'Brunetti? Paxton. I just heard from Anderson.'

* * *

'You're not listening to me,' Laver said. He and Flipper were standing in front of Ned Kelly. At least, the famous bushranger's bullet-pocked iron armour in a glass case, high up above the reading room of the State Library: a permanent exhibit that didn't attract many tourists early in the day. At 10 am, Laver was in full bike gear, just started on a day shift, and Dolfin was in his usual immaculate dark suit but looking like he hadn't slept for days.

'Cecy made some calls. Two men, Stig Anderson and Colin Wilde, were both presumed dead although not formally iden-tified in a fatal,' Laver continued. 'Killed and burned beyond recognition in a car crash near Nimbin. Their driver's licences miraculously just clear of the flames. And now two guys of exactly their description are walking the streets of Fitzroy and Collingwood. They're not dead, Flipper. They're down here and they're trying to sell drugs to the owner of the Heidelberg Groc-o-Mart. My informant overheard the actual deal taking place.'

'Your informant being a nerdy check-out kid with the hots for a hippie chick who, last we saw, was up close and personal with one of your zombie drug-dealers.'

'He heard what he heard. And I've seen what I've seen, which includes a couple of guys following Anderson and Wilde around. A couple of guys who I might add sound extraordinar-ily similar to the men you described walking into the airport taxi rank from outside the airport.'

Dolfin snorted. 'Medium height, in grey suits, with dark hair, no decent look at their faces? Yeah, unmistakably the same blokes.'

'Flipper, I know you're still snaky on me after what hap-pened when we fronted Stig in such a half-arsed way but think about it. Thirsk was sniffing around and he ended up dead. These guys are hooked into a major drug ring and faked their own deaths. Jake and Lou are in danger, plus I've got these dickheads knowing where I live. This thing could go up any moment. Mate ... I'm making our call. I'm saying this is nuclear.'

And that's when Flipper lost it. 'Fuck you, Rocket,' he said loudly, then remembered the library rules. He hissed, 'This is not nuclear. This is nowhere near nuclear. You and I invented "nuclear" for within situations. When you're moments from being shot, in a siege situation, then you can yell nuclear. With bullets flying. In genuine fear for your life. When immediate action is required, no questions asked. It was not created to force me, a mate, your last surviving bloody mate in the Force, to risk my career chasing your increasingly tiring stupid and wild theories.'

They stood, five metres apart, mutually fuming.

Laver finally said, quietly, 'Okay. Fuck, you're right. I'm sorry. I shouldn't have said nuclear. But shit, Flipper, you don't know the frustration of not being listened to, of not being respected, even by you.'

'Mate, I do—'

'No you don't. You fucking don't. I've laid this out for you as plainly as I can and you won't even run the names Anderson or Wilde through a computer to see that yes, they are dead men mysteriously alive and a long way from their former home, with mysterious products they're trying to sell. What will it take? You want Jake or Lou to do a Thirsk before you'll believe? Pick me up in the middle of the night to go and ID one of these innocent kids? Or, better, you want that big gorilla turning up at my place when Mrs Macleod happens to be asleep in front of the tellie and I'm not ready for him?'

'You don't have evidence, Rocket. You've grabbed a bunch of strands and built a hypothesis. You only know Wilde's name because you had a known perp pickpocket him. Christ.'

'How did he know where I live, mate? Come on, Flip. Just answer me that. How the fuck could a gorilla like Wilde turn up at my home?'

'That is strange,' Flipper nodded. 'But he may have followed you.'

'I wouldn't spot a tail, after all these years? And somebody as distinctive as that?'

'As distinctive as you say he is. Nobody else has seen him.'

Laver wanted to belt his mate over the head with Ned's helmet. It looked heavy. 'Seriously? Except Lou, who is scared of him. And Jake, who is terrified of him. And the guys in the Ford, who are following him.'

'You believe.'

'Yes, I believe. Oh and Cecy, who's a good cop. And a used-car salesman who may or may not be eating solids again by now, after being woken from an induced coma.'

'Unsolved. Again, only according to you.'

'Yes, with my previously respected cop instincts that are completely redundant, apparently.'

'We caught that serial rapist that time because he went to the same general store as that Soggie.'

That stopped Laver cold. 'What?'

Flipper said, 'Remember? Lacey or whatever that guy's name was. We were looking everywhere for him, had an entire taskforce devoted to the job for three months, and then Tiny, a Soggie from a few years back, saw him in the same queue at his local shop, waiting to buy milk and bread.'

'What the fuck?'

'I'm saying, the gorilla could have found you like that. Sheer luck.'

'Mate, somebody within the Force told him my address.'

'You think,' Flipper said. 'You choose to believe. Fuck it, mate, I'm sorry. You just won't let it go. But I can.'

'Flipper, if you don't believe me now, if you won't help me, I honestly don't know what to do. It means I'm totally abandoned as a cop, and by you. Shit Flipper, by you!'

'Then see a counsellor and stop being a cowboy.'

Dolfin's phone made a low buzz, vibrating. He checked it and looked at his mate.

'I've got to go. The real world is calling. And don't ever call nuclear on me again, unless it really is. Because you know what will happen if you pull that stunt again?'

'What?'

Dolfin gave him a long heavy look and said, 'I'll be cross.'

'Flipper, we're not done with this.'

'I am, mate. I totally am,' Dolfin said.

And walked away.

* * *

Wildie put down the Xbox controller, his hangover fading, and looked with something approaching disgust at Stig Anderson: sprawled, legs askew, on the couch and smoking his third joint of the day. Before lunch.

'Good plan, brains. We just sit here until they kill us. Get a little high while we wait.'

'Steady, Wildie. Everything's in order.'

'Which is why you're smoking yourself to some kind of oblivion.'

'The deal is done. Midnight tonight. Heidelberg. My head will be back in shape by then.'

Wildie's rough voice sounding almost gentle as he said, 'Mate, you're losing it. I'm sorry, but you fucking are. Jenssen's men are in town and you know who those guys are. We're blown and that means we'll be dead.'

Stig waved a vague hand. 'Paxton got rid of them. Says it's cool. Deal's still on.'

'We have to leave. Now.'

'Tonight.' Stig was now waving his hand gently in the joint's smoke, watching the small clouds twist. 'We do the deal tonight and then drive right out of here.'

'Tonight's a set-up.'

'Crap.'

'Paxton hasn't got the balls to do a deal while Jenssen's hit men are in town.'

'Says they're gone. To Adelaide.'

Wildie snorted.

Stig took another toke. 'Tonight's our best chance, mate.'

But the Wild Man stood up, hands on hips. 'Stig, you're done. I don't know when it happened, but it's happened. You've lost it. Is there anybody else you can ring as an emergency back-up plan? Arrange a fire sale price before tonight?'

Alarm and something resembling panic fighting its way to the front of Stig's addled brain. Wildie watching his stoned partner finally shrug and say, 'Dunno. Maybe.'

Wildie reaching for the car keys and Stig just managing to raise his head, asking, 'Where are you going?'

'I'm going to cover our tracks.'

'What does that mean?'

'There are loose ends. There are people who know we're in town. There are things to be done if we're going to stay alive. Enough of your sit-on-your-arse way. Stop smoking that shit and turn back on.'

Wildie stalking off to the bedrooms and coming back with two packages wrapped in towels. Unrolling one to reveal a pistol, and handing it to Stig.

'Given how high you are, try not to shoot yourself to see how pretty the bullet is.'

Stig sitting up straighter now, staring at the gun. 'What the fuck? Where did you get this?'

'You mean "these".' Wildie unwrapping the second gun and stashing it down the front of his jeans, under his belt, and placing his singlet over it. 'This shit's getting real and we need to be able to defend ourselves.'

Stig looking up at him with wide eyes, like a rabbit.

The Wild Man standing, hands on hips, shaking his head in disgust. 'Wake up, right now, Anderson. Hit the phones and do a deal that doesn't involve this Paxton bloke. If it's a crap deal for less than we should take, who gives a shit? I'd rather be alive. Do the deal and then we're going. This is not a debate. I'll be back in a bit.'

And he was out of there. Slamming the door and stalking to the latest car, a red Holden ute, very powerful, parked illegally on Rathdowne Street. The Wild Man in control at last and feeling better for it. Clear in his mind. He fired up the car, listening to the rumble of the engine, and decided the first stop was the Groc-o-Mart. The little cop-dog assistant manager. Then to Friends of the Planet to pick up Stig's little hippie cutie. Wildie wanted to make sure she was second on the list. That part of what he had to do he planned to have time to enjoy.

CHAPTER 31
TAKING CARE OF BUSINESS

Jake finished lunch, his standard ham sandwich at his desk, with a Big M chocolate milk to wash it down, and looked out the window of his office at the car park. A white Ford was parked midway back, two men sitting side by side, behind dark glasses.

Jake could feel his heart start to pump. He reached for his phone, found Laver's number and dialled.

Laver was sitting in the Mobile Public Interaction Squad office with Cecy, contemplating asking if she'd like a lunchtime beer, thinking she'd frown, and picked up on the second ring.

'They're here.'

'Who's here? Jake, is that you?'

'It's me. I'm at work. Those two men. They're here. They've got to be here for me.'

'Mate, calm down. Where are they? In their car?'

'Yes. Watching the door. What do I do?'

'Stay put. I'll be there inside fifteen minutes with another officer.'

Cecy's eyebrows raised as Laver put the phone down. 'Would that be me?'

'Yep. The one day I decide to ride the bike to the office. I need you to drive me. I'll explain on the way. But first, let's lose the lycra. You might be about to meet some real criminals. Best not to look like a couple of noobs.'

* * *

Cecy pulled into the car park and they spotted the Ford immediately. With Laver directing, she parked two rows back, three cars to the side. Out of the range of the Ford's mirrors. The men would have to turn their heads to see them.

Laver was already dialling. 'Jake? We're here. You good?'

Jake's voice, sounding shrill, said: 'Just a moment.' Then distant, as though his hand was covering his phone. 'Yes, sir?'

Laver listened to a muffled voice, heard Jake say, 'Okay, sure,' and finally had Jake back on the line, whispering.

'That was Barry, my boss. He said a couple of guys are about to be here for a meeting in his office and he is not to be disturbed. Definitely do not disturb. Could it be them?'

'Dunno. Let's get you out of there, either way.'

Laver had the door open and one leg out when Cecy put a hand on his arm and said: 'Rocket.'

He followed her gaze and saw a blue Commodore, rental sticker on the back window. A deeply suntanned man, wiry but well dressed, in sunglasses, his long hair pushed back from his forehead, getting out of the car. The men in the Ford sat up straighter, gave him their full attention.

Laver got back in the car and slid down in his seat. 'Who the fuck is that?'

'Did you catch the slight nod to the Ford?' Cecy said.

'Oh yes, I did.' Laver put both hands over his mouth and breathed into them for a moment. 'You know who this guy is? He's the boss.'

'How could you possibly know that?'

'I just know. The Ford crew work for him. You watch. Shit.'

Laver thought hard for a few seconds. 'Have you got a Dictaphone?'

'No. Jesus, Laver. A Dictaphone?'

'Okay, show me your phone. Now!'

Cecy handed her mobile over, thinking yet again that this was the strangest cop she'd ever met.

Laver's eyes had a new look in them. A hard gleam. He was dialling his phone, even as the tanned man walked over to the Ford, leaned in to talk through the driver's window.

'Jake? It's Laver. Okay, you have to move fast and I promise I'll get you out of there safely. Don't say anything, don't argue, don't debate. Just do what I tell you. Got it?'

'Okay.'

'Where's your boss?'

'Barry? He's just leaving his office. Heading downstairs.'

'Take your phone, and don't hang up this call, whatever you do. Go into his office right now, and leave the phone somewhere not obvious – but on speakerphone so it will pick up the conversation.'

'Wha—'

'I said don't debate.'

'But it's a brand-new iPhone.'

'Good, it's definitely got speakerphone then. I'll get you a new phone if I have to.' Laver calm, so Jake would be too. 'Do it now, then head to the toilet and wait until you know they're all in his office. Then go straight to your car and drive to the Clifton Hill McDonald's. Where Queens Parade and Heidelberg Road split. You know it?'

'Yes. But listen, Detective Laver, I don't think I ...'

Laver watched the doors of the white Ford open.

'Jake, there's no time. Things are happening and the pair from the Ford is on the move. Do it now. Do not leave the McDonald's until I get there. And don't hang up this call. Barry's office now! ... GO!'

Cecy watched Laver switch his own handset to mute and then to speakerphone. The sound of Jake breathing hard filled the car. They heard a door open, winced as something banged loudly against the phone, heard a rustle, then Jake hissing: 'It's set.' Then silence.

The men from the Ford were following the tanned man through the front door.

Meanwhile, Laver was cursing at Cecy's phone.

'Where's "office tools" in the menu? Is it the clock?'

'That's the alarm,' Cecy said. 'It's the calculator thingo.'

'Come on, come on.' Laver was pushing buttons. 'Voice recorder, perfect!'

The speakerphone picked up the click of a doorhandle being turned and then movement. Cecy, looking up to the first floor, could see the outlines and occasional features of the men in one of the office windows. Saw the suntanned guy who Laver said was the boss move past the window, then watched a man in shirtsleeves, presumably Jake's boss, pull down a white blind.

Laver huddled over Cecy's mobile phone. Hitting 'record'.

Then hearing a man's voice say: 'You're in town? I had no idea.'

Another voice saying, 'Nobody does, Barry. Except us.'

'To what do I owe this honour?'

The second voice saying: 'It's not an honour, Barry. It's a fucking mess is what it is.'

Barry spluttering: 'I can assure you, I'm very confident of reeling in these two, Anderson and Wilde. Your associates here, Mr Wilson and Mr Brunetti, believe they even have the correct address.'

'Actually they don't. Mr Wilson has informed me moments ago that the merchandise remains unlocated.'

Laver, listening as he watched Jake emerge from the sliding door, crouching low as though trying to duck helicopter blades as he headed for his car. Laver thinking, 'Good boy.'

On the speakerphone, nestled up to Cecy's voice-recording phone, the same voice saying: 'It would be fair to say I've lost confidence in how you're running the Melbourne end of things, Barry.'

Barry sounding angry. 'Lost confidence? Like I'm not trying to find them?'

Laver watching Jake fumble and drop his keys, then bend and finally open his car door.

The other voice saying, 'Barry, we know there's been contact.'

'I swear,' Barry's voice pleading. 'I have not laid an eye on them.'

'Not you.' A new voice, hard and with a slight British accent. 'Your assistant.'

'My assistant? I don't have an assistant. Karl knows that.'

'Your assistant here. At the supermarket.'

That brought a silence over the phone.

'Jake? Jake, from here? Bullshit.'

The British voice saying, 'Not the time for debate, Barry.'

'You're saying Jake has been seen with Stig Anderson? That is just fucking ridiculous.'

Jake's car driving away.

The other voice, the boss, saying, 'Who's this Jake?'

The British voice saying, 'He's in the next office, boss. He's been seen with Anderson and Wilde.'

'Okay, we'll meet him in a minute.'

Barry's voice saying, 'I had no idea.'

The boss's voice: 'Well, that's not exactly a shock, Barry. You don't seem to know shit, even when it's right under your nose. This is a clusterfuck and I'm closing down the Melbourne end immediately.'

Barry, sounding ever more shocked and confused, saying: 'Closing down Melbourne?'

The boss: 'Looks like the Groc-o-Mart will have to go back to making profits off frozen chips.'

'That's crap.' Barry getting angry. 'Moving your gear is the only reason I've even kept this fucking supermarket open.'

'Well.' The boss sounding tired. 'No need for any of us to worry about that anymore, really, is there?' Laver closing his eyes as the boss said: 'Especially you, Barry. Mr Brunetti?'

Cecy seeing the flash against the window at the same time as the speakerphone made the sound of a soft punch, dissolving briefly into static.

Cecy stifling a scream and immediately feeling embarrassed. Laver looking at her and mouthing 'Silencer' even though the phone was on mute. Putting a hand on her shoulder. Cecy realising she'd been holding her breath.

The speakerphone silent, except for the sounds of movement.

'That'll do it,' said the British voice.

'Be sacked if I needed two shots from that range,' said a new voice.

'What now, boss?'

'We need to stomp on Anderson and Wilde, immediately. Let's start with known associates. You know where to find this Lou woman you spoke about?'

Sounds of a door opening.

'Yeah. I'll check her house, and work. She's been seen with the kid from this place too.'

'This man, Jake?' The boss sounded surprised.

'Yeah, the one who works – worked – for Barry.'

'And he's in league with Lou, who appears to be close to Anderson? Why haven't I heard about him before today?'

'Didn't think he was a serious player.'

Footsteps and the third voice saying, 'Jake's not in his office. His jacket's gone too.'

The boss saying: 'Jesus Christ. Is he here? We need them both: him and the chick. One should get us to Stig. It's time to end this. You good to clean this up?'

'Of course.'

'I'm leaving. I was never here.'

The British voice asking, 'How long are you in town for?'

'Till we've sorted this shit and not a second more. Ring me when you have either or both of them. Take them somewhere safe and I'll meet you there. Tell nobody that I'm here.'

Laver clicking the red hang-up button on both phones, praising an unknown divinity that the batteries held out on all handsets. A minute later, watching the suntanned man walk calmly to his car, get in and drive away. Laver hating having to watch his taillights disappear, knowing the rental plates would bring back John Citizen, or maybe J Smith, tied to a bogus credit card.

One of the two other men emerging now, heading towards the white Ford.

'What do we do?' said Cecy, still barely able to breathe. 'A man just got killed.'

'We phone the uniforms as we drive.'

'Shouldn't we tackle him now? He's getting away.'

'I'm not allowed to carry, remember? And these guys are killers.'

'Tony, we're police officers. We can't just watch them drive off.'

'We'll get him, and the bloke tidying up. Don't worry. But we can't now.'

'Which means what?' Cecy asked, still staring at him.

'Which means I have to get to Lou before they do. Look, you stay here and meet the uniforms when they arrive.'

He could see her brain racing and gently placed a hand on her cheek, stopping her cold. 'Cecy, listen to me. You're going to be a very good cop but you are not ready to tackle either of those two. I'm not good enough without a gun.'

She swallowed and nodded. 'Fair enough. I'll call Homicide.' Then asked, 'What are you going to do?'

Laver watched the white Ford start to move.

'I'm borrowing your car. I have to get to Smith Street. Fast.'

Cecy got out and Laver switched to the driver's seat, heading towards the Heidelberg Road exit.

He had swung a hurried right-hand turn towards the city about thirty seconds before a red Holden ute pulled into the car park.

CHAPTER 32
77 SUNSET STRIP

Lou was behind the counter of the Friends of the Planet, selling an anti–Japanese whaling T-shirt to a chick she took to be a uni student, almost certainly media or arts, when she saw the bike cop come through the front door. Not in uniform, but definitely him, and looking intense.

Lou in disbelief as he grabbed her upper arm, hard, and handed the T-shirt to the girl, saying: 'Here, it's yours, for free. Damn the Japanese and their fake research. Wear it proud.'

And started marching Lou towards the street.

Lou finally managing to plant her feet enough to slow him down, and screaming the first thing that came to mind: 'What the fuck?'

The cop not letting go of her arm but looking directly into her eyes. 'Lou, this is serious. Some people are coming for you. Right now. They might kill you. Almost certainly will. We have to leave.'

'I'm in charge of the shop. What people? Who wants to kill me? You're insane.'

'I'll explain. In the car.'

Lou twisting and lurching to free her arm, Laver feeling surprisingly strong arm muscles under her jumper.

'I'm not going with you. Who the fuck do you think you are? This is police harassment.'

The cop shaking his head and almost smiling as he started dragging her towards the door again. 'Technically maybe, but it's more personal assault, because I'm not acting officially here.'

'Listen, you pig arsehole—'

He stopped again and regarded her, never letting go but relaxing his grip. 'Lou, if you make me shoot you to get you into the car, it would sort of defeat the purpose of what I'm trying to achieve here. We've got maybe one minute.'

'You don't have a gun.'

'Very observant. Let's move.'

The student with the T-shirt, watching all of this open-mouthed, finally managed: 'You want me to call the police?'

'He *is* the fucking police!' yelled Lou, being dragged bodily to the street, Laver's arm now around her waist as she struggled.

'Pigs, man,' said the student hotly. 'The damn pigs.'

'You said it, sister,' Laver agreed and was finally out the door.

Getting her into Cecy's car took some work, so Laver could have kissed Jake for being right where he was supposed to be, in the Clifton Hill McDonald's car park.

Lou, after listening to Laver's story on the way to the McDonald's, had said flatly: 'That is so much bullshit. Nobody was coming for me. I don't know them, whoever they are, and Stig is not a drug runner.' But thinking to herself: so, it's all true.

Now watching Jake, inexplicably in his stupid hat, locking his car and diving into the back seat, looking like a ghost as he registered Lou, still tight-lipped and furious, in the front passenger seat. Laver wondering if the white Ford had made it to the Friends of the Planet yet.

The traffic wasn't as bad as it could have been, Laver weaving through the lanes expertly but leaving little room for error as they sped past the university, wound around the zoo and finally took the up-ramp onto the Bolte Bridge. Peak hour not yet in full choke mode as they cleared the Westgate Bridge and set sail for Geelong, going at least a hundred and thirty.

Lou, arms crossed, face like thunder, hissing: 'I still say this is kidnapping and I'm laying charges.'

Laver sitting totally upright in the driver's seat, the early afternoon sun still high enough to be thwarted by the sun visor. 'Fine. Later, you can do whatever you like. The beauty being you'll be alive to feel angry. For now, just let me drive.'

Jake looking white as a sheet and young as he huddled in the cramped back seat. Once, he tried, briefly, to put a comforting hand on Lou's shoulder – which was why her arms were now folded tightly across her chest.

Trying to make sense of the last hour, of feeling so *violated*. Bodily dragged. By a cop.

But also trying to sort out what the cop had said and feeling unsettled by Jake's shaken manner. Trying to just take deep breaths and get her head around it, all the way to the Torquay Road out of Grovedale.

Laver driving with a sharp but easy concentration, apart from when his phone rang and he drove one-handed, saying into the phone: 'Has Homicide put an APB on the Ford and the Commodore?

'Did the recording come out okay?

'Have you got hold of Flipper yet? ... Sorry, Detective Senior Sergeant Dolfin. With an f, not a p-h.

'It wasn't a kidnapping. Tell Slattery I don't need to turn myself in. ... Yeah? ... In that case, tell him to shove it where the saddle usually goes. Like I have time for that bullshit.

'I'll keep you out of whatever happens from here, I promise.

'Your car is fine. You could wash the windscreen occasionally.

'Cecy? I might not get another chance to say this so ... Thanks.'

Laver hung up.

From the back seat, Jake's voice said: 'Did you say "homicide"?'

* * *

The Wild Man parked the ute illegally on Smith Street, about five shops up from the Friends of the Planet. Still pissed off that the kid hadn't been at the Groc-o-Mart. Not entirely believing the check-out chick who'd said he wasn't answering his phone upstairs, but not about to kick in the door to the office area and cause a scene when he was pretty sure the kid's face would be in the news in a day or so. Also noticing that the kid's car wasn't in the car park.

So he'd changed tack and headed for Lou. The kid might be with her anyway, if he was lucky. But instead was almost at the door when, shit, he saw one of Jenssen's enforcers, Wilson, about to leave the shop. Wildie ducking into a gallery of street art, heart thumping and barely able to believe Wilson hadn't seen him. Placing a hand on the pistol in his belt just in case.

But now watching Wilson crossing the road and getting into the white Ford, heading north.

Wildie leaving his car and running the four blocks to Louie's house in Fitzroy. Hammering on the door until it was eventually opened by a guy in a stripy T-shirt and board shorts, wearing a blond, scruffy student beard and glasses.

'Like, what's with all the commotion?'

Wildie pushing straight past him, stiff-arming the guy against the wall on the way past.

'What the—'

'Where's Louie?' The Wild Man's voice even more of a growl than usual.

'Lou?'

'Where is she?'

'Not here. I don't know.'

'Where's her room?'

'Dude, you can't just come in and—'

'Where is her room, dipshit? You have five seconds. In fact, fuck that. You don't.'

Wildie punched the housemate hard in the stomach. He crumpled to the floor, moaning and writhing.

'Which fucking door?'

The housemate, gasping for air, lifting an arm from his gut to point to a door down the corridor. Wildie barging through the door and finding himself in a woman's bedroom. Organic face creams and other potions on a chest of drawers.

A cupboard full of multi-coloured clothing. A dream catcher floating on a piece of string from the ceiling to above the pillow of the double bed. No signs of somebody having packed a bag. No sign of flight.

The housemate on his hands and knees in the corridor. 'You can't just come into a guy's house, man, and ...'

But the Wild Man could. He grabbed the housemate by the throat, just to feel the rush of violence, lifted him to his feet, just like that, and held him for a moment, before slamming him against the wall.

'You might want to think about re-letting her room,' he said. And left.

Knowing he shouldn't have let himself go like that but then thinking he was leaving Melbourne forever tonight. Let the cops look.

By the time Wildie got back to Carlton, Stig looked slightly less stoned than he had, pacing the lounge room. But shook his head when Wildie raised an eyebrow.

'Nobody wants to know. Jenssen's blokes being in town has everyone spooked. Barry's our one shot. Tonight.'

'He's definitely on?'

'I think so. I tried to double check but he's not answering his phone.'

* * *

Through Geelong, they had taken the Torquay turnoff and passed through that town, past the giant surf retail outlets, past the footy oval and then sweeping right past the golf course, until they turned left into Jan Juc.

'We're going where?' asked Lou.

Laver grinned from the driver's seat. 'You won't believe this but we're going to 77 Sunset Strip.'

Lou and Jake stared blankly at him.

'You don't know that TV show?'

They still stared.

'Shit, it was before my time too, but at least I know it. You don't even know the jingle? The music?'

He gave up.

They pulled into a side street and then a driveway to park behind a weather-beaten timber house with a sprawling backyard featuring a Kombi, a partial motorbike that was either half-dismantled or half-rebuilt, a couple of pushbikes and a quiver of longboards. There was also a lot of unmown grass, and a rolled-up hose.

Dogs inside the house started barking like mad until a male voice snarled: 'Carl! Benji! Quiet!'

Laver got out of the car and stretched, breathing the sea air, as the house's back door opened and the dogs, a kelpie and a pug, shot out, heading to the car, barking insanely, noses twitching. A man appeared, tall and suntanned and with surf-bleached dreadlocks. He was wearing a faded green singlet and board shorts, and a couple of necklaces featuring wood carvings and possibly something hewn from bone. Tribal tattoos sprawled down his left shoulder.

'Dogs. Shut up!' he roared, and they did.

Now he stood watching Laver tickle Carl the kelpie under the chin, Benji the pug trying to nuzzle in for some of the action, flipping over on his back and lifting a paw for better tummy access.

'Well, well, well. If it isn't the killer cop,' the man said.

'Charming,' replied Laver. 'Your body count beats mine, prick.'

'Nice to see you too,' the man grinned. 'A bloke could ring first.'

'Sometimes it's best not to trust a mobile phone.'

'Oh. Like that, hey?'

'Yep.'

Jake had gotten out of the car and was standing, two dog noses sniffing him, as the cop shook hands with the surfer dude.

Laver turned and said, 'Jake, this is Bushy. He used to be one of us but now he's an ambo.'

'Ambo?' asked Jake faintly.

The surfer's eyes were surrounded by creased skin, laugh lines on his face. 'Yeah, a paramedic. Drive an ambulance.' He twirled a finger. 'Woo woo woo woo woo?'

'I know what an ambulance is,' Jake said dumbly.

'Well, a bloke can't be sure,' said Bushy.

Laver looked around then walked over to the car and opened the passenger-side door. Lou was still sitting in there, arms folded.

'And Bushy, this is Lou, who's not thrilled to be here, but needs to be.'

Bushy folded his arms, shoulders and biceps bulging, and tilted his head to look at her.

'G'day Lou. I don't bite,' he said.

Lou was giving him looks, despite herself. 'What does "one of us" mean? You said he used to be "one of us".'

'Oh,' Laver said. 'Former cop. A Soggie. But retrained for the ambos.'

Bushy shrugged. 'Once I decided I was up for a sea change, I realised there was a lot more call for medical support than Kevlar vests out here. Although that could be changing.'

'Yeah?' Laver raised an eyebrow.

'Torquay pub on a Friday or Saturday night is getting hairy, even for me. You want a cuppa?'

'Mate, I can't. There's things happening in Melbourne that I need to get back to, but I need a favour. These two need to be babysat.'

Part of Lou bristled at the word, but she'd grown genuinely worried over the last few hours. And another part of her was noticing everything about Bushy. How he stood. Those surfer shoulders. How he wore those board shorts. The legs under them.

Bushy's face had taken on a harder edge, all business. They moved away from Jake and Lou. 'How long, Rocket?'

'Not long; tomorrow. We're close to closure on this one.'

'Want to let me know who I'm looking out for?'

'Could be any of four. Two forty-year-olds in a white Ford. Or another guy a bit younger than us, with a surfer look but not one. And his mate, tall, orange mohawk, prison tatts, hard to miss, very dangerous.'

Bushy chuckled. 'Rocket. I'm an occasionally stoned and permanently retired surfing bludger.'

'Of course you are. Gentle and helpless as a kitten if these two need protecting.'

'Against four. Shit.'

'Not four. Two or two but, honestly, I'm not expecting any of them to show, mate. I haven't told a soul where we've gone, I wasn't followed and I haven't mentioned anywhere west of the Bolte Bridge on a phone. I just want these two safe so I can concentrate on the rest of it.'

Bushy and Rocket gazed at one another and then the surfer nodded. 'Of course, mate. You know I'll help.' He turned and called out, 'Come on, you two. Let's get inside, hey.'

As Jake walked past, Laver put a hand on his shoulder: 'I promise it will only be overnight. Trust me.'

'Yeah, I do,' the kid said. ' I guess I have to.'

'And one more thing. I need your hat and your car keys.'

'My hat?' Not even waiting for an answer, Jake handed it over with the keys, clearly watching Lou and their host regarding one another. Jake gave Bushy a final look as he walked through the door and into the house, but he went.

Lou hadn't moved from the car. Bushy wandered over and leaned down. He smelled like salt.

'If it helps convince you, I might have a cigarette that tastes a bit funny if you like tobacco, but will relax you quite a lot.'

Lou looked at him now and said, 'Aren't you an ex-cop?'

'Yeah, strong emphasis on the "ex". And what? You think no member of the constabulary has ever smoked a joint? Anyway, I'm long retired. Come inside and let's get to know each other.'

Was that a pick-up line? She was being kidnapped by a strange renegade cop and now his friend was hitting on her? Even weirder, she found herself giving Bushy a little grin in return. She got out of the car.

'Don't think I've forgotten that you forced me into this car and coerced me here against my will,' she said to Laver on her way past.

'Coerced. Good word. Potentially saved your life too,' he called after her.

'Potentially?' Bushy raised an eyebrow.

'Hopefully better than potentially,' Laver said. 'At least I'm directing traffic for the next bit.'

'Well, go get 'em, tiger. The swell's shit anyway, so I'm happy enough to stay close to home.'

'I can always rely on you, mate, as long as the waves aren't running.' Laver stopped at the car door and said, 'Bushy. By sundown tomorrow, if you haven't heard anything? You might want to ring Flipper.'

'I thought you were going to turn up.'

'Let's hope.'

'Shit, Rocket. You know what you're doing?'

'Yeah, I do. The only thing I can.'

Laver didn't drive straight to the main road. From the end of Sunset Strip, he turned left and away from Jan Juc on country roads, eventually sweeping around a long right-hander, the ocean huge in front of him, and parked at Bells Beach.

He got out of the car and sat on the bonnet, watching the sluggish waves struggle through one of the world's most famous surf breaks – currently subdued by a south-westerly wind and a meagre swell.

Laver sat and took in the sea, the air, the sounds of the waves. Watched the patterns on the water. Felt a slight chill in the air as the breeze started to bite. He wrapped his arms around himself and took a deep breath. Laver took it all in: the very fact of his own breathing, his heart beating.

Then got into the driver's seat and drove back out to the Great Ocean Road, turning towards Melbourne and to everything that was to come.

* * *

Laver sat outside his apartment for fifteen minutes, watching the street and the parked cars. Finally, he approached the building from a side gate, still moving slowly and watching the doorways. A gun would have been comforting – but then again, what would be the point?

Inside his apartment, he showered for a long time and changed into fresh jeans and a T-shirt. Purple with a logo of Roger Ramjet on the front. He looked steadily at himself in the bathroom mirror, eyes empty in the reflection, and thought in a removed kind of way: Is this what I want to be wearing? Is this appropriate?

Then thought, why not? What was he going to wear – a suit?

He pulled on his favourite runners, a pair of Nikes he'd bought in New York a few years ago, exclusive to the Fifth Avenue store. Collector's items. From what now seemed the golden age of him and Marcia. He thought of them exploring Brooklyn together, in love. He made himself stop thinking about her.

In the lounge room, he pulled a notepad over from the other side of the table, and a felt pen. Then sat for the longest time, staring out the window until he was ready to write.

Dear Callum,

    I don't know why I'm even writing you this letter except that I have a feeling my worst fear might be realised and I may never actually see you again.
    I guess what I want to tell you is that it was never my intention to not be a part of your life. That decision was taken from me, like so many things in life are, whether we like it or not.
    As I write this, my life is a mess and the way forward is unclear. I hope so much that we can be together one day and I can talk to you about the kinds of things a father wants to say to his son. But I suspect that's not going to happen.
    If I'm right and we don't get that chance, try to live a great life. Remember that an honest life is harder but simpler. Be honourable and true to those you love. Try to avoid the sort of mistakes your mother and I made.
    And seriously reconsider any desire you might have to be a member of any kind of police force.

I love you,
Dad

He placed the letter in an envelope and wrote 'Callum Laver' on the front. Then placed it on the mantelpiece along with an envelope containing other documents people would be looking for.

He poured himself a big whisky, still with room for three blocks of ice, aware he was putting off the phone call. But finally he sighed and dialled.

His father answered on the fourth ring.

'What?'

'Dad, it's me.'

'Ah, the stranger. Don't have time to come and see your old man anymore, hey.'

'I was there just the other day.'

'For three minutes. That doesn't count.'

'Dad, I don't want to fight.'

'Who's fighting? I'm just making a point.'

Laver listened to his father's raspy breath down the line. TV chatter in the background.

'Dad, I want you to know that I appreciate the job you did in raising me, once Mum wasn't around.'

'Eh?' He could almost see the squinting scowl enveloping the old man's face.

'I know it was hard for you. Things weren't always perfect. They still aren't. But I know you tried.'

'Eh? What is this, boy? Hang on, I'll turn down the tellie.'

Laver heard fumbling, heard the TV noise fade and heard Daisy's voice in the background, rising in inquiry.

'The boy's going soft,' his father said, voice away from the phone. Then back to the receiver, saying: 'All this murdering people getting to you, is it, son?'

'Jesus, Dad.'

'No need to blaspheme. You've got enough sins on your plate just now.'

'Dad, will you shut up long enough for me to say what I want to say?'

'Daisy thinks you should get out of the Force. Thinks that shooting is the start of a life decline unless you leave the job.'

'What do you think, Dad? What's your opinion?'

A pause as he thought about it, then said speculatively, 'Plenty of fellas shot blokes in the war and lived good lives.'

'You weren't in any war. Which war?'

'Didn't say I was, you little smartarse. But I know men who were. You remember Bob Johnston from my work? There was a story where—'

'Dad, I want us to be peaceful with one another.'

'Eh?' His dad sounding pained. 'Son, what's this about?'

'I love you, Dad.'

That brought nothing but stunned silence. Tony hadn't said that since he was maybe twelve years old.

'Dad?'

'You're starting to scare me, son. Are you okay?'

'I think the correct response is, "I love you too, son".' Rocket going for it, now he was out there in this uncertain place. But there was more silence.

'Can't you say that, Dad?'

'Well, of course. You know I do. I don't know why we need to—'

Time to end his father's misery. 'Relax Dad, I have to go. Give Daisy a huge hug for me. If you get a chance, tell Callum I was a good man.'

'Callum? You've heard from Callum?'

'No Dad, but you might. Goodbye.'

Laver hung up and could feel tears in his eyes. All he did lately was cry or try not to cry. Christ.

He stared at the phone and thought about phoning her. But why? He scrawled on a piece of paper: 'Marcia. Good luck with the shit for brains from your work.'

Then screwed it up and put it in the bin. Fuck it. What was the point of making her feel guilty? She'd left just in time.

He was almost done. Laver moved to the door, having one last look around the apartment, when he suddenly put his keys back down on the table and headed to the kitchenette. He ran hot water and dishwashing liquid into the sink and then slowly, carefully, washed and stacked the dishes and hung the washing-up gloves over the tap to drip-dry into the sink.

And then he left his flat.

CHAPTER 33
INCIDENT ON RATHDOWNE

He had to drive two laps of the Groc-o-Mart car park in Jake's car before Brunetti and Wilson picked him up, the white Ford falling in behind.

'Very slack,' thought Laver. 'Asleep on the job.'

He was wearing Jake's ridiculous reggae beanie, hunched over the wheel. He wondered what was going on ahead of him. Flipper had refused to help him stop this, so Laver had decided his mate might as well watch the show. The calls had been made and Laver knew where to drive, not too fast in case they lost him. Lucky they were driving towards the city, against the flight of the after-work traffic.

Rathdowne Street was moderately busy; not bad for peak hour. Laver turned right out of Alexandra Parade and slowed, even smiling when the white Ford clearly ran the red light to make the turn. Saw the flash of the camera on the pole – one last traffic infringement to complete their criminal history. They were almost there.

Dolfin was in his car, with the house in the sights of his binoculars. A Soggie was planted on either side, three full houses away so they couldn't possibly be spotted, as per Rocket's instructions. Flipper was now seriously concerned about his best mate on the Force and was definitely going to be speaking to the police counsellors about him, whether Rocket liked it or not: the equivalent of a police intervention. But first, there was this house. When Laver had said 'nuclear' this time, there had been a note in his voice that Flipper had never heard before. After their meeting with Ned Kelly earlier that day, Dolfin knew Laver wouldn't have used the word this afternoon unless he meant it. But he still had no idea why, or what was about to happen. Knowing only that he had to be outside this house. Watching as an old Mazda pulled up – Laver getting out of the driver's door, wearing a ridiculous beanie.

Another car pulling up behind him, two men in suits, as Laver went through the front gate of the house and, without looking back, hammered on the front door. The two men opening the doors of their car, but not getting out – sitting and watching.

Flipper concentrating the binocular lens on the front door instead and seeing it open to reveal half of a big man, bare-chested and bald. But not bald. A flash of orange, vertically down his head. A mohawk. Something dull and grey and solid-looking in his hand. Dolfin knowing a gun when he saw one.

The man and Laver staring at one another, Laver just standing dumbly with his arms dangling by his sides. Laver saying something Dolfin couldn't hear. The big man's face beginning to react.

Flipper saying, 'Oh fuck.' Far too late.

* * *

Stig, sitting at the kitchen table, stoned. He'd promised Wildie he'd have it together for the sale to Barry tonight, but hadn't been able to get Paxton on the phone all afternoon and had started smoking joints as nerves took hold. Losing the will to stop lighting just one more up, and then another.

Now looking at the world through a familiar haze, rais-ing his head, hearing Wildie open the door and a voice say, 'Thought it was my turn for a home visit.'

Wildie snarling, 'You've got to be kidding. You are so fucking dead.'

At the front door, the cop just looking at Wildie, not saying a word as the Wild Man grabbed him violently by the shirt, dragged him into the house and landed a vicious right hook to the cop's face with the butt of the pistol he was holding, a blow so hard the Wild Man felt it right to his shoulder. Blood exploding from the cop's temple, but the cop not attempting to fight back. Wildie transferring the gun to his left hand

and punching him twice more, savagely. The cop staggering but not falling, blood pouring from somewhere on his face, breath rasping. Wildie moving the gun to the dazed cop's temple but just now beginning to wonder why he didn't seem to be armed.

Oh no. At the kitchen table, Stig knew. Just knew. With a dull certainty that went way beyond the fog of the drugs.

It was like a dream sequence as Stig rose from the table, a gun magically in his hand – he'd forgotten he was even holding it – and took three lazy steps towards the front hall even as he heard the Wild Man fighting somebody: the hard smack of solid punches. Wildie grunting.

And then was in the hall just in time to see Brunetti and Wilson, Jenssen's men, as they burst through the front door; the thought occurred to Stig that he really should raise his gun, a moment before he saw the flash from Wilson's handgun and felt himself punched in the stomach harder than he'd ever been punched before. Stig dreamily letting off a shot and watching the plaster above Wilson's head explode as Brunetti's gun flashed and he was punched even harder in the right side of his chest.

Stig now feeling his legs fall away and dimly aware of the floor meeting his back. Surprised to feel floor against his temple. How did that happen? Stig thinking special effects never really prepared you for the reality; a moment of adrenalin, registering what it's really like to be shot. Stig all wide-eyed on the ground, watching Wilson's head explode as the Wild Man finally returned fire before Brunetti stepped all the way inside the door, hiding, and turned to look back outside where Stig vaguely registered shouting.

A cop in full Kevlar bursting past the door and the concealed Brunetti to shoot the Wild Man three times fast to the body and head. Wildie toppling noiselessly. Or maybe Stig wasn't hearing anymore? he wondered. Dreamily, he watched Brunetti about to unload on the cop from behind the door but then saw a red explosion on Brunetti's chest.

Stig slipping away but seeing the bike cop on the floor with Wildie's gun, still trained on Brunetti who was sliding down the wall, hands scrambling stupidly at the hole in his chest, a river of red and bodily gunk snail-trailing down the wall as he fell.

Stig going blank for a moment but then aware of two faces, in black cop helmets, looking down at him. Seeing their mouths move. Not hearing anything. Stig now not seeing anything. Stig remembering his mother once telling him, after his uncle died, that death was like crossing a road. Stig still wondering what that meant, wondering what came next. Stig feeling light, free of his body. Stig feeling a pang – of what? Regret? Fear? Surprise?

Stig feeling nothing.

* * *

Dolfin walked through the front door in his usual suit, no Kevlar, gun drawn but not fired. He surveyed the bodies: the gunman against the wall was gurgling and whimpering, but one look told Dolfin that would be short term. He'd already radioed for paramedics and back-up: Shooting in progress, potential member down. They'd all be here in minutes.

Laver on his hands and knees, a handgun lying on the floor beside him. Laver, with scarlet red on his face, vomiting savagely into the hall's carpet.

Beside him the body of the orange-haired man. Colin Wilde, Laver had called him. The Soggies were shaking their heads from above the body of the one who must be Stig Anderson. Another body a metre or so inside the front door, now with pulp where the right eye and temple should have been. The untouched left eye staring.

And there was Laver, who had seen it all coming, who Dolfin hadn't believed, retching on the carpet.

But alive.

Flipper dug into his pocket and found a handkerchief, crouched and handed it to Laver.

'Just gimme a minute,' Laver said hoarsely. The blood was coming from a cut above his left eye, among other places.

Dolfin said, gently, 'Rocket, you fucking idiot. That was suicide.'

'You wouldn't listen.' Laver more moaning than speaking. Semi-conscious. 'Nobody would listen.'

'Where are the hippie and the nerd?'

'Safe.'

Dolfin knelt beside Laver, still on his hands and knees, bleeding, panting, possibly about to be sick again. Probably concussed. The closest thing to a brother that Dolfin had. Alive.

'Mate, next time, I promise I'll listen.'

Laver gasped, 'Next time.' And almost attempted what might have been a laugh.

Dolfin could hear sirens. Knew there would also be unmarked cars, with Broadbent, the media liaison, probably that politician cop arsehole Strickland from the ombudsman.

He stood back up and looked again at the bodies. The man against the wall was no longer gurgling. The Soggies were standing silent, just another day at the office, guns relaxed, waiting for the sirens to arrive.

Dolfin looked at the fired gun next to Laver's hand.

'One thing's for sure, Rocket,' he said. 'If your career wasn't fucked before, it is now.'

CHAPTER 34
PUNCHING YOUR WEIGHT

Laver didn't get out of hospital until after midnight. Cecy was there when he got wheeled in on a bed after getting stitches for the cut above his eye, along with other patch-ups. She hugged him, really hugged him, and he could feel her trembling. Felt tears against his neck and felt his own eyes getting moist. Cecy was looking older than her twenty-something years, and Laver felt a pang that she was so much younger than he was, and another pang that the job was already ageing her. She'd been fast-tracked on the realities of police life in a big way since they'd heard Barry Paxton being shot. God, lunchtime that day.

The good news was that most of the initial grilling from Strickland and co, as well as Broadbent, had been able to happen while he waited for treatment and had his concussion assessed. There would be more meetings in a day or so, but for now he could rest up. Plus, as a bonus, he could argue later that the comments directed at Strickland were the result of a scrambled brain developing a concussion.

He crashed at Dolfin's house, half-expecting Coleman's ghost to be joined by Brunetti, with Stig, Wilde and Wilson maybe along for the ride – enough spectres for a card game – but surprisingly his brain relented and he actually slept. He started the drive to Jan Juc after ten the next morning, driving carefully, his head throbbing like a bastard, hoping his reflexes would not be tested on the way. The day had broken clear and warm, and Laver wondered briefly if he could stay for a surf before turning back towards Melbourne and everything that wasn't waiting for him there.

It was just after 11.45 am when he arrived at Sunset Strip. The house was quiet, curtains drawn. He knocked on the back door, which was never locked, and walked in when there was no reply. Smelled the fog of dope the moment he entered the house.

And burst in on a naked Bushy and a topless Lou, blinking with sleep, desperately fumbling for clothes on a fold-out couch in the lounge room.

'Oh shit, Laver. What time is it?'

'So you two have gotten to know each other then?'

Bushy sniggered, stoned. 'Looks like it. It was an entertaining evening.'

Lou struggled into a singlet, spectacular breasts disappearing before Laver's eyes. Also now giggling, pupils dilated. 'I'm feeling very protected.'

'And where exactly is protected person number two?'

Bushy looked slightly alarmed. 'I guess he's still in bed. He took my room. We were sort of fooling around on the couch after a couple of joints and he didn't look too happy.'

'Poor Jake. He's going to think I'm a bitch now.' Saying to Laver, 'I never said I liked him. I never gave him hope. I didn't.'

Bushy, trying to get it together, squinted at Laver. 'Shit, Rocket. What happened to your face?'

But Laver was already gone, walking to the bedroom where the bed was still made, unslept in.

'Shit, Bushy,' he yelled. 'He's not here. I wish you'd paid equal attention to both parties.'

Lou giggling and saying, 'That would have been difficult.'

Laver was back out the door, grabbing Bushy's bike, a surf cruiser covered in rust but good for riding to the beach. A bike that Laver used to find difficult to ride, its single gear a pretty heavy one. Now, his legs stronger from his job, he was able to ride it easily to the cliff tops overlooking Jan Juc back beach.

He saw Jake down below, sitting on the sand, knees tucked under his arms, watching surfers battling chopped out, messy waves. The dogs, Carl and Benji, sniffing and running along the water's edge in front of him.

Laver came down the long steps from the cliff top and sat down beside him. The dogs ran up for pats.

'Sounds like you had a rough night, Jake.'

Jake swallowed hard, staring determinedly out to sea. 'It was always going to happen. I was a dickhead for holding out hopes.'

'I'm sorry, mate. It's a shitty truth: you can't make a woman like you.'

'I know. I just fooled myself, you know, and then she took one look at your friend and I knew in my gut what was going to happen, even before it did. And then I had to watch it unfold.'

'Oh man, that is brutal.' Laver lay back on the sand, feeling the sun on his face. 'It's too early for the pub to be open.'

'I don't drink.'

'Of course you don't.'

Jake suddenly looked at the cop lying next to him, saw the massive bandage and the bruises. 'Geez, what happened to you? What happened in Melbourne?'

Laver squinted open an eye against the sun and looked at the silhouette of this kid, this almost-man. 'They're dead, Jake. All of them.'

'Who? Lou's boyfriend?'

'And his mate. And the two guys in the white Ford. And Barry.'

Jake couldn't speak.

Laver told him loosely what had happened, about the Groc-o-Mart being a front for a drug baron, and about Jake being wrongly thought to be a spy.

They walked the dogs back to the house where, mercifully, Lou was now fully dressed. Laver noticed she was laughing a little too loudly, not looking Jake in the eye. Eventually, Jake went and sat in the back seat of Laver's car, waiting to go.

Laver sat down in the lounge room and broke the news about Stig and the Wild Man to Lou. Told the whole thing. Lou seemed horrified and truly shocked that Stig was so bad, so into the criminal world. Turned pale and shook when Laver described the shoot-out. Bushy asking lots of cop questions, like: 'And the boss guy in the rental car?'

'Like smoke into a cloud,' Laver sighed. 'Never seen again.'

'Ah, that hurts.'

Laver nodding. 'I suspect he was a significant fish. Not often you get a look at one like him. And he got away.'

Bushy also gave Laver sympathetic looks when it got around to what the whole scene meant for his career prospects.

'Mate, I could ask my mate who runs the surf school if you could add a bike arm to it. Life's pretty sweet down here.'

'Thanks Bushy, but I'm a city guy. I might have more free time to visit though.'

'Always welcome,' Bushy said. 'As are you, Lou.'

'Thanks,' she said, kissing him softly on the lips. She promised she'd be in touch, but her eyes showed she was already somewhere else, closing down as Stig's death sunk in.

They stood up to go but Laver had to try at least once. 'Lou,' he said. 'Your mum worries about you and Jake really likes you. It's up to you how you treat the people who care about you, but maybe do me a favour and be a little more gentle with Jake out there, huh? You owe him a lot – quite possibly your life.'

'Men and guns,' she said with venom. 'Cops and robbers.' And stalked to the car, leaving Bushie and Laver to stare at each other. They walked to the back door, stopping in the doorway.

'You two are going to be very happy together, Bushy. She'll be a treat at the Soggie reunions.'

'Get fucked. And sorry I got distracted. I'm getting unprofessional in my old age.'

'Yeah, you are, you prick.'

Bushy looked towards the car and started to smile as he said, 'I'm not that sorry.'

'Selfish bastard.'

The pair hugged, and Bushy said, 'I'm glad you're alive, Rocket.'

'Thanks, mate. Me too, I think.'

The journey back to Melbourne was silent as the grave: Laver, feeling his concussion, head still pounding, exhausted and as lacking in conversation as the two passengers. Not even able to face music, which showed he wasn't well.

At Lou's house, she opened the door and got straight out.

'No need to say thanks for saving your life,' Laver called after her. 'Really.'

She gave him a look: a dead grey-eyed stare from under a green-and-purple fringe. And then was gone. Jake got the briefest of glances as she walked through the front gate.

'You want to sit up front?' asked Laver.

'No, I just want to go home.'

'Fair enough. Jake, do you know the old boxing saying, "You've got to punch your weight?"'

'Not really.'

'Well, you're way better than her division. Aim higher.'

Jake said nothing for a few long seconds. 'Yeah, you know what? You're totally right,' he finally said, not believing it for a second.

Laver didn't either.

CHAPTER 35
THE PERFECT SHOT (REPRISE)

'So some details about highly unethical behaviour such as money laundering and organised-crime activities that may well include somewhat damning evidence against a then–Assistant Commissioner of the Western Australian police force start to trickle in from Perth,' Flipper said, putting sugar in his cappuccino.

Laver wondered if his mate was the only guy who still hadn't made the switch to a caffe latte or a flat white.

Flipper continued, 'Our finest local dogs start following Mr Strickland, who of course would have no way of knowing this fact because the tail is highly classified and the Victorian police force is spotless when it comes to integrity.'

'Goes without saying,' Laver nodded, lining up the six ball, cursing inwardly that the Red Triangle pool hall, three storeys up off Brunswick Street, remained an alcohol-free zone.

'The difference,' Flipper said, 'is that this time the dogs are joined by Internal Affairs detectives, carrying a warrant for Mr Strickland's arrest, on quite the list of charges. The party is swollen by the novelty value of arresting a senior member of the ombudsman's staff. Doesn't happen every day.'

Laver narrowly missed the ambitious double on the six, wandered over and picked up his coffee. Raising the cup, he said, 'To justice.'

'To justice,' Flipper agreed, pulling out a hip flask to add whisky to his coffee.

'Oh, bless you!' Laver held out his cup, checking the teenager at the counter wasn't watching. 'So let me guess. They lost him and he's now holed up at the Unknown Pension, somewhere in Buenos Aires?'

'Better. He gets a phone call – from who, it remains unknown, but the smart money is on Lonigan—'

'The media and comms guy?'

'Yeah, they're tight.' Flipper lined up and nailed the twelve ball down the length of the table. 'Then again, only five or six people officially knew about the surveillance, which means everybody. Anyway, his mobile goes off, he doesn't break stride but decamps briskly to Parliament Station.'

'Briskly.'

'Very briskly. Never quite breaking into a run. Our boys are decamping in an equally brisk manner and are not far behind him on the escalator travelling down to Platform Four. Sandringham line. Strickland has never been one for public transport, being more your chauffeured-limo kind of guy, so the dogs are on full alert.'

Laver sipped his coffee, feeling suddenly tired. The stitches above his left eye aching.

'You know what Strickland does?' Flipper frowned at the fourteen ball, then planted both hands on the cushion and looked directly at Laver. 'He walks straight up to the vending machines, on the crowded peak-hour platform, and pulls his gun. Empties the entire clip into CC's corn chips and also fatally wounds several Mars Bars. Then carefully puts the gun on the ground and lies down on his stomach with both arms spread out. When our boys descend, he looks back over his shoulder, looks them straight in the eye and says: "I don't seem to be my usual self. I think I might need to see the police counselling service."'

Flipper, shaking his head, bent to look again down his cue at the fourteen. Missed the shot.

'Time off for mental health recuperation,' Laver said after a while.

'For starters. Full disability pay, open ended.'

Laver sunk the two but missed a difficult long shot on the four ball. 'Only thing missing is a Governor's Medal for working heroically while under duress.'

'No chance of charges being laid until extensive and full psychological tests have been conducted. Could take months. And they might not ever be able to fully explain whether said party was mentally on his game when certain, umm, events transpired.'

Laver fell into one of the old theatre chairs that lined the walls and closed his eyes.

'Makes you proud to be a police officer, doesn't it?' said Flipper.

'Mate,' Laver replied. 'I don't think that's a problem I'm going to have to wrestle much longer.'

Dolfin pausing, coffee halfway to his mouth. 'Should I warn the town's remaining vending machines?'

'Nah, I'll leave them for the Stricklands of the world. But I think it's time for something else.'

'Rocket, you're a career cop. Anyway, who's going to shoot people down at the rate you have been? Political scapegoats aren't that easy to come by.'

'I'm sure they'll find somebody. They always do.'

Dolfin got up. Jawed but failed to sink the eleven ball. Cursed enthusiastically, then returned to his coffee. 'What else would you do? If you weren't a cop?'

'Dunno, but I must be good for something. Bike courier maybe?'

Laver stood, walked the table and squinted at the six ball: now out of position, no realistic shot available. And then shrugged. He calculated cavalier angles and then struck the cue ball hard and watched the six ball double, then triple the length of the table – before falling sweetly into the top pocket, nothing but net.

Flipper put down his coffee to break into spontaneous applause.

'Rocket, old boy! That was the perfect shot.'

ACKNOWLEDGEMENTS

ACKNOWLEDGEMENTS

This book was a long, long time in the making.
Many people have been there for the entire ride, giving me friendship, love, support, laughter, tears, sharing life's roller-coaster and often supporting a writer's insecurities or providing timely advice. A big shout out to Belinda Byrne and Phil Hudson, for example, who both read early drafts or excerpts of this book and had the courage to tell the truth: that it was not yet up to scratch.

I hope it is now, BB and Huddo.

Shaun Kinna, Anna Heywood, Michael Roberts, Richard Hinds, Jen Storey, Katey Slater, Richard Glasson, Ros Willett, Richard Stubbs, Pip Mushin, Simon Coronel, Brett Wiencke, Phil 'Cat' Campbell ... so many muses, friends and creative companions on the road to this novel. I can't name them all but you know who you are. And my parents, Ron and Judy, and my sister, Amanda – even if my mum did want me to publish under a nom de plume because she thought the book was 'funny, but disgusting'. Thank you to Chloé Brugalé, mon amour.

My aim was always to try and bring authentic police humour and sensibilities to this book. With that in mind, things became truly surreal the day that I found myself sitting across a coffee table from a real-life version of Tony Laver. I was several years into writing the manuscript when I happened, through my day job, to meet a former Victorian cop who had shot a man and been sent to cop purgatory while politicians got involved. I quoted the scene where Laver's new boss tells him to keep his head down, log in and log out, but don't cause trouble, and this ex-cop laughed and said I was almost word-for-word correct.

'You've been in my head for a decade,' I said and he grinned, frowned and then said: 'So if I told you some of the real stories, could you use them instead of stuff you've made up?' And so we had a beer, with another ex-policeman, which led to a lot of the details within this fiction being absolutely real, even when unlikely. Laver asleep seconds before shooting Coleman, for example? Pretty much as it happened. A man behind a door being shot repeatedly by a high-powered SOG gun, but not physically appearing to have been hit, until he toppled? Real. Sadly, I promised these men that I would not mention their names but I do want to say thank you, for the wild stories, for a lot of laughter and most of all for trusting me with such intimate details of real-life police work in my city. Given they were talking to a former (if brief) police roundsman, who had covered the official version of some of the anecdotes, now telling me what really happened and how things unfolded – this trust was no small thing.

And the book is a lot better for the insights. Thanks again.

While I'm on mysterious acknowledgements, cheers to a leading police reporter and friend for 'the Italian job' story. And, for that matter, to all the fellow hacks of my time at the *Herald* and *Sunday Age* newspapers.

A final thankyou to the staff of Media Giants for covering for me when I needed it so I could complete drafts of this novel. Especially to Alex McNab for reading the final first draft and giving me some great insights. And to everybody at Hardie Grant for taking a chance on an attempt at an entertaining crime novel without the words 'Under' or 'Belly' somewhere in the title. A huge thankyou to Fiona Hardie and Sandy Grant for agreeing to read the manuscript, to publisher Fran Berry, editor Rose Michael and copy editor Allison Hiew – especially for agreeing to stomach my attack on auxiliary verbs. (And to HG's Jane Grant, and my legal advisors Greg Sitch and Luca Costanzo.)

Last and not least, thank you to the Bangers for their friendship and lace-out passes, and to the ice hockey Rookies for endless adventures.

And to my brother, Shonko, for 'Frankie' (short for Frankenstein), my city-cruiser bike made entirely out of parts of other bikes and still my transport of choice around my hood.

If you're not yet convinced, I fully recommend bike riding as a way to get around your city. The air feels great on your face and you notice the details of the streets. Long may your wheels roll.

Nicko Place